All Roads Lead Home

Diane Greenwood Muir

My deepest gratitude goes out to friends and family who have given me time to hide away and write and have encouraged me to be more than I ever dreamed.

Thank you!

This is a work of fiction. Names, characters, places, brands, media, and incidents are either the product of the author's imagination or are used fictitiously. The author acknowledges the trademarked status and trademark owners of various products referenced in this work of fiction, which have been used without permission. The publication / use of these trademarks is not authorized, associated with, or sponsored by the trademark owners.

All rights reserved. No part of this book may be reproduced in any form or by any electronic or mechanical means, including information storage and retrieval systems, without permission in writing from the publisher, except by a reviewer, who may quote brief passages in a review.

Cover Design Photography by Maxim M. Muir

Copyright © 2013 Diane Greenwood Muir

All rights reserved.

ISBN-13: 978-1482021806
ISBN-10: 1482021803

CONTENTS

CHAPTER ONE

"Hallooo! Is anyone here?"

Polly nearly fell off the ladder hearing a voice come from the main level, then muttered, "I'm going to have to get a dog." She brushed her hand across her face, pushing her hair back and madly looked around for a place to prop her paintbrush. Things had been so quiet and she hadn't expected anyone to show up. Her heart racing, she glanced around, trying to think, and then saw the paint can on the floor. Well, that was obvious, where was her head? Skittering down the ladder, she placed the brush across the top of the can and headed for the main stairwell, arriving in time to see four women ready to mount the staircase.

"Hi there!" she said.

"Are you Polly Giller?" said one of the women, stepping up on the first step.

"Yes, I am. Can I help you with something?"

"We're here to welcome you to Bellingwood. We figured you might enjoy a few meals, so we brought enough for the next few days." The women each had their hands filled with grocery bags and casserole dishes wrapped in brightly colored slings.

"I'm Lydia Merritt," said the woman, "and this is Sylvie Donovan,

Andy Saner and Beryl Watson. We're the welcoming committee!"

Polly walked down toward the women and stopped a few steps from the bottom.

"Wow!" she said, "I wasn't expecting this. Thank you!" She motioned around the stairway to the back of the hall. "The kitchen is back here. Let me show you."

Polly stepped in between two of the women and led the way. Renovation of the old school kitchen was nearly complete since it was the first room she'd attacked. The back wall, filled with windows and painted a soft yellow, looked out onto the old playground. A counter which was currently being used to store small appliance followed the back wall to an eight-foot pine trestle table which sat next to the door. The window and counter at the front of the kitchen remained in place from the days of serving students. On the left as they entered, was a wall filled with pantry cupboards trimmed in dark walnut around glass doors.

On the right were two stainless steel refrigerator / coolers and a separate freezer. A large cast iron commercial stove and oven stood on the far right wall. Deep sinks were on both sides of the kitchen and under the counter, which wrapped around to the right wall where an industrial dishwasher stood. A massive preparation space with sink on each end and storage space beneath filled the center of the room.

"I'm sorry this is the only livable room right now," Polly said. "There is so much to do yet."

"Oh, don't worry, Polly," said the petite woman identified as Andy Saner. "No one in town can believe you are taking on such a big project. You know, we all went to school here."

Polly spun around. "Of course you did!" she exclaimed. "Oh, I would love to hear stories you have about the building when it was filled with kids."

A rumbling chuckle came from Beryl Watson. "Do you want stories that are clean or stories that are true?" she said, her voice filled with mirth.

"Stop it, you," teased Lydia. "You don't need to start telling tall tales before the poor girl gets to know us."

The women bustled in and filled the center of the prep table with the items they'd brought.

"We can leave this here for you, but we'd be glad to put it away if you don't mind us opening your cupboards." This came from the last to be heard from, Sylvie Donovan. She looked to be about eight years older than Polly. Her eyes were bright, if a little sad. Her blue corduroy jacket covered a green plaid flannel shirt and loose fitting jeans. She wore old tennies on her feet and her long, brown hair was pulled back with a loosely tied, crocheted hair ribbon.

"Oh," said Polly, "I can do it. This is so amazing; I don't know what to say."

"Really, Polly," assured Sylvie, "We're going to be in your way while we bother you for a few minutes, we might as well take care of it."

"Alright," Polly responded. "I'll turn the coffeepot on. Would you like some?"

"Now you're on the right track," said Lydia. "We're all coffee drinkers, aren't we?" She looked around at the other three who nodded in agreement while opening pantry doors and unpacking bags.

"Coffee would be great," said Beryl. "Now, Andy, did you bring your label maker? I can't imagine you will let us stuff things in here willy-nilly, will you?"

The petite woman chuckled and said, "Don't you think it would be appropriate for the owner of the pantry to establish her territory before I start labeling everything? She might not like my methods of organization."

Polly looked up. "I do pretty well, but if you have a good idea for organizing a large pantry, I'd love to hear it!"

Beryl wrinkled her nose, "You might not want to say that to this woman. She has a," she paused and thought, "we'll call it a flair for putting things in order. It's a sickness, you know. We keep telling her she should turn that sickness into a business. Other people ... normal people who don't feel the need to alphabetize their refrigerators ... might want a little of her influence."

Andy threw a box of crackers at her friend. "I like things to make sense. A pantry isn't simply organized alphabetically; it's organized by how you use it. And then, it's organized alphabetically."

Beryl caught the box out of the air and stuffed it onto a shelf. "Well, there's the 'C' shelf. I don't care what you do after that."

Polly watched the two women banter and then turned to see Lydia and Sylvie simply taking things out of bags while watching the entertainment.

"Do I step in here?" she asked Lydia.

"Not unless you have something important to say. However, Andy will give a lot of thought to organizing your space if you let her. Just say the word, and you will never lose anything again. I keep her out of my kitchen though. Sometimes I like the adventure of wondering what will pop out at me when I clean the shelves!" Lydia smiled at her friend and winked.

"Wow, I suppose I should have asked you to help me with this before I started," Polly said.

"Oh! Don't say that. You've got a wonderful place here." Andy started pulling things back out of the cupboard. "But, if you move this here with the chocolate and put these over here, then if you make sure this cupboard is used for your spices and over here you could put all of your canned vegetables ..." She turned around to see everyone staring at her.

"Oops. Sorry."

"No! That's great!" Polly exclaimed. "It's all yours now." She laughed and pulled a stainless steel cart out from under the front counter. "Here, we'll put everything on this and you can have a ball."

In a few minutes, every cupboard door was wide open and supplies unloaded. Beryl had found the coffee mugs and pulled five out. She gathered plates and napkins, and after discovering a platter, filled it with scones and cookies. The chatter of the women as they worked in her kitchen made Polly giggle. It seemed surreal. Women she'd never met before had walked in and made themselves at home.

Lydia was stowing casserole dishes and plastic ware-filled containers in her refrigerator and freezer. "The dishes are clearly labeled. You shouldn't have to cook for a while unless we keep showing up," Lydia remarked. "And this kitchen is amazing! I'd show up every day just to cook here."

She walked over to the stove. "Andy, did you see this thing? It's got everything you could want in a stove!" To Polly, she asked, "How much did this cost?"

At Beryl's gasp, Lydia's face fell and she shook her head. "I'm sorry. I've never seen anything like this in someone's home."

Polly chuckled. "If I'm going to pull off what I want to do here, it needs to be this big."

Lydia asked, "What exactly are you hoping to do?"

"A little bit of everything," Polly responded. "A little bit artist's retreat, a little bit community center, a little bit bookstore, a little bit crafting. Yeah, that." She clicked off the coffeemaker, reached into a drawer for a trivet and carried both to the table.

Polly went on, "I haven't even thought about cooking since I got here. I appreciate the chance for good food."

She sat down on the far side of the table and the women gathered around. Andy kept glancing at the pantry shelves until finally Beryl said, "Enough, girl! I'm sure Polly will let you come back with your label maker and turn it into a thing of organizational beauty. Right, Polly?"

Polly took a bite out of a scone. She moaned a little as the aroma of raspberry and sugar filled her senses. "What? Oh. Sure. You can come back any time. Excuse me a moment while I enjoy this," and took another bite.

Lydia was the next to interrupt Polly's reverie. "The whole town is dying to know what you're doing here. There are a lot of rumors. Most of the guys working on the renovation are from around here, but you know men. They never get it right and they never know what questions to ask to make us happy."

Andy said, "My daughter's boyfriend, Jimmy, has been working in here lately. I keep telling him to ask questions, but he's shy."

Polly nodded. "I know who that is. He is shy. He walks past a room where I'm painting, hesitates as if he wants to step in and speak to me, then shakes his head and goes back to where he was working. He seems like a nice boy, though."

"I'm glad he has a good job. He has to wait until my daughter is finished with college before he asks her to marry him. He knows I'll kill her if she doesn't graduate, so he's trying to be patient."

"Polly, why did you buy this old school?" Lydia pressed a little harder.

Polly sat back in her chair, holding her coffee mug between both hands.

"I wanted to live in Iowa again. I realized one day how much I missed being around real people. Mom died twenty years ago and then three years ago Dad was killed in a car accident. They owned a farm over by Story City. Dad sold out to his brothers about ten years ago - he made a really good deal. He moved into a little house in town and had a great time there. He loved working with wood, so he had a small shop in his garage. Christmas was his favorite time of year. He'd dress up as Santa Claus and take the toys he made to shelters in the area.

"I'd gone to Boston to college and got a job out there, working at the Boston Public Library. It was absolutely wonderful. I loved everything about it, but I missed the quiet of the farm and being around people who loved me only because I was family. I came back after Dad died and cleared out his house. I put everything in storage, went back to Boston and realized that what I loved about the library was the solitude I found in the stacks.

Then, something happened and I realized how much I wanted to be here. I started scouting around for a small town and the son of one of Dad's old friends is a realtor. When he sent me pictures of this school and I realized how close it was to Ames and Des Moines, I decided I didn't need to work at the library any longer and I didn't need to live in Boston either. I gave them my notice, packed my stuff and made the move."

"What happened to make you suddenly leave Boston?" asked Sylvie.

"Oh, nothing much. It was the right time for me to go." Polly's eyes misted a little bit and they noticed her slight shudder. She averted her eyes and took another bite of the scone.

"So, how long have you been in Iowa?" Lydia asked, moving the conversation along.

"I left Boston in April, rented an apartment in Ames while the purchase of the school went through and began making plans to renovate it."

"You surely aren't going to live in this big ole place by yourself, are you?" Beryl's eyes were huge.

"This is exactly what I want," Polly replied. "I'm putting an apartment upstairs and turning the downstairs into my dream. I'm going to play and invite everyone else to play with me. Someday it will have everything in it I've ever wanted; a little craft shop where we can teach knitting and crocheting, cake baking and other cooking classes, and maybe a little library and bookstore. Open computers and Wi-Fi if people have their own. Comfy chairs and tables all over the place. Kind of like a community center, but more."

She went on, "We will host parties and events in the auditorium and on the stage. In the other three rooms upstairs, I'll have space for artists and authors and anyone who needs a getaway for a while."

Polly sighed, "It's a dream I have and now I'm going to go after it."

"Wow," said Andy. "That's a pretty big dream. I hope your Dad left you lots of money."

Beryl scowled at Andy. "You girls are awfully personal today." She looked at Polly. "You'd think they'd never been out in public before."

Polly's eyes sparkled as she laughed. "He left me plenty to do this and even screw it up a little."

"Don't you have any sisters or brothers?" asked Andy.

"No. I was an only child," Polly replied. "That's probably what makes me so comfortable in the quiet."

She looked around the table, then said, "I don't know anything about you all, except you're courageous enough to walk in on a strange woman. Oh, and that you went to school here. Tell me things I should know about you."

Lydia said, "I'll start. My husband, Aaron, is the sheriff. He's a good old guy, even if he seems a little gruff. We have five children. They're all grown up and two of them have gotten married and have kids of their own. If I start telling you about my brood I won't stop, but the youngest, Jim, is over at Iowa State in his last year. He's already got a job lined up when he graduates. We're pretty proud of all of them.

“My oldest daughter, Marilyn, lives over in Dayton. They have twins and even if I got to see those cuties every day, it wouldn't be enough. The next daughter, Jill, lives in Kansas City. Her husband works there. They have one little boy. I wish they lived closer so I could spend more time with him. After Jill is Daniel, who lives in Des Moines and then Sandy. She’s in Minneapolis. As for me, I don't do too much. Just wait for my kiddos to show up!"

Beryl smiled at her friend, "Lydia does everything. She organizes meals for shut-ins, manages the Sunday School program at the Methodist church, drives some of the widows whenever they need to shop. Heck, she shops for those who don't want to get out. Don't let her fool you! She's everyone's best hope for the good life, it seems."

"Hush, you," said Lydia. "That's enough."

Andy laughed. "Don't you love them already, Polly?"

Polly smiled. This felt right. "What about you, Andy?"

"Well, I'm a widow, but I'm not one of those ladies Lydia has to take care of." She stopped, looked around the table and said, "Am I? Oh no. I'm not, am I? That's not why I'm here with you?" Her voice began rising until Lydia lightly punched her in the forearm.

"Stop it, you fool," Lydia said. "We've been friends since elementary school."

"Oh," responded Andy. "That's right."

She went on, "I've been feeling a little old lately and sometimes a little lonely. Fine, I got stupid for a minute.

"I'm retired, I guess. I used to be a high school English teacher. I taught here in this school, right up at the top of those stairs for years. When they closed the building, I taught in Boone. My husband, Bill, died about five years ago. He was a wonderful man. He farmed and we raised three great kids out there. The two older boys, Billy and John, run the farm with their families. Melanie, my youngest is in grad school in

Iowa City. I moved into town so Billy and his wife could have the farmhouse and it's probably a good thing. I miss the farm, but at least I'm close to my friends."

Beryl waited for a breath, then said, "My turn! I'm single and I love it. I kicked my first husband out thirty years ago and then when I thought I'd found a great man a few years later, he up and died on me after only two years. I decided to say 'to hell with it.' I'm great all by myself and I'll stay that way forever. If a man wants to hang out with me, fine, but he can own his own house and live his own life."

Polly couldn't help it. She burst out laughing. "Well, that's a great way to look at it!"

"You're damned right it is. If I want to run naked through the house in the middle of the night, there isn't anyone to stop me or think I'm trying to get them all turned on."

By now, all of them were laughing, Beryl included.

"I do like living by myself. I have a cat to keep me company and all that solitude gives me plenty of time to paint."

"You're an artist?" Polly asked.

Lydia answered, "She's a great artist. She even has art hanging in a gallery or two in your little town of Boston! We're pretty proud of her."

"I'd love to see your work sometime, Beryl. Maybe you'd allow me to hang a few things here." Polly said.

"Polly, dear. I'll choose one for you to hang before you open those doors." said Beryl.

Sylvie had been quietly enjoying the banter of the other four women. Lydia turned to her. "It's finally your turn, Sylvie. You have to fess up and tell your life story now."

She began rubbing her right thumb across the forefinger. "I don't have much to tell. I work at the grocery store and take care of my two boys, Jason and Andrew. They're still pretty young and need me at home. I spend a lot of time going to their school activities. There's not much time for other things with work and their lives. If I didn't have these ladies around, I don't know what I'd do!"

Polly looked at Lydia, as if hoping for a little more information, but it didn't look like she was going to get much more.

Andy reached out and patted Sylvie on the shoulder. "We love your kiddos and are glad you choose to hang out with us old ladies. You make us feel young again!"

Beryl laughed again. It seemed there was always an undercurrent of laughter in her voice. "That's right, Sylvie. Us old, decrepit ladies certainly do like having you around to make sure we don't drop over into our graves when we walk past the cemetery."

Polly's puzzled look signaled more laughter. "Oh, you don't know," Beryl said. "Andy lives past the old town cemetery. We tease her about it all the time. She says the ghosts don't bother her, but one can never be sure what's going to pop out, can one?"

"Stop it, you crazy person," said Lydia. "You're nuts.

"So," Lydia went on. "We're your welcoming committee. We'll probably keep bothering you until you get this place finished. Andy, Beryl and I have known each other forever, it seems. Sylvie was in one of Andy's last classes at this school ... isn't that right, girls?"

Both women nodded. Sylvie responded. "Mine was the last graduating class. After we left, everyone else was bused into Boone. I loved it here and I can't wait to see what you're doing with it."

Lydia stood up. She really was in charge. "Alright, we've kept you long enough. I suppose it's time we let you get back to whatever you were doing." She pulled a 3 x 5 card from her wallet and wrote down some numbers. "Here are our cell phone numbers. Now that you know us and have been thoroughly entertained by us, I fully expect you to take advantage of these and call us if you need or want anything, even if it's only company."

She handed the card to Polly. "And if I don't hear from you before the weekend, I'm coming back to check on you. My house is always open if my car is there. I drive a blue Grand Cherokee. If it's not there, well ... who knows where I am!"

Beryl jumped in. "I'm always home, unless I'm with blue Grand Cherokee here. If you stop by my house and I don't answer the door, walk around back. My painting shed is out in the garden. I spend most of the time out there, even in the winter."

Andy looked at Polly. "You're never going to find my house until you've been there a couple of times. It's kind of like looking for the blue bird sitting on a fence post. Hey! I should buy a blue bird and put it on my fence post. Why haven't I thought of that before! But, once you do find me, you're always welcome."

Sylvie started to speak and then stopped. Then, she started again. "I don't ever seem to be home, but when I'm there, one of these nuts always finds me. I work in the grocery store downtown, though. Stop in and say hi, okay?"

Lydia started walking out of the kitchen and the rest of the ladies stood and followed her out into the main hallway. She said to Polly, "You know, I'm can't wait to see what you're planning to do with all of this. All these painter's cloths aren't telling me a thing!"

Polly said, "I'll tell you what. Give me a few more days and I'll have you back over. Everything is going to come together quickly in the next month and it will start making sense."

Lydia gave her a quick hug. "Do that. We're glad you're here. This is going to be fun."

Beryl grabbed Polly's hand as she walked past and gave it a quick squeeze. Andy patted her on the shoulder and Sylvie winked at her as they all followed Lydia out the front door. There was a blue Grand Cherokee parked in the front lot beside Polly's red Ford pickup. As the ladies got in, she waved and watched them drive away.

Polly walked back in, shut the door and returned to the kitchen. She poured another cup of coffee and sat down again, thinking over her first encounter with new friends. It wasn't quite what she expected, but then, honestly, she had no idea what it was she expected.

As she drank her coffee, Polly remembered the open paint can upstairs. She dumped the rest of the coffee in the sink, sluiced some water around to rinse it out and took off up the steps at a run. When she got to the door of the room she had been painting, she stopped to take in its beauty. With tall ceilings and glass windows, sunlight streamed in everywhere. The light grey walls were going to be perfect for her bedroom, and it was time to finish so Henry could begin working.

She thought back for a moment to her last life. Sunday afternoons and evenings were usually spent with Joey, doing something in and around Boston. Since she hadn't grown up on the east coast, he loved to act like tourists and take her to see all the sights. Whether they were on the swan boats in Boston Common or out in Concord, or walking through some author's home, it was always fun. Then, when evening came, they would pick up a pizza and carry it back to her apartment and watch television. Her Sundays had been filled with fun and relaxation.

This was much better, though. She worked herself to exhaustion and slept like a worn out puppy every night. She was glad she'd finally moved her things to one of the rooms across from her apartment. Even if everything but her bed and a table was still in the basement in storage, at least she was living in her own place.

She grabbed the brush, climbed back up the ladder and finished the last of the second coat. It would dry overnight and tomorrow, Henry would hang moldings and begin framing the doors and windows. They'd talked about hard wood floors in this room and she planned to check out some old barn board he had found on a farm south of Boone. If it was what they both thought, it would be perfect.

Polly cleaned the brushes and rollers, washed out the trays and sealed up the paint can, and then walked across the hall to where her bed was and stripped down. She took a quick shower to rinse of the splatter, walked over to a box of books on the floor, shut her eyes and pulled out a book. When she looked at the title, she giggled. "Anna Karenina, eh?" she said out loud. "Thanks. This will put me right to sleep."

She set her alarm for six, snuggled under the covers and opened the book. "Happy families are all alike; every unhappy family is unhappy in its own way ..."

"Well, that's one way to start a book," she thought and continued reading. After a few short minutes, her eyes began to droop and she mustered up enough energy to drop the book on the floor and turn out the light.

CHAPTER TWO

Early the next morning, Polly was in the kitchen when she heard the front door open.

"It's me, Polly!" Henry Sturtz's voice rang through the building. There was no drywall hung in the main level yet, so sounds tended to echo.

Polly walked out. "Hi, Henry, coffee is made if you want it." When she had realized how much coffee it took to renovate a building, she'd purchased a large 40 cup pot. Some days it took several of those pots to keep everyone moving.

"I had to stop at Casey's for a large coffee already. This weekend must have kicked me around a little!" he said.

"Oh!" she laughed. "How was it?"

Henry had told her a little about his sister, Lonnie, on Friday before he left for the day. She lived in Ann Arbor with two of her best friends, was finishing her doctorate and planned to continue teaching at the University of Michigan. The three loved to torment Lonnie's older brother whenever possible. They often came to Iowa and discovered ways of making Henry do girl-stuff. Then, after exhausting him, they'd head back to Michigan, knowing it was a job well done.

"I think we saw every antique store between here and Iowa City. She kept finding things she wanted me to restore. I told her I was too busy. Needless to say, I have a cherry sideboard and hutch sitting in my shop now. I hate refinishing furniture. I hate it," he said.

"But, I guess you're going to do it anyway?" Polly snickered.

"What else can I do? I can't say no to that girl." Henry looked at Polly for sympathy.

"Oh, you'll get no sympathy from me," she laughed. "You're a big boy and you know how to put 'no' into a sentence. If you haven't figured that out by now, it's no one's problem but your own." Polly smiled and turned to head into the kitchen.

She heard him mumbling as he followed her.

Henry looked at the shelves in the pantry.

"What happened here?" he asked. "Did you go shopping? I thought you were painting all weekend?"

"Oh, some of the ladies from town happened here. Yesterday." she said. "There were four of them. They kind of tornadoed in and I didn't know what to say!"

"That's great," he laughed. "They probably could hardly wait. Let's see. Lydia Merritt was the leader, wasn't she!" His mouth opened up in an immense grin and he could barely hold back the laughter.

"Yep. It was Lydia and let's see if I remember," Polly stopped and thought. "Beryl someone, Andy something, and Sylvie Donovan. She didn't seem to fit in with them, but it looked like that wasn't going to sway the others. They had her firmly in hand."

"I don't know Sylvie, but those other three women are a threat to your peace and quiet. Once you are their friend, everyone will know who you are and will be interested in what you are doing."

"What?" She asked, a little panicked.

"Oh, don't get me wrong," he said. "They're amazing and three of the best people I've ever known. They will take care of you."

He stopped speaking and a little chuckle bubbled out from behind his lips. "I call them the Musketeers. If one of them thinks something should be done or someone needs something, the others stand with her and the next thing you know, the world is different. It's like magic.

He continued, "All I'm saying is that your quiet little life here is now officially over. I hope you're ready. Now, before I say anything more, I need coffee."

Henry had been in the kitchen enough to know where the mugs were. He pulled one out and walked over to the pot to fill it.

"Since Lydia was here, did she bring anything good to eat for breakfast?" he asked.

"Oh, that's funny," Polly replied. "We had cookies and scones yesterday. I'm sure there is something else in the fridge, but I haven't had time to look."

"Well, let's fix that," Henry said and pulled open the door of the first refrigerator. "Huh, Andy's been busy. Everything is neatly labeled.

"Taco meat, spaghetti sauce, meatballs, shredded lettuce, sliced tomatoes, chopped carrots and celery. Good heavens, lunch and dinner are certainly ... oh, here we go! This has potential!"

He pulled out a large plastic container filled with small bags.

"What does it say?" Polly asked.

"'Breakfast sandwiches.' We have ham, bacon and sausage. All you have to do is microwave them." He said.

"How do you know that?"

Henry tipped the container so she could see. Each bag was individually labeled and on the underside of the lid was an instruction card.

"I'm not even sure what to say," Polly laughed, "but I'll heat some up. Do you want one or two?"

"I want two of these," and he began flipping through the bags. "Here, sausage and ham for me. What would you like?"

"Let's make it even and give me a bacon sandwich." Polly tore open the bags and placed the sandwiches on a dish and into the microwave.

Henry returned the container to the refrigerator and pulled out another.

"Would you like some fruit as well?" he asked.

"Sure!" Polly took out plates and opened the silverware drawer. She put everything on the table and pointed at a chair, so Henry sat down. When the microwave announced its completion, she took the plate out and walked back to the table.

They sat in silence for a few minutes while eating and drinking. The quiet was broken by the sounds of more vehicles pulling into the lot out front and workmen bringing their tools and supplies in to the building.

Polly looked at Henry, shrugged and said, "I'm sorry ... I need to handle this." He took one last bite and gathered up the dishes.

"Just drop them in the sink, I'll deal with them later," Polly said as she headed out the kitchen door.

Walking out into the main room, Polly saw Jerry Allen, her electrical contractor. "Hi Jerry! What's up for you guys today?"

"Oh, we've finished the big rooms upstairs, we still have to rewire the bathrooms up there, but we're working on the main level. I want to make, sure there is good power in the basement as well." He turned to Polly. I'm glad you aren't asking us to go through all of this concrete. It would take forever and make a real mess."

She smiled. "You do whatever is right and I'll be fine. I think the plans we have in place will work." She shook her head. "I still can't get over how little people expected to be using electricity in a school. If I had my way, there would be quad plugs every two feet."

"We'll get it done, Miss Giller."

She stopped him, "Please ... it's just Polly."

Polly started up the steps, then said, "You know where the coffee pot is in the kitchen. Help yourselves!"

She went on up to her room. She shut the door, changed into slacks and a red blouse, and then grabbed her sweater. When she got back downstairs, she ducked into the classroom where Henry had set up his shop.

Several other men had arrived and were measuring and sorting through the moldings. They looked up at her arrival and each nodded a hello.

Polly recognized them and after her encounter with the women over the weekend realized she should pay attention to their names, especially since she would probably see them on a regular basis.

"I'm sorry, guys. Will you tell me your names again?" she asked.

One by one the three men stood, "I'm Marvin Davis," the first said with a bit of a drawl and held out his hand to shake Polly's, "but the guys call me Peaches."

Polly cocked her head and asked, "Why would they call you Peaches?"

"Oh, because they think I sound like I'm from Georgia. Like anyone around here knows what a guy from Georgia sounds like." He scowled at the two other men. Marvin was in his mid to late fifties and looked like he'd spent a lot of time working outside.

"Peaches here got his name 'cuz he's such a sweet guy, just like peaches and cream," drawled the next guy, who came up to stand next to him. His voice straightened out as he said, "I'm Leroy Forster. Call me Leroy."

"Okay, I'll do that!" Polly replied with a smirk. Leroy was no spring chicken. He had terrible scars on his hands, but tattoos on his forearms covered any scarring which might have been there. When he shook her hand, she felt a great deal of strength radiating from him.

The third man said quietly, "I'm Ben Bowen. I'm the guy who does all the work around here while these two chat it up with pretty women."

Leroy said, "Yeah, we call him Pretty Boy."

"But, you can call me Ben." He took Polly's hand in both of his. "Thanks for renovating this school ma'am. It's a real pleasure to be bringing the old place back to life. I went to school a long time ago in this place and it's nice to know it will see people again. I appreciate the work, too."

"Thanks Ben, Leroy, Marvin. I promise I'll remember from now on!" Polly said and then walked over to Henry. "I'm heading out to see what those barn boards look like for the floors. Anything else I need to know?"

"You should be fine," he responded, "I've talked to the guy and had

Butch stop by as well. Since he'll be doing the milling, I wanted him to see things before I talked to you. He said they looked good as long as you like the color."

"Great. I'll see you later!"

Polly walked to the front door and turned around to look at her home. The morning was starting to buzz. She loved her Mondays now. Each week, workmen came in and started on a project. It was exciting. There was always some interesting decision to make, like the week she had to pick out the kitchen appliances. She had nearly cried with joy every time she got to choose the perfect large appliance for her kitchen. Things she had only dreamed about having were finally showing up in her home.

She pulled the door shut behind her and walked down the front steps to her truck.

It took about twenty minutes to get to the farm where the barn boards were located. Polly pulled into the drive. This was hard for her. Even though she knew she was expected, knocking on a stranger's door felt weird. She thought about it on the drive down and decided it was also weird that she was uncomfortable with this. She'd grown up on a farm and when she was young, her parents never had a problem with people knocking at the door.

Polly’s mom had died when she was twelve and they'd had a housekeeper who spent her days at the house. Her husband had been Polly's father's right hand man on the farm. The two of them, Sylvester and Mary Shore, arrived every morning at 6:30 and left after supper every evening. They'd never had kids and had been friends with Polly's parents long before she was born. After Polly's mother died, Mary quit her job as a doctor's receptionist and made sure the young girl was healthy and happy. It had been a pretty good life.

But now, it was time for Polly to walk up to a stranger's door. No one ever went in the front door when she lived on the farm. It seemed like everyone knew you went to the back door. But, Polly had been away for a long time and she had no idea if that was still the right thing to do. She sat in her truck for a few minutes trying to figure out the lay of the land. If she went in the front door, they might think she was trying to be too formal, but she didn't want them to think she was too forward by going to the back door. Oh, she hated this part of getting to know people.

As she was putting her hand out to open the door of her truck, the back door of the house opened and a young woman walked outside. Polly pulled the latch and stepped out of her car.

"Are you Polly? Polly Giller?" asked the young woman.

"Yes, I am." Polly said with more than a little relief.

"Brad's in the barn. He told me to keep an eye out for you. It’s this way," the young woman said. "By thc way, my name is Lee. I hope you like these boards. I think they're beautiful, but Brad says there is no reason for us to keep them. This old house already has nice wood floors, so I guess I don't need them."

Lee had shoulder length blonde hair and her eyes were already smiling. Before they got to the barn, Polly’s insides jumped when Lee let loose with a shout, "Brad! Brad! She's here!"

There was some rustling in the barn as the two women entered. A good looking young man in jeans and a plaid shirt looked up from a pile of hay he seemed to be arranging.

"That stupid cat had kittens in here last night, Lee."

"Well, if you wouldn't feed that stupid cat, she might not think you were hers," Lee retorted.

She turned to Polly. "He likes us all to think he hates small animals, but we know better. He's a big softy. He'll be out here every night making sure they're warm and safe. What do you want to bet he builds a pen around this pile of hay so nothing can get to them."

Polly smiled at the two and leaned over to look inside the space Brad had been working on. There was a mama cat with five tiny balls of fur gathered around.

"Oh, they are adorable, aren't they? I haven't had cats in years!"

Lee got a hopeful look on her face, "Would you like one or maybe two when they're old enough to be weaned?"

Polly laughed. "Let me think about it, but I bet they'd be wonderful at the old school house. I'll let you know."

"Alright, alright, Lee. Leave her alone. Cats come and go so fast around here we don't even bother naming them," Brad said.

"Oh, don't let him kid you. He named mama cat the first time he saw her." Lee responded.

"I don't think 'stupid cat' is actually a name, Lee." Brad said.

"No, it's not. But, Snuffles is and she loves you." Lee poked her husband in the arm and he yanked it away.

"Whatever."

Then he said. "The barn boards are over here." He walked to the other side of the barn and there were a number of beautifully grayed and weathered boards propped against the wall. Polly gasped. "Those are gorgeous!"

Lee said, "I know. They really are. When we pulled the barn down and I saw them, I thought they'd be perfect. A little work and they'll be even more beautiful."

"I want them all," Polly said. " I need to get someone down here to pick them up, but I want every single one of them. Anything I don't use on my floors will be used somewhere else."

She reached in her jeans pocket for her checkbook. "I'll write you the check today, but it might take a few days for me to round up a truck and some guys to move these. Is that alright?"

"That will be fine," said Brad. "I won't need this space for a few weeks or so. Call when you're coming to get them and we'll get you loaded and ready to go."

Polly wrote out the check and before Brad could put his hands on it, Lee took it. "I'll make sure this gets in the right account, honey. I don't think you need to put it in one of your little savings accounts. We can use this in other places."

Brad shook his head and smiled at his wife. "She's always telling me what to do. Thanks a lot Miss Giller and if you want a couple of cats, I'll gladly bring them up. Both of us would like to see what you're doing with that old school house. It was sure a shame when it closed down and even more of a shame to see it sitting there all boarded up."

"I'll call later this week and I will think about those cats. But, you two are welcome to come any time. When the floors get laid, I'll let you know so you can see where your boards are living!"

Lee and Polly walked out of the barn while Brad went back to work, setting up the home for the kittens.

"Would you like to come in for some coffee or tea?" Lee asked.

"I don't think so today. It's been nice to meet you though," Polly said. "I need to get back to the craziness on the home front. I like to remind them I'm still around and they can't make decisions without me!"

Polly turned to go back to her truck.

"Oh, Lee, I have a stupid question," she said.

"Yes?"

"If you hadn't come out of the back door, I would have had no idea which door to use. It's been so long since I've been in the country." Polly said.

"That's hilarious!" Lee laughed. "I suppose I would have answered the front door just like I do the back door, but now that you've been here once, you never have to use the front door. You're a friend."

"I'll see you another time, then!" Polly said and opened the door to her car. As she sat down and turned the key, it occurred to her she still hadn't gotten a good answer. It wasn't going to be any easier the next time she had to go to someone's home.

Polly backed down the driveway and out onto the main road. If she hurried, she would have time to stop at the Post Office before lunch. The building got quiet during the lunch hour and she liked having some of the foremen and contractors show up at her kitchen table to tell her what they'd been doing during the morning.

Her dreams were all coming true. It seemed like life couldn't get any better.

CHAPTER THREE

Heaving a sigh, Polly dropped into a chair in the kitchen. She was going to have to get more furniture pulled upstairs. She didn't have a comfortable chair anywhere. It was either stand, sit in the kitchen or lie down in her bed, unless she was driving somewhere to get something for someone. Now that she lived here, her days seemed long and the nights were short, which was strange because outside, the nights were long and days were much too short. She was never ready for the sun to set so early in the evenings.

They still had a great deal of work to do on the old bathrooms upstairs. They were completely gutting the rooms and would turn each of them into a spa bathroom.

Painting those classrooms had been an incredible feat. Fourteen foot ceilings weren't an easy reach, but she knew she needed to keep going. This was one part of the renovation she could do and she wanted to not only make decisions, but be part of the work. She knew it might seem strange to some, but before she chose the paint for a room, she tried to imagine the room filled with children as they learned from their teacher. Each room seemed to tell a story and she was happy with how things had turned out.

Henry had been busy this week. The rooms upstairs framed and trimmed and bookshelves built into the walls. He shaped each of the pieces in a classroom on the main floor and then took them upstairs for installation. His two young assistants, Jimmy Rio and Sam Terhune, were more than willing to traipse up and down the steps all day.

The week had been long. Electricians and plumbers were working on the lower level trying to get everything in place before drywall was hung. They had two more weeks before that was scheduled, but they had been all over the place every day of the week.

As she sat, staring out the window at the broken down playground, her cell phone rang. She sighed. There was no more room left in her mind to make another decision, but knew if someone had a question, it was her job to come up with an answer. She didn't recognize the phone number, so offered a tentative, "Hello?"

"Hi Polly, it's Lydia Merritt. How are you doing?"

Polly shook her head. She pulled the phone away, stared it, took a deep breath, then came back to the conversation.

"Hello, Lydia! I'm doing alright. How are you?" She felt badly that her voice didn't sound energetic, but that was all she had left.

"Well, I'm probably doing better than you, dear. I haven't had a building full of workers all week. Are you exhausted?" Lydia asked.

"Honestly, Lydia. I really am. Times like this I wish I had a bathtub, a soft chair and someone to rub my feet."

"I have a bathtub and a soft chair and I could probably be talked into rubbing your feet, but I suppose you might not want to be around anybody at all this evening."

Polly wasn't sure how to respond. She hesitated before answering.

"I don't know if I have the energy tonight for people," she said.

"I didn't figure you would. Whenever you get up, check outside your front door. I left you some dinner. You shouldn't have to do anything. It's simple."

"Oh, Lydia, you didn't have to do that. You guys already left me a lot of food." Polly said.

"I know. But it's Friday night and you can take this up to your bed, curl up with a book and fall asleep. That is, if you don't mind a few crumbs in your bed," Lydia said. "And, I have another reason for pampering you a little and then calling you.

She went on before Polly could speak, "Tomorrow evening I have tickets to a play over at Iowa State University. Beryl and Andy are going. I asked Sylvie if she wanted to take her kids, but it sounds like her mother is coming into town, so she declined. We thought we'd make an evening of it. Dinner and the play and maybe drinks or something afterward and then ... you come stay at my house for the night. Pack a bag. We're going to have a slumber party. You'll get a real chair to sit in, carpet under your feet, a bed you don't have to make in the morning and breakfast on the table. How about it?"

"I'd love to go out with you, but a slumber party? I don't think I'm ready for that." Polly said.

"Sure you are. It will be great," Lydia responded, "The girls and I plan to hang out in front of the fireplace. The old man is leaving town tomorrow and won't be back until Sunday night. I thought we could have some fun."

Lydia's enthusiasm was contagious. Polly hadn't been to a slumber party since she was in elementary school and she certainly hadn't been to one with women who were so much older. What was she supposed to think about all of this?

She opened her mouth, but before she could respond, Lydia said, "You have to. You have to!"

"Alright, I'm in." Polly said, then continued "Lydia, this has to be the craziest thing I've ever heard!"

"Oh, honey," Lydia said. "You just wait. Crazy is what we do when we get bored around here. And don't think the play will be the most wonderful thing you'll see tomorrow. Wait until Beryl gets a couple of my famous chocolate martinis in her! That will be wonderful."

Polly had stood up while she was talking and walked to her front door. She opened it and there was a small, square, blue basket with a pretty red checkered napkin wrapped around its contents. She picked it up, pushed the door shut, clicked the lock and walked to the stairs. She sat down and opened the napkin.

"Lydia!" she exclaimed.

"Yes dear?" Lydia asked.

"I opened the basket. This is beautiful! Thank you!" Polly said.

"Well, you have a good night. Sleep well, sleep late and be ready for us to pick you up at four o'clock tomorrow afternoon. Beryl's driving, oh lordie, so the rest of us can start the party at the restaurant. She'll catch up when we get back to my house," Lydia responded.

"Thank you so much, Lydia. I'll see you tomorrow!" Polly ended the call, and then went back into the kitchen to shut the lights off. She'd clean the coffee pot out tomorrow morning. She slipped in past the plastic draping to Henry's temporary shop and saw everything was tucked in and turned off for the night. Walking back to the main floor switches, she flipped them down and walked up the steps to her room.

Brad's Monday telephone call, telling her he had a buddy with a big truck and would take the boards to Henry's friend Butch for milling on Wednesday, had gotten everyone moving. She peeked into the room and smiled. Just getting the wood frames built around the room made it feel warmer already. She turned the light back off and wandered across the hallway to her bed.

Slipping off her shoes and tucking them under the table, she set the basket on the bed, then took her clothes off and walked back across the hall to the shower in her apartment. There was nothing better than practically scalding, hot water pouring over her head after a busy week. This shower was one of her personal luxuries. Water flowed from the ceiling of the shower as well as from the walls, along with a regular shower head. When she turned it all on, the water massaged every ache and pain that painting and hauling and cleaning and scrubbing had delivered to her this week. She didn't indulge in the whole thing very often because she generally stayed in there so long her skin became prune like, but tonight, it seemed like just the thing.

Finally, she turned it all off, stepped out of the shower and wrapped a towel around her body. She picked through her hair with her fingers and grabbed another towel to wrap around her head. Walking back across the hall, Polly picked her robe up from the end of the bed, dropped the towel on the floor and crawled in. Now, she could tear into the basket of goodies waiting for her.

The first thing she touched was a partially frozen bottle of water with a few chunks of ice floating around. There were two small sandwiches cut in half with crusts trimmed away. She sniffed the bread … homemade. Wow.

The first sandwich was ham and Swiss, and smelled glorious. The second was a delectable roast beef that threw off its aroma as she unwrapped its plastic wrap. Beneath those she uncovered a container of crackers with cheese cut to size and one more container of grapes. Another package contained chocolate chip cookies and on the bottom of the basket was a napkin wrapped around a little freezer pack, resting on a rectangular cutting board. A plastic bag contained plastic ware and packages of mayonnaise, butter and mustard were tucked in the side of the basket. Lydia thought of everything.

Polly wondered if she took care of everyone in town like this and then quit thinking after taking a bite of the roast beef sandwich. It was amazing. She felt decadent and spoiled.

How had she ever hit this woman's radar? She was never going to be able to say thank you enough for what Lydia was doing. Then it hit her. No one had done this much for her since she left Iowa the first time. Mary had loved her like a daughter and Polly missed having someone around to mother her. This felt good.

She finished what she could of supper, scrubbed the towel through her hair again and tossed it on top of the first. She was going to have to do laundry sometime this weekend. Polly set the little basket on the floor under her bed, not wanting to go back downstairs.

She opened her book and read until she nodded off. The last time she glanced at the clock it read 9:18. She hadn't fallen asleep so early in a long time.

When Polly opened her eyes again, she was surprised to see it was 7:05. What had Lydia put in those cookies? She never slept all the way through the night and ten hours of sleep was glorious. She stretched and yawned, feeling quite lazy and content. No one was going to be in the schoolhouse today. It was all hers. She could do whatever she wanted and she decided she didn't want to paint today. She pulled the blankets up under her chin and looked around. The sun was out and flooding the floor of her room. Finally she couldn't stand it any longer, sat up, grabbed her robe and went into the bathroom.

One look in the mirror over the sink had her laughing out loud. "Well, that's why I don't take a shower before I go to bed," she said to herself. Turning on the shower head, she ducked in and rinsed through her hair one more time. This time, she brushed it out and tied it into a braid. It wasn't that long, just past her shoulders, but the wet braid would give her some body for this evening's dress-up affair.

Back in her room, she pulled on jeans and a t-shirt, and then filled a laundry basket. One basket wouldn’t do it, so she stuffed a pillowcase with the excess. She'd been living here for three weeks and suddenly realized she didn't know where to do her laundry, so she picked up her cell phone and called Lydia.

"Good morning, Polly! Did you sleep well?" Lydia asked before Polly could say anything.

"I did! What did you put in my cookies?" she asked.

"Oh, a little love, nothing more than that." Lydia said. "You're still coming out with us this evening, aren't you?"

"Oh yes! Absolutely! Say, I was wondering if there was a Laundromat in town. I am in desperate need of clean towels." Polly said.

"No, we don't have one. The town is too small. Boone is the closest town with a decent place to do your laundry," Lydia responded. "But, what are you talking about! You can do your laundry at my house tonight, unless you need something clean before we pick you up."

"Oh, Lydia, no. You've done so much for me. I’d hate to do that." Polly said.

"Stop it. There is nothing I love more than taking care of people and one of these days you aren't going to need me anymore, so let me help you." Lydia's voice had gotten a little pouty. "If you don't let us do things for you now, how are we going to feel when we want you to let us sleep over at your place?"

Polly laughed enough to snort, "You have me there," she said, "I'll bring the clothes with me when you pick me up. Does Beryl have enough room in her car?”

“Oh, dear. That plan changed. We’ll be in my Jeep. Beryl panicked at the thought of driving in Ames. You know, the big city. She gets lost in Bellingwood, so it’s better for all of us if we don’t push her too far outside her box.”

"Thank you again, Lydia. I'll see you later," Polly said.

"Have a great day, you might want to take a nap this afternoon. Know what I mean?" Lydia responded.

"I suppose I do," Polly laughed. "Good-bye."

"Good-bye, dear."

Polly pulled the overflowing basket and stuffed pillow case out of the room. She went back in, picked up the little basket from last night’s supper, stuffed her phone in her jeans and headed for the stairs.

She'd always done things in one trip and knew she could do this too. Polly tucked the laundry basket under her left arm and with Lydia’s basket in her right hand; grabbed the pillow case and began bouncing it down the steps behind her. When she got halfway down the steps, she heard a noise and dropped everything in fright as a head popped around the corner of the stairs.

"I'm sorry! I'm sorry!" It was one of Jerry Allen's young apprentice electricians.

"What are you doing here? I didn't know anyone was working today!" Polly's voice was a little stricken.

He started to walk up the steps to help her with the laundry, when both of them realized her underwear and bras had been strewn all over the steps. He hesitated, looking at her with panic in his eyes.

"I'm so sorry!” he exclaimed. “Billy left the power stapler here yesterday and we need it for a job out on Bob Miller's farm.” The young man began backing away from the stairway and Polly's obvious discomfort. She walked down the steps with the bag of towels and set them beside the door, then grabbed the basket, which was upside down on the floor.

He went on, "I knocked on the door and no one answered. I thought I'd come in and grab it and it wouldn't be a big deal."

"It's alright," Polly said. "I now have a weakened heart, a red face from dirty laundry and a notion that the next best item to install will be a doorbell. Do you want to tell Jerry it needs to happen Monday rather than later?

"What is your name, by the way?" she asked.

"It's Doug, Doug Randall. I'm so sorry!" He kept backing toward the door and when he could, he opened it and stepped out. Then, he poked his head back in. "I'm sorry," then a sneaky little grin lit up his face, "but I've never seen anything like those purple things!" He ducked out quickly and pulled the door shut behind him.

Polly looked up at the steps. Her eyes lit on the purple underwear with hot pink bows. She didn't think they were anything special, but decided if they gave a young man something to think about, she'd try not to be embarrassed every time he looked at her. Then it hit her - great, he was going to wonder every day if she was wearing them.

She gathered up the laundry, tossing it into the basket, then pulled a towel out from the bag and tucked it in around the top.

"What a way to start a day," she laughed as she walked into the kitchen with the little blue basket of goodies in her hand.

While her bread was toasting, she dumped coffee grounds out of the pot and put it into the deep sink, filling it with water. She put a dab of soap in and let the water run until it was filled. The toaster popped up and she turned off the water. It could soak for a few minutes while she ate. Saturday morning was a good day for a soda. Diet Mt. Dew could always be found in the bottom of her refrigerator and rather than wait for coffee to be made, she grabbed a can and her toast and settled in at the table.

Looking out again at the broken up playground, she began to dream of possibilities for that space. Weeds had broken through the cracks in the blacktop and the pieces of playground equipment still there were rusted and broken down. The teeter-totter only had one hinge left and the merry go round was rusted and tilting to one side. Those needed to be dealt with before winter came so next spring she could look out on grass rather than this mess.

She opened her soda and took a bite of toast. Then, she pulled everything out of the basket. She was going to try to return the basket, napkins and cutting board to Lydia, but figured it would be a losing battle. She'd try anyway.

Her phone rang, "Polly? This is Jerry Allen. Doug told me what happened at your house and I have to apologize. If I'd known he was going to be there, I'd have called you first. I'm sorry!"

She laughed out loud. "I'll bet he was as startled as I was. It's no big deal. I'm fine. He was probably more embarrassed than me. So, I'm fine."

"My wife is going to be in Des Moines this morning and will pick up the door chime we had discussed. Yes, we'll install it on Monday and try to avoid any more surprises," he said, then went on. "Oh, you might be meeting her this evening."

"I will?" Polly asked.

"Oh. Uh oh. I didn't say anything. Good-bye! I'll see you Monday and I'm sorry about Doug!"

Jerry hung up abruptly and Polly wondered what in the world he was talking about.

CHAPTER FOUR

“I’m here, Come in!” Polly called out when she heard a knock at her door that afternoon. She’d slung her overnight bag over her shoulder, grabbed up the bag of laundry in the hand holding her clutch and balanced the basket on her left hip. There was no way she could open her front door. This might have been carrying self-reliance a bit too far.

The door pushed open and all three ladies were standing there. Andy took the basket from her, Beryl reached for the pillowcase and Lydia asked, "Is that all you have? You must have tiny, tiny laundry."

Then, she took the overnight bag off Polly's shoulder and headed out the door.

"Wait! I could have carried my stuff out."

"Why yes you could," said Beryl, "but then you wouldn't be able to shut and lock your door, would you! Now, let's go!"

They dropped her things in the back of the Jeep and Andy and Beryl both hopped into the back seat while Polly stood there feeling a little discombobulated. All she could think was, "What happened here?"

"Let's go!" said Beryl from inside the vehicle.

Polly pulled the door shut, checked her purse to make sure the keys were there and trotted to the Jeep.

"Can't even give a girl a moment to get her wits about her, can you?" she said to the back seat as she jumped in and pulled her seatbelt across her shoulder.

She turned around, "You know, I'm younger than any of you, I could have sat back there."

"Don't even start with us. Just sit there and enjoy the ride." That came from Beryl.

"So, Lydia told me you weren't driving tonight, Beryl," Polly said.

"Lydia is such a downer. She knows I get lost wherever I go," Beryl started and then Andy interrupted.

"And when you get lost, you drive faster, thinking that will get us unlost. You aren't safe."

Polly craned her neck to the back seat. "But I thought we were going to Ames. How hard is that?" she asked.

"Oh trust us, Beryl gets lost in Bellingwood. Ames is nearly impossible for her and Des Moines? Nobody lets her drive down there." Lydia chuckled as she backed out of the lot.

"I guess I didn't even ask," Polly said, "What play are we seeing tonight?

Lydia was the one to respond, "The tickets are in my purse. I'm not sure what it is. But, whatever, it will be terrific and we'll have fun."

"I hear you have purple undies," said Beryl quietly from the back seat.

Polly didn't even bother to look up. She shook her head and started laughing.

"Nothing gets by you guys, does it?" she said.

"Not if we can help it," Andy replied. "You know, when you get to be an old lady, you have to have something going on all the time!"

"Okay, whatever," said Polly. "You do give a new definition to the phrase little old lady, I guess."

The four women chattered all the way to Ames. When it came time to pay for the meal, the receipt arrived at the table with the word "Paid" on it, handwritten by the waitress.

"What is this?" asked Lydia. "Who did this?"

The waitress said nothing as she gathered up the plates.

"Really. Who did this?" Lydia asked again.

Beryl and Andy both had shock on their faces and they all looked at Polly.

"Uh huh. So, that's how it is," said Beryl.

"Just so you know, you ladies are old and out of touch. I took care of it when I went to the bathroom. Did you really think I needed to do that? I'm still young enough to sleep all the way through the night without a bathroom pit stop." Polly laughed, then said, “Gotcha.”

They were all laughing as they returned to the Jeep and headed to the Iowa State Campus. Polly looked at it a little wistfully. She had considered coming to school here, it would have been close to her family. She and her dad had come down for a campus tour, twice, because he wanted to make sure she liked it. When the scholarship arrived from Boston University, all their plans changed and she had never looked back. Everything had seemed so perfect and the opportunity to live on the east coast was something Polly hadn’t wanted to pass up.

Her mother had grown up in one of Boston's suburbs and Polly had been out there a few times as a young child. Her application to Boston University was sent in as a lark. The acceptance and subsequent scholarship made everything real.

Lydia parked the Jeep at Fisher Theater and everyone was still giggling back and forth as they found their way to their seats. The play wasn't anything familiar to Polly, but she enjoyed the production. As they left, Beryl and Andy were commenting on the scenery and costumes. It seemed both found something to enjoy and couldn't stop talking about it.

"It's not like we don't get out," Beryl laughed. "You'd think we had never seen a play before!"

"Do you remember when Rent came to Des Moines?" Andy asked, "That was amazing! There is nothing like watching professionals do their thing, is there! Such a smooth presentation. I still cry every time."

Polly didn't say anything. She'd taken plenty of opportunities to see live theater in Boston and on several occasions even went down to New York to see shows on Broadway. Andy was right. When professionals did a great job on stage, everyone in the audience became engaged in the story. There was nothing like it.

"Maybe we'll take a road trip to Chicago one of these days." Lydia announced, "How about it, ladies?"

They got in the Jeep and headed home. The stars were bright and the sky was clear as they drove across Highway 30. Lydia ducked up an access road to pick up Highway 17 and go north. The four women talked about the play and dinner until they arrived in front of a deceptively large home in Bellingwood. From the front, it looked like a normal split level home, but the lights filling the yard showed it to be a much larger home than could be seen from the road. The garage was on the lower level behind the house and as they drove down the hill, Polly saw several cars parked.

"Are all of these cars yours?" she asked Lydia.

"Oh, no. Beryl and Andy both drove over." Lydia said rather smugly.

"But, that's still a lot of vehicles."

"We have a couple of extra cars around, I guess."

It didn't seem as if Lydia planned to share anything else, so Polly followed her to the back of the Jeep and grabbed her overnight bag and the laundry basket. Beryl promptly picked up the pillow case as Andy tried to wrestle the basket out of Polly's arms.

Lydia unlocked a side door to the house and they entered through the laundry room. Beryl dropped the case and Andy placed the basket on top of the dryer. "Leave your laundry here and we'll let you come back to start it after we all get settled in. I think I heard something about chocolate martinis!"

Polly let them walk her through the hallway which opened into a darkened room. As Lydia flipped on the light, Polly's eyes tried to take in a room filled with women of nearly every age.

It was ten o'clock on a Saturday night and there had to be fifteen women in chairs and couches, at tables and behind the bar in the room.

"Hello?" she said. She didn't recognize anyone.

Lydia held up a hand and the room went quiet. "Alright, ladies. This is Polly. You all know she owns the old school house and is renovating it. But, she doesn't know any of you."

She turned to Polly and said, "Gotcha." Then, she smiled and walked away. Polly turned to Beryl and Andy for some support and they shrugged. Beryl lifted the overnight bag from Polly's shoulder and followed Andy further into the room. "You'll never get to one-up that one, girlie. Don't even try!"

Polly stood in the doorway and while her head told her to turn and run, it also told her she had nowhere to run to. She smiled at the ladies, who didn't seem to be making a mad rush at her. In a moment, though, one of the younger women came up to introduce herself.

"Hi, I'm Marian Allen. My husband, Jerry is doing your electricity," said the rather plain looking, but confident woman.

"OH! Did he tell you he nearly blew the whistle on this?" Polly asked.

Marian coughed. "No. He didn't. What did he do?"

"Oh, it was no big deal. He said you were going to be in Des Moines and would pick up the door chime so he could install it on Monday,"

Marian interrupted. "Oh, that's right! Because poor Dougie saw your underwear! That boy's mama is at the table in the purple shirt." Marian snorted. Then Polly realized everyone in the room had something purple on with hot pink accents.

Her face flushed and she started laughing. "You're all in purple!" She looked at her three new friends. They'd changed into purple shirts and each had a hot pink bow clipped in their hair.

"This is never going to go away, is it!" she laughed. "How did you do it on such short notice?"

"Oh, a few phone calls here, a few texts there and everyone was on board," said Beryl.

A very short woman with a pink scarf around her neck, stood up. "I'm Dougie's mom, Helen. He was absolutely mortified he'd freaked you out and saw your dainties." she said. "It does make a mama's heart feel better, though, that he's never seen anything like it before. Whew!" She laughed and sat back down.

For the next hour, Polly moved from person to person, meeting women and spending a few moments making connections. Wives and mothers of people who were working on her school house; women who worked in shops around town or lived on farms not far from her home; others who worked in Ames or Boone, a couple in Webster City; everyone wanted to be sure she would recognize them the next time they met.

Polly knew she wouldn't remember all of their names, but that soon became a non-issue.

Lydia stood up. "Alright everyone, it's time to begin the game," she said.

"While you're here and awake, you all have to try to find something interesting out about Polly. When you do, write it down on the piece of paper with your name on it and then we'll take a picture of you with your sign and Polly. The most interesting and unique story about Polly will win the prize."

"What's the prize?" came from a few of the women around the room.

"You're going to have to wait and see. We'll announce it when everyone has had their picture taken." Lydia responded.

As the women went to the table and began shuffling through the pile of papers there, Polly turned to Lydia. "Do you do this for everyone who moves in?"

"Well, maybe or maybe not. Though there have been some who don't get into the spirit of things." She patted Polly's arm. "You've been a good sport about everything. Now get yourself a chocolate martini from the bar and settle in. People are going to start asking you questions!"

"Wait," Polly said, "Is this going to go on all night? Are all of these ladies spending the night here?"

"Well, a couple of them might have to leave so they can get some sleep before church tomorrow, but they have Sunday School classes to teach. Did you meet Angela Boehm? She's the Methodist pastor's wife and she's staying all night. She told him she might make it to the 10:30 service or she might not. He chose to be fine with it." Lydia laughed as she gave Polly a nudge toward the bar.

"Coming right up!" said Andy, as she swirled some chocolate sauce in the glass and poured a martini from a shaker. A squirt of whipped cream, and a little more chocolate sauce topped it off before she handed it to Polly.

Polly took a sip, "Whoa! What's in here?" she asked.

"Oh, vodka and chocolate liqueur," Andy replied. "Enjoy! And come back for another when you're done."

Polly found herself pulled to the couch and women began asking questions about her family, her school, her last job and anything else they could come up with.

She did her best to anchor names with people. Two women sat down beside her. They'd already introduced themselves once, but she looked at them quite pitifully and the older woman laughed. "You don't remember any of our names, do you?" she said.

Polly looked down at the sheet of paper in the woman's lap. "Oh, sure I do. You're, ummm ..." she glanced down again.

The woman laughed and said, "Oh, now you're cheating! Yes, I'm Linda Morse and this is my sister, Sarah Conyers. We're both so glad you've bought the old school. It will be wonderful to have that old place renovated. It's been such a depressing sight out there all by itself with boarded up windows. The city only got around to mowing the yard when it was shaggy, so you never knew if it was going to look nice or not."

"You two are sisters?" Polly asked, ready to let anyone talk if it meant she didn't have to for a while.

"We sure are," said the younger one, Sarah. "We've lived here forever, raised our kids and had good lives. I think you're going to love it, even if we don't have wild old lady slumber parties every week."

"How many kids do you have, Sarah?" asked Polly.

"I've got two boys. My oldest boy is at Iowa State and my youngest is a junior in high school. Both boys help their dad out a lot on the farm. Ben, the oldest, plays football some in college. We love going over to see the games. I was lucky today was an away game so I could come out here, though," replied Sarah.

"How about you, Linda?" Polly pushed.

"Oh, I've got five kids. I guess it never felt like I had enough. I loved having them around as little kids, then I enjoyed having them grow up some and now I've even got some grandbabies who like to visit me," Linda said.

Then, Linda stopped. "Wait, this is supposed to be us finding out about you. So, Sarah, do you have a question for Polly?"

Sarah gave a wicked little smile. "Alright Polly, here's one for you. Who is the first boy you ever French-kissed?"

Polly giggled a little. "Really?"

Sarah said, "Yep, really. We want to know something a little wicked about you."

Polly laughed. "Well, it had to be in the back seats of the band bus. Which one was my first?" and she winked at the two ladies who were sitting with her.

She went on, "No, I do remember. It was my freshman year in high school and it was on a band bus. We were coming back after an out of town football game. I have no idea where we'd been, but it was dark and chilly, we had our blankets and were all snuggled in. There had been a lot of chattering until finally everyone was worn out. I suspect there was more going on in the seats behind me, but Darrin, the boy I wanted to be dating at the time, was sitting with me. He started out by holding my hand and I think when he took my hand under the blanket, everything in my stomach did a flip flop. We were talking quietly because we didn't want anyone to hear us. I doubt it was anything important, but all of a sudden, he leaned over and kissed me. First it was a sweet kiss, and then all of a sudden it got a little more passionate. We did a lot of kissing on that band trip and on the rest of the trips that year. But, we broke up after the winter dance. Yeah. That's a sweet memory."

Polly turned to Linda, "Okay, it's your turn, I guess."

Linda asked, "What's your favorite childhood memory of your mother?"

Polly stopped for a moment and thought. "You know my mom died when I was twelve, right?" Both women nodded and then she giggled and went on. "Oh, this will work right in with tonight's theme. I rode the bus to school every day. Mom always had questions for me before I walked out the door. Did I brush my teeth, did I wash my hands, did I have my school bag and one I could never figure out. She asked me every day if I had my panties on.

"Well, every day, when she went down the list, I said yes, yes, yes, yes and trotted out to wait for the bus, but I think I must have been showing my rebellious streak early, because one morning when I was in first grade, I decided I wasn't going to do what she asked. I was going to lie and tell her I'd done all of those things. I did have to take my bag with me, because she would have noticed, but I didn't do anything else. I went skipping out to the end of the lane to wait for the bus and all of a sudden I realized how uncomfortable I was. What if my dress went up and the boys saw? I started crying and crying. I could see the bus coming down the road and I knew I couldn't get on it without my panties. I had to make a decision. Mom would be easier to handle than the embarrassment facing me otherwise, so I ran back up the lane, sobbing. Mom came out to meet me and waved off the bus. I fessed up to her and she smiled. We went inside and I ran upstairs to my dresser to get some panties, then she came up and I washed my hands and face and brushed my teeth.

"She didn't say much to me, just knelt down and put her arms around me and told me she loved me and was proud of me for making the right decision. Then she drove me to school and dropped me off. She never said anything to me about it again and she never again asked me if I was wearing panties. I don't think she ever quit asking me about washing my hands and brushing my teeth, though."

Polly hadn't been paying much attention to her surroundings with so many of the women stopping by to ask her questions and try to get to know her. As Angela Boehm sat down beside her, she heard Beryl cough and say, "Excuse me, excuse me!"

Everyone stopped and looked up. I thought you all should see what embarrassed little Dougie Randall this morning ... well, yesterday morning, since it is already long after midnight. She stepped to one side as Andy and Lydia held up either end of Polly's bright purple underwear with hot pink bows.

Polly leaped off the couch and ran at the women, who darted to the side. Andy tossed the undies over Polly's head to Lydia who caught them and stuck them under her shirt. "Are you going to come get them now, girlfriend?" she taunted.

"But, they're dirty!" Polly cried.

"Oh, hell no, they're not," said Beryl. "While you've been in here partying and drinking up all of those ... how many has she had, Andy? Three ... martinis, we finished your laundry for you. And if those are the fanciest panties you own, we're taking you to Victoria's Secret next time we go to Des Moines."

Polly made a dive for Lydia, who backed into a cluster of women standing in front of the bar. They gave her a little push back into the center of the room and she faced off with Polly. All of a sudden chants of "Fight! Fight! Fight!" surrounded the two who were dancing around each other.

Lydia pulled the panties out from under her shirt and tossed them up in the air. Polly leaped for them and grabbed them.

"No fight today, ladies, back to your party." Lydia said.

She walked to Polly with her hands up in surrender. As she got closer, she said, "I'm sorry, Polly. I couldn't resist. I hope I haven't embarrassed you too much."

Polly shook her head. "I don't know what to do with you! You are like no one I've ever met!"

Beryl had walked up as she said the last, "And it's a very good thing, too, Polly. She keeps us all on our toes!"

The rest of the night passed quietly. Polly answered questions and suddenly felt as if she were at home. These women wanted to be her friend and were having a good time, all because of Lydia Merritt. They genuinely liked Lydia and Polly found she couldn't imagine living here without knowing this wonderful lady. At one point, she sat back on the couch and looked around. Women were laughing and eating, drinking and talking. No one paid any attention to who was drinking alcohol, water or soda. It was a wonderful party.

Polly checked her cell phone for the time. Two in the morning. She should be asleep. A few of the women said something to Lydia, who then turned and announced to the room. "It's time to pick a winner. Who has the best story about Polly?"

Each story was read out loud and Polly posed with the woman after she read her story so Lydia could snap a picture. Then it was time to vote. Polly expected the women to yuck it up with the panty story she had told Linda Morse, and it did come in second, but the largest round of applause went to the story Adele Mansfield told about the first morning Mary had shown up to make breakfast and ensure Polly got to school on time.

Polly listened as Adele read what she had written down:

"Mary had never had children of her own and both of Polly's parents had always let her be part of Polly's childhood, so she felt as if she knew the little girl well already. She worried, though, that Polly would resent her in her mama's kitchen. She got everything together at her own house so she wouldn't make too much of a mess and clutter up the counters. All she had to do was reheat the gravy and pour it over some biscuits. When she set the table and everyone sat down, Polly sat down beside her. She reached out with her little hand to hold Mary's while her daddy offered grace. When he said "Amen," Polly squeezed the woman's hand and smiled up at her."

Polly looked over at Adele. "That's not the story I told you," she said, with a quiver in her voice.

"No it's not, honey. Your Mary was my sister's best friend. She told me that story and I thought I'd share it with you today. She loved your mama and she loved you and would be awfully proud of you, I think."

Polly stood up and walked over to hug Adele. "I'm glad you're getting the prize. That's the best story of the night," she said, tears threatening. "Will you promise to tell me more about Mary and your sister someday?"

"I certainly will. Maybe you can come over for lunch one of these days when you're not too busy." Adele responded.

"It's a date. I'll call you," Polly said.

"Well, Adele," said Lydia. "It looks like you're the winner!" and she pulled out a beautiful satin, purple robe with a hot pink sash. All of the ladies laughed and then oohed and aahed over the robe.

Since Adele was one of the women who was heading home for the night, Polly gave her a quick hug before they all left by the back door.

When they were gone, Lydia said, "I can put a movie in, or you can all go to bed. Most of you know where the bedrooms are upstairs. Anybody who wants to crash on the sofas down here is welcome to do so. No one has to worry about cleaning things up. From here on out, you can do whatever you like and tomorrow morning there will be coffee and cinnamon rolls at the bar."

A few more women, who decided their own beds sounded like a good idea, said their good-byes. Several went upstairs and crashed in beds and still others snuggled into the sofas and recliners in the basement. Polly stayed awake for a while longer, talking with some of the women and before she knew it, she saw sunlight.

She tiptoed over to the bar where Lydia and Beryl were setting coffee and breakfast pastries out and whispered, "Do you ever sleep?"

Beryl laughed, "Don't kid yourself, tootsie pop, when you are gone, Lydia will sleep the rest of the day. That woman prowls around at all hours of the night and always seems to find plenty of time to sleep."

Lydia poked her friend's arm, "It's that whole menopause thing. I figured I didn't need to fight it, just roll with it. It keeps everyone around me happier."

"Here, Polly, have coffee. You might need it. You're looking a little ragged."

"Well, I did have … how many was it, Beryl? Three martinis." she said. Then, she blinked her eyes. "And my head hurts."

"Polly, I know you're pooped and you have a big week ahead of you. Drink your coffee and Beryl will take you home. She should be able to get there without getting too lost. I'll get everyone else on their way.

And then, check your email later, the pictures will show up."

"That sounds wonderful," Polly said. "Lydia, I don't know how to thank you for last night. It has to be one of my top ten extraordinary life experiences! You are a wonderful, wonderful friend." She reached out to hug the woman. "I don't know how to say thank you for everything."

"There is no need, honey. I love doing this stuff and having someone new around to appreciate it makes it that much more fun for me! Now go home and rest up for your week. I'll check on you later."

Polly and Beryl went back down the hallway and found not one, but two laundry baskets filled with her clean, neatly folded clothes. Beryl picked one up and before Polly could protest, said, "Just be quiet. If she didn't have people around to take care of, she wouldn't know what to do with herself. Lydia Merritt has more energy than she knows what to do with and her dear, sweet husband spoils her rotten. She has to turn it around on everyone else so he doesn't turn into a marshmallow. Take the basket and thank her later."

Polly picked up a basket and her overnight bag and followed Beryl to her car.

Lydia was right; she did want to go back to bed, so after hauling the laundry upstairs, she left it at the end of the bed, dropped in and promptly fell asleep.

CHAPTER FIVE

Despite a building full of people, Monday morning found Polly in the basement looking through boxes for heavier blankets for her bed when she heard a crash and then a very masculine screech. She ran up the steps to the main level to find everyone else heading to the second floor. She followed the crowd and when she got upstairs, the activity was in the old girl's bathroom. Doug Randall was limping out, his hair and clothing filled with plaster dust. Jerry Allen was right behind him with his hand on his back.

"Okay, buddy. Breathe. Just breathe."

"Did you see that?" Doug asked. "Did you see that? There were bones and skulls!"

Polly pushed through the people standing around.

"What are you talking about?" she asked.

"Bones. And skulls." He took a breath. "In the ceiling!"

Polly cocked her head and looked at Jerry quizzically. "In the ceiling? I thought it was concrete and they were going to drop a new one to hold the infrastructure."

Jerry shook his head. "So did I. Doug must have pushed in the right place, because what we thought was concrete wasn't at all. It was dry wall made to look like concrete. Someone dropped that ceiling years ago."

Doug sat down on the floor. "Bones. And skulls." he said again.

Polly tried to step past Doug and Jerry to get into the bathroom. She wanted to see what in the world had happened.

Jerry stopped her. "Are you sure you want to see this?"

"I think I need to!" she said.

He let her through and followed her back into the bathroom. The ceiling had taken a beating when Doug pulled his hand back out of the drywall. It looked as if he had grabbed the ceiling to maintain his footing on the ladder and pulled an entire section down on top of him. He was absolutely right. Two skulls had fallen out of the ceiling onto the floor, as well as a number of bones. Polly saw there were books and clothing as well. She started to step further in, but Jerry stopped her again.

"We need to call the police. You shouldn't disturb anything." he said.

"Right. Right. Alright. You're right." She used her phone to snap pictures of the room, the floor and the mess as well as the ceiling. "I wonder if the other bathroom's ceiling is this low," she said out loud.

"That's a good question. I can't believe no one ever noticed this." Jerry said.

"I suppose the only person who might have noticed it would have been the custodian." Polly mused, and then said, "Who are these people and what are they doing here?"

"We aren't going to know anything more until the police show up and start investigating," he said. "Do you want to call them or should I?"

"Oh. Yes. That." Polly walked back out into the main hall. "I'll call them. Will you take care of making sure no one else goes in there and messes things up?"

She looked at her phone. In all of her life, she'd never had to call the police. Should she call 9-1-1 or contact the police department. And which police department handled something like this. She walked over to the top step and sat down.

Then, she realized she wasn't thinking straight at all and dialed the number of the one person who could help her.

"Hello, dear. How are you today?" said Lydia when she answered the phone.

"Lydia, I need your husband. How can I reach him?" Polly asked.

"What? You need Aaron? Whatever for? Are you alright? Did someone break in and steal something?"

"No, Lydia. Doug Randall broke my ceiling and two skeletons fell out on the floor," Polly said.

"Well, leave it to Doug. Wait, did you say skeletons? Are they real?" Lydia gasped.

"I don't know anything other than that there are two skeletons in my upstairs bathroom and I think I need Aaron to get over here as quickly as possible." Polly's body shook as a small shiver passed through her.

"Don't worry," said Lydia. "I'll call him and get him over there immediately. Tell everyone to stay away from it. I know those boys and they're going to think this is fascinating!"

"Fascinating. Yeah. That's exactly what I thought," Polly sighed. "Thanks Lydia. I'll talk to you later."

She pressed the 'end' button on her phone and turned around. Everyone was still standing around, talking quietly about what was in the bathroom. Doug wasn't paying any attention to the conversations taking place over his head, he just sat there.

Polly stood up. "Jerry?"

"Yes, Polly." he responded.

"I think Doug might be in shock. I know I'm a little shook up. But, he might need to be distracted or something. Would you send someone downstairs for something hot to drink for him and some sugar? I know there is plenty out on the table." Polly had taken to putting baked goods on the kitchen table so the guys who were working could have snacks with their coffee. She figured she was spoiling them, but they certainly didn't mind eating the sweet stuff and she was glad they kept showing up and working.

One of the other electrician's apprentices, she thought it must have been Billy of the lost power stapler, took heed of Jerry's nod and started down the steps. Then, he looked at Polly. "Can I bring you something too?" he asked.

"Sure," she said. "Coffee would be great."

She watched as another man followed him down the steps. In her shock she couldn't remember his name. Oh yeah, it was Marvin. He was one of the guys who spent a lot of time in the kitchen making sure the coffee pot was full. He and Billy could make sure there was coffee coming.

Polly sat back down on the step to wait for Aaron Merritt to show up. She was a little ashamed that her next thought was about how this was going to mess up her work schedule. She just knew they'd be investigating for weeks and wouldn't let any work continue. Then, her subsequent thought was about whether or not they would let her stay in the building.

"Damn," she said out loud.

"Ma'am?" said one of the workmen, Leroy, who heard it. Even with the distraction, it occurred to her to be proud that she'd remembered two names today.

"Oh, sorry," she said. "Just thinking out loud."

“Are you sure you’re alright?” he asked again.

“I’m sure. A little shook up is all.”

She was going to have to find a place to stay. There was no way they would let her stay here while the investigators were in and out, was there?

"Breathe, Giller. Just wait until Sheriff Merritt shows up. Then you can ask questions." She muttered her words quietly under her breath, looking around to see if anyone heard her. Leroy was still standing there watching her, but he turned around and began talking to someone else

Billy came back up the steps with a cup of coffee and some cookies. She took the cup from him and he put a cookie with a napkin in her hand. "I'll bet this will help you too, ma'am," he said and smiled a sweet little boy smile.

Marvin carried another cup and walked over to hand it to Jerry, who had his hand out, then stepped back.

Polly smiled back at Billy and he walked over to kneel in front of Doug. Jerry knelt down and pressed the coffee cup into Doug's hand. "Drink the coffee, Doug. Eat a cookie."

Doug shook himself a little and looked up at Jerry. "Coffee? Okay."

Billy set a napkin with three cookies on Doug's leg. Doug took a drink of coffee and looked around the large hallway.

"Did I really pull bones out of that ceiling?" he asked.

"You really did, dude," said Billy. "That's so cool!"

Polly chuckled. She was only ten or twelve years older than those boys, but they seemed so much younger. Both were good kids. She thought it was great Jerry was teaching them a trade. He treated them like they were his own sons and both boys seemed to like him a lot.

She heard the door open and got up again. Walking down the stairs, she hoped it was Lydia's husband. No one else needed to be here now. When she got to the front door and opened it, both Lydia and Aaron were waiting there.

"Polly," Lydia said, "I don't believe you've met my sweet-ums yet, have you!"

Aaron looked down at his wife. He was a tall man, probably about 6'1," with a big barrel chest and immense forearms. He didn't look like any sweet-ums Polly had ever met and it didn't seem as if he necessarily appreciated the affectionate banter.

"What have I told you about using those phrases, woman," he said to his wife as he grinned at her.

"You've told me that I'll be in trouble later," she said, and then in an aside to Polly, "That's why I keep using them. I like being in trouble."

Polly giggled and felt a little uncomfortable. This seemed inappropriate for the momentous occurrence upstairs, but it also seemed as if there was no stopping the woman.

"I don't ever take her with me when I have a crime scene, because this is her behavior," Aaron said. "She embarrasses the hell out of me, so it's easier to leave her at home!"

Lydia patted his backside and said, "I think all of the excitement is upstairs, pookie. Go do your thing. I'll be down here telling Polly all about the trouble you like to give me."

Aaron shook his head and walked away. He went upstairs and Polly could hear him greeting the men gathered in front of the bathroom door. She desperately wanted to be up there seeing everything going on, but didn't know what to do with Lydia.

"Oh, go on," Lydia said. "I know you want to be up there. I'll sit down here in the kitchen twiddling my thumbs. I do know better than to be involved in anything Aaron is doing. I only pick on him for the effect."

"Really? Are you sure?" Polly asked.

"Absolutely. Go. I'll be fine."

Polly ran up the stairs and heard Aaron Merritt telling the workmen they might as well go home. They weren't going to be doing anything else today. A few of the men broke off from their clusters and headed downstairs to get their things. Doug was still sitting on the floor and Billy was hanging pretty close to his friend. Jerry and Aaron were talking.

"No," Jerry said, "After Doug and I came blasting out of there, no one else went in. Polly and I looked in at the mess, but we didn't go beyond the door."

"Alright then," Aaron responded. "I'm going to call DCI and have them get someone over here. I want to talk to Doug and make sure you and he have given a statement. Then you can get out of here and he can get cleaned up. Make sure the kid is okay, though, before you send him home to his mama. I don't want her worrying."

Aaron stepped back toward Polly and punched a button on his phone. She was close enough to hear a woman's voice on the other end say,

“Iowa Department of Criminal Investigation, how may I help you?”

Well, at least she knew who DCI was now.

"Hey Arlene, Can I talk to Digger?” Aaron asked, then paused for her response, “Oh, alright. Put me through."

He turned to Polly. "You know, this is going to take a while. You might want to pack some things up and if I know my Lydia, the reason she is here is to take you back to our house. You’ll need somewhere else to sleep tonight."

"Hey buddy!" he said back into his phone. "I have some old bones over here and I need a team to come clean things up and check it out."

He listened for a moment, "Yep. As soon as possible, I guess. Somebody pulled the ceiling out of the old school building and it looks like a couple of bodies.

"Oh crap!" he blurted. "I know whose bodies these are. Crap. Crap. Crap. Crap. Dammit. I don't want to have to deal with this.

"Digger, get a team over here as soon as possible. Yeah. This is an old, ugly case and I'm going to need everything done right so we can figure out what happened."

He listened again and said, "Thanks, buddy. And by the way, it's time for you and Ellen to come back to dinner. Is it okay if I have Lydia call your wife?

"Thanks again. I'll see you later." Aaron put his phone back in its holster on his belt, then turned to Jerry.

"I want to let you go home, but we're going to wait for DCI. They'll check the two of you over to make sure nothing important fell on you and then one of their people will listen to your story and get it written down. They should be here in a half hour or so.”

He looked at Polly in apology. "Polly. I need a key to the place. And you're going to have to go home with Lydia. But, before you do, I want you to meet the guys from DCI so you know who will be wandering around your home. Why don't you go ahead and pack up any things you might need for a couple of days."

Turning back to those still standing around, Aaron said, "The rest of you need to leave now unless you have something important to tell me."

The few men who were there took the hint and headed downstairs. In a couple of minutes the parking lot was empty.

Polly went into her room, shut the door and sat down on her bed. 'Dammit' was right. She felt like she'd barely gotten started and now everything was in an uproar. She wanted to throw something, so she grabbed a pillow and flung it across the room. That didn't help, so she opened her overnight bag and began flinging things into it. She picked up the purple underwear and laughed aloud. She tossed them in, then walked back across the hall to the bathroom and pulled out her travel kit. It went in on top of the clothing and she zipped it shut.

"Well, that didn't take very much time," she thought and looked at her watch. Half an hour, huh? She had another fifteen minutes before people started kicking her out of her house.

It had taken a while, but this schoolhouse was starting to feel like it was hers. All of a sudden she realized she couldn't stand the thought of people walking around here with everything in such a mess. She gathered the towels and draped them over the shower door, rinsed down the sink and ran the scrubber around the toilet.

Then, she walked back across the hall, barely acknowledging the people there and shut the door to her room behind her. She picked the pillow up off the floor where she'd thrown it and straightened the bed. She stacked the laundry baskets in the corner of the room and arranged everything on the floor beside her bed as neatly as possible.

As she opened the door to walk back out with her bag, she saw five people come up the stairs. Great. They were here and she had to leave.

As soon as she thought those words, she realized she was being pissy. But, who wouldn't be? There were skeletons in her bathroom and strange people were kicking her out of her home. Pissy was going to be her privilege. At least for a few minutes.

She stood in her doorway and watched them take over. Aaron excused himself and walked toward her. "Polly, I'd like you to meet Danny Boylston. He's going to be in charge of this whole thing," he said as he waved his hand back at the bathroom.

"Danny," Aaron called out. "I'd like you to meet the new owner of the school, Polly Giller. This is her place and she should know who you are before you start tearing through her stuff."

Danny Boylston was even taller than Aaron and thin as a rail. He had jet black hair and dark black eyes which looked almost sad, like a bloodhound's eyes, Polly thought. She dropped her bag and put her hand out to shake his. His fingers were as long as he was tall, but his grip was firm and warm.

"Nice to meet you, Polly. I'm sorry it is under such messy circumstances. We'll do our best to be efficient and get out of your way as quickly as possible."

"Alright," she responded. "I guess that's all I can ask for."

Without any further conversation, he turned around and walked back to the bathroom. One of the women was checking Doug over, brushing some of the dust and particles off into a bag. Finally she motioned to another woman, who spoke quietly to Doug, then looked up. "Is there anywhere I can go to talk to the kid?" she asked.

Polly looked at Aaron, who nodded at her. "I suppose the only place with chairs and a table would be the kitchen," she said. " There's coffee there, if you want it, but I'm going to turn it off before I leave."

"That will be fine. Doug?" and she motioned for Doug to follow. He picked up his coffee cup and stuffed the napkin he'd been gripping inside it. Polly walked over to him and took the cup out of his hand. "You'll be alright. You have nothing to be freaked out over at this point, am I right?" she asked.

"I guess. I've never been interviewed by a cop before," he said.

"And you've never had bones fall out of the ceiling before either," Polly said. "You got through that, you'll get through this. And I'm going to get you and Billy a steak dinner in Ames when this is over. I promise."

Doug laughed, then shook his head.

"What?" she asked.

"Oh, nothing. I was only thinking about purple ..."

"Stop it!" She laughed. "You already got me into a ton of grief." She punched him lightly on his arm. "Now, go. Get this over with and then go home and get a shower."

She followed the two downstairs and Lydia met them at the bottom of the steps.

"Are you ready to go, Polly?" she asked.

"Well, I need to clean up the coffee pot when they're done," Polly said.

"I've already taken care of it. I poured the rest of the coffee into the two big thermoses you have and those are on the table with the cookies. It will be fine until tomorrow."

Aaron Merritt had also come back down the steps. "Lydia, I told her you wouldn't let her stay anywhere but our house. Was I right?"

"Oh, you know me so well, punkin'," she said. "Come on, Polly, we're taking your truck. And Aaron promises to tell us everything when he gets home for supper, doesn't he!"

He chuckled, then sobered as he said, "I'm sure I already know who it is, Lydia. You aren't going to like it."

Her face fell, "You're serious, aren't you, Aaron."

"Yes, I think I am. I'll know more when we get a little more information from DCI, but that's what I'm thinking. It looks like we've finally found them."

"Oh dammit, Aaron. Everyone was normal again. It took thirty years for that family to start living. I don't know whether this will help them or make them miserable."

Then her face brightened up. "Be on time for dinner, tonight, Aaron. Remember, we have company!"

He stopped as they got to the door. "Polly? Do you have an extra key?"

"OH!" She said. "There are a few extra keys in the newel post over here." Polly walked over, gave the newel post a quick turn and revealed a small pocket. There were four keys in there and Aaron took one. "I've already checked them. Everything works."

He took one more. "I'll give this to Boylston and we'll get it back to you when this is over."

CHAPTER SIX

Enjoying Lydia's commentary, Polly followed her directions as they drove through the streets of Bellingwood.

"Now that you've made the drive with me, do you think you can get to my house on your own?" Lydia asked.

"I hope so. That's one of those things I haven't done yet," Polly said. "I haven't taken the time to drive around town and get familiar with all the streets and what we've got here."

"It's not a very big town," Lydia said. "If you were able to drive around Boston in this truck, I bet you'll be able to get around this place."

"Oh, I sold my car in Boston, Lydia. This was Dad's truck. I don't know why I didn't sell it when he died, but he'd just gotten it and loved it so much, I couldn't bring myself to get rid of it."

Polly could no longer contain her questions. "What in the world were you and Aaron talking about? Do you know whose bodies those were in my ceiling?"

"I'm afraid so. I really am afraid I do. It's so horrible. No one is going to want to believe they've been here all this time, hidden away in the school," Lydia said.

"Okay, you have to give me more information than this. You're killing me!" Polly gasped at her obvious faux pas, "I mean. I'm dying here." She stopped again. "I'll shut up. It seems like you knew them and I'm not helping."

"Turn left here at this corner and you'll see the house," Lydia said. "Once we get inside and get you settled in your room, I'll tell you the whole story. Then, when Aaron gets home tonight, we'll see for sure if I'm right."

Polly turned the corner and saw Lydia's home. Now she knew where she was. She turned into the driveway and went around back, like they had done the night of the slumber party. Lydia climbed out of the truck and waited while Polly grabbed her bag and jumped out to follow her. Rather than using the entrance through the laundry room, Lydia pushed open a sliding glass door and they walked right into the family room.

"Come on upstairs," Lydia said.

Polly followed her up the stairs and into the kitchen. The back windows looked over the garages and out onto a grove of trees. The kitchen was done in country blues and was quite warm and homey, exactly what she would expect from Lydia.

"This way, Polly. I've got a couple of rooms upstairs you can choose from."

Polly followed her through the dining room, past the formal living room, to the steps. Upstairs there were four bedrooms and those doors were all standing open.

"The back bedroom is ours, but any of the others would be perfect for you," she said. "There's a bathroom here," and she opened a door, "or the two bedrooms on this side share a bathroom. Since no one else is here, you might want one of those rooms."

Polly looked in the first room and it was decorated in rich burgundy and green. The wooden bedroom set was a beautiful deep mahogany which complemented the other colors in the room.

"Oh my, this will be wonderful," she exclaimed.

"Terrific. Why don't you drop your stuff and I'm going to go back to the kitchen to make a few calls. Come find me whenever you're ready."

Polly recognized that Lydia was a little distracted. While she was welcoming and gracious, all of her extra joy and sass seemed to have washed away. Whatever she knew about those two bodies had upset her and Polly didn't know how to help. So, she sat down on the bed and dropped her bag beside her.

She opened her bag and looked inside it, then realized she had no idea what she might be looking for. She pushed it away and flopped down.

"Wow," she said out loud. "That's a nice bed!"

Polly turned over on her right side and looked around the room. There were two abstract floral prints hanging on either side of the mirror over the dresser. Everything seemed to be unique, yet perfectly coordinated. She wondered if Lydia had done this or had hired someone to decorate her home. She got back up and walked into the bathroom. Bright yellow and cream were perfectly accented by the sunshine streaming in the window over the sink. Mirrors on either side brightened the space as the sun glinted off them, throwing rays all over the room.

Then, she peeked into the adjoining bedroom. This room was done in deep blue and ivory. The wooden bedroom suite was done in walnut and white maple. The room was a play of striking contrasts and took Polly's breath away. She was going to have to either hire Lydia to help her decorate the school or find out who she'd found to do this work.

Polly walked back into her bedroom. She figured she had probably spent enough time up here for Lydia to make her calls and walked out in the hall. As she started down the stairs, she heard Lydia saying, "I understand. We'll see you when you get here. Just don't forget to come home, okay?" There was a slight pause. "I love you too and I'm sorry you have to do this alone. You know ..." another slight pause. "Alright. Tell the girls if they need me, all they have to do is ask. Good-bye."

The sound of a chair scraping across the kitchen floor and cupboards opening and closing accompanied Polly as she traversed the rest of the steps and made her way into the kitchen.

"There you are, Polly," Lydia said, turning around from the stovetop. "Would you like some tea? I have water brewing. Or anything else we can find in the refrigerator."

"Tea would be great. Can I help you?"

"No, I think I have everything out."

Polly looked at the kitchen table. Yes, Lydia had everything out. There was a small plate of cookies, a basket with several different types of tea, fancy napkins and china all sitting on the table. Polly couldn't help herself. While Lydia was pouring the water into a teapot, she flipped a plate over. "Of course it is," she thought, then said out loud, "My mom always served on Wedgwood."

"Oh!" said Lydia. "Those have been in the family for years. I think they were my mother's wedding present."

"My mom's too!" Polly agreed. "I have them somewhere. They've been in storage so long, it will be good to see them again. They were only used when company came, though."

"Well, you're company and family all at the same time, here," said Lydia, and she set the teapot down on the table. "Here, sit down and we'll talk. I'm sure you are," and she looked at Polly with a little bit of a smirk in her lips, "dying to know what's going on."

"I'm so sorry, Lydia. Sometimes my brain and my tongue don't seem to agree about what should be out in the world," Polly apologized. "You obviously know who those two people were and I should have been more sensitive."

"Oh, don't worry about it. It's alright. The day brought me a little shock, that's all." Lydia said. "Actually, I suspect it brought you a shock as well, though, it was probably different." Her voice trailed off for a moment and Polly saw Lydia's lower lip tremble. She reached out and put her hand on top of her friend's forearm.

"I'm sorry, Lydia. Who was in the ceiling and how do you know them?"

"Goodness," Lydia said, "It's been over forty years ago. You'd think I could manage better than this." She held out the basket of tea to Polly, who took a bag, opened it and placed it in her cup. Lydia took another and then poured hot water into both cups. She stirred hers around a little and looked up again.

"Forty-one years ago. It was the worst thing I'd ever faced. We didn't know what happened to them. No one did. The police questioned all of us trying to find out something, but no one knew anything at all.

"It was the summer after my freshman year in high school, 1971. We didn't have a large class, there were only sixty-two of us. I'd had a great year and was getting ready to have a great summer. Mom and Dad had scheduled a big vacation to South Dakota and Wyoming and I was going to go to a camp in Colorado before school started that fall. I didn't have a care in the world. Dad had hooked me up with a great job at the drug store and I was ready.

"We left for vacation and had a glorious time. We saw everything that year. We were driving back home and Dad decided he needed to call his partner to make sure everything was alright. I think he wanted to make sure the building still stood.

"When he got back in the car, he just sat there. Then he told us what he'd heard.

"Do you remember meeting Linda and Sarah?" Lydia asked Polly.

"Sure, they are sisters, aren't they?" she responded.

"Yes, but they had twin sisters who were my age. Jill and Kellie. We'd been together since Kindergarten.

"While we were gone on vacation, those two girls disappeared. The police were there, the whole town turned out and searched the fields and the woods; everywhere they might have gone. There were all sorts of rumors. A poor drifter who was in town at the time was thrown into jail for a while, but he didn't know anything. When they couldn't find any evidence to hold him, they had to let him go and he left town.

"People thought they saw the girls get into someone's car, other people thought they saw them in Des Moines. We had calls come in from Omaha and Minneapolis. Their parents never quit looking. They were wonderful people, but I think it destroyed them in ways no one can ever understand. Linda had already graduated from high school and was at the University of Iowa. Sarah had just graduated. It nearly killed her to go away to school, but her parents didn't want her to sit around moping and made her start her life. She didn't go too far, though, just down to AIB in Des Moines. She came back after a couple of years and started working for Dan Timmons. He had an insurance business. When he retired, Sarah's husband bought the company and they got married.

"The girls' dad died about fifteen years after this all happened and then their mother died maybe ten years ago. When she was gone, the girls finally settled down and released all of the pain. They relaxed for the first time since that summer and I know this is going to start all of their pain up again."

Lydia paused and said, "Aaron has to go tell them now their sisters were in the old high school all this time. I wish he'd let me go with him, but he told me I didn't need to go through this tonight. He called Rev. Boehm and he'll meet Aaron at Linda's house. Oh, this is killing me! I should be there!"

"Do you want me to take you over there, Lydia?" Polly asked quietly.

"No, he's right. I'll let them deal with this tonight and stop by tomorrow. Maybe I'll feel more like my normal self, and I won't fall completely apart."

Polly held on to Lydia's arm, and then moved her hand down to clasp Lydia's fingers.

"Tell me about the girls when they were in school," she said.

"Kellie and Jillie," Lydia smiled. "That's who they were to us. They were horrid brats and we all loved them. They were identical and played that up at every chance. I know they drove their parents crazy, alternating personas. They made their mother cut their hair exactly the same and when she tried to do something different to one of them, they'd figure out a way to fix it so they looked the same. Even if you got to know them well, it was difficult to tell until you spent a few moments. They were constantly pulling dirty tricks on teachers. The school tried separating them into different sections, but then they would take each other's place in the classroom, waiting for the teacher to say something.

"They seemed to have a second sense about each other. If one of them got sent to detention, you knew the other was going to show up there before too long. Both were smart as a whip and did well in school. When they got older, they finally began separating their interests. Jillie loved playing basketball. Kellie played, but wasn't very good at it. Kellie loved to sing. Jillie sang in the choir, but didn't have a very good time. Jillie was totally in love with every boy in the school. When she got into eighth grade, she made it her goal to dance with every single unattached boy before the fall sock hop season was over. Kellie was more of a wallflower and didn't care whether or not the boys paid any attention to her."

Lydia paused and grinned. "Then, Kellie figured it out our freshman year. Things got much worse for the boys. They didn't know which sister they were asking out most of the time. And it was very possible they would ask Jill out and Kellie would show up at the front door for the date. One time, both girls decided to go after ... who was it?" Lydia mused. "Oh, I think it must have been Bob Andle. Yeah, that was it. They separated and began talking to him at different times. He didn't know who was talking to him. They set up a date with him to go to Boone for a movie. He showed up at the house and both girls were dressed and ready for him.

"Most boys would have thought that was so cool, but Bob took one look, realized what had happened and left them at the door. The next day, his sister, who was a senior, found the two girls and told them they had pulled a dirty trick. I think she scared them. They apologized to him, but he never looked at either of them again."

"Oh, Polly," Lydia sighed. "If it is this hard for me; imagine how hard it is going to be for Linda and Sarah."

"I know," Polly said and squeezed the hand she continued to hold.

"Did they suspect anyone other than the drifter or did they think the girls ran away or what?" she asked.

"They did ask about the possibility of them running away. That didn't make sense, though. There was nothing wrong in their house and if they had run away, it would have been for a fling to Des Moines or maybe even Omaha. Then they would have called and come home after having had a little bit of fun.

"With all the rumors of them showing up in these other cities, I suppose the police thought maybe the girls had been kidnapped. I know that for the next year, all the girls in high school were very careful. There was a lot of talk about white slavery, you know, girls being taken away to live in foreign countries. We all made a big deal out of it and were frightened of our own shadows," Lydia responded.

"What about anyone else in town. Was there anyone that would have deliberately hurt them?"

"Well, they'd tortured nearly everyone around them with their twin antics, but I don't think there was anyone who had enough reason to want to hurt them, much less kill them," Lydia responded.

"Kellie had started dating a junior in high school about the time of the Winter Ball in January, right after we got back from break. Buddy Landers. They got pretty hot and heavy. Jill didn't like him very much, but we all figured she was mad because Kellie had a steady boyfriend. Buddy was destroyed when the girls went missing. It was as if his heart had broken in two. He didn't come back to school that fall, but I think he ended up graduating with the class. The police were pretty rough on him and it messed him up emotionally. I think I remember his mom worked with the teachers to get work for him and then he had to see a counselor in Ames. He finally showed back up at the school the next January and though he didn't say much to anyone, ever, he got through the year and got his diploma.

"Wow, I hadn't thought of him in years. After graduation, he left town. I heard he ended up in Florida somewhere, but I have no idea what he's doing now. Heck, I don't even know if he's still alive. His parents moved away back in the 90s when his dad got a job in Denver. So, unless he has stayed in contact with a classmate, we don't know where he is or what he's doing.

Polly heard the front door open and then Beryl's voice, "Lydia? Girlfriend? Where are you?"

Lydia stood up and walked to the door of the kitchen. "I'm in here. Come in and have some tea. Polly's here and I'm telling her about Kellie and Jill."

"So are you doing alright?" asked Beryl. "I can't believe it is true. Really?"

"I'm afraid so," said Lydia. "Poor Dougie Randall pulled a fake ceiling down this morning and their remains tumbled out. Polly's been kicked out of her home until they get it all cleaned up and sorted out, so I get to have her stay with me!"

Beryl pushed Polly's shoulder a little, "Well, ain't that the best deal you're getting today! Are you sleeping in one of those five-star luxury rooms upstairs?"

Polly laughed. "They are beautiful! And that bed may never let me leave in the morning."

"Now you see why we like sleepovers here. Which room did you take?"

"I'm in the burgundy and green room."

"Oh! I love that room. As soon as Lydia's Jill moved out, she ripped it apart and re-did everything. You'd never have known it was the same room. That girl liked pink! I thought she would have grown out of it, but that room was seriously sick. It was ... yep ... it was Pepto-Bismol sick," said Beryl.

"She loved all that pink," said Lydia. "I was so glad to have at least one daughter who was all girly and frilly. Marilyn was happiest in blue jeans and Sandy wouldn't be caught dead in a dress.

"Okay, you named your daughter Jill," Polly exclaimed. "Were these girls the reason?"

"Actually, they were. Jillie and I got pretty close when Kellie started dating Buddy. I'm not sure why. We'd never been that close before, but we drifted together. I'd had a steady boyfriend for a while and we broke up right after Valentine's Day. I was whining about it one day, Jill thought it was funny and then asked if I wanted to come over and shoot some hoops after school. I was terrible! But, she kept inviting me over and so I went."

Beryl put her arms all the way around Lydia. "I don't think anyone realized how much you missed her the next year, honey."

That was all it took, Lydia fell apart and began to cry. Polly didn't know what to do with herself while the two women held on to each other and she was saved by a soft knock on the door sill. Andy had come into the house and her face was drawn.

"I was with Sarah today in Ames. She wanted me to go to lunch with her and talk about some English tutoring for her youngest. He wants to go out East to college and needs help prepping for the SATs. Aaron called her and asked her to go to Linda's when she got back to town. I dropped her off and went in with her when he told them what had happened today. I figured the next place I needed to be was here, after I sat with her for a while."

"How are they doing?" asked Lydia.

"Actually, they're doing pretty well right now. Rev. Boehm is there. Angela went with him. Aaron was doing a great job. He's pretty awesome, Lydia."

"I know. He really is." Lydia snuffled a little and Polly automatically handed her a cloth napkin from the table.

Beryl snorted with laughter. "Blow your noise baby, that's the most action that napkin has seen in years! At least this time when it hits the laundry, it will have something to do!"

All four women cracked up. Lydia tried to be dainty and pressed the napkin against her nose, but finally looked at the others, grinned and blew it.

CHAPTER SEVEN

Siting at the kitchen table with Lydia and her friends, Polly listened while the others reminisced about their school years, and especially those years with Kellie and Jill Stevens. There were no more tears, but she recognized the wistfulness of lost opportunities with people you love. She'd felt it often enough at the loss of both of her parents. Soon, Beryl looked at her watch!

"Ladies," she said, “it's 5:45 and there isn't a thing to eat on the table. What are you going to do, Lydia, when Aaron comes home and you have nothing to feed him? Aren't you worried he'll become a beast?"

"No, the beastly stuff comes after you've all gone home to your sweet little beds." Lydia giggled and even blushed. "I can't believe I said that."

She pulled out her phone, "Let me see what he's up to, just a second" and she texted her husband. In a moment, he returned the text.

"He says he's about finished. Do you want to go to Davey's for dinner tonight?" she asked the table.

"Oh, that will be perfect," Beryl responded. "They have a new bartender I'm dying to try out."

Polly looked up at her, a little bemused. "You want to try the bartender?"

"Well, hell yeah, toots, he has to be at least one third of my age. At least! And I hear he's cute."

Polly looked around the table at the other two, who were sitting there grinning.

"She has a few drink recipes she loves tossing at bartenders. Beryl, here, says any bartender worth his salt will know how to mix them properly and if they don't, she's glad to teach them, isn't she, Lydia!" declared Andy.

"And she's been known to walk around the bar and start mixing drinks like a pro. Every restaurant and bar owner from here to Davenport knows about Beryl. If they're smart, they make sure to get her favorites trained from the beginning. If they want to watch their bartender squirm, they say nothing. Davey will have said nothing. Beryl's attack on his new bartenders is one of the favorite parts of his day."

Lydia texted Aaron again and said, "Alright! Let's go! I'll drive, unless you want to crawl in the back of Polly's truck."

Andy laughed. "You know, someday I could drive. I have a perfectly good car."

Beryl poked her in the arm. "Your perfectly good car might hold us, but it wouldn't go very fast with four people in it. And I hate unfolding myself out of your stupid back seat. The last time I nearly broke a nail! The front seat isn't much better. I've kissed a lot of ugly in my life, but I'm not particularly fond of your front windshield. You might want to wash the inside sometime."

Andy sighed. "Oh, whatever."

Lydia laughed at her friends. "Let's take my Jeep. Unless you guys want to drive separately and then go home after we're done. "

"Oh no," said Andy. "If Beryl starts testing drinks, your husband would flip a lid if she drove. We'll bring her back here and figure it out from there."

"Hey!" cried Beryl, then she stopped. "Oh. You're probably right." Then, she stopped again and looked at Lydia. "You know. We drive right past my house. Why don't I drive there and then you can pick me up."

"Alright, fine," said Andy. "I'll drive by myself and head home from the restaurant."

"You wanted to bring the party back here, didn't ya, dollface?" asked Beryl, sidling up to Andy. "I know you. You thought you'd get me all drunked up and have your way with me in Lydia's comfy bed upstairs."

"Oh!" snorted Andy. "You're impossible. It's a good thing I love you. Now get, before I kick your ass."

"Kick my ass? You and ..." Beryl looked at her friend. "Yeah. You could take me. It's happened before."

She picked up her purse and headed back out the front door. Both she and Andy had parked in the half-circle driveway in front of the house. Polly ran upstairs to get her wallet and her phone. She saw there had been two missed calls, but didn't take the time to look at the numbers. She jammed it in the back pocket of her jeans and ran back down the steps. Lydia was waiting at the bottom and they went to the lower level together.

"You know, I could drive if you want to ride back with Aaron," Polly said.

"Oh, no. I don't even know if he'll be coming back here for a while. They're still at the school. He's making them work longer hours so you can get back in there. Otherwise, those kids would find a way to keep you out of there for a month." She chuckled. "Okay, maybe not that long, but he's pushing for you!"

They picked Beryl up and then went on to Davey's. Polly had driven past the restaurant, but hadn't taken the time to explore. For that matter, she hadn't taken time to explore much in Bellingwood. She'd run into the grocery store once to pick up some essentials, but had found she liked the Hy-Vee store in Boone. She missed the variety she'd found in the supermarkets in Boston, but even there, most of her shopping was done in small local grocery stores.

Lydia opened the immense door. It was covered in red quilted vinyl. The foyer was dimly lit and the carpet on the floor was dark. Polly could only imagine that if smoking inside restaurants was still legal, heavy smoke would pour out when they opened the next door. When they pulled those wooden doors open, she was pleasantly surprised to see a beautifully finished counter for the register. There was nice blue carpet on the floor and she looked into the main dining room. Quite a few tables were filled. The hostess recognized Lydia and said, "Aaron is already here. Let me take you to his table."

Lydia remarked, "Andy is going to be right behind us, will you let her know where we're sitting?"

"Of course, Mrs. Merritt. Right this way."

She showed them to a round table. Aaron was talking across it to a couple at another table. When he saw them come in the door and head for him, he stood up. Lydia went over to sit beside him and he pulled her into a hug. "Did it finally hit you?" he asked.

"Yes. You knew it would." Then, she looked at Beryl. "Did he call you?"

"Absolutely not," came the response. "He texted me."

Andy came up to the table. "Who texted you?"

"While you were delivering Sarah to her sister's house, Mr. Hot Stuff over there texted me to go make his wife cry so she could get it all out and get over it."

"I did not!" Aaron exclaimed.

"Well, those may not have been your words, but we all know that was your intent. You certainly don't want to have to deal with those tears." Beryl said.

Aaron pulled a chair out for his wife, then waited while the other three sat down. "I got soft drinks for everyone. Polly, she's bringing you coffee, because the boys say you drink a ton of it. If you want something else, though, just say so. Soup should be here in a minute and the special is some weird chicken thing."

Lydia interrupted, "By weird chicken thing, he means it's not steak. We'll ask again when Amber gets here."

Amber was pregnant ... very pregnant. She waddled to their table carrying a tray of drinks. When she put coffee in front of Polly, she asked, "Did you want something else? Sheriff Merritt wasn't sure."

"This will be fine," Polly said. "Thank you."

"Does anyone else want something different to drink," Amber looked around the table and her eyes stopped on Beryl.

"Oh, yes, I do, sweetie! Let's see, what shall I have tonight?" After thinking for a moment, she said, Andy, this one's for you, since you got me all hot and bothered back at Lydia's house," then turned back to Amber. "I'd like to order a Red-Headed Slut."

Amber giggled and said, "Oh, I can't wait to tell him!" She started to walk away, then turned back. "I'll be right back with your soup."

Beryl watched Amber waddle away and said, "As long as she doesn't give birth between here and the kitchen, we're gonna be fine." Then, she leaned back in her seat and stretched her arms open wide. "I can't imagine being pregnant and waiting tables. Someone needs to help that girl out!"

Everyone looked at her.

"Oh. Me? I should help her out? What am I supposed to do?"

Andy muttered, "Shutting up would be a great place to start."

"Hey!" Beryl laughed, then thought about it and said, "You're probably right. I think I will."

"Yeah," Andy retorted, "I'll believe that when I hear the silence."

Beryl dramatically went through the motion of zipping her lips shut and sat back in her seat. Polly watched Aaron to see his response. He hadn't paid one bit of attention to Beryl's antics. While Beryl was chatting it up with the world, he had leaned into his wife and was talking quietly with her. Polly saw tears threatening Lydia's eyes and she leaned on her husband's shoulder as he pulled her chair closer to his and put his arm around her.

Then, Beryl unzipped her mouth.

"See, Polly. That's why our girl has so much energy to take care of everyone else." and she zipped her lips shut again.

Another waiter brought the soup out and passed it around the table. As he left, Amber brought Beryl's drink to her. She set it down on the table and then wandered to the other side to watch Beryl. The entire table focused on her first sip.

Beryl picked the glass up and bumped it against her closed lips. She grinned, then unzipped her lips. "Oh, I forgot," she said and took a drink. She swirled it around in her mouth, raised her eyes as if contemplating the ceiling. She swallowed and emphasized it with a gulp. "Hmmm," she said. "Let me try another sip."

She went through the same motions again. She set the glass down and got up out of her seat. Andy grabbed Polly's arm, "Come on, you don't want to miss this."

They followed Beryl to the bar which was back through the front entry. There was an absolutely adorable young man behind the bar, who looked up at them as they entered.

Beryl sat down on a stool in front of him and said, "Alright, who told you?"

His head pulled back and his eyes got big, "I'm sorry, ma'am. What?"

"Who told you?"

"Who told me what?"

By this time, several more people had gathered around. Andy poked Polly and pointed at a man in his fifties. "That's Davey." Polly nodded and turned back to the bar.

"Where did you learn how to make a Red-Headed Slut?" Beryl asked the boy. "No one in this town has ever made one of those before."

His shoulders went back and he got a little cocky. "That's because I'm not from around here." he said.

"It was perfect and I want to know how you knew what to do," she asked.

"Maybe a bartender needs to keep his secrets," he retorted.

Beryl turned on Davey. "Did you tell him about me?"

"I did not," Davey said. "I did tell him to be ready for anything, though."

"So you're ready for anything," she said, flipping back to the bartender.

"I guess I am! If we have the liquor in stock to make what you want, I can make anything. I guarantee it."

"Well!" Beryl huffed and spun around on her stool. She walked out of the bar and back into the restaurant.

Polly walked up to the bar and said, "Okay, how did you do that?"

"Don't tell her," he said, "But, I'm not stupid. I actually had heard about her from some other patrons. They've been asking me all week if Beryl had come in yet. I brought insurance." He reached under the bar and pulled out a computer tablet. I have the whole internet here. I can make any drink she asks for and I can make it perfectly."

He laughed out loud as he put the tablet back under the bar. Polly and Andy chuckled as they joined the others at the table.

"Well, what's so funny," Beryl asked, continuing her huff.

"You are, my dear." Andy said. "You've been trumped by a very young, very smart man. I never thought I'd live to see the day."

"Whatever." Beryl pushed the drink away. "Well, that's no fun now. Here Polly, you drink it."

Polly looked at the women, then picked the drink up and took a sip. "Whoa! That's good!" she said. "What's in it?"

"Peach schnapps, Jagermeister and cranberry juice." Beryl responded. "The little runt got the recipe exactly right, too."

Amber came back and took their orders. The weird chicken stuff was Chicken Marsala and Polly gladly ordered it. As expected, Sheriff Merritt had a steak, while Lydia ordered a salad. Beryl and Andy both had pasta dishes and ordered wine.

As they waited for their food to arrive, Polly asked, "Aaron, how were you able to verify the remains were those of Jill and Kellie Stevens?"

"Believe it or not, their purses were with them up there. Whoever killed them must have gathered everything they had and then put it up in the ceiling."

"How in the world did someone have time to re-do the bathroom so no one noticed it was different?" asked Andy.

"We don't know all of the details yet. We're going to have to go back through school records and talk to people who were in charge back then. I hope we're able to find everyone. Forty years is a long time to wait before returning to an investigation. But, we've got an awful lot of reports from those days. We'll start there. They talked to practically everyone in town, so there should be some good memories written down. I've already got Melanie pulling up the boxes from the basement and DCI is pulling out their documentation. I've talked to the State Patrol and we'll get it all coordinated. Everyone has something and I'm telling you that somewhere there is a clue we need in order to figure out what happened to those girls.

"Did they talk to you girls that summer?" he asked.

Lydia responded first, "Since I was in Wyoming, they didn't have much to ask me, except who the girls were friends with and if they'd ever talked about anyone strange hanging around. There wasn't much to tell. All of my friends were their friends."

Beryl said, "Sure, they talked to me, but I didn't pay too much attention to those girls. I was a little caught up in my artsy-fartsy self and didn't engage with people if I could help it. If Lydia hadn't made sure I got out and around people every once in a while, I might have been a terribly boring human being!"

"I was friends with Sarah, so I spent a lot of time with the family that summer," Andy reflected. "It was worse than you can even imagine. Her mom sat in the front room in a blue chair, staring off into space. When Linda or Sarah would try to get her to eat or drink something, she would do what they asked and then go back into the silence. Their dad wasn't much better. At least he could leave the house for a while to go to work. After the first week they'd been gone, he didn't know what else to do. His wife was broken and he couldn't help. The police seemed to spend a lot of time there for a while, but then, there was only one detective who continued to show up on a regular basis and then after a while, even he didn't know what else to do to help look for the girls. They'd done everything they could.

"Neither of the older girls wanted to leave for college, but their Dad wouldn't let them stay home. He hired someone to come in to the house to keep it clean and make sure their mom got up in the morning. She finally snapped out of it around Thanksgiving. It was like a light bulb finally flicked back on.

"She called me the week before Thanksgiving and told me Linda and Sarah were coming home and she'd like to have a party that Friday night for them at the house. Would I be able to round up some of their friends? I was so shocked to hear her voice, much less hear her planning a party, I simply said yes.

"I made some calls and we had a pretty good turnout." Andy turned to Lydia. "You were there, weren't you?" she asked.

"Yeah. You called me. I probably wouldn't have gone otherwise. Most of those girls were older than me. But, I dragged you to that one, too, didn't I, Beryl!"

"I remember!" Beryl said. "I wasn't sure if I wanted to go, but you picked me up and I couldn't say no to you. That was actually a pretty fun evening. Linda brought her boyfriend home and that shocked her parents."

Andy went on, "The girls were surprised to see their mother so alive again. She told them that one night, in the middle of the night as she lay in Kellie's bed, not sleeping, she figured if they were ever coming home, the last thing they needed to see was a Mom who was nuts, so she was going to quit being nuts. And if the girls never came home, then her other two daughters didn't need a crazy person for a Mom either. She'd fallen apart and now she was going to stop it. It took her nearly six months, but she figured it out and decided to start making a life again.

"I don't think either of them was ever really happy again though. You could see it in their eyes. But, they made an attempt to have a normal life. They were good grandparents to Linda's kids and tried to make both Linda and Sarah know they were loved."

Andy stopped. The table had grown quiet.

Amber brought the two pasta dishes to Beryl and Andy. She asked, "Is it true, Sheriff, they found bodies in the old schoolhouse?"

She turned around and took two plates away from another server who had followed her over, placing the salad in front of Lydia and walking around to set Aaron's steak in front of him.

"Yes, it is true, Amber. We were just talking about it. I'm sure you'll hear all about it tomorrow when the news starts spreading around." he replied.

Amber put Polly's dish in front of her. "I heard it was the twins who everyone thought ran away forty years ago."

"We think that is true, Amber. Thank you for bringing our meals out."

She looked a little confused, knowing she'd been dismissed. "Is there anything else you need right now?"

Everyone shook their heads. "Okay," she said. I'll be back in a bit to check on you."

Lydia looked at Aaron, "It's a good thing you don't have any reason to keep a tight lid on this."

He chuckled. "There's absolutely no reason to do that. After the number of people who saw what happened at the school this morning and the speculation already pervading the community, it's best to tell the truth so stories don't start running rampant.

"Do you remember when Stanley Borts hit a deer out by the lake? He mushed that thing up bad. There was blood all over the car. He parked it out in front of his house when he got home and by the next morning, everyone had him murdering his wife, running over her fifteen times."

Lydia laughed. "Well, she is a terrible bitch and she treats him terribly! I remember listening to her scream at him in the post office because she hadn't picked the key up to their post office box. He ran out to get it for her, it was right there in the car, but she called him terrible names."

Beryl said, "Stupid old biddy, she's mean to everyone. Maybe he should have run over her."

"Well," said Aaron. "With something like this, it's important to keep the town calm. They can take care of Linda and Sarah and their families and we can do whatever it takes to get the investigation going. And, as long as everyone knows what is happening, maybe they will go back through their memories of that summer and click on something new. Especially now they know the girls were killed here in town and hadn't been taken away to serve as sex slaves in some foreign country." He winked at his wife as he said that and she poked him in the ribs.

They finished dinner and Andy took Beryl home. Aaron followed them both to make sure they got safely home. Polly and Lydia were on a couch in the downstairs family room when he walked in the door. "Would you girls like some water or a soda?" he asked.

"Not for me," said Polly. "This has been a day. I'm about to fall asleep."

"Thanks, sweet-ums," Lydia grinned. "We're fine."

"Alright. I'm going upstairs and watch some television. Turn it off if I've fallen asleep, would you?" he patted Polly's shoulder as he walked past her, then kissed his wife on the top of her head. He locked the doors and shut off the outside lights. Then, Polly heard him walk upstairs, check the doors there and make his way up the second flight of stairs.

"He's pretty wonderful to you," she said to Lydia.

"Yes, he is. He'll take good care of you and the school and I can promise we're going to figure out who hurt my friends." Lydia's voice was firm and strong. "I'm not going to let this go another year. Now that those girls have been found, we're going to find their killer, too."

She stood up. "Well, let's go to bed." The two walked to the steps and Lydia flipped the lights off. She turned lights off on the main level and followed Polly on up to the second floor. Outside Polly's room, she reached out and hugged the girl.

"I'm glad you're here tonight. Now, sleep well and we'll see you in the morning. Get up whenever you'd like. I'll be downstairs around six or so. But, please don't be in any hurry. We don't have much to do tomorrow."

"Good night, Lydia. I'm sorry about your friends, but I'm glad you have these amazing women around you now."

Lydia smiled. "They are pretty amazing. And look, you're one of them! Goodnight."

She went on to her room and Polly could hear her talking to Aaron as she shut the door. Polly walked into her own room, closed the door and turned on the lamp beside the bed. She walked back to turn off the overhead light and then sat down on her bed.

All of a sudden she remembered the missed calls and checked her phone.

"God damn it," she said. "God damn it. I can't believe it."

She pulled the cord out of her bag and plugged her phone in, then set it on the table. After cleaning her face and pulling a night shirt on, she crawled in between the blankets.

"I'm not thinking about anything except this comfortable bed. Nothing is going to make me not enjoy sleeping here tonight," she said to herself.

Polly reached up turned the light off, turned over and fell asleep.

CHAPTER EIGHT

It was only five thirty in the morning. Polly stretched, rolled over and looked at the clock. She had a little more time to sleep, so she opened the alarm clock on her phone, set it for 6:15 and curled back into the soft and wonderful smelling blankets. The next thing she knew, her phone was singing her awake. Daylight Savings Time hadn't yet ended, so it was still dark outside as Polly slipped off the bed and allowed her toes to curl up in the cushion of carpet. Padding across the room to the bathroom, she listened for any noises in the house. She couldn't hear anything, but trusted that Lydia and Aaron were up and moving.

After a quick shower, she pulled on fresh jeans and a green blouse. Since there was no possibility of working at the school today, is wouldn't hurt her to look a little more feminine. She put her shoes on, pulled the covers back up on the bed and tucked things in. Then, she opened the door to her room and peeked out. Lights were on downstairs, so she walked down and found Lydia alone in the kitchen, where smells of bacon and something sweet greeted her as she got to the doorway.

"Good morning," she said.

"I heard you coming. Coffee is already on the table and I'll have muffins out in a moment," Lydia said.

"Has Aaron already left?"

Lydia laughed. "No, that slug won't be down for another half hour. Don't be fooled, he's a terrible morning person. I've made him crazy for years, but he appreciated it when I was up with the kids. He could come down long after we'd all fought getting ready for school, then enjoy breakfast and kiss them all before he left. Dirty rat. Now he knows I'll have the house warmed up, coffee made and breakfast ready for him, so he can be a leisurely slug."

Polly took a drink of her coffee. "Do you ever sleep?"

"Oh, I sleep like a log. From the moment my head hits that pillow until 5:45, I'm out. Now, if you must know, I take a 20 minute nap every afternoon." Lydia looked around the room, then whispered, "I don't tell just anybody that. I like them to think I am cheerful from dawn 'til dusk!"

"Well, aren't you?" Polly asked.

"I suppose I am," Lydia responded. "It's so much easier than being grumpy all the time. And people like you a lot more if they don't have to feel sorry for you. They generally have enough feeling sorry for themselves going on."

Polly giggled. "I guess you have people pretty well figured out."

"It is human nature to need attention turned on ourselves. Whether you are being whiny or filled with drama or a plain old bitch, people pay attention to you, which reinforces their bad behavior. My mama taught me that the world desires sunshine and I could choose to be sunshine for people or rain on their parades. I decided sunshine would be a lot more fun."

Polly heard footsteps on the stairway and looked up as Aaron entered the kitchen. "I'm early, woman. Where's my breakfast? What have I told you about treating your lordship right?"

He swatted Lydia on her backside, then leaped backward as she swung on him, spatula in hand. "My lordship needs a haircut. So there," she said.

He stood there and looked at his wife, then reached over, pulled her close and dipped her. Winking at Polly, he kissed her and said, "Good morning, snookums."

Polly giggled and watched as Lydia dropped like deadweight in his arms. He scrambled to bring her back to an upright position and she wiggled away from him. "Good morning to you, you nut. Now, sit down and I'll feed you as soon as food comes out of the oven. What in the world are you doing up ..." she turned and looked at the clock on the wall, "at 6:40 in the morning?

"I thought since we had company, it would be a good idea to impress her with my prompt arrival."

"Honey, you're always prompt, we just had to figure out what time you would start your day."

"Okay, I know." he replied. "I woke up and started thinking about the Stevens girls and couldn't go back to sleep after you vacated the bed. Your side got cold and my toes didn't like it much, so my brain clicked on. I couldn't turn it back off."

Lydia pulled muffins out of the oven and set the pan on a rack to cool. She checked the timer on a second oven and, slicing a loaf of bread, dropped two pieces in a toaster. Then, she pulled a glass container of orange juice out of the refrigerator and asked Polly, "Would you like some?"

Polly shook her head and said, "No thank you."

Lydia poured juice into two of the glasses she had sitting beside the refrigerator and put one in front of Aaron and the second at the empty space.

"What were you processing on about the case, Aaron?" Lydia asked.

"Was there any time during those years that the school was closed up long enough for someone to work on the ceiling? That would have taken some work. He would have had to get supplies and haul everything in, then work without discovery. I thought the custodians or someone was always in the building."

Lydia said, "I don't honestly know. As soon as school was out for the summer, I was gone. They could have held bonfires on the playground and danced naked around them and I would never have known.

"Doug Leon is still around town. He was one of the custodians when I was there. In fact, I think they even interviewed him at the time, but he didn't have any motive. And now, he's an old, lonely guy. You should probably talk to him about when the school building was closed up."

Lydia thought about it for a moment.

"You know, I was one of the weird ones who left school behind when I was done in May every year. There were a lot of kids who had to go to summer school and others were hired by the school to do yard work. I think there were even a few hired to wash windows those summers. Andy helped out with a couple of tutoring and day care experiences for the younger kids, but I don't know if she worked at the elementary or the high school. You'd have to ask her."

She paused and thought again, then said, "How in the world are we supposed to remember things from forty years ago?"

The timer on the oven chimed and she pulled out a breakfast casserole. Aaron grinned at Polly. "I never get fed like this unless someone is here. She makes me suffer with oatmeal or toast."

Polly shook her head and laughed at him. "You look quite deprived."

"Doesn't he though? His mouth tells you he's a terribly abused man. His eyes tell you he is easily amused by himself." Lydia chuckled as she cut the casserole and brought it to the table. She went back to the counter to get the muffins and brought those over.

Polly felt her phone buzz in her back pocket and pulled it out. "Geez, it's not even seven o'clock here. Who's calling me?"

She stepped out of the kitchen into the living room and said, "Hello?"

She heard Joey's voice on the other end. "Polly? Did I finally find you?"

"Hello, Joey." Her voice lost its luster. "How did you find me?"

"Oh, I badgered Janet until she finally gave me your new number. Why haven't you contacted me? It's been six months. I've been worried sick."

"I'm sorry, Joey. I've been busy and are you kidding me, we broke up. It didn't occur to me you would want to, much less need to know my new number."

"I can't believe you did this to me, Polly! This isn't like you at all. It's like you dropped off the face of the earth."

"Joey, I'm in the middle of breakfast with some friends."

"Is it a new boyfriend? Is that why you left me? Did someone tell you he was better than me? Because I've been working on it, Polly. I've been seeing a counselor and taking the anger management classes like I promised."

"Joey, there is no one else. I'm glad you're doing better. But, I have to go now. I will call you later when I have time."

"No, Polly. Don't go! I want to talk to you for a minute and tell you how much I miss you and how I know that I screwed up badly. Dick says I've come a long way since last February. I'm a whole new person."

Polly took a breath, "Joey. I have to go. I said I would call you later and I will. Good-bye."

She cut him off when she ended the call, then walked back into the kitchen and sat down. She felt sick.

Lydia put her hand out and touched Polly's arm. "Are you alright, dear? We couldn't help but overhear."

"Oh, I'm so sorry. I didn't mean for you to have to hear my garbage. You've got enough going on. I'm alright. It's just something I thought I put behind me."

"What we have going on or not going on doesn't make a difference right now. You've got this going on. Are you alright?" Aaron's concerned eyes made Polly's lip quiver and before she knew it, she was crying.

"I'm sorry," she said again. “It's been a weird year and I hoped when I moved back to Iowa, some of the weirdness would stay in Boston. But, he found me and I'm pretty sure he's going to make it weird all over again. He called last night and I missed those calls. I saw them before I went to bed, but hoped it was someone else. I didn't have the energy to even look. And now, he has found me."

"Polly," Lydia said, nodding to her husband, "He's the sheriff. We can help. Did this guy hurt you?"

Polly looked at them, startled. "Oh no! Not me. I'd kick his ass." Lydia chuckled and Aaron snorted with laughter.

"Of course you would, dear," Lydia said. "So, what's wrong?"

"Well, it wasn't me. Joey was ... is ... quite jealous. At first it was sweet. He kind of swept me off my feet. He didn't want anyone else looking at me or taking care of me. He swooped in and did everything for me.

"Then, after a few weeks, it got worse. I couldn't talk to a taxi driver or a doorman without him asking what was going on. I told him he couldn't harass me about the men who were at the library. It was my job to help anyone who was there. I tried breaking up with him a couple of times, but he always promised he would be good."

She looked at the two of them. "Oh, I know now that is classic victim talk. But, damn, he was hot and he was sweet to me.

"One night we were in a club to hear one of my favorite bands. I left the table to go to the bathroom and somehow I tripped. A guy on the dance floor caught me before I hit the ground, then when he pulled me back up; he spoke into my ear asking if I was okay. He had to get that close because the music was so loud. Well, Joey had a little too much to drink. He'd never done anything completely stupid before, but that night, he attacked the guy and beat the hell out of him. Security broke it up and called the police. The guy pressed charges and Joey was in jail for the rest of the weekend until I could get him bailed out on Monday.

"I was so pissed off. But, he calmed me down. I stuck around through his trial and then he had to serve thirty days. Part of his sentence was taking an anger management class along with seeing a counselor. As long as he was doing something positive, I was fine with staying with him. I thought I loved him.

"Then, one day, he showed up at the library. One of my regulars stopped me in the aisle to thank me for recommending a book. He was kind of cute and we laughed about something. I was supposed to meet Joey for lunch at a cafe down the street, but didn't know he had come in to the Library. The guy left and Joey stopped him outside and threatened him, shoving him up against the building.

"I walked out to go to lunch and saw the whole thing happen. I pulled Joey off, apologized to the guy and then the two of us went to the cafe. He admitted he'd quit going to counseling and the anger management class had ended. I broke up with him. I was done. I told him I had taken it for long enough and that he and I saw the world differently. Then I told him if he ever tried anything again, I would contact the police myself.

"He was like a hurt puppy. He sat there and cried. He begged and begged, promising he'd fix it. Finally, I got up and walked out.

"I called my boss and took the rest of the day off, called a locksmith, who met me at my brownstone, changed the locks and changed my telephone number. There were a couple of nights I was pretty sure he was outside my house. I found flowers the next morning. He sent me long letters, pleading with me to come back. I ignored it all.

"One day, my boss called me in and asked if I was doing alright. She told me I had lost weight and looked miserable. I went into the bathroom and took a long look at myself in the mirror. I decided I didn't have to live like that, so I went home, figured out what was important; decided my life was important and I had enough money to start dreaming big. I quit my job, packed my stuff, put it on a truck to Iowa, rented an apartment in Ames and left town. I gave my phone number and address to my boss and it sounds like Joey convinced one of my coworkers into finding it.

While Polly told her story, Lydia had placed a section of breakfast casserole on her plate and had opened a blueberry muffin and spread butter on it. She picked Polly's fork up and put it into her left hand. "Eat something. I promise it will help."

Polly giggled, "You sound like my Grandmother Giller! Food fixed everything for her. There was never a time we were at her house when there wasn't food being cooked or cleaned up. She annoyed my mother so much because Mom always felt like she had to be in there helping and she hated being stuck in the kitchen while there were other things going on."

Polly looked at the fork in her hand and took a bite.

"Oh, that's good. You're right. I don't need to think about him while I've got all this other stuff going on." She broke off a piece of the muffin. "I wish it were that easy. I've kept pushing him to the back of my mind for so long, I think I believed it was behind me and he would forget me. I can't believe this is going to start all over again." She dropped the food back onto her plate.

"It's not going to start all over again, is it Aaron?" Lydia said.

Aaron looked up from his plate. "Polly, we can do a lot of things to protect you. The first thing you can do is contact your cell provider and block his phone number."

"Oh, that won't do any good. He goes through cell phones all the time. He'll get another one. I suppose I could get another number. It doesn't matter for the Library any longer. I'm done with everything there now."

"I tell you what. Why don't you and Lydia head over to Boone for another phone. I'll take yours and will manage your calls today. As soon as you get a number, let me know and I'll forward the local calls to you. Anything coming in from Massachusetts, I'll answer." Aaron said.

Lydia chuckled, "Well, that ought to scare the poor kid to death." She mimicked answering a phone using a deep voice, "Polly Giller's phone, this is Sheriff Merritt. Can I help you?"

Polly giggled along with her and whether it was from nerves or relief, she began laughing so hard tears streamed down her face. Lydia joined her and soon the two of them could barely breathe. Every time either one of them could gasp in enough air to speak, they spoke in deep tones, "Sherriff Merrit," they said and burst into laughter again.

Aaron looked at them helplessly. Then, shook his head and ate his muffin. With a few big gasps, the two women stopped laughing and held on to their sides.

"Oh, that was painful," cried Polly.

"I haven't done that in years," Lydia agreed, still bubbling out a few giggles.

"You two are a little scary. I was afraid I might have to call for help!" Aaron admonished.

"Yeah. You look terribly frightened with your mouth full of muffin." Lydia said.

"Well, I was a little scared. But, as long as you weren't turning blue, I knew I could wait." He stood up from his chair, taking one last drink of coffee. "Well, since I got such a nice, early start, I am going to head over to the schoolhouse before heading into Boone. Stay in touch with me today, okay?"

Polly handed him her phone and then stood up. She hugged him and he let her. "Thank you so much," she said. "I do appreciate this."

"No problem. Give me a call when you get your phone." Aaron went downstairs and they heard the door close.

Lydia said, "Polly, I'm not leaving until you eat more than one bite of breakfast. So, eat what you can, then we'll head in to Boone and get you set up."

Polly obeyed and ate a few more bites of the breakfast casserole. She drank her coffee and absentmindedly ate the muffin while Lydia cleared the table and began putting food away.

"Do you wonder if life will ever be normal again?" Polly mused out loud.

"Life is what you make it," Lydia replied. "I know it seems like Joey has had power over you in the past and is in power right now, but Polly, you can do anything with your life that you like. You're building a pretty good support group here. Take advantage of us and be strong like your parents taught you."

CHAPTER NINE

No more waiting! It was Saturday morning and Polly was ready to go out of her mind. Thursday had been fun, traveling around with Lydia. They'd gotten a new phone and yes, Aaron had taken one call from Joey. He was pretty sure he'd freaked the young man out. Polly contacted nearly everyone who needed to know what her new number was, so now she was headed back to Boone to get the new number programmed into her old phone, since they had a seventy-two hour replacement policy for something like this. She was glad to get all of her contacts back and was also glad to quit worrying about any more calls coming in from Joey. It was time to let that chapter of her life be finished.

At breakfast, she'd asked Aaron about getting back to work on the school. He thought they'd be able to have access to most of the building on Monday and if Polly wanted to move back in, she could. They planned to keep the bathroom closed off from remodeling until they were completely finished. He didn't know how long it would take.

She really wanted to be able to get everyone back to work, though. Now that things were moving along, she was chomping at the bit to keep them going.

While she was driving, her phone rang. It was Beryl.

"Are you ready for another sleepover tonight?" she asked.

"Oh, good heavens, no!" exclaimed Polly.

"Well, that's good. At least I don't have to plan that. I don't have nearly as many friends as Lydia."

"That doesn't sound like you, Beryl." Polly responded.

"Oh, trust me, it does. I don't like people as much as she does and they seem to sense it when we're in a small room together. They think I'm nuts. They might be right."

Polly laughed. "They just might! So, what's up?"

"Well, Sylvie is free tonight and we found a babysitter for her. Would you like to come over to my house for dinner?"

"You cook?" Polly asked.

"Of course I cook! I'm a great cook!" Then, Beryl stopped. "I make a helluva salad. I'm wicked good with a knife. Sylvie is bringing dessert, Andy is bringing vegetables and Lydia is doing something. I have no idea what, but it will be wonderful, I'm sure. I can heat up an amazing spiral cut ham. I've got this all figured out.

"So, what are you going to bring, Polly?"

"Oh, Beryl" Polly snorted as she laughed. "I'll bring bread and ..." Polly drew the thought out for a few moments.

Beryl interrupted, "Oh, and I've got the liquor covered. I saw you enjoying my red-headed slut the other night."

"You know, Beryl. I looked it up on the internet. It's also called the red headed princess!"

"Yeah. I'm never ordering it using that terminology. It's not nearly as much fun," Beryl retorted.

"You bring bread and anything else you come up with that might be fun," she continued. "We're only going to sit around and fingerpaint, so be at my house around, oh, say, 6:30. We'll have plenty of time to eat and get ourselves in trouble."

"Alright. Wait. Fingerpaint?" Polly wasn't sure what she was getting into.

"Trust me, you'll have fun. Bring yourself and your food! Tra-la-la!" Beryl hung up and Polly caught herself staring at her phone.

"I have the weirdest conversations with people," she thought and realized she was coming to a stop. If she remembered correctly, a right turn and then a left turn onto Story Street would get her downtown and to the telephone store.

All of a sudden she realized she had no idea where Beryl lived. She dialed the number right back and she heard Beryl's voicemail, "Polly, you have no idea where I live do you? My address is 928 North Walnut. It's the cute little brick house on the south side of the street. Wait, they're all cute little brick houses. Well, anyway. You'll find it. See you tonight. OH, leave me a message so I know you got this and can erase it."

Polly said, "I got this. Erase the message."

"Thanks girlfriend!" Beryl said.

"You're absolutely insane, Beryl!"

"I know, it's my best quality. I'll see you tonight." and Beryl was gone again.

When Polly got back to her school, she went upstairs to check on the bathroom. Sure enough, the door was closed and there was a new lock on the door. Crime scene tape stretched across it and sealed the door closed.

"Cool," she thought and pulled out her telephone, shooting several pictures. "This is definitely going in my scrapbook!"

She opened the door to her bedroom and found everything as she had left it. Dumping her bag on the bed, she flopped down and looked around. "I've got to get more of this place put together so I can bring in more furniture!"

Polly poured things out of her bag at the end of the bed and put the toiletries back in the bathroom. That didn't take long, so she went downstairs to the kitchen, the only fully finished room in the place. It was actually in pretty good shape, though she supposed no one had spent much time in there since Lydia cleaned it up on Wednesday.

First things first. She measured ingredients into her bread machine and turned it on. Two hours and then she could shape it and let it rise once more before baking. She had plenty of time.

Sitting down at the table, Polly flipped her laptop open and decided to respond to a few emails. It was a pain to do it on her phone and nothing had been urgent. A few of her friends out east were asking questions about all of her exploits in the middle of the country.

No one understood why she had wanted to come back. They couldn't imagine living without the excitement of the city around them day and night. Polly wasn't sure she wanted to tell them she'd had more excitement since she moved back to Iowa than in all the years she'd lived in Boston.

Sal Kahane had been her roommate in college. Sal didn't like Joey at all and if Polly was leaving Boston to get away from him, she was fully behind the decision, though she told Polly she missed her like crazy. Things weren't the same out there any longer. Polly thought about it. They had known each other for ten years and Sal hadn't said a word when Polly called her and told her she was leaving Boston behind. She came over and helped her pack her stuff, and then hugged her good-bye on the morning she left the city.

Bunny Farnam wasn't quite as supportive, but then she wouldn't be. That poor thing always needed to be the center of attention. Polly was fine with letting that happen. Bunny could draw a crowd and she knew Polly would be there to take care of her, cheer her on and tell her she was the greatest girl ever. The last email from Bunny had been filled with all of her woes and tragedies. Her work was so hard, her boss hated her, her mother had set her up on yet another blind date and he was totally disgusting! Nothing new there.

Drea Renaldi was a young professor at Boston College. They'd met at the library and about five years ago had started going out for coffee. When Drea introduced Polly to her very Italian family, they all decided the innocent young thing from Iowa needed a big family. It was Drea's family who embraced her after her father died and taught her that family was more than flesh and blood.

Drea had two brothers, the older one had promised to hurt Joey for

Polly. She told him she had it taken care of. He didn't believe her, but left the boy alone. The Renaldis weren't too happy with her decision to leave them. That's how they saw it. None of their family ever left Boston, so how could she? But, Drea told her it would be alright and was there with Sal to help her pack. Those strapping brothers of hers and a few cousins made sure everything was packed into the truck correctly, because no one was messing with their Polly.

She took the time to write chatty notes to all of them, including pictures of some of the renovation. She didn't want to tell them about Joey or the murders, so she left that out. Joey didn't have this email address, so she hesitantly opened the one that he and she had communicated on during their time together. She'd left it off her phone, not wanting to even deal with him. There were 94 emails in there. She quickly got rid of the spam and random junk, leaving sixty-seven from Joey. She hadn't checked this account since late June and was surprised he continued to send emails even when she wasn't responding.

Polly shook her head. How could he not understand it was over?

The subject line of the last email read, "I'll find you." It was dated this morning.

She opened the email and her heart sank.

"Polly I miss you so much. I can't believe you won't talk to me. I also can't believe you told the Sheriff to answer my call. I've never hurt you before and I wouldn't hurt you now. I have to find you. I have to talk to you. We have to straiten {sic} this out. I love you with my whole heart and I only want you to be happy. Love, Joey"

There was a sour taste in her mouth. She closed the email and then closed the tab in her browser. She sat there staring at the screen and finally shut the computer down and closed the lid. Dropping her head into her arms on the table, she shut her eyes and tried to relax.

The door chime woke her up and she glanced at her watch. It was 3:30, she'd been asleep for over an hour. She shook her hair back, fluffed it with her fingers and tried to come fully awake. The door chimed again and she got up and trotted to answer it.

When she saw it was Henry, she said, "Hi there! What are you doing here?"

"I was checking to see if I could unload some flooring. I just picked it up and if I don't have to carry it home and then back over here, that would be great. I didn't know if the DCI was going to let you back in until I saw your truck parked out front."

"Sure! Do you want to drive around to the side doors and I'll open those for you?" she asked.

"That would be great. I'm going to call Jimmy and Sam to see if they're free." He pulled out his cell phone and dialed as he walked back down the steps to the truck. Polly shut the door behind him and walked through the main area to the side doors beside the room where Henry had his temporary shop set up. She opened one door and saw there was a large rock already in place to hold it open. Another rock was there to hold the other side open as well. She propped the two doors open and waited. Soon, Henry backed up a small panel truck, parked it and got out.

He opened the back doors and said, "They're both going to be here in a couple of minutes. I'd asked them to meet me at my shop, but this will be better.

"So, we're going to be able to get in and get started Monday morning?" he asked.

"Aaron says the bathroom is off limits. Heck, it's all sealed up. If anyone tried to get in, the DCI would know about it. But, other than that we get the place back." Polly's heart brightened as she thought about getting back to work.

"Are you staying here now?" He asked.

"Yes. Even though nothing is finished, it is beginning to feel like home. I want to be able to bring some furniture up so I can be more comfortable upstairs and I can't wait to get into my apartment!"

"I know," he said. "But, it's going to take several weeks before we get those floors installed and ready for use."

"That's alright. I'm excited that we can get started again. I know we only lost three days, but it was three days!"

"We'll make those days up in no time. Don't worry about it. You know, we could throw a rug down in the office area down here and bring some of your stuff up so you have a little more space to spread out. Or, if you want some more things in your room, we could bring those up and move them across when the real bedroom is finished. We'll have your living room and bedroom done all at once."

"I might go downstairs tomorrow and pick a couple of chairs out to take upstairs," she said." It would be nice to have something comfortable to sit on and read. I did buy a space heater today. It's starting to get chilly."

"Yes, it is. I think you're going to love the radiant heat in the floor, though. That was a great choice for this old place," he said.

Then he asked, "Are you doing alright with this craziness? I wish I would have been here the other day. I felt badly you had to face that."

"Oh, I was fine. It was poor Doug who was so shaken up. He wasn't that freaked out when he saw my underwear!"

Henry laughed, "Polly, that story has made it all over town."

She blushed and dipped her head. "I know."

"People definitely know who you are now. Maybe infamous is the word we should use to describe you."

"Oh, crap," she muttered. "Of all the things I wanted, notoriety over purple panties came nowhere close."

"Well, since you were such a good sport about it, I think you gained a lot of points … if that makes you feel any better."

"Not really," Polly sighed. "But, oh well."

"So, Pol, tell me the truth. How are you doing with everything that has happened around here?"

She looked at him and smiled. "Wow, Henry. No one has called me Pol since Dad died."

He stuttered. "I'm sorry. I hope I didn't offend you."

"Oh no!" she exclaimed. "It was just strange to hear someone use that name. Sometimes I miss him. And yes, I'm really okay. I know Aaron is around and Danny Boylston seems to know what he's doing. The whole thing is just sad. Lydia and Andy were both close to the family, so I feel badly for them, but I'm fine."

Five men drove up in two old pickups. Sam and Jimmy got out of the driver's seats and said, "Hey, Henry. We brought extra help because we figured there would be a lot of boards!"

"That's a great idea guys. Thanks. We'll get this unloaded in no time." Henry pointed at the wall and said, "Sam, why don't we stack it right here. You know how I like it."

Polly pulled Henry back a few feet. "I've got some cash if you want to pay these other three today,"

"No, I've got it, Polly. We'll get this done in a few minutes," he replied. "I'll take care of it."

"Alright, if you're sure," she said.

"I'm sure."

The six of them unloaded the truck of the wood Polly had purchased from Brad Giese. It was beautiful and it looked like there was enough to cover the two rooms, but it didn't look like it was everything she had purchased.

"Is this it, Henry?" she asked.

"Oh no. This is the first round of milling Butch finished. He called me, knowing we wanted to get started right away. I'll pick up more from him next week. There will be plenty. No worries."

"I wasn't worried, just curious," she said.

When everything was neatly stacked against the wall, Henry walked outside and handed each of the guys some cash. He thanked them and they left, then he walked back in.

One of them called out, "Ms. Giller?"

"Yes?" she asked.

"I'm going to use the bathroom off the stage, if that's okay." he said.

"Oh," she called. "Sure! No problem. Thanks a lot."

Henry said to her, "You know, Davey's serves prime rib on Saturday nights. Are you busy for dinner tonight?"

"Oh, Henry. Yes I am. Beryl is having some sort of girls' night thing at her house and though I'm a little afraid of what that means exactly, I'm going to show up. I'm so sorry. I would have loved to go. We were all there Wednesday night and it was terrific."

"No problem," he assured her. "I didn't want you to have to sit at home alone on a Saturday night. No one should have to do that unless they want to!"

"Well, I'm not going to be alone, that's for sure." Polly jumped when she heard a tone ringing. "Oh! My bread! I'm making rolls to take tonight. We're doing potluck!"

They heard the front door open and close. Henry said, "That must be him leaving. Just a sec." He ducked out the side door and looked around the building, watching the second pickup drive off."

"Yep, that was the rest of them," he said coming back in the side door. "I'll shut the doors when I leave. And, Pol?"

"Yeah?" she said.

"If you need anything, please call me. I'm not that far away. I should have said something earlier. This is a big, damned place and you're here all alone."

"Thanks, Henry. I appreciate it. Trust me, if I need you here, I won't hesitate to call. But, I'm fine. I kind of like it. The feeling that somehow all of this is mine. I love being back in Iowa, feeling safe in a little town where people pay attention to each other."

"Have a good time tonight, Polly," he said as he picked up a rock and set it aside so the door could close, "and do me a favor? You have to tell me stories on Monday about what happens with those ladies tonight."

She giggled, "Absolutely!" Then she stopped. "Unless I can't because they're too embarrassing."

Henry pushed the second rock out of the way and let the door close behind him. She heard him tug on the doors to ensure they were locked shut and then heard him drive away.

Polly went back into the kitchen, pulled the dough out of the bread machine and shaped it into rolls on a greased baking sheet. She covered them to let them rise and went upstairs to take a shower.

CHAPTER TEN

Polly pulled into a spot on the street behind Sylvie, who was getting out of her car. Sylvie popped open the trunk and pulled out a platter. Polly could see her hesitation as she tried to figure out how to gather something else into her arms and jumped out. "Can I help you, Sylvie?"

"I can't figure out how to pick these other things up. I suppose I could make two trips," she paused. "Yep, that's what I'll do."

"No wait. I've only got a couple of baskets," Polly said. "I can help you."

She slung the baskets over her left arm and slammed the door shut on her truck. Approaching Sylvie's trunk, she saw the problem. The tray Sylvie had picked up first was a little front heavy and everything was coming off it if she wasn't careful. There were two grocery bags and another platter still on the floor. Polly slipped the loops of the bags over her right hand, then picked up the second platter, which she discovered was heavy!

"Okay, wow. What is on here? Lead weights? You're going to cause me to gain fifteen pounds in one evening," and she smiled as she looked up at Sylvie.

"Most of the weight is decoration. I probably didn't need to, but I don't often get to show off any of my nice things." Sylvie reached up and pulled the trunk lid closed.

"Thank you," she said. "The boys helped me load things and I didn't even think about carrying all of this in."

"I feel a little paltry with my pathetic baskets of bread," Polly lamented.

"Oh, don't. No one cares whether you bring anything or not, and you know," she winked, "Lydia and Andy love to cook. The only thing we can do is show up and enjoy their parties. You have to love 'em!"

Andy came out of Beryl's front door, a bright red with ivory vines painted up the side panels. Even though it was dark, Polly began to see the effect of Beryl's artistic taste on the front of her home. The shutters were painted, red frames and ivory panels to match the door. The pillars on the stoop were wound tightly with vines entwined with red and white lights. The three half moon steps up to the stoop were edged in multi-colored bricks. There were sprays of dried flowers coming up out of immense vases with drops of lights through each of them and a matching wreath on the door.

Andy crossed the yard to the two girls and taking one look at their offerings, grabbed the platter out of Polly's arms.

"It's about time the two of you showed up," she admonished. "We were beginning to wonder!"

Polly turned her arm and looked at her watch, "But I'm still five minutes early!"

"That doesn't matter," Andy said and flung the door open.

"There you are," sang Beryl! "We were just talking about you two."

"We're not late, are we?" Sylvie asked.

"Oh, honey. Even if you were, you wouldn't be. We can hardly wait to get the evening started. Come in, come in!"

Beryl took the platter out of Sylvie's arms and headed off into the house. Lydia came into the foyer and hugged the newcomers.

"Hello there, girls! It's going to be a feast tonight!" She took the bags off Polly's arms and then took hold of the baskets. "Drop your jackets on the chair there and get inside. We'll get everyone warmed up in a minute."

Lydia left the two alone in the foyer and they looked at each other. Taking a breath, Polly asked, "Have you ever been here before?"

"Nope," Sylvie said hesitantly, "We seem to have been left alone, though. Shall we enter?"

Polly went first and then stopped as she looked into a room off the entrance hall.

The front room was enveloped in color. There was no good place for her eye to land first. She breathed and tried to take it all in. There were four wing chairs. They were all the same shape, but each was covered differently. Reds and blues, greens and burgundies, yellows, oranges, deep purples and browns. Some of the patterns were geometric, there were fleur de lis and other shapes as well. Nothing matched, but it all fit together. There were several rugs piled on each other in places. Wooden side tables were filled with vases and candlesticks, picture frames and other knick knacks. A long table was pushed up under the front window and on it were plants and small china dolls. The front window was covered with sheer panels, and then burgundy and blue fabric was draped from the curtain rod. From the ceiling a chandelier covered in crystals softly lit the space and an immense mirror at the far end of the room reflected the entire effect, making the room seem quite deep. The walls were covered from floor to ceiling in striped blue and ivory wallpaper which seemed to shimmer in the light.

Five paintings were hung on the wall opposite the window. Polly stepped in to look at them more closely. Yes, there was Beryl's signature at the bottom of each. The center painting was the largest with two smaller paintings on either side. The large painting was of a tree in a meadow. At least that is what Polly saw when she looked at it closely. It was a little abstract, though she felt pretty confident she recognized the image. The four other paintings were obviously painted as complements, pulling their main color from one of the colors of the central painting. When she looked more closely, she saw that Beryl had taken a section of the tree and enlarged it, showing detail of what might be happening in the branches: a few birds and even a squirrel; a section of the meadow with a mouse and some other creatures, the sky with the sun glinting off clouds and the trunk of the tree with bugs and snails crawling through the bark. All abstract, all precise.

"Look at this, Sylvie," she whispered. "Just look at this!"

The two of them were staring at the paintings when Beryl peeked into the door.

"You girls haven't gotten very far inside. This is going to be a long night if you stand around gaping at everything."

"Beryl," Polly exclaimed, "this is absolutely amazing!" She looked back at the wall, “It's amazing!"

"Enough. Come on, let's get going." Beryl said and when she walked over to them, she took both by the arm and propelled them back into the hallway.

The hallway opened into a very comfortable living room. The decor was quite different from the first room. Great, big comfortable couches were covered with quilts, knitted throws and pillows. Once again, multiple rugs covered the floor, overlapping each other. The theme for this room seemed to be denim. Huge pillows, covered in various shades of blue denim were positioned around the floor, tall candlesticks rose up from behind sofas and chairs with white candles standing on them. There was a fire in the fireplace and oversized lamps scattered around the room. The wooden tables were rustic and had magazines and art books scattered across them. Behind the sofa on the frontroom wall, an enormous bookshelf filled the space. Polly, distracted, walked over to peer behind the sofa. Two wooden stepstools invited someone to look at the top shelves, but Beryl was impatient.

"Polly. Really." she said.

"Are you kidding me with this, Beryl?" Polly asked. "You can't bring me into a place like this and not expect me to look around. There are so many amazing things."

The walls in this room had no room for paintings, but Polly saw there were several smaller pieces amongst the things on the mantel of the fireplace. She started to walk over there to look at them and Beryl took her arm again.

"That's enough. Come on," she said and tugged Polly towards the stairs leading down to another room. Polly saw there was a set of stairs leading up and assumed those went to bedrooms, but it didn't seem as if Beryl was going to let her explore. A small hallway wound to what Polly figured had to be the kitchen. She was dying to know what Beryl's kitchen looked like, but she was led down the steps into a fairyland.

Twinkling lights were draped and swooping from lowered rafters. Another fireplace was filled with a crackling fire. A small kitchen and bar was tucked in under the stairway and a roomy table was elegantly set up with candles and flowers. It seemed every space on every wall in this room was taken up with paintings. A plush multi-colored carpet was underfoot and the overhead lamp was muted, bathing the room in a golden glow. Bookshelves lined the lower three feet of the room and as Polly glanced around, saw they lined the entire lower level of the house, even the front of the bar of the kitchen.

Before she could take off to look at anything in the room, Andy had pressed a glass of something in her hand. "A toast," she cried, "to Saturday night!"

Polly brought her attention back to the group of women and raised her glass. Drinking it, she nearly choked, "What's in here?" she asked.

Beryl smiled, "Maybe I overdid it with the tabasco? It's a bloody martini."

Polly took a sip, "It's pretty good if I sip it. But, wait. What else is in here?"

This time Beryl laughed out loud. "I found Bacon Vodka! Isn't it great?"

All of them laughed with her and then she said, "Okay. The first game for the evening is for you to figure out which seat is yours. It shouldn't be too difficult, but you have to guess and then open the box on your plate. If it's yours, you'll know and you can sit down. If it's not, you have to shut the box quickly so no one else can see and then look again."

The four women giggled and went over to the table. Each of them looked around, there were no clues, so they picked up a box and looked inside. Polly found a baby rattle. That made no sense to her, so she closed the box and put it back on the table, then looked at the others.

They were all snickering, but it seemed as if Andy's snicker was a little bit pointed toward her. No one had chosen the right box, so they picked up their glasses. Polly went to where Andy had been, and dammit, sure enough. Inside was a bright purple bra. She closed the box and sat down.

"Aren't you going to show us?" Beryl asked.

"Hell no. You are all awful. If I show you, you're going to want me to put it on." Polly said.

Andy picked up the box Polly had opened, looked at it with some confusion and then closed it and put it back down. "Oh my, I hope not," she said.

Neither of the others had landed on their box yet, so they moved again. Sylvie opened the box at the place on Polly's left. She sat down with a smile on her face. "You shouldn't have," she said.

Beryl was standing behind her and patted her on the shoulder. "Of course I should, you deserve it."

"What do you have?" Polly asked, leaning over to look in the box. Sylvie pulled a chain out with two charms on it. Her boys' initials were on each charm. Between them was an amethyst and on either side were two other stones, a ruby and a diamond.

"Birthdays?" Polly asked again.

"Yes. Mine is in February, Jason's in July and Andrew's is April." Sylvie turned to look up at Beryl. "Thank you so much." Beryl patted her shoulder again.

"Alright ladies. Are your gifts right? Andy?"

Andy sat down in the chair and opened the box. "Yes, this is so me!" She pulled out a set of salt and pepper shakers. When they were placed together, two black cats wrapped around each other.

"You have cats?" Polly asked.

"Yes. Chaz and Addams," she said. "I'll show you later."

Lydia had a puzzled look on her face, "I guess this is mine, but I don't get it," she said.

"Sit down, grandma. I have some news for you," Beryl said.

"Really? Who?" Lydia asked.

"Marilyn called me yesterday and asked if I could find a creative way to tell you that she and Brian were pregnant again. They're coming over tomorrow after church, but she thought I could have fun with this. And I did!"

A small smile lit Lydia's face. "I can't believe it. I didn't even know they were trying. After they'd worked so hard to have the twins, I didn't think they'd be able to have anymore." She looked around the room. "Girls, I'm going to be a grandma again!"

Then she said, "Thank you, Beryl. I hope it is okay that this will be one of the baby's first gifts!"

Beryl threw her arms around her friend. "Of course it's okay! Now, drink up, ladies, I have pitchers more of this stuff in the refrigerator." She walked back over to the bar and Lydia got up as if to help.

"Nope, sit still. All I'm going to do is grab a few things. I can do this by myself."

Picking up one of Polly's baskets of bread, she set it on the table and then brought over an antique blue and white covered soup tureen.

"First course, bread and soup," and with a flourish she whipped the lid up and steam poured out. "It's a theme. Potato and bacon soup."

The rest of the meal was served from the bar, brussels sprouts, asparagus and beans were Andy's offering. Lydia had brought mashed potatoes and roasted acorn squash. Small covered dishes at place settings were filled with fresh bacon crumbles and Beryl's ham was heavenly. By the time dinner was over, Polly was sure she would burst. She looked at Sylvie and said, "I don't know how I'm going to eat any dessert tonight."

"Don't worry, I think we have a little time before we have to worry about that," Andy said as she stood and started to gather up the dishes around her.

"Stop that," Beryl said and pushed her hand back down. "You know better," then she called out, "Deena? Meryl?" Two high school girls came down the steps.

"Did you have a good supper?" Beryl asked the girls.

"Yes! It was awesome! Thank you," one of them said and the two girls started clearing the table.

"They live in the neighborhood and help me out a lot," she said. "They take art lessons from me. It's kind of nice having two excellent protégés around. I appreciate everything they do. It's kind of like having," she paused, "I was going to say a wife, but they don't nag me. Well, anyway, they'll take care of all this and we should go back upstairs. Leave your boxes. They'll make sure everything is ready to go when you leave."

Polly put her napkin down beside her plate, stood up and followed them upstairs. While they had been eating, the main room had been transformed. The rugs were pulled up and large tarps covered the floor. Four easels were set up with 20 x 30 canvases on them and stools were placed in front each canvas. Wrap-around aprons lay across a small stand beside each stool and an array of paints, brushes, charcoal, pencils, chalk and pastels was laid out on a card table.

Beryl said, "Pick a medium and an easel."

Sylvie looked at her, stricken. "I'm not an artist!"

Polly interjected, "And you're intimidating!"

"Oh, stop it," Beryl said, a little disgusted. "You are all creative and I don't care at all what your canvases look like. Splatter color on them. All that matters is your hands get a little dirty and you make something happen between your mind and the canvas. If you want help, I'll help you, but I know you can all do this. Now get moving!"

They jumped at her command and scurried over to the art mediums. Sylvie fingered the charcoal before picking up a piece. She chose the easel as far away as possible from Beryl. Lydia grabbed a few of the pencils, then thought about it and took a few more.

Andy laughed and started squeezing acrylic paint onto a palette. "I've done this before, I know what to expect and I know what to do, too!" She picked up a few brushes and made her way to another easel. Polly stood in front of the different mediums looking shaken, Beryl said, "Take the pastels. They're perfect for you."

Polly did and sat in front of a blank canvas, not knowing what to do.

Beryl said, "Shut your eyes, all of you." Polly shut her eyes and listened. "Think about a place you love. Look at the colors, or the shapes. Are there people or animals? See the background in your mind." She was quiet for a few moments, then said, "Now open your eyes. You may not make a perfect piece tonight, but all I want you to do is enjoy yourself. Get a feel for the medium in your hands, play with it on the canvas. Put color where you want it, put another color where you think it should be. Draw random shapes or something which fits with the color. Really ... all I want you to do is get the feel of touching the canvas."

Polly picked up a light blue and moved it across the canvas. It felt wonderful. She picked up a different shade and blended it into the first, then continued to work. The house had gone quiet, except for the girls working downstairs. She heard a low conversation across the room and looked up. Beryl was standing beside Sylvie, moving her hand back and forth on the canvas. "Yes," she said, "you're seeing it." Then Beryl walked past Lydia and hugged her. "You're a good grandma," she whispered as she moved to Andy.

"Oh, Andy, I can always count on you. You should have taken more art in college," she said as she picked up the canvas and turned it so everyone could see it. "This is what I had to compete with while we were growing up." Polly burst out laughing. Andy had painted a hideous looking clown face.

"How is THAT some place you love?" Polly asked.

"I know better. Beryl gets all artsy fartsy on nights like this. I have to remind her I hate this crap."

"Whatever," Beryl retorted. "You were pretty good. If you'd kept at it, who knows what you might have done. But, at least we know what it is. You are such a brat."

"Me?" Andy sneered. "I knew what was coming tonight and I showed up. I think I'm the good girl."

Beryl stopped behind Polly. "What do you have happening here, girlfriend?"

"I'm not sure? I got all caught up in the colors and the way they worked together."

"Okay, then, that's perfect. Color it is!"

Everyone went back to their canvases and continued to work. Deana and Meryl brought up four large canvas bags and set them in the hallway, then returned to the basement. They continued bringing things upstairs and chattering away.

Beryl said out loud, "Do we know anything more about the Stevens murders?"

Polly looked up, she'd practically put the whole thing out of her mind, but Lydia responded.

"Aaron called before he left Boone. The DCI is still processing everything they found. There were fingerprints, but of course, they don't know if they belonged to the girls, to someone else or the killer. They don't match anything in the system, so that wasn't helpful. I don't know how much he'll tell me, but I doubt they know any more now than they did on Wednesday."

Polly looked up, "Did they ever have a funeral for the girls?"

"No," Lydia said. "They weren't sure if they were dead, so I think everyone hoped someday they would finally show up. Rev. Boehm will talk to Linda and Sandy about it. It's so sad. I'm sorry their parents aren't here to be able to finally have closure, even if it was this."

Andy spoke up, "I suppose it's better to believe they figured it out when they got to heaven and found the girls. We can't think about what might have been, especially since they've died."

She put her brushes down and declared, "I'm done and I want something sweet to eat. When are we having dessert?"

Polly looked at her watch. It was ten o'clock. "Wow! Where did the time go?" She put the sticks of color back in their slots, then stood and stretched. "Ow, my butt," and she arched her back, stretching again.

Beryl gathered the canvasses and stood them up against the hallway wall. Andy's clown was a hideous face, Lydia had drawn a large baby quilt, filling in squares with soft pastel colors. Polly's attempts at blending colors looked silly to her, but the others seemed to like what they saw. Sylvie's charcoal was rough, but Polly saw waves crashing on a beach.

Lydia said, "Beryl, do you see what I see?"

"Sylvie?" Beryl asked, "Have you ever taken any art instruction?"

Sylvie laughed. "Of course not! I don't have time for that and I couldn't afford it anyway."

Beryl said, "Well, honey, you've got some talent. You and me? We're gonna talk."

She walked into the kitchen muttering, "I hate it when talent hides. Schools don't know what they're doing. Stupid teachers, stupid schools."

The rest of them looked at each other and giggled, not knowing quite what to say. Then Beryl called out, "Sylvie, could you help me in here?"

Sylvie jumped up and ran to the hallway and into the kitchen. There was some giggling and muttering, enough so that Lydia called out, "Do you need any more help?"

Sylvie called back, "No, we've got it! Just a minute!"

Deena and Meryl quietly walked into the room and folded up the easels, setting them aside. They carried all of the supplies out and downstairs and then came back and folded up the tarps. While they were working, Polly looked at the other two women in the room, "Is it just me or do you feel useless?"

Andy laughed, "It's not just you. Can we help, girls?"

One of the girls said, "Oh no! You sit still."

"Alright," Lydia said, as she lifted one foot and then another while the tarp was pulled away, then folded up. "Are you still alright in there?" she called out again.

"Hush your mouth, woman! Sit still for once in your life." Beryl's laughter rang out.

"I'm not sure if I know how to do that, but I'll try," Lydia said.

The girls had removed the tarps and tossed the rugs back around the room. The hard wood floor looked comfortable enough, but the random piling of the brightly colored rugs certainly kept the room looking warm. After they finished, they brought the coffee table back in and placed the magazines back on it. One stacked them neatly, the other reached over and gave them a push so they scattered. "Trust me," she said to her friend as they walked out to the kitchen.

Sylvie walked into the room with the platter Polly had carried in. Adorable little pewter towers ranging from a quarter inch tall to two inches settled into indentations in the platter and each had something on top. There were cheesecake bites and mini cream puffs, chocolate chip cookies and brownie bites, fruit tartlets and even tiny pumpkin pies. Beryl had in her hands another platter with little bowls filled with chocolate sauce, berries, crème fraiche, whipped cream, butterscotch, granola and other toppings. Deena and Meryl followed with plates, silverware and napkins.

"Wow, Sylvie. You're an artist with food, too!" exclaimed Lydia.

Sylvie beamed.

"Did you make all of these separate dishes for tonight? There's only five of us! That's a lot of work," said Andy, "and a lot of money." Lydia tried to shush her.

"Eat up," Sylvie laughed and the others took a plate and began picking out bites and covering them with toppings. Beryl handed plates to Deena and Meryl who sat down on the floor and ate while they listened.

"Cooking and baking is one of the things I CAN afford." Sylvie, said, "Sam gives me an amazing discount on things. And don't worry. I decided this was a perfect time to make some gifts for the kids' teachers. It isn't a holiday, so they won't be expecting anything. It will be a nice surprise. Tomorrow, they're going to help me deliver some treats to a few women around town who probably don't get things like this anymore."

"Oh Sylvie, that's so sweet!" Beryl said.

"It's nothing, just something Mom used to do."

"I remember your mom," Andy said. "She was wonderful. OH! I remember her treats, too!"

"She loved baking, so we ended up sharing all the time!" Sylvie said. "Sometimes it feels like all I ever do now is work and run around after my kids. I don't get enough time to spend with other people."

"You're here with us tonight, Sylvie. That's a pretty good thing," Lydia said.

"I know, and I appreciate you inviting me. It was great to get out and be normal. The kids are old enough to let them have a little freedom from me. I guess I'm not sure how to be anything other than their mom anymore."

"They're good kids and lucky to have you. You've done a good job with them. And trust me; we'll make sure you get a life if that's what you want. We're good at life, aren't we?" Beryl asked looking at Lydia and Andy.

"Well, we've certainly seen a bunch of it," Andy laughed.

"So, what are you doing for the rest of the weekend, Polly?" Lydia asked. "It's going to seem weird for you not to be at my house tomorrow morning."

"Oh, you and Aaron have been so good to me. I can't get over it. I've only been in town a few weeks and I'm already spending nights at someone else's house. But, I honestly don't know what I would have done these last few days." She paused. "I could have gone to a hotel, but wow, you guys took care of me in so many ways. Thank you!"

"Oh, I loved having you there," Lydia said. "My old fart is always so much more fun when there are other people around."

"I'm sure that's not true," Polly scolded, "You two are kind of crazy about each other."

Lydia got a warm look on her face. "You know, I nearly lost him once. I don't take him for granted now, but I'll tell that story another time." She looked at Polly, "So what IS up for you the rest of the weekend?"

"Henry is going to have his guys help me bring up some more furniture on Monday, so I have a place to sit upstairs. I'm going to go down in the basement tomorrow and try to figure out what I want. I feel like my life has been in boxes for so long and I don't see much chance that's going to change until after the New Year!"

Sylvie looked up, "Would you like some help tomorrow?" she asked timidly.

Beryl and Lydia were sitting a little behind her and nodding wildly at Polly.

"I'd love that Sylvie! Would you like to bring your boys?"

"Could I?" she asked. They've never been in the school and I've talked a lot about it. I had so much fun when I was there, and now that those girls' bodies have been found, it seems like that's all they ever talk about at home."

"I've got plenty of food for lunch. Why don't you come over about noon? We'll make lunch and then go attack my stuff."

CHAPTER ELEVEN

Lifting a box to the floor, Sylvie said, "I don't think I was ever down here when I was in high school." "Old Mr. Leon was kind of creepy and no one wanted to be around him. I think some of the boys came down to do industrial arts stuff in that part of the basement," she pointed to the back, "but the rest seemed like it was his territory."

"Was he the only custodian here?" Polly asked.

"No, there were two other guys. Let's see, what were their names?" Sylvie paused in thought. "Darren something and Ken Malotte." It seemed like he made them do all the dirty work. They weren't very old, probably in their 30s at the time. I remember them hating phys ed testing, they were forever sweeping up vomit." She looked at Polly. "Do you remember the smell of the sawdust stuff?"

Polly laughed. "I think every kid in school does."

"So what are we looking for down here?" Sylvie asked.

"Well, I want to drag the two green chairs over to the stairway so the guys can carry them up for me tomorrow. We're going to have to haul stuff off them and stack it up somewhere else. Then, I would like to find the boxes with my winter clothes. It's going to get cold pretty soon."

They'd already taken the tour. The boys had the run of the place with strict orders to leave the upstairs bathroom alone and they seemed appropriately intimidated by the crime scene tape which sealed the door shut.

"There's so much space here, Polly. I can't imagine only one person living in this place!"

"Oh, I hope it doesn't take long for things to get busy. If I have my way, the place will be full all day long and then, if I can get a few artists to come live in the rooms upstairs, it will never be completely quiet. I'll probably miss all of this alone time." Then she said, "Not that I've had very much. With all the noise of construction, I find that I like my weekends."

"Mom! Miss Polly! You have to come see what we found!" Andrew and Jason had been messing around in one of the back rooms of the basement space. Polly had given them a couple of flashlights and their mother had admonished them to be careful.

"Hold on a second, boys." Polly turned on a Coleman Lantern she had and handed Sylvie another large flashlight. They wove through two smaller rooms until they got to what looked like a crawlspace.

"What's in there?" Sylvie asked.

"It's another big room," Andrew said, "but you have to crawl through this part first." He got down on his hands and knees and crawled into the space. He turned around and shone his flashlight back out at them. "Come on! It's no big deal. It's not like there are rats or anything down here."

Sylvie looked at Polly with a smirk on her face, "Yeah. I want to get into a small space behind my son, who thinks rats are cool because it's not like there are any down here." She sighed. "Alright. Here I go." Down on her hands and knees she went, then sat up and slipped her flashlight into her waistband and began crawling through the hole.

"It's cool, Polly. The crawlspace is only about three and a half feet long."

Polly got down, and pushed the lantern in front of her while she crawled through to the other side.

The crawlspace opened up into a room, each wall about eight feet long. There didn't seem to be any light other than the lantern she had and the three flashlights. Crates lined the outer edges of the room, stacked three and four high. At the opposite end of the room from the crawlspace was another full size door Jason was attempting to open.

"What is this place?" she asked and turned to the crates at her right. Lifting the top one to the floor, she began rifling through it.

Sylvie had walked over to where Jason was trying to pick the lock on the door and then tapped on it. There was a dull thud. "Jason, honey. I don't think anything is behind this door. It sounds like it's been walled up.

"Well, why didn't they take the door out?" he asked.

Sylvie turned around a couple of times. "This door would face the old gymnasium. I don't remember there being an entrance to the basement out there, but I suppose at one time there could have been." Then she said, "What are you finding, Polly?"

Polly said, "It's the weirdest thing. It looks like detritus from kids' lockers. I can't tell if this is stuff left behind at the end of the year, lost items, or what? But there are scores of crates in here and I can't believe there hasn't been more damage."

"You know what?" Sylvie said. "I think this was an old root cellar. They closed it up long before I was around. Something tells me it was before I was even born. Kids used to talk about it being down here, but I don't remember anyone ever knowing where it was. And I NEVER came down to the basement, it was way too creepy. Those old boilers made weird sounds and I didn't like the janitors ... I mean, custodians."

She started peeking through some of the crates, then heard Andrew say, "Look! Cool!" He pulled a microscope out of one of the crates. "Can I have it mom?"

"These things aren't ours, honey. Let's wait before we start taking stuff out of here."

A muffled sound came through the crawlway. "Oh!" Polly said, "That's the door chime. I'll be back. I don't think I need a light to get out, so I'll leave the lantern."

She crawled back into the main portion of the basement and ran for the stairs. When she arrived at the top, she opened the door to find Aaron Merritt standing there.

"Aaron! What are you doing here today?"

He was dressed in jeans, so she was fairly certain it was nothing official.

"Oh, I wanted to return your key. I don't need it any longer. I've got my son in law in the Wrangler and we're going to do some fishing, while the womenfolk," he chuckled, "are talking about babies."

"Are you in a real hurry?" Polly asked.

"No, I don't suppose so. We needed to get out of the house. Is something up?"

He pulled the key out of his pocket and handed it to Polly. As she walked over to the newel post, she said, "Well, I found something interesting in the basement. Actually, Andrew and Jason Donovan found it. There's a room tucked away in the back and it's filled with ..." Polly gasped as she looked in the space in the newel post. Then, she shut her eyes and thought for a moment.

"No, I'm right. There were two left."

"Two what, Polly?" Aaron asked.

"There were two keys left in here when I gave one to you and Danny Boylston. Now there's only one. I don't know who could have been in here and taken it since Wednesday. There's been no one around!" She took the remaining key out and pocketed both.

"Oh, I hate that," she said. "When was someone around to take a key and why would they want one? I mean, this place is wide open all week long."

Aaron said, "Why don't we call a locksmith. I can have someone here right away. I don't want you in this place alone without knowing where your keys are. Are all the doors keyed to the same lock?" He asked.

"Honestly, no. I had the rest of the doors keyed differently because I didn't want anyone coming in without me knowing. This key only unlocks the front door. Maybe I forgot and gave someone else a key and didn't count correctly."

"It's okay, Polly. We'll get a locksmith here and he'll make new keys for you. Then, I'll call Boylston and tell him he needs to see you before he can get in again. It's no big deal. Give me a minute to make some calls and then you can tell me what you found in the basement." Aaron walked outside and put his cell phone to his ear. Polly went back downstairs and over to the crawlspace.

"Sylvie? Can you hear me?" she called.

In a few moments, she heard, "Yes. What's up?

"Aaron Merritt is here. I'm going to bring him down to see what we've found. You know you don't have to stay in there if you don't want to."

Sylvie responded, "Oh, we're fine. I've told the boys to make sure things go back in the crate they've removed them from. I think there might be some kind of organization with it, but I haven't figured out what it is."

"Alright. We'll be in there in a few minutes."

Polly went back upstairs as Aaron was walking up the outside steps with a big, blonde young man.

"Polly," Aaron said, then gestured to the young man, "I'd like you to meet my son-in-law, Brian Erikson. Brian, this is Polly Giller."

Brian stuck his hand out to shake hers and she found her hand enveloped in an immense, warm paw. His hands were calloused and strong and his face was ruddy. He had bright blue eyes filled with laughter.

She looked at him and then she said, "Don't tell me. You know, too."

"No ma'am. I don't know anything about anything," he said.

Aaron clapped him on his back. "That's the smartest thing any man can ever say, especially when the alternative is walking into a trap."

Polly shook her head and backed up into the school.

Aaron said, "Lance Alston is going to be here in twenty minutes or so to change the locks on this door. He said he should be able to re-core the cylinder. He'll make keys for you and you'll be ready to go.

"So," he went on, "what did the boys find?"

"Well, there's a crawlway back into what might have been an old root cellar and there are some things in crates back there that don't make much sense to me."

"What kind of things, Polly?"

"It looks like stuff that belonged to kids through the years. I can't imagine all of this stuff was left in lockers at the end of the school year. Why would anyone want to keep it?"

She gestured through the basement door and the two men went down the steps.

Polly crossed in front of them and wove her way through the boxes and furniture to the crawlway. "Sylvie?"

"We're still here, Polly."

"Aaron and Brian are coming in." Polly yelled.

Brian got down on his knees and crawled into the space.

Aaron looked around. "Hmmm, no one would have seen this when the boilers were sitting here," he remarked.

"Okay," Polly responded. "I wasn't sure what was up."

Aaron picked up an old piece of plywood. "I'll bet the boys pulled this off the wall to find the space."

He gestured for Polly to go on through, so she did and he followed close behind her. When they stood up, Jason and Andrew were still carefully digging through crates. Sylvie, though, was holding a jacket and had a strange look on her face.

"What's that, Sylvie?" Polly asked.

"It's my jacket. I didn't leave it in my locker. It was stolen." she said.

"Are you sure it's yours?" Aaron asked.

"I'm sure." She put her hand in a pocket and pulled out a small plastic case, with what looked to be a picture of a boy band on its face. "This was a Christmas gift and I carried my lip gloss in it." She unzipped it and sure enough, several tubes were inside.

"I also found two CDs in the same crate with Barb Pierce's name inside the case. She would never have left them in her locker after school was out. She was particular about her CDs." Sylvie thought for a moment. "I think someone was stealing from us and these crates are from different years. I'll bet if we get it figured out, we'll find a long history of stuff in here."

"Okay, boys," Aaron said, air chuffing out of his lungs. "I need you to stop playing in the crates."

Both boys looked chagrined, but stopped what they were doing.

"Polly, I know you didn't expect all of this when you bought this old school, but I'm going to bring in some people to run tests on these things and see what's going on. It does seem odd there is such a large collection down here and I want to make sure it's all normal stuff. What a historical treasure, though. I'll bet there are years and years of items. The statute of limitations on theft is only three years, so I suppose we aren't going to prosecute anyone."

"Sheriff," Polly said. "After you've done all the investigating down here you need to do, we could probably haul these crates up to the auditorium and let people look through them. Maybe we could get them organized by their decade and photographed and see what we find!"

"That's a great idea. I know a few people who might enjoy doing just that. I'm sorry boys, but I have to get everyone out. Take your flashlights with you."

Sylvie was still holding her jacket. "Sylvie. I promise you'll get that back," Aaron said.

"No, I was thinking about the day I discovered it was gone. I had to ask for a ride home because it was so cold and I didn't have a coat. Principal Mayfair was going to take me, but luckily Crystal Jensen overheard and took me home. Mom and I had to go out that night to buy a new coat for me. We couldn't afford another school jacket. I can't believe it's here. I never thought I'd see it again. I assumed someone else was wearing it. Weird." She laid the jacket back on top of a crate and followed her sons out of the room.

Brian went next, then Polly followed with the lantern. Aaron was right behind her. When they all got into the main basement, he asked Brian to go up and grab a hammer and some nails. They closed the basement off again from the strange little room.

Sylvie looked at the Sheriff. "You know, Aaron. I hate to say something terrible about someone, but Doug Leon always had dirty or ripped knees in his pants. We figured it was because he cleaned the floors or something. Everyone talked about it. Neither of the other janitors' was that bad. But, I suppose none of them worked here as long as he did either."

"I'll talk to him, Sylvie. If he can tell me what this is all about, we'll figure the matter is settled. If he can't, we'll keep looking." Aaron ruffled Andrew's hair as he walked toward the steps. "You boys don't need to go looking for anything else around here, but you did a good job today. That was a good find."

Brian followed him up the stairs and they walked outside.

Polly said to Sylvie, "Oh, I'm getting the locks on the front door changed. I wonder if the guy is here yet."

"Why are you doing that?" Sylvie asked.

"I'm missing one of the keys in the newel post. I'd left them there to hand out to some of the workmen and one is gone. I don't know who would have taken it, but Aaron thinks it's better to be safe."

"He's right. Here, let Andrew go up and watch for you. He'll come down and get you when the guy shows up."

Andrew and Jason both ran up the steps, then Andrew came running back down. "He's here, he's here!"

Polly said, "I'm sorry. This isn't getting much done down here."

"Send the boys back down. We'll move things you obviously aren't going to need for a while so you can get to the other stuff. That will help you when you come back."

"Thank you, Sylvie," and Polly went up the stairs to find the boys waiting in the outside doorway. "Andrew and Jason, thank you. Would you mind going back to help your mom?"

Both boys looked at her in shock. Jason said, "But we want to watch!"

She laughed. "Of course you do. Alright, no problem." Then she called down the stairs. "The boys are going to stay and watch. Come on up, you don't have to stay down there by yourself doing my work!"

"I'm fine," came Sylvie's voice from the depths.

Polly laughed and turned around. A young man was pulling things out of the back of his van as he spoke with Aaron. Then, he turned to walk up to the door. Aaron and Brian got into the Wrangler and waved as Aaron gunned it in the gravel, spinning his tires.

"Hi," the young man said. "I'm Lance."

"Thanks, Lance, for coming out in such a hurry." Polly said.

He laughed. "Are you kidding me? When Sheriff Merritt calls, I don't mess around. I obey."

"Oh, I hope we didn't interrupt anything," she said.

"No, I was on call this weekend. Just watching a little football. Gotta see if my Browns will ever win. Since we're guaranteed there's no chance of that, it makes it easy to leave the game. This will take a few minutes and then I'll cut you some keys and everything will be back to normal."

He turned to the boys, "You can watch if you like."

Jason said, "There was a door in the basement we couldn't open. Mom says there's only dirt on the other side of it, but she doesn't know everything."

"If you'd like, I could take a look at it," Lance directed the question at Polly.

"No, that's alright." she said and sat down on the step to wait.

"The sheriff locked up the room anyway, so we can't get to it, but maybe he'll call you to look at it another time!" Jason said excitedly.

"Maybe," Lance replied, and went back to his work. After pulling the locks and changing the cores on both doors, he went back to his van. "Boys, I'm going to cut some keys. Will you test them for me?" They followed him and after some grinding and no small amount of giggling,

Andrew brought the first key up. "Can I try this, Miss Polly?"

"You sure can, Andrew. Thank you." She watched as he tested the key first in one door, then in the next. When the locks flipped closed, then open, he announced. "It's perfect! Do you need to test another one?"

"Jason gets the next one. And yes, we should check every key I cut," Lance said, winking at Polly. "How many would you like to have me cut today?"

She put her head down and flipped her fingers as she thought through her needs, then said, "I think eight might be necessary."

"Alright," he said, "Eight it is. Are you ready for this, boys?"

Once the boys had pronounced a key good, they dropped it in Polly's outstretched hand. She'd never been around boys before and found she loved their energy. These were good kids.

When the last key dropped into her hand, Lance came over with his receipt book. She jumped up, “I'll go inside to get my wallet."

"Oh, no need. I'll give you this and you can send us payment later. I don't need to be running around with your money today."

He turned to leave. "Let me know if you need anything else! I'll even come running if it's you on the other end of the phone and not the Sheriff!" He smiled.

"Thanks so much," she said and walked back inside with the boys. Putting the keys in her back pocket away from the others, she went back down to the basement behind Andrew and Jason who bounced down to tell their mom all about their adventure.

CHAPTER TWELVE

"Absence makes the heart grow fonder," Polly thought as she looked back at her bed. She was up and ready to go early, knowing that no one could get into the school since she'd changed the keys. She turned the locks on the front door and went in to the kitchen to turn the coffee maker on and then began rummaging in the refrigerator for something to eat. Nothing appealed to her, so she opened the freezer and there, like a little ball of sunshine was a fresh container of breakfast sandwiches, with Andy's labeling talent all over them. She pulled the container out and selected a sausage sandwich and stuck it in the microwave.

How had she ever thought she would be able to do all of this on her own? In a few short weeks she had made a number of new friends, met more people than she could possibly remember and when things got weird, those new friends showed up to take care of her.

Polly thought back to the year her mother died. There had been darkness and sadness after the death, but it didn't last long. Her friends and teachers, her parent's friends and random people from town had all been there. As she needed them less and less, they'd gone on with their lives, but it had seemed seamless to a twelve year old girl. She'd never felt alone. Mary and Sylvester were always there, she never had to eat breakfast by herself when her dad was in the fields. Mary was there when she got home in the afternoons and if she had a problem or forgot something at school, which she often did, Mary took care of it.

When she'd gone away to Boston for her first year of college, Mary called every week and sent care packages. Polly's dad was always involved, but she knew he was busy running the big farm and she was glad he'd been around as much as he had. He never let her hang up the phone, or go to bed or leave the house without telling her he loved her. She missed them all. Time had done a number on her family and when she stopped to think about it, it didn't seem fair that at the age of 32, she had no more family left. Her parents hadn't lived to see her get married or do anything big with her life.

The microwave dinged and she drew a cup of coffee from the pot. Sitting down at the table, with dawn breaking, she felt a tear escape. Brushing it away, she said out loud, "Stop it. You're fine. You have friends and people who care about you now. Just stop it."

She chuckled a little as she remembered her father's trick to help her stop sadness from becoming overwhelming. He knelt down in front of her, pulled her arms over her head and said, "Who's the goose who's loose?" Then, he'd tickle her sides and chase her when she ran. A quick hug and a tap of his finger on her nose and the world would seem to tilt back to normal. Even when she was older and feeling sad, all it took from him was a quick, "Who's the goose ..." and the two of them would laugh. Sometimes he'd stop in front of her and lift her arms over her head, but then they'd laugh and hug and her world would seem normal again. No one else had ever known that trick with her and she missed him today.

Polly heard clattering from the front hallway and got up to go look. Doug Randall and Billy Endicott were laughing as they picked up coils of wire and bags of supplies dropped on the floor.

"What's up, guys?" she asked.

Doug blushed at seeing her. Billy said, "We bet each other we could get all the way in with this stuff without dropping it. We made it this far." He gave his buddy a push and Doug landed on his backside when his feet couldn't negotiate the mess of things in front of him.

"Thanks a bunch, dude," he said and swept Billy's feet out from under him. "There, serves you right."

"Are you two alright?" Polly asked.

"Oh, we're fine," Doug said. "I'm sorry. It's his fault. Everything he does gets me in trouble."

He scrambled and began picking things up off the floor. Billy looked a little chagrined and shrugged a quick apology to Polly. "Is coffee ready? We're here because we're starting in the auditorium today. Jerry said we had to get an early start."

"Yep," she laughed. "It's ready to go. Can I carry anything?"

Both boys looked at her in shock. "No!" they said, "We've got it." Doug scurried to drop his first load inside the doors of the auditorium and dashed back out to pick up the rest of the packages. Billy carried his armload of items in, set them down and came back out, watching Doug gather things up. "I guess we needed three people, eh, dude?" he said.

"Whatever, Billy." Doug replied. "We need to get this organized before Jerry gets here or he'll have our heads. Go back out to the truck and get those sawhorses."

Billy took off and Polly laughed. "What, you didn't try to bring those in, too?"

Doug looked up, mischief on his face. "Oh, we thought about it, but aside from putting them around our necks, it wasn't happening." He went in the auditorium and came back out, heading down the outside steps. Passing Billy, he reached his hand out and swatted his friend's belly then went to the truck and hauled out a piece of plywood. Lifting it over his back, he walked back in.

Billy had already spaced the sawhorses out and Doug set the plywood across them. Then they began pulling their bags open and dumping packages out, arranging and rearranging as they went.

"I'll be right back," Polly said. She went into the kitchen and poured off two cups of coffee then carried them back to the boys. "Here, it's the least I could do."

"Thank you, ma'am," said Billy, as he accepted the cup.

Polly had been walking back toward the door when she heard that and spun around on her feet.

"Billy?" She chided.

"Yes, ma'am." he responded.

"You can call me Polly or Miss Giller. You can call me Miss Polly or even hey you, but will you please stop calling me ma'am? It makes me feel old and I'm only ten or twelve years older than you."

"But, ma'am, some of my teachers in high school were only ten years older than me. You are old!" He giggled and ducked behind the table filled with supplies. "Now, you wouldn't want to make a mess in here by knocking the work table over, would you?" he asked. "Jerry would kill us and then there wouldn't be anyone to do your electricity."

Polly walked over to him. He stood up and faced her. "Don't ma'am me," she said and pushed the cup of coffee so it splashed down the side of his jeans. As she turned away, she heard Doug laughing quietly.

"Hey!" Billy said, "That's wet! And hot! Hey! And now I don't have any coffee!"

By the time she got to the front door, she heard him muttering at his friend, who continued to laugh.

Polly started to push the doors shut when she noticed the lock was scratched up. She looked a little more closely and decided she didn't remember it looking like that the day before when the locksmith left.

Well, that was creepy. She thought about it for a minute, and then looked at her watch. It was only 6:45 in the morning. She wondered if it had been Doug and Billy, so she went back into the auditorium. Billy looked up at her and wrinkled his nose. Doug grinned.

"Guys, did you try to unlock the door this morning?" she asked.

They looked at each other and said, "No. It was unlocked when we got here."

"But, you didn't try to stick your key in the lock?" she pressed.

"No, I don't think Doug even thought about it. He reached for the handle and opened the door. I have the key," Billy said and reached into the wet pocket. "It's a little wet, though," and smirked at her.

"Alright, I was only checking. You might as well give me the key. I changed the locks yesterday." she said.

"Really? Why?" Doug asked.

"I think someone stole a key and now I'm worried they tried to use it to get in last night."

Both stopped what they were doing. "What?"

"Oh, don't worry. They couldn't, but I'm a little freaked out by it."

Billy handed her the key, then said quietly, "I'm sorry for calling you old. I deserved the spill."

"Yes, you did," she said and took the key from him. Then, she punched him lightly in his arm. "I might have to hire you two guys to be my night watchmen!"

"Oh, that would be so cool!" Doug said. "We'd bring our sleeping bags and eat your food and camp out here. We'd totally do that!"

Billy nodded. "I'd bring my dog. He's a great dog. He'd let us know if anyone tried to get in."

Polly laughed. "Well, if I decide I'm too wimpy to stay here by myself, I'll let you know. Thanks guys." She turned away to walk back out. "I mean it. Thanks."

Jerry Randall was getting out of his truck as she walked back to the front door. "I see my boys are already here. Are they doing alright?"

"They're getting set up," she said. He grabbed tools from the bed of his truck and walked toward her.

"Jerry?" she said.

"Yes?"

"I think I had a key stolen from the newel post and someone tried to get in last night." His face took on a look of shock. "Anyway," she went on, "I had a locksmith here and he changed the lock yesterday. Your key won't work any longer. I have the one Billy was going to use and need to give you a new one."

"Are you doing alright?" he asked. "This is a lot of crazy stuff happening here at the school. It's been quiet for twenty years and now there are bodies and stolen keys. Anything else?"

"Oh, you won't even believe it," she said. "We found an old boarded up root cellar yesterday. It looks like someone had been stealing things from high school kids for more than forty years and storing it down there."

"What!" he exclaimed. "Girl, you've got some serious courage, sticking around through this."

She laughed. "I'm not sure whether it's courage or stupidity or sheer bull-headedness. I guess I've decided this place is mine and it's going to stay that way."

"Here, let me set these things down and start the boys moving. I'll be right back." As he walked into the auditorium, Polly saw Henry pull up in his truck. He waved to her as he got out, then walked across the parking lot toward her. Jerry and he met at the door.

"Good, you're both here at once," Polly said. "I need your old key, Henry." He looked at her with some confusion.

"I think someone stole one out of my newel post ... and," she pointed to the locks on the doors, "I think that person tried to get in last night. Fortunately, Aaron Merritt was here yesterday when I discovered it and called in a locksmith. So, new keys!"

She handed one to Jerry and held one out to Henry, who dug around in his pocket, then said, "Just a second." He trotted back to his truck and jumped in, digging around in the console. "Got it!" she heard. He came back and put it into her hand, taking the new key. "Sorry about that, I never seem to need it. You're always here." He jammed the key down in his jeans, then said, "What do you mean someone tried to get in last night?"

"Well, that's all I can think. I haven't called the locksmith." She looked at her watch. "7:15 in the morning seems a bit rude. But, I'll double check with him to make sure it wasn't all scratched up when he left." The door is pretty new and shouldn't look like this, should it?" Polly looked at both of the men, who then bent over to inspect the damage.

"You should call Merritt, too, Polly." Jerry said. Looking at Henry, he said, "Did you know they found a secret room in the basement yesterday, too?" he asked.

"Polly!" Henry exclaimed. "Are you sure you want to stay here?"

"I guess I am now," she responded. "Hopefully, we're through the worst of it."

Aaron pulled up in his Ford Explorer. "Well, good morning, all!" he said, walking towards them.

"We were just talking about you, Sheriff!" Henry stuck his hand out. Aaron reached forward, took the hand, then patted him on the shoulder with his left hand.

"Were you!" He shook Jerry's hand and nodded at Polly. "What did I do?"

The two men looked at Polly, who said, "Aaron, would you check out the locks on my door? It looks like someone tried to use that key, but I don't know if I might be crazy. Would Lance have damaged it when he rekeyed the locks?"

Aaron bent over to check out the lock. "Hell no!" he exclaimed. Then he asked. "Have any of you touched these?"

"Not the locks," Polly said. "I don't think, anyway. Did either of you guys?"

They both shook their heads in the negative. She went on, "I suppose Doug and Billy would have touched the handle trying to get in this morning. They're in the auditorium."

"Alright. This is just damned well enough!" Aaron declared. He stalked back to his Explorer and pulled the radio out. Polly could hear him asking for a team to come up. Then, he pulled his phone out and made another call.

When he came back to the steps, he didn't seem any calmer.

"Polly, I don't know what is going on, but I do NOT like the idea of you spending another night here alone until we figure out what is going on."

Polly didn't figure the two men on either side of her were about to disagree with the sheriff, so they wouldn't be any help.

"Ummm, Aaron. Whoever it was didn't get in last night because we changed the locks. I'm tired of living everywhere but my home."

Henry started to interrupt, "But, Polly … " was all he got out before she shushed him.

"I know that in every murder mystery where the poor, stupid girl says she's going to be brave and stay in her own place, she ends up with her throat slit, but please guys. The bodies in the bathroom were there before I got here and the crates in the basement were here a long time before that. I'll make sure the doors are locked and leave the outside lights on," she pleaded.

Doug and Billy had come into the hallway and were listening.

"Sheriff, we told her we would stay here. We'll camp out for a while. Billy will even bring Big Jack!"

The sheriff shook his head. "I don't like it. And Lydia isn't going to like either." He gave Polly a sideways glance, hoping that mentioning his wife might change her response.

"Yeah," she laughed. "That's not fair. But, I don't care if the boys stay here with me. They can be first on the firing line."

The two boys grinned at each other. "Cool!" Billy said. "Camping and I don't even need a tent!"

Polly shook her head as Jerry strode in to the auditorium with his apprentices following.

Henry said, "I've got a lot of guys coming in today to get the radiant floor laid upstairs. They'll be here around eight." He turned to the sheriff, "Excuse me, "I'm going to head up and start getting things together. Talk to you later, Sheriff. Don't let her be stupid, okay?"

"Got it. I'll do what I can, and if I can't do anything, I'll sic the girls on her." Aaron winked at Henry.

"I'm not happy about this, Polly," he said when Henry was gone, "We don't know who stole that key or why they want to get back in the building."

"Maybe the boys will find out tonight if that person tries again!" She laughed.

"Polly, it's not funny," he scolded.

"I know. I'm not going to get too excited about this, though. Everything happened years ago. We don't even know if the killer still lives around here. And that stuff downstairs isn't a big deal. Do you think the person who collected those things is the killer?" she asked him.

"No, you're right about that. I can't imagine someone with that kind of a cache would move to murder, but I also don't know what he or she would do knowing you're in here if they could find a way to gain access to it." Aaron responded. "I don't like it, Polly." he said again.

"I know, Aaron. But do you not like it enough to force me into a different decision?" she asked.

He shook his head in frustration. "Probably not."

Cars began to pull into the parking lot.

"Well," he said, "It looks like DCI is back to work upstairs and there are some of my boys. We're going to make a decision about the crates in the basement. I'll talk to you about that later, alright?"

"Thanks, Aaron. I'm going to be fine. I promise," she assured him.

"First of all, Polly, I'm supposed to be telling you things are going to be fine, not the other way around." He surprised her by hugging her. "And if something were to happen to you, even if it was only a scratch, my life wouldn't be fit to be lived any longer, trust me."

With that, he walked out to begin directing all of the police activity in her crazy schoolhouse.

Polly turned around, walked back into the kitchen, put the coffee pot on the counter and pulled trays of cookies out of the refrigerator and set them out with napkins and cups. This wouldn't be the first pot of coffee made today. Then, she filled her mug, sat down at the table and sighed.

CHAPTER THIRTEEN

In just a week, things felt like they were finally coming to an end. Floors were being finished in the apartment, the DCI had finally released the upstairs bathroom and workers were gutting them. Ugly institutional bathrooms would soon give way to a couple of exotic spa bathrooms for Polly's future guests.

Doug and Billy had made an adventure of their nights on her main floor. They'd brought a gaming system and screen and two cots and had camped out in the future office space. She heard them up late into the night and wondered how they ever got enough sleep to be going by the next day, but they were out every morning to go home and shower, then back by eight o'clock to go to work. She'd have to do something wonderful for them.

Aaron's people had gone through the root cellar with a fine tooth comb, looking for any clue as to who had taken the items; then brought the crates up to the stage. Screens were set up around the stage to keep curious eyes away as much as possible and while workers were in the building, there was always someone from the Sheriff's Department there to ensure no unauthorized person gained access.

Lydia, Sylvie, Andy and Beryl had all joined in cataloging the items at various times throughout the last few days. The crates were all numbered as to the area where they had come from in the basement. Each item was photographed and labeled. If a year could be identified, it was. Any names or other information found was also logged. So far, they'd only gotten through about a third of the crates, but the process continued.

Polly couldn't get over the vast amount of stuff contained in the crates. It was an incredible timeline. Shoes, items of clothing, novels, textbooks, 45s, LPs, cassettes, CDs and even 8tracks were all part of the collection. There were a few yearbooks, some old pom pons, a flute, drumsticks, hair bows, quite a few spiral notebooks, old games, decks of cards, lunch boxes, trophies and plaques; the list kept growing.

Since today was Friday and it seemed like everyone planned to be at the schoolhouse, Polly got up at 5:30 and was in the kitchen before the boys woke up. The bread machine was busy kneading dough when Billy looked in from the counter. "What are you doing up so early, ma ... I mean, Polly?" he asked.

"Oh, I thought I'd make cinnamon rolls for breakfast."

"Really? Wow!"

"They will be ready when you get back this morning."

"Cool! Okay, I was just checking to make sure everything was alright," he said.

"I think the entire town knows you guys are here to protect me," Polly said. "Unless the creep is from Mars, he knows it too and isn't going to try to get in."

Billy threw his shoulders back, stood up a little straighter and grinned. "That's us. Knight Protectors!"

She laughed. "And I appreciate it. A lot."

"Well, we did find out you are a great cook." he said. She'd cooked every night this week, making everything from homemade pizza to steaks on the stove top grill. It had been fun having someone else to cook for, especially a couple of young men who ate their weight every night. She'd given them run of the kitchen and pleaded with them to clean up after themselves. They'd taken advantage of the stocked pantry and refrigerator and she loved it. They were good guys and Polly was glad to have them around.

"Okay, we're out of here. We'll be back before eight. I can't wait for the cinnamon rolls!" He waved and went to roust Doug.

Polly pulled the first batch of dough out of the machine and added ingredients for the next. This was going to be a bit of a process, but she had to do something to let people know how much she appreciated their work. She heard Doug yell, "See ya later!" and the door slam behind him.

She was rolling out her second batch of rolls when she heard the door open again. Looking up at the clock, she saw it was seven thirty. That was about right. Henry was nearly always here about this time and there were rolls and coffee sitting on the counter waiting for the early birds. She figured the smell of baking and cinnamon would draw people back to the kitchen, and wasn't paying attention. She slathered butter over the dough and began sprinkling the cinnamon mixture when she heard a familiar voice.

"Hi, Polly."

It was all she could do to not drop everything in her hands. She knew she had set her jaw, but she closed her eyes, took a deep breath and looked up.

Joey was standing in the window of the kitchen, watching her.

"Joey." She tried to keep all inflection out of her voice. "What are you doing here?"

"Polly. I've missed you. I had to see you."

"Why, Joey? We're finished."

"I don't think we are, Polly. I know I screwed up, but we had something great. I mean, you are amazing. How could any smart man let you go?"

She put her hands down on the workspace in front of her, bracing herself.

"When did you get in?" she asked.

"I flew in last night and stayed in Des Moines. I rented a car, got up early and here I am!"

"Joey," she said with all the patience she could muster, "how in the hell did you find me."

"Polly, can't you be glad to see me and tell me we can spend some time together talking things out."

"Oh, Joey," Polly sighed, "Why couldn't you have left well enough alone? I broke up with you and I left Boston! I'm done dealing with your stuff and with you. I don't have anything left inside for you."

She looked down at the work table and began rolling up the dough.

"Polly, I don't believe that," he protested. "I can't believe that! Please tell me you'll at least give me a chance to show you things are better."

Polly looked up. Joey wasn't whining or crying at her. He seemed more like a normal person than he had when she left him earlier this year.

"Joey, I don't care if you stick around, but you're going to have to find a place to stay. You aren't staying here. You can get a hotel down in Boone or over in Ames. If we can find time to spend together, that's cool, but you have to know I've got a lot going on and I'm not changing my world around because you showed up. I didn't ask you to be here and I don't really want you here."

She sliced the rolls and put them on a pan, covering it and setting it near the oven so the dough could rise.

"That's great, Polly. I want you to see that we still have something great and we can be together."

"Good morning, Polly! Who's your friend?" Henry came up behind Joey and rested a hand on his shoulder. He reached out with his right hand to shake Joey's. "Hi! I'm Henry Sturtz, pretty much in charge of construction around here."

Releasing Joey's hand, he picked up a cinnamon roll in a napkin. Without waiting for an answer, he commented, "Wow, Pol. Homemade cinnamon rolls? What's the occasion?"

For the first time since Joey showed up, Polly heart felt like it belonged in her chest. The strain washed away and she smiled at Henry.

""Well, everyone has been working so hard this week, I thought I would do something a little special. So, breakfast it is!

"Oh!," she continued. "And this is Joey Delancy from Boston. He's decided to see what I'm up to out here in the middle of the country."

"Then, welcome to Iowa, Joey Delancy!" Henry said, clapping him on the back again. "Here, have a cinnamon roll! I hear our Polly is a terrific cook and it looks like I get to be the first to try her baking!" Henry took a bite from the cinnamon roll, licked his lips loudly, then put it down on the counter. While he was swallowing, he picked another up in a napkin and handed it to Joey.

"Wow," he said. "Those are amazing. You wouldn't want to miss out on something this wonderful, would you Joey?"

Polly looked at Henry a little oddly. He'd never been quite so effusive, but then, she'd never seen him around people he didn't know.

"Polly girl, you're amazing. How long do those have to rise?" he asked, pointing at the rolls by the oven.

"I suppose about fifteen more minutes."

"Then, that's perfect! Can you come upstairs for a minute? I need to show you what we're working on today in case you want to make some changes."

Polly cocked her head to the side, trying to understand him. Neither his body language nor his eyes said anything was out of the ordinary, but his request certainly was.

"Sure," she said. "I'll be right there. Let me wash my hands."

He poured a cup of coffee and walked away. "Sure are great cinnamon rolls, Polly!"

"Joey." Polly said, "This place is about to get busy. I've got workmen and some friends coming in. I'm not going to have time to talk to you today."

"That's alright, Polly." He looked around. "Is there anything I can do to help?"

"Ummmm ... no," she said. "Look, why don't you head to Boone. There's plenty to do down there. I'll drive down and meet you at the Giggling Goat about seven tonight. You have all day to find it. I'll see you there."

"Uh. Okay." he hesitated as he spoke. "I was kind of hoping we could talk this morning, but if you're busy."

"Yep. I'm busy. You can see I've got a million things going on. So, you go to Boone and I'll see you this evening."

She walked out of the kitchen and waited for him to follow. He picked up the cinnamon roll Henry had given him and walked to the front door. She stopped at the steps, about to head up. Joey stopped as well and put his arm around her waist, trying to pull her in for a kiss.

"No, Joey. Just. No." She pulled away and moved up one step.

"Alright, Polly. I'm sorry. I've missed you so much and it is so good to see you." He walked to the door, then turned to look at her. "I guess I'll see you tonight."

"Goodbye Joey." She walked up the steps and heard the door shut behind her. She glanced around to make sure he was gone and then heard a car turn on and drive away.

Henry was waiting at the top of the stairs. "Is everything okay, Pol?" he asked.

"Oh," she said with a faked brightness, "Everything is fine! Now, what did you need to ask me?"

"Polly. You know better than that. I've got this covered up here. Who was that and why was he asking if you guys could still be together?"

"Oh, you heard that."

"Yes, I heard that. Who is the guy and why is he here?"

Polly backed up and stood straighter. "Look, Henry. I know this town has somehow decided I need to be taken care of and I love that everyone here is so friendly, but this is a little out of bounds, don't you think?"

"Polly. I'm sorry," Henry said. "He was making you uncomfortable and it seemed as if you didn't want to talk to him. It also seems as if you two have a history and he's trying to reignite something. If you had wanted to make something happen with him, you might have stayed in Boston. But, you didn't. You came out here. Now, if you're hiding out here to get away from him, you're spending a hell of a lot of money on it. And that seems stupid."

Now Polly became infuriated.

"Look," she spat. "It's none of your damned business how much money I spend or what I spend it on. I'm not a stupid young girl who needs a man to advise her about what to do with her life. I've been doing that all on my own for a long time. I don't need you or Sheriff Merritt or Lydia or anyone else thinking I can't manage my life. If I want your help in my life, I'll ask for it. Otherwise, I'm paying you to work on my building. So, if you don't have a question for me, I have things to do."

She strode back down the steps and realized the tension which had left her when Henry showed up in the window of her kitchen was now back in triple measure. She wanted to cry and scream and kick something. Instead, she went back into the kitchen and pulled the third batch of dough out of the machine. She punched it a couple of times on the work table, and then grabbed the rolling pin and hit it with some force before rolling it out.

"Whoa! Who are you trying to kill?" Doug picked up a cup and poured coffee into it.

"Anyone who gets in my way." She looked up, "Are you going to get in my way?"

"Oh, hell no!" he said. He put the cup down and raised his hands in mock surrender. "I know better than that by now. What in the heck is wrong? You were fine when we left and that was, what?" he glanced at the clock, "an hour ago? Not even that. What happened this early in the morning?"

"Nothing," she snapped. "I'm just tired of people thinking I can't take care of myself."

"Okay," he said. "I'm gonna take my coffee and a roll - they smell awesome, by the way - and go to work. Billy," he said as they passed in the hall, "don't even start with her. She'll deck you with her rolling pin."

"Whazzup, ummm, Polly?" Billy smiled at her until he saw the look on her face. "Oh, Doug wasn't kidding. Anything I can do to help?"

"No, take your food and go," she muttered and rolled out the dough.

"Okay. I'll do that. If you need us, you know where we are."

"Yep, you're in my world. Everyone is always up in my world. I don't even get to sleep in my own place anymore because everyone is all up in my damned world." She hit the dough with her hand as Billy grabbed his coffee and a roll and took off.

Batch number two had risen so she put them in the oven and turned the timer on. Then she took a breath. This wasn't going to do her any good. She'd learned long ago to not get physical when she was mad, it only broke things she loved and didn't actually help matters. She took another breath and then a third deep breath. Alright. That was better. The idiots weren't going to take her down. That was her mantra for the day. And holy smokes, she had a lot of idiots in her world. They were mostly male and she was mostly tired of them.

She slathered up this batch, sprinkled the topping on and rolled it. Then she cut the rolls out and put them in the pan and covering it, set it aside to rise. She ticked off numbers in her head and decided she'd put one more batch in the machine. Too many was better than too few. While everything settled around her, she sat back down at the table with a cup of coffee. Polly took a drink and looked out on to the back yard. She couldn't wait to get that playground out of there and get some color and beauty going, but for now, at least she could see beyond to the trees lining the creek.

Polly put her head into her hands and shut her eyes. How did her life get so weird? She took a few more deep breaths and tried to force herself to relax.

"Polly?" Her head snapped up. She hadn't heard anyone walk in. It was Henry.

"Polly, I'm sorry," he said, contrition in his voice. "I didn't mean to push you so hard about your friend."

"Oh, it's alright. And I'm sorry for freaking out. My frustration blew all over everything." She laughed. "I suppose I should go and make sure

Doug and Billy are okay. They both might be afraid of my rolling pin now."

"They'll be fine. I am sorry. I should not have pushed you. Your life is your life and I have no right in it. I know that."

"Henry. Stop. It's alright," Polly said. "I've never had people in my life who gave a hoot what I did or what happened to me. And honestly, the last guy who did was Joey and he beat someone up because he was jealous the guy helped me up when I tripped. I had to bail him out of jail for that one."

"Were you guys dating?" Henry asked.

"Up until he threatened another guy simply because he thanked me for helping him find a book." She paused. "In the library where I worked!

She continued, "We broke up. I don't know why he's here, but I can bet it isn't to tell me what a great idea he thinks I've had putting all of this together." She put her forehead back into her left hand, rested it, then pushed her hair back.

"I suppose I was mostly angry because you were right. I probably am hiding out here from him. I didn't tell him where I was going and I didn't give him my phone number. I just left. If he hadn't pulled all of that crap, I might have stayed in Boston a while longer. I always knew I was coming back to Iowa someday. As much as I loved it out there, it wasn't my home. Even with my family all gone, my home is still here."

Polly balled up her fist and rested her cheek on it, then opened the hand and rested her chin in the palm. "Everything was going so well. I was having fun meeting people and making decisions about this place. For the first time in my life I can't wait for Monday mornings because I get to be with new people and do new things. Now it all seems so upside down."

Henry sat down beside her and said, "You know, Pol, when you moved into Bellingwood, you leaped into the hearts of a lot of people. If we get a little pushy, it's because we're crazy about you. When you're upside down about everything, the rest of us are upside down too because we like you. A lot. We tend to take care of the people we like."

She laughed. "Yeah. I'd forgotten what it was like to have so many people who know you around. In Boston, people stare at the ground so they don't have to look you in the eyes when you're on the street. Out here? I drive down the road and complete strangers are waving at me! If I tell people I live in Bellingwood, they start asking me about the school that's being redone. When I tell them who I am, they want to know everything!

"It can be a little overwhelming, but I'll get used to it again." Polly sighed and then sat up straight.

"The rolls are going to be done any second. Thanks Henry, and I am sorry."

"You're one resilient girl, Polly. You'll be fine and I'm sorry too. So, now that we're a pair of sorry people, it's probably time to get back to work." He stood up and held out his hand. She took it and he gave her a little strength while she stood. They both looked at each other and then broke as they heard the front door open and workers begin to come in.

Henry walked out and said, "Hey guys! Polly made cinnamon rolls. You're going to want to get 'em while they're hot!"

The timer dinged and she pulled a batch out of the oven, while sliding the third batch in. She reset the timer, then slid fresh rolls onto a plate. After a few minutes, she glazed them and put them on the counter.

CHAPTER FOURTEEN

Not only were the cinnamon rolls a huge success, but the coffee maker was ready to be emptied again. It wasn't every day Polly stood around serving the people who were working, but it felt right today. She chuckled and thought to herself that it might be penance for throwing a tantrum first thing in the morning.

Over the last few weeks, several people had asked if they could help with the coffee and she gladly showed them where to find supplies. This meant things were always cleaned and set up for the next day. All she had to do was flip a switch in the morning. Coffee was an easy way to keep a building full of workers happy.

One of the older guys, Marvin, had taken control of the pot and its cleanup. He told her he liked having an opportunity to do things for people and he didn't get to do so often enough. Polly declared it was his territory.

At nine o'clock this morning he'd come into the kitchen to check the pot. "Have you been the one making coffee today, Miss Giller?" he asked.

"Yep, that was me, Marv. Sorry if I got in your way."

He laughed. "Oh, it's your kitchen. I was only trying to be helpful. Would it be alright if I went ahead and started another one?"

"You know better than I do what these guys will drink," she smiled. "Do your thing."

"So, Miss Giller," he commented as he rinsed the parts of the pot in the large sink, "Are you doing alright with everything that's been going on in your school house? This has to be pretty upsetting."

"It is, Marv. I'm still glad that I bought it and started this project, but sometimes I wonder what I thought I was getting in to!"

"I was upstairs when Dave pulled down those skeletons. That had to freak you out. I'm sorry you had to see that. You've been good to all of us and a girl like you shouldn't ever have to see that stuff. Death is a terrible business, isn't it?"

Polly looked up at him. "Yes, it is, Marv. It really is."

He didn't say anything else, finished setting the coffee up and went back to work.

Polly glanced up at the clock. Her friends were showing up at any moment to work on the items in the crates. They'd worked Monday and Tuesday afternoon, but each of them had been busy the last couple of days with their own lives. Polly looked forward to digging back into the crates. This time capsule of pop culture dated back through the sixties. When she pulled something like a charm bracelet or a framed photograph out, she wondered about the original owner and what they'd been like and what they would think of their possessions now. Would they even remember owning those things?

The first day had been an exercise in patience as the database was designed and protocols set in place for recording all the data. She wasn't sure what was going to happen to everything once it was cleared for release, but they certainly were going to have detailed records of it all. Even when they weren't working in there, a guard was left in place. She supposed that made sense. There were so many people coming and going throughout the day, it would be easy for anyone to mess with it. Every night, the guard locked all the doors to the auditorium. He took the memory card from the camera and the external drive hooked into the computer. He unlocked the doors in the morning, inserted a new card into the camera and a new external drive into the computer. Polly thought it might be overkill, but Aaron Merritt had told them that until the murder was solved or they were absolutely certain neither had anything to do with the other, this procedure was in place. She just smiled and nodded.

She poured two cups of coffee, grabbed a cinnamon roll and started making her way to the stage. She had volunteered to take computer duty today. Beryl would take the camera, Andy would tell them all how to make sure things were organized and Sylvie and Lydia would work.

"Good morning, Stu," she said to the guard. "Would you like some coffee and a cinnamon roll? It occurred to me that no one probably brought you anything."

"Thank you, Polly," he replied as he took both from her. "So are you and the girls back at it today?"

"As soon as they get here. It's going to be the whole crew. You know what that means, don't you?" she laughed.

"Oh, I'm afraid I do. Sheriff Merritt has his hands full with that team." He chuckled and took a bite of the roll. "Oh, that's good! Thank you. My wife isn't much for baking. She loves to cook and can make a mean lasagna, but she says we don't need dessert in the house. I think she doesn't like spending any more time in the kitchen than she has to. One of these days maybe I'll talk my boys into trying some recipes. Then, things will get better." He winked and smiled at her.

Polly knew he had three little boys. They were all much too young to be in the kitchen yet. "So, maybe an Easy Bake oven for them? You could at least get a miserable looking chocolate cake."

"Hey, that's a good idea! I just wish there wasn't so much pink," he laughed.

Polly snorted. "Oh, that's hilarious. There were even some of us girls who didn't like all that pink, but no one seems to have ever figured that out. I spent more time in the dirt and in jeans than I did in little pink, frilly dresses, but I loved being in the kitchen with Mary."

"What is that wonderful aroma? It smells like someone baked this morning!" Sylvie walked into the auditorium followed by Andy.

"Good morning girls. There are fresh cinnamon rolls by the coffee. I ended up making six dozen this morning." Polly said.

"Six dozen what?" Beryl had arrived on the scene. "Wait, let me see if I can tell." She wrinkled her nose up and down and turned to face toward the kitchen as if being led by that same nose. "Girl, you baked a little heaven this morning, didn't you!"

She actually skipped across the floor to the stage, dropped her bag at Polly's feet and said, "I think I'm going to bury my face in something with frosting. Should I bring any back for the rest of you? Deputy Stu will you eat another one if I bring it?"

He looked sideways at Polly, then smiled. "Absolutely. Everyone is already jealous that I'm here, thinking I have the easy assignment this week. They're not going to believe this."

"So, my skinny little friends," Beryl said, "Can I bring one for you or will you reject this amazing gift Polly has offered us?"

"Wow," said Andy. "If you put it like that, how can I refuse? Even if I did just have breakfast with the Queen of England."

"Oh, that's your answer for everything," Beryl said. "You spend way too much time with that woman, but we're glad you've come back down to play us common folk. How about you, Sylvie?"

"I'm starving. It was a scramble to get two boys out the door this morning. For some reason they decided to sleep late and hate everything I offered for breakfast. It was joyous." Sylvie grumbled.

Beryl skipped through the door and was back in a few minutes with napkins and a plate of rolls.

"I suppose we ought to stay down here and eat these, then wash our hands, eh?" Andy said.

"Of course we should, Andy. Wouldn't want to get any sugar on the loot." Beryl sounded a little sarcastic and Andy reacted.

"That would be awful, Beryl! Who knows what we're going to find and we don't want to contaminate it with sticky fingers," she said.

Beryl rolled her eyes at her friend. "Andy?"

"Yes, brat?"

"Okay, just so we're clear who is the brat and who is the insane person," Beryl said.

"I'm clear. Sorry," Andy said.

Lydia and Aaron walked in to the auditorium together holding hands.

Beryl spoke first, "Good morning, you two! Don't tell me you are just getting started on your day. Did you have a late night?" The tone of her voice implied something fun might have occurred last night.

Aaron shook his head. "Your friends are going to give me a heart attack someday, Lydia."

"Not if I can help it," she replied. "I intend to keep that heart well-oiled and exercised."

"It's not right," he protested. "It's just not right. I get no respect from any of you."

Lydia reached up and kissed him on the cheek. "Oh, we all respect you and love you. We simply aren't afraid of you!"

"Stuart Decker?" Aaron commanded.

"Yes, sir." Decker came to attention.

"You've neither seen nor heard any of this. Got it?"

"Umm, sir?"

"Yes, Deputy Decker?"

"That actually doesn't work for me."

"Why is that, Deputy Decker?"

"Because," and the deputy dropped out of his attention stance, "they do this to you all the time."

"I know," Aaron sighed. "I know. It's a good thing they don't spend any time at the office or on the road with me. I'd be toast."

"Yes sir," Decker agreed.

"How are things going here?" Aaron asked around the room.

Lydia responded, "We're going to have a full day ahead of us. We'll see how far we get into it. I'm sorry we took a couple of days off. There were so many things that needed to be done. Beryl has a show coming up in Kansas City and Sylvie had to work."

"Whoa, baby." Aaron said. "No worries. I was only asking if anything had popped up yet."

Everyone else laughed and Lydia said, "Well, excuse me for feeling guilty for not doing the work you asked me to do!"

"Whatever," Aaron responded. "I'm heading down to Boone. If you need me, call." He bent over to kiss his wife and she turned so he got her full on the lips. She threw her arms up around him and kissed him until Beryl had to say, "Alright, already! Give it a rest, girl. You'll see him tonight. Sheesh!"

Lydia pulled away and smiled sweetly up at her husband. "Have a good day, dear."

"Yeah. I'll do that." He spun around and Polly heard him sputtering as he left the room.

"You torment him, don't you?" Polly asked Lydia.

"Every chance I get. I have fun!" she said, then looked at Beryl. "Well, where's my cinnamon roll?"

"Umm," Beryl looked around at everyone else. "Are you all as distracted as I am at the moment? Ah hell, I seem to have lost my mind." Then she looked at the plate still in her hands.

"Here," she said. "Here is your cinnamon roll. Get your own coffee." She looked at Andy, "Whew. I think I need to splash some cold water. How about you?"

"Cold water is a great idea," Andy replied. "It's too early for that stuff, Lydia. You can't do that to us."

Lydia just smiled. "I'll be right back with coffee. You girls settle for a moment."

She came back into the auditorium with coffee and they sat on the edge of the stage drinking and eating. Polly gathered up the waste and took it to the kitchen. She was in the middle of washing her hands as the others came in and followed suit. It was time to get to work. They pulled plastic gloves out of a box and started digging into crates.

Each item received a number and tag; it was photographed from several angles and then entered into the database, bagged and returned to the original crate. They worked for a couple of hours while chattering away about their week when Andy said, "Guys. Stop. I think I found something."

Beryl was photographing a TEEN magazine from 1969. Polly entered the tag number and details and dropped it into an evidence bag, handing it to Sylvie who dropped it back in its original crate.

"What is it, Andy?" Polly asked.

"This doesn't fit at all. I'm looking at a crate of stuff from the early seventies. It might even be 1971 or 1972 and this shirt and coat are in here. She held up a t-shirt with Pearl Jam on the front. The coat was blue wool and had Members Only on the side pocket. Neither of those items had existed in the 70s.

Stu walked over and looked at the items. He snapped on a pair of gloves and took the items out of Andy's hands. Looking closely, he ran his thumb over a stain on the coat.

"Andy, I don't know what you've found, but I'm glad you did. Other than this, are things in the other crates pretty much in a logical order?"

Andy nodded. "So far it is. We haven't gotten deep enough for me to say that with one hundred percent certainty, but yeah, that's probably right."

"Thank you. I'll take custody of this. Let me fill out the tag and get it photographed. Beryl, are you ready for me?"

"Oh, baby," Beryl said. "That was a loaded question. But yes," she got serious. "I'm ready any time."

She shot pictures of each item with their respective tags. Polly entered the information into the database, then Stu placed them into large evidence bags and made a quick phone call. He picked up two more evidence bags, asking Beryl to pull the memory card out of the computer and Polly to unmount the external hard drive.

"I've got replacements in the car," he said, "but I'm waiting for someone to show up and take charge of these things. Can you all keep yourselves busy until then?"

Lydia laughed. "I think we can handle that. Do you want us to stay in here with you or do you care?"

"No, you can do whatever you'd like. I'd appreciate it if you wouldn't say anything to anyone, though."

Beryl gave him a scowl. "Really, Stu? After all this time we've been together? You still don't trust me? I haven't told anyone about those quiet moments we spent together."

He shut his eyes and dropped his chin into his chest, "I asked for that. Sometimes I forget you guys are not like the rest of the people," he paused for effect, "in the world!"

"Would you shut the doors? Someone should be here soon and we'll get you set up to go again right away. Thanks, girls."

"Oh, isn't he sweet," Lydia said. "He called us girls. Other than Polly and maybe Sylvie, he's the youngest person in this room. Come on, 'girls,' let's see what damage we can do to Polly's kitchen."

It was nearly noon and the building was starting to get quiet as the workers stopped for lunch. Marv had obviously started one more pot of coffee. Polly turned the hot water on in one of the deep sinks, and then dropped the baking pans in after filling it with hot sudsy water. Lydia filled a smaller sink while Andy gathered the platters. Sylvie sprayed the countertop down and wiped it clean while Beryl pulled out some dish towels. Soon everything was cleaned up and back to normal and Aaron walked in.

"You missed me so much you had to find a reason to bring me back, didn't you," he teased. Sylvie was the closest to him as he walked in the door and giggled. He pulled her into a side hug and said, "I knew you girls couldn't live without me."

He went on, "Well, you're set up to go again on the stage. That was a great catch, Andy. I guess that's why I'm glad you all are doing this. You're making good connections. The things are on their way to the DCI in Ames for testing. We won't know anything for a few days."

Lydia asked, "Why did you come back into town? I thought you had to be in Des Moines this afternoon."

"Oh, any excuse I can get to see you, I will take." He walked over and flicked Lydia's hair, "I just wanted to tell you all that you'd done a great job. And I still have time to get to Des Moines for my meeting." He checked his watch. "But, I had better go now. See you later!" He kissed his wife again and this time she let him get away with a quick kiss. He smiled at the rest of them, and walked out of the kitchen toward the front door.

Two of the men who worked for Henry, Leroy Forster and Ben Bowen, came down the stairs as the sheriff was leaving. They walked back to the kitchen to fill their cups with coffee.

Leroy asked, "What was the sheriff doing here again? Did you guys find something in the crates?"

Polly froze, hoping nothing showed on her face. She wasn't quite sure what to say, but Andy broke in, "We were so busy this morning, we needed a new memory card. I guess they're pretty choosy about what they want us to use, so they brought one up. As for the sheriff, I think he wanted another kiss from his honey!" She chuckled and waited for that little bit of information to embarrass the man.

Ben laughed and poked his friend, "You want a honey to kiss, don't you, Leroy."

"Uh huh. I guess so." Leroy said and turned around to head back up the stairs.

Ben followed him, then turned around. "By the way, Miss Giller. Thanks for the cinnamon rolls. It isn't every day I get to eat homemade treats!"

"You're welcome, Ben." Polly found her voice again.

After they heard the men go up the steps, she wilted a little and said, "Thanks Andy, I had no idea how to respond. The only words I had in my head were Stu telling us not to tell anyone."

Beryl opened up the refrigerator. "Well, what shall we have for lunch today?"

Polly walked over and stood beside her. "I should have lunchmeat in there and I made a fresh loaf of bread last night. Sandwiches?"

"That sounds great!" Sylvie responded. "I have chips here in the cupboard."

Before long, they'd assembled lunch and were sitting at the back table.

Henry walked into the kitchen and grinned. "Of course," he said. "The musketeers are here when the cops show up. I think it is you guys causing all the trouble for Polly. Until you showed up, everything was just fine." He pulled up a chair at the other end of the table, then turned to Polly.

"Don't mind me. I'm about to get myself into huge trouble."

Stricken, her eyes pleaded with him to say nothing, but he ignored her.

"Did she tell you yet who was here this morning when I arrived?" he asked, looking at Lydia.

"That apology?" Polly remarked, "Is off the table. You can't be trusted." She tossed her sandwich on her plate and stood up. "It's no big deal," she said as she walked over to the cooler and pulled out a Diet Mountain Dew.

"Yeah, that no big deal nearly got Doug's head bashed in with a rolling pin as I understand it," Henry said.

"What?" Lydia asked. "What happened?"

"Damn it," Polly cursed and stalked out into the hallway.

"Polly! Come back here." Beryl called after her.

"I did this, I'll take care of it." Henry said.

"Why is she so angry? Who showed up this morning?" Lydia pressed.

"I think it's her old boyfriend from Boston. She sent him away, but he had her pretty worked up and she jumped down my throat when I confronted her about it." Henry responded. He got up and walked out to the hallway where Polly was pacing.

"You couldn't keep your damned mouth shut, could you? When did this become your business and who in the hell do you think you are spreading my business around like manure?" She was furious.

"Polly, they're your friends. Honestly, I couldn't imagine you hadn't already told them. You guys spent most of the morning together."

"Well, what if I wanted to deal with this and get him sent on his way? I don't get to do that now, do I? I'm so glad you have it all figured out for me." She stalked to the other end of the hallway and slammed the side doors open. She stepped out on the back stoop, then spun back to face him. He'd been following pretty closely.

"Now, I have to explain myself to them and for some reason, I feel like you are asking me to explain myself to you and all I want to do is make this go away. If this is what your friendship means, I want nothing to do with it."

"Alright, I get it. I stuck my nose in where it didn't belong. What can I do?"

"Not a damned thing right now. You're an ass. It might help both of us if you just leave me alone." When he hesitated, she said, "And by leave me alone, I mean get out of my face so I don't have to see you." She fluttered her fingers at the inside hallway. "Go away. I don't want to discuss this any longer with you!"

"Really? We can't talk about this?" he asked.

"Not right now," she hissed. "I'm so angry at you I want to throw a rock at your head. Be gone!" She flicked her fingers again and he looked like he was in pain, but turned around and headed for the steps. After he walked upstairs, she took a deep breath and then another. Then Polly set her shoulders and shut her eyes. She did not want to listen to her friends press her on this issue, but she knew she couldn't run away, so she gathered herself, pulled the door shut and walked back to the kitchen.

Beryl looked up when she came in. "Damn girl, you got some spitfire in you! I think Henry might feel like he started draining testosterone away after that encounter. I hope he can get the wound closed or he'll be singing with the women come Sunday morning!"

Polly couldn't help it, she laughed uproariously.

"Are you kidding me?" she asked with a snort, "That's what you have to say? You are insane. And thank you."

Lydia came up to her and patted her on the back. "Alright," she said,

"Let's get back to work and see if we can crack any more cases wide open."

CHAPTER FIFTEEN

Stopping what she was doing, Polly coughed to get everyone's attention. "You're going to let me get away with not telling you what happened?" she asked.

None of them said a word; they kept moving items around and talking about the pieces they were seeing. Beryl was shooting a picture of a Mickey Mouse Pez dispenser while Sylvie waited to bring it to Polly for input, Lydia was looking at a little pink sweater and Andy was putting away a Newsweek magazine from 1984 which had already been photographed and inventoried. She pulled out a can of hairspray and giggled, "Some little girl didn't have a chance to put her hair back together that day."

Lydia looked up, "You know, there is nothing worth anything in these crates. It's as if the thief deliberately took things that weren't terribly important. That's probably why he or she was able to get away with it. No one paid much attention to what they lost."

Sylvie responded, "And if it was something bigger, we assumed a classmate had taken it. I was annoyed when my jacket was gone, but I couldn't prove anything, so I moved on."

Polly stood up, "Alright. Fine. I get it."

"What dear?" Lydia asked.

"I was mean to Henry. But, he shouldn't have said anything. It wasn't his story to talk about. I would have told you when I was ready. I wasn't ready yet." The slight whine in her voice annoyed Polly, but she couldn't rid herself of it.

"You're absolutely right. Henry shouldn't have said anything. He's a dumb, stupid man," Lydia responded.

"And you told him so in no uncertain terms," Beryl laughed.

Sylvie turned to Andy. "She scared me and I was far away!"

Andy giggled. "Yep, I guess we know who the scary one is in the bunch. We're siccing her on men we want to send screaming home to their mamas."

"Hey!" Polly laughed. "I'm not that mean."

"Do you want us to go ask Henry?" Beryl asked.

"Fine. I was pissed off and I was mean."

"Oh, we got that. And we're not going near the conversation. At least not without chocolate." Andy laughed.

Lydia said, "We understand that you don't want to talk about this right now. You don't know any of us well enough to trust with it, much less all of us as a group. It's your story and when you're ready to talk, whomever you choose to talk about it with will listen."

Polly stood up and smiled. "I'll be right back." She left the stage and walked into the kitchen and returned with a large bowl of chocolate candy.

"Here," she said. "First of all, I'm sorry you guys got splattered. I'll deal with Henry and his bad behavior later."

She passed the bowl around.

"Why do you have all of this candy?" Beryl asked.

"Um, hello? Tomorrow night is Halloween," Polly said.

"You're going to open the school for kids?" Andy asked. "No one knows that or it would have been a big deal!"

"No, I'm not going to open up or anything, but just in case kids show up, shouldn't I be ready?" Polly said.

"Well, you won't be if we eat everything this afternoon. So, is this going to be a long conversation?" Andy queried.

Polly sighed then looked at Lydia. "Did you tell them about the phone call last week?"

"Oh honey, no!" Lydia was shocked.

"Really? Alright, well, here's the deal." Polly repeated the story she had told Lydia and Aaron the morning Joey had interrupted their breakfast, then went on.

"This morning, Joey showed up here at the school. I don't know how he tracked me down. I didn't tell anyone in Boston where I was going. It completely freaks me out that he found me, but I sent him to Boone to get a hotel room because it doesn't look like he's going anywhere until we talk this out.

Andy interrupted. "You do know your purchase of this place is public record, don't you. All he had to do was a little bit of searching and he could easily find you."

Polly looked up. "And he knew Sheriff Merritt's name since he answered my phone that day, so he knew what county to look in. Alright, while that's creepy, at least it makes sense."

"How long has he been around?" Beryl asked.

"Well, he said he flew in yesterday and got a hotel in Des Moines, then drove up here early this morning. That sounds about right. He gets something in his head and then charges off and does it."

She looked around at her friends, "I don't want to go out tonight, but I've got to deal with him or he'll be up here haunting me all the time. He doesn't take no for an answer."

"Is he the reason you left Boston?" Sylvie asked quietly.

"I guess he is. It's not like I was planning to stay there forever. I knew someday I was coming back to Iowa. But, before all of that happened, I had planned on being out there a few more years. I like it there a lot and I have good friends there. I had a great job and I adore exploring all the history. But, I was getting tired of the noise of the city and was ready to be back where people thought about others every once in a while.

"I wasn't here when Mary died and I wasn't here when Dad died. Those were awful phone calls to get, knowing I hadn't had a chance to tell them one more time how much I loved them. Especially Mary. She took such good care of me when I was young. I suppose I told Dad every time we were on the phone, but it was still hard closing out his house, knowing I'd missed the fun part of his life after he quit farming.

"We had talked a lot about when I found the right guy and had kids. We talked about me coming back here and living close by so he could make toys for them. He'd bought plans to build beds and changing tables."

Polly giggled, "It's probably just as well he didn't find out I wasn't in a hurry to get married and have kids. He'd have been disappointed."

"No, he wouldn't have," Lydia said. "He'd be happy to have you around, no matter what you were doing."

"Well, this place is kind of my response to him, I guess. And as mad as I get at Henry, he's a lot like Dad. The glint he gets in his eye when he talks about making things out of wood is so much like Dad. Damn. I'm going to have to apologize to that stupid man again."

"Again? You ripped his balls off twice today?" Beryl looked shocked.

"Yeah. He got all up in my business this morning when he walked in on me talking to Joey."

"Wow," Beryl said, "He's dumber than I thought. Most men would only set themselves up for that abuse once in a day."

"He's not so dumb," came a voice from the auditorium floor. Polly pulled back the curtain to see who was there. It was Henry. He continued, "It got you talking to your friends. Don't forget ladies, I have a younger sister who lives to torment me. These balls are made of pure titanium." He chuckled, turned around and left the hall.

"Crap," Polly said. "How long do you suppose he was standing there?"

Stu Decker answered her. "Oh, pretty much through your entire conversation."

"And you didn't tell us?" Lydia asked.

"Ummm, no?" he responded.

"Well, you're not much protection at all, are you?" Beryl said.

"Look, the guy needed some kind of relief after the takedown he'd had. We men have to stick together. It seems to me he needed more protection than you."

Beryl turned her back on him and thrust her hand in the air as if she were dismissing him completely.

"What are you going to do if this Joey character won't leave you alone?" she asked Polly.

"I dunno," Polly replied. "I'd like to think he would be reasonable, but obviously he's not if he's out here trying to talk me into getting back together with him. I don't know how many times it's going to take for me to turn him down before he gets it.

"And honestly, ladies, I have absolutely no idea why he is so obsessed with me. We were only together for about five months and we hadn't ever talked about long-term goals in our relationship. He had dated plenty of other women before he met me and I know there is one other girl at the library who was interested in him. This just seems so odd."

Lydia said, "That's exactly right. This is odd. Honey, if you can't get him to be reasonable in a hurry, you might have to admit you can't handle his level of crazy and get some help with it."

"What would we do? Put him in jail? That's not going to help," Polly said.

"Polly, if you think for a minute that his anger won't turn on you at some point, you're flat out wrong. Just because he is nice to you right now doesn't mean he'll be nice to you when he doesn't get his way." This came from Sylvie. "Before you know it, you're the target."

"So where are you meeting him tonight? Tell me you're not meeting him at his hotel." Lydia said.

"Oh! No!" Polly exclaimed. "I told him to wander around Boone today, there's plenty to do there and he's as much of a history nut as I am.

He'll probably end up at Mamie Eisenhower's house and lose track of time. We're going to meet at the Giggling Goat at seven o'clock. It's the only place I knew he'd easily find. That should be alright, don't you think?"

Lydia looked at the other three women. "That should be fine. So, would you freak out if you saw some friends having a drink and a sandwich there?" she asked pertly.

"Yes, Lydia. I might." Polly responded.

"Oh, well darn. I'm pretty sure some of us would like to know what this guy looks like so we can keep an eye on him if he shows up."

Polly sighed. "Are you going to be upset if I tell you not to eat there tonight?"

"I don't think that upset is the right word," Lydia replied. "Disappointed, maybe," and she looked hopefully at Polly.

"Fine," Polly said, her lips pressed together. "But, you can't sit at the table next to us and you can't sit with us and you can't blatantly eavesdrop."

Then she sighed, "In my entire life I have never met people as pushy as you when it comes to my life."

Beryl giggled. "Who? Us? You're the most excitement we've had in years!" She laughed out loud. "It was getting pretty boring around here. All we did for fun was tease Lydia and Aaron about their nightly escapades and after this long, even that has gotten pretty boring."

Lydia swatted her friend's arm. "I want Aaron to see this guy and I want this guy to see Aaron and know you are our friend. After that, your evening is your own. Whatever you decide, we will try to live with it."

"Do you mean like take him back?" Polly sounded surprised.

"Yes, like take him back. You're not a stupid girl, Polly. If you liked him once, you had to see a lot of good things in him."

Polly thought about it. "You're right. He is witty and smart about all sorts of things and he loves history, probably more than I do. He took me to a lot of weird little hidden away haunts in the Boston area. He loved to read and liked the same kind of movies I like. He created these wonderfully romantic outings, taking me all over the region. It was like New England was his to show off. He is a great cook and things seemed to be pretty good."

"He sounds great," Lydia said, "What does he do for a living?"

"Well, I'm not sure," Polly said. "No, it's not like that." she assured them, seeing the shocked looks on their faces. "His parents have a lot of old family money and he doesn't need to work. He's spent most of the last few years going to school. He has a couple of Master's degrees - one in Art History and another in Literature. He's decided he is fascinated by ancient languages and is working on a degree right now as well as spending time at the Peabody Museum in their collections."

"Do you know his parents well?" Andy asked.

"I met them a couple of times. His mother is active in Boston's Junior League. She spends most of her time volunteering and doing social things. I didn't fit in with their idea of a spouse for their son, but they were nice enough to me."

"Well, what do you believe they think about him being out here and what did they think about his jail time?" Lydia pressed.

"I don't know if they even knew he was in jail. I had to bail him out the first time around." Polly paused and thought, "Huh. I guess I don't know. I didn't see either of them at his trial and after that I guess I didn't ever see them again." She shrugged her shoulders. "I have no idea what they thought and I bet they don't know he's here in Iowa. They didn't pay much attention to his life. Both times I met them it was at some charity event he took me to. He had to show up or he told me they would cut him off."

"Sounds like a spoiled, entitled brat to me," Beryl muttered.

"Stop it." Lydia hushed her.

"Oh, you're probably right," Polly continued. "It never showed itself that way. He was always polite and a gentleman. We never did anything I didn't want to do. He always asked me first unless he was surprising me with something and there were often fun surprises. He didn't go overboard buying things, it seemed like he knew that would put me off. He was nearly perfect. If he hadn't lost his temper, heck, in a few months

I probably would have asked him to marry me.

"So, I'm glad I saw the real Joey when I did. The first time I thought I'd provoked his response. It came out of the blue. He'd never behaved like that before. So, I figured somehow it was my fault. However, the second time? I wasn't buying it. There was no provocation that time on anyone's part and he crossed the line when he came into where I worked and threatened one of my patrons."

"Do you think he has gotten any help?" Sylvie asked.

"He said he has been through an anger management class and spent time working with a counselor. But, he quit both of those even after they were mandated by the court the last time, so I don't know if I believe him." Polly replied.

"So," Lydia said, "What is your plan for tonight? What are you hoping to accomplish?"

"I don't know. I'd like him to be honest with me first of all. This morning when I asked how he found me, he avoided the question. I want him to hear himself say that he is stalking me. Then, I want him to tell me why he thought it was appropriate to track me down more than six months after we had broken up. I think he made a lot of this stuff up in his head and hasn't thought about the reality of his actions. He's not this stupid! At least I didn't think he was this stupid."

She sighed, "And if he is having some kind of emotional or mental breakdown, damn. I don't know what I'll do with him."

"Do you know how to reach his parents?" This came from Andy.

"Well, I suppose I could track them down. I don't have any direct numbers for them, but I'm sure there are ways to reach them. Yeah. I know enough about them to be able to contact them."

"Then that should be a backup plan," Lydia said. "Make his parents deal with him. They put him out there in the world like this and they can take him back. It's not up to you to fix him up. Just remember that."

"I know, Lydia. That makes a lot of sense. It isn't easy for me to take my hands off a situation I was involved in, but I don't need this."

They went back to work, talking more about Joey and Polly and making plans for dinner. Lydia texted her husband to let him know what the plans were for that evening.

Soon enough, Stu stepped up on the stage and said, "Ladies, it's 4:30. My shift is nearly over and guys are packing it in for the weekend. Can you get to a stopping place?"

"Wow!" Polly said. "That went fast. Just a couple more pieces and we'll hand everything over." She finished entering the information about a Han Solo action figure and saw that Beryl was photographing a small camera. When they were finished, Beryl pulled the SD card out and handed it to Stuart, Polly logged off and unmounted the hard drive and handed that over as well. They gathered up their stuff, walked back into the kitchen and waited while he shut the lights out and locked up the auditorium.

Sylvie was the first to leave. "I'm sorry I can't be there tonight. I haven't spent any time at home with the boys this week, so we're going to watch a movie and make popcorn. I hope it goes well for you." She hugged Polly and waved as she left.

"We'll see you later, Polly," Lydia said. "We're going to get there around 7:30 or so. We'll pop by like casual friends, then watch you like a hawk from across the room. How's that?"

Polly laughed. "You guys are too much. You do know that I'm 32 and have been living in Boston for the last, oh, fourteen years?"

Lydia smiled at her, "Uh huh. You're in our territory now. Thirty-two is like fifteen to us. And besides, what else are we going to do on a Friday night? Like Beryl said, you're our entertainment now."

"Okay," Polly said, "I guess I'll see you later!" She watched them leave and shook her head.

Then she realized she had one more thing to do. As she was heading up the stairs, Marvin, Leroy and Ben were coming down.

Leroy said, "What in the hell, lady? You're tough! Henry has been limping around all afternoon from the beatdown you gave him."

"Yeah," she retorted, "And don't you forget it. Cross me and it will be painful."

She watched them leave and made her way up the steps. Henry was sitting on a five gallon bucket drinking a bottle of water.

"Hi there," he said. "Want a seat?" and he gestured toward another upside down bucket.

"Here I am again," Polly sighed. "Telling you I'm sorry, the second time today. I shouldn't have gotten so angry at you."

"Well, I suppose I deserved it. I'm not used to being around a woman who gets all fiery like that. You're kind of scary."

"That's what everyone keeps telling me. I'm sorry. Okay?"

"It's alright. I'm sorry too. We're going to have to stop doing this or people will talk, though." He laughed.

"Talk? About what?" Polly was astonished.

"About us." he replied.

"What about us?" she asked.

"Oh nothing. No big deal." Henry shook his head as he stood up. He swallowed down the last of the water and tossed the bottle into a bucket.

"Look, I need to be in here tomorrow to check this first coat of finish. I won't show up until after 8:30. Will that be okay?"

Polly looked up at him, still processing on the 'us' comment. "Sure," she said distractedly. Doug and Billy will be gone by then. You have a key, right?"

"Right. I'll see you then. Make sure the doors are all locked up tonight before you leave."

"What?" She asked, "Oh, alright. Sure. See you tomorrow."

Henry walked downstairs and she heard the door shut behind him. She walked back down to find Doug and Billy standing in the door to the room they had claimed as theirs.

"I'm going out tonight, guys. Sorry about that. There are frozen pizzas in the kitchen and plenty of chips and pop. There's also candy and stuff in there too."

"What time are you leaving?"

"Oh, probably about 6:30, why?"

"Do you care if we bring some friends over to play video games? We'll be done by eleven or so ... maybe midnight," Billy assured her.

"That's fine, but I don't want people on the floors upstairs and I don't want people in my room or in Henry's stuff over there." She gestured to the room Henry had claimed as his workshop. "You can have free run of the kitchen, though."

"Great! We're going to head out and get our stuff for the night and we'll be back before you leave, we promise!"

"Guys, you are being awesome about this. I'm sorry you have to play baby sitter to an old lady."

"Are you kidding? It's like we're on vacation! Our parents aren't bugging us to help around the house, you have great food, we can play games and watch TV whenever we want. This is great!"

"Well, one of these days I will take you out for dinner," she said. "Anything you want."

"Cool!" Doug said, "We'll be back in a bit." They took off and shut the door. She locked it behind them and went back upstairs. She lay down on her bed, her eyes burning from exhaustion. She set her alarm for 5:45 and dropped off to sleep.

CHAPTER SIXTEEN

It had only taken a few minutes for Polly to pull out a feast of goodies and put them on the counter in the kitchen for the boys and their friends. She had also brought in some extra soda from storage and filled the refrigerator. The guys had spent enough time in the kitchen with her and were comfortable with the stove and knew where to find everything, so she wasn't too worried about them having a party. From what she could tell they were more interested in playing games than getting drunk, so she didn't even have to be concerned about that. However, when she saw them coming in the door with card tables and chairs, she was more than a little curious.

"Exactly how many people are you planning to have here tonight?"

"Oh, no worries," Billy said. "There are only going to be eight of us, but we decided to hang out here in the hallway in front of the food. We'll get everything hooked up, the guys are all bringing their own laptops and it'll be cool."

"Alright," she said, "I'm trusting you."

"Really, Polly, no worries. We're only playing games."

"Okay then. I'm outta here. Let me know if anything explodes, alright?"

"Cool. Wait," Doug stopped. "Where are you going?"

"I'm going to the Giggling Goat in Boone. It looks like everyone is going down there tonight. I'll see you later."

"Cool." And with that he was setting up chairs and tables and pulling extension cords to the wall sockets. Polly hoped they didn't blow her school up, but it did make her smile. This was one of the things she looked forward to in the future. Hopefully a lot of people would find reasons to use her school for different activities, even if it was just the guys coming in to play games.

She got in her truck, headed up to the county road, turned west and drove until she ran into the next one leading directly into Boone. She'd driven this road enough it was starting to feel familiar. She turned south on Story Street. One of these days she was going to have to ask some questions about the big, old, beautiful homes in this town. Sometimes she drove around just to look at them. But, tonight she was too distracted to do anything other than acknowledge their existence.

She stopped and waited while a train passed in front of her, then crossed quickly over the tracks when the arms went back up and headed for the restaurant. She parked her truck and went inside. Joey was already at a table and stood when he saw her. He walked over to greet her, kissed her on the cheek and took her arm to escort her to their table. The waitress showed up immediately with a glass of water and asked if she wanted anything else.

"No thank you, water will be fine," she said.

"Are you sure you don't want a drink?" Joey asked.

"No, water is fine." she repeated. The last thing she wanted to be was out of control tonight.

"I ordered onion rings. It seemed like something I could recognize on the menu."

"Oh, don't be a snob, Joey."

"I'm sorry," he said. "Have you eaten here before?"

"No. But, everything should be good. This place is always busy. You should probably have the steak. You're right in the middle of the country, where beef and pork actually live."

"Alright," he laughed. "I'll have a steak sandwich. What about you?"

"Have you ever had a pork tenderloin before?"

"Probably," he responded.

"Not like this! I'll order one and you can try it. You can be guaranteed that if that is on the menu in an Iowa restaurant it will be great. These people like their pork tenderloin sandwiches."

When the waitress returned with their onion rings, Polly asked for a cup of ranch dressing and Joey placed their order. She had gotten used to him ordering for her, so she let it happen without saying anything.

"It's good to see you, Polly. You look amazing tonight," he said.

"Thank you, Joey. It was nice to get dressed up. I've been so busy with construction, I haven't done this in a while." She paused. "I went out with some friends a couple of weeks ago, but that was only girls, so maybe it didn't count."

"Well, you are absolutely beautiful. I've really missed you."

He seemed to be waiting for her to reciprocate, but fortunately, the waitress stepped in with the dressing and a pitcher to refill Polly's water. "Anything else?" she asked.

Polly shook her head and Joey ignored her, so she walked away.

She looked back at Joey and he reiterated. "I've really missed you. I couldn't believe you left town. I wish you would have called to let me know you were thinking about leaving."

Polly looked at him a little perplexed. "Joey, we were no longer together. Why in the world would I have called you?"

"Oh, come on, Polly. We both know that was only a little bubble in our timeline. I'd been waiting my whole life for you and when I met you, I knew there would never be anyone else for me."

"Oh, Joey," Polly sighed. "How is that even possible if I'm certain you're not the one for me?"

Joey's eyes got hard and his mouth set into a thin line. "Are you telling me there is someone else in your life already?"

"Stop it. Just stop it." Polly's voice got low and threatening. "There is no one else, but I am damned well certain you aren't the person I'm supposed to be with for the rest of my life. I don't know why you are here and I don't like it. I broke up with you and I left Boston behind. I'm starting a new life here and you aren't part of it. Don't you dare get pushy with me."

"I'm not getting pushy, Polly. I want you to understand how important you are to me. I will do anything to make you happy, as long as you don't send me away."

"Do you hear yourself, Joey? I'm telling you we aren't together and you keep ignoring me!" Polly was certain that her frustration with the situation was going to explode all over him if he didn't begin to hear what she was saying to him.

"Polly Giller! How are you this evening?"

Their conversation was interrupted by the overwhelming presence of four people surrounding their table.

"Who's your friend, Polly? Are you going to introduce us?"

The anger that had been building inside her was released and she said, "Sure! Everyone, this is Joey Delancy, a friend of mine from Boston. Joey, this is Beryl Watson, Andy Saner and Lydia and Aaron Merritt."

She pointed at each of them as she introduced them. Joey stood up and shook the hand of each of the ladies and then Aaron. If he recognized the name, he didn't flinch or say a word.

"Joey," Polly said, "These are friends of mine from Bellingwood. These ladies have been taking great care of me and it's been fun getting to know them."

Beryl cut in, "She didn't have a chance. We made sure she was going to get to know us. Since she started renovating that old schoolhouse, all sorts of excitement has been happening in out little town. We tell her she's our entertainment. And look, here she is again with someone new! It looks like we might have even more entertainment!"

"No, not tonight, you goofball. We're going to get our own table over here and enjoy a good dinner. What are you having tonight, dear?" Lydia asked Polly.

"I haven't had a pork tenderloin since I got back to Iowa. Any chance I get to have one, I'm taking it, at least for a while." Polly said.

"Well, that sounds terrific. In fact, that's probably what I'll have as well. You two enjoy yourselves this evening!" Lydia turned to Joey. "We've taken a liking to this little girl, you take care of her, okay?"

"Alright," he said, a little shaken. "I'll … I'll do my best."

They scurried away to their table, out of Joey's line of sight, but Lydia and Beryl planted themselves at the table so they could see everything that was happening as well as make faces at Polly.

Joey sat back down and said, "Those are your friends? Aren't they a little old?"

Polly looked across the table at him, letting her disgust fill her eyes. Then, she took a breath and said, "You never did tell me how you managed to find me. I know that none of my friends have talked to you."

"Honestly, Polly, it wasn't that difficult." he replied. "Once I had the Sheriff's name, the rest came together pretty easily. Your little friend at the library thought it was great fun to track you down. She told me it was a shame we were no longer together, especially since I'm so gorgeous."

Polly made a mental note to call her old supervisor. Good heavens, it was astounding how stupid people could be.

"Joey. Do you hear this sounds? You are stalking me and asking other people to help you do it. This is not normal. This is not how normal people have relationships." She was doing her best to maintain some level of patience, but this latest bit of news was almost too much.

"Polly, you left me, your friends and your home in Boston! You had a great job … a job you loved. You had a great little home and when we get married you are going to have the opportunity to make a beautiful home. Our children will be happy and you'll never miss living out here in the middle of wherever we are."

Polly stood up. She had finally reached her limit. "That's it. I came down here to try to talk to you and get you to see some sense. I wanted to give you the benefit of the doubt and I wanted to believe you really had been going to counseling and would be sensible about what had happened between us. What I see now, though, is that you are even more delusional than you were last spring."

He reached across the table and grabbed her forearm. His voice got quiet and smooth as he said, "Sit down. Don't embarrass us, especially in front of your friends. I'm not threatening you or anything. Let's have a nice dinner."

Polly looked over his shoulder and Lydia's hand was on Aaron's arm. He looked as if he was ready to explode out of his seat, but she held him back. Her eyes were questioning Polly. With a slight shake of her head, Polly sat back down.

"I'll have you know," she said. "That it is only because I don't want to see you pulverized by my friends that I'm going to sit back down. Your attitude is completely unacceptable and if you can't understand that and get past it, I will be glad to turn you over to the Sheriff and let him put you on a plane back to Boston."

"Oh, Polly, stop it." Joey's tone had become patronizing. "You are over reacting. I'm not going to hurt you. Have I ever hurt you? You mean the world to me and I can't imagine living without you in my world. So what am I going to have to do to make that a reality for both of us?"

At that moment the waitress came back to the table with their food. Polly's stomach was so tied up in knots, she couldn't imagine eating anything. She opened the sandwich and layered the lettuce and tomato on one side with a little mayo, then flipped it over and put ketchup on the bun, followed by onion and pickles. This really was her favorite sandwich and she was furious that the idiot sitting across from her was going to make it a miserable meal. She poured ketchup onto her plate beside the fries, then cut her sandwich into quarters.

She sat back in her chair and tried to relax. Picking up one of the quarters, she took a small bite and rolled it around in her mouth. She forced herself to breathe slowly, then smiled a little as she realized this was now the third time today she'd had to force herself to relax. Men drove her over the edge and the one across the table exuded pure insanity. So, how was she going to get rid of him? After a few more deep breaths, which Joey had the courtesy to allow her to have in silence, she was ready to deal with him again.

"Okay, how long are you planning to stay in Iowa?" she asked, and then cringed as soon as it was out of her mouth. She knew exactly what he was going to say and he didn't disappoint her.

"I will be here as long as it takes to convince you to come back to Boston with me," he replied.

"Yeah. That's what I thought you were going to say. I don't even know why I asked. But, what are you doing about your classes or your work at the Peabody?"

"I scheduled a sabbatical for this fall. I don't think anyone really cares if I'm gone as long as I am happy when I return. I'll be happy if you return with me. Hopefully, we can get you home and settled in Boston within the next month or so. I'd like to get started again with my work by the middle of January."

"Oh," she said.

She bit her lower lip; the dry weather was starting to crack them now and she hadn't brought any protection with her this evening. She wondered what the boys were doing back at the school house. Then, it occurred to her that one of these days she was going to have to come up with a cool name for that place. Her mind began wandering through some of the fun places she'd seen while driving around the countryside. Most of those wouldn't make sense in Bellingwood. She was going to have to come up with the name of the school all on her own.

"Polly? Are you listening?" Joey was looking at her.

"Oh, I'm sorry. What did you say?"

"I asked how you liked your sandwich. For a joint like this, mine is pretty good."

"Oh. Yeah. It's fine." She looked down and saw that she had finished the quarter sandwich she had in her hand and was automatically eating fries. Wow. She'd wandered away from the entire evening.

"So, Joey. How are your parents?" she asked.

"They're fine. Mother is gearing up for the big Christmas ball. She started working on that in June, I believe. Father is planning a trip to Italy for them after the holidays. You know, he had a heart attack this summer."

"Oh, I'm sorry to hear that. How is he doing?"

"I suppose he is fine. I don't get up to the house very often, but Mother calls me once a week to remind me that I have responsibilities and to let me know what is happening in their world. She was concerned that you had moved out west. She said something about Indians and cowboys. Even I know that is nothing to worry about."

Polly smiled and nodded. "No, there aren't too many battles this side of the Mississippi anymore. We even have automobiles and electric lights now." She shook her head, then pulled out her phone. Her mind wondered if she could still outthink the jerk.

"So, I got this new Samsung phone the other day. What are you using now?" she asked.

"It's the same old thing, just updated." He pulled his phone out.

"Can I see it?" and she held out her hand. When she had her hand on the phone, she bumped his glass of wine into his lap. Keeping hold of the phone, she said, "Oh, Joey! I'm so sorry!"

"It's no problem. I'll be right back. Don't even worry about it," he said.

He left for the bathroom and she rapidly began scanning his call history. She found his mother's name and phone number as well as the phone number of the little bimbo from the library who had been helping him. She also landed on a phone number for a clinic in Cambridge and entered those all into a note in her own phone. Sending it on, she cleared back to the main screen and set the phone back near his plate.

Lydia and the others had watched the entire process take place with what seemed to be proud grins on their faces. Polly felt much better. She had people to contact who might help her handle whatever Joey had managed to plan. She felt badly that his Dad was dealing with heart issues and his mother a big soirée, but Polly's life was about to crash right into their carefully laid plans.

She winked at her friends and picked up another quarter of her sandwich. Funny how her appetite returned once she started taking control again. Then, she had one more thought. Pulling her phone back out, she switched to the voice recorder. As Joey walked out of the bathroom, she clicked it on and set it in her lap and then picked the sandwich back up and took a bite.

"I really am sorry about your pants," she apologized.

"Don't worry about it, Polly. I brought plenty of clothes. If it takes longer than a week to convince you to return to Boston, I'll find a dry cleaner. For that matter, I suppose even Des Moines should have some department stores which would take my money."

"Joey, I'm not going back to Boston."

"Oh, honey," his voice turned to velvet and it made her want to slap him. "I know that you think you are going to do something with that little school up in that strange little town, but you and I both know that you are much better off with me than by yourself."

"No, Joey," she pushed now. "I'm not better off with you and I will repeat myself one more time. I broke up with you. I left you and I left Boston. I want nothing more to do with you. I want you to get on a plane back to Boston tomorrow and leave me alone. Do you understand?"

"Polly, I have no idea why you are saying these things to me. You and I are a match made in heaven. I've told you over and over again that I waited a lifetime for you to show up and I'm not about to let you go. I will do anything to convince you to return with me. Do you want me to buy you out of your little school? I'll do that. Do you want me to find a building in Boston for you to renovate? I'll do that. But," and his voice took on a sinister tone, "you are returning to Boston with me. You are going to be my wife and you are going to be the mother of my children."

"Joey, I have no idea what makes you think any of that is true," she started.

He interrupted, "Because I say that it is true. For god's sake, Polly. I don't know why you can't get on board with this. No one has ever said no to me before and I'm not about to let it happen now. I love your spirit. It is going to be a wonderful thing in our children, but you have to get over this crazy notion that you are going to live without me. I won't have it!" He pulled his napkin out of his lap and flung it on the table.

"Look," he said loudly. "You have made me lose my appetite. This was a perfectly decent dinner and your continual insistence that you and I aren't going to be together is infuriating me. I'm tired of listening to you say these things."

"Now who's embarrassing who?" she calmly asked. "Sit and calm down, you fool."

"How do you think you can get away with talking to me like this?"

"What?" she asked flatly. "Are you planning to beat me up?"

He wilted. "Polly, I would never lay a hand on you. You know that. And those times with those guys. I was so jealous that they got to spend time with you when I didn't or that they were touching you when I wasn't. It didn't seem fair."

Polly decided to try one last push, just for the fun of it. "So, you have to be with me all the time in order for you to be normal, is that what you're saying?"

He thought about it for a moment. "Well, truthfully, Polly, that is when I feel the most normal. As long as it is only you and me and there is no one else around to take your attention, things are fine. Anything else isn't right. Don't you feel the same way about me?"

"No Joey, I don't and I have to tell you that your attitude and behavior makes me wonder if you were seeing a normal counselor. Anyone who would let you get away with believing those types of things is irresponsible."

She waved as the waitress walked past. "Could we get the ticket, please?"

"Joey, I'm going home now. I don't want you to follow me or try to see me. Ever again. You have made a couple of mistakes and if you cross the line with me, I will be glad to have you thrown in jail. Stay away and don't push me to do something that neither of us want me to do. Will you do that?"

"Sweetheart, you're not going to throw me in jail. You were the one who bailed me out the last time I was there. You stayed with me through thick and thin and I trust you completely."

"Well, that's just foolish." The waitress placed the ticket on the table and Polly grabbed it. Joey tried to take it from her and grabbed her wrist. "You want to let go of that right now, Joey," she said. When he didn't, she repeated, "Right now. Let go or things are going to get ugly in a hurry." She glanced over his shoulder and he turned around. Aaron's face was bright red with fury. "Right now," she said again. He released her wrist.

"You know," he said. "Your friends aren't always going to be close by."

"Don't try to frighten me, you idiot. You have no idea how close my friends are."

She looked at the ticket, counted out cash, found the waitress and pressed it into her hand, saying "Thank you."

Polly picked up her purse, dropped her phone in on top of everything else and strode out of the restaurant. She got into her truck, backed out of the parking place and started the drive home. It wasn't until she pulled into her parking lot that she finally breathed normally again. She looked up, saw the entire place lit up and smiled. It was good to be home.

CHAPTER SEVENTEEN

"Get up, Polly!" Her eyes opened. What? She heard it again.

"Oh, Polly! Get up!"

What in the world? She looked at the clock beside her bed. It was eight o'clock. EIGHT O'CLOCK! Henry was going to be here this morning to check out the floor and she was still in bed.

"Polly!"

"I'm up! I'm up," she shouted out the door.

"You're not really up. Get up!"

Could she live without a shower this morning? Damn. She couldn't think straight. She shook her head, trying to clear the cobwebs, then sat straight up in bed. She threw the blankets back and dropped her legs over the side of the bed and tried to think.

It was Saturday morning, she'd come home in a foul mood last night, but then had stayed up much too late with Doug and Billy's friends. They'd even talked her into baking for them. Bunch of mooches. Then, at some point, she'd left them to their noise and come upstairs. That had to have been ... right after one o'clock. She'd known it was a mistake then and now she was sure it had been a mistake. Who knew she could be so fuzzy with no alcohol in her system. Then, she smiled. It had been a great time. There were boys and girls sitting around tables in her hallway, laughing and playing games. She had no interest in what they were doing, but loved that they felt comfortable enough to spend time in her place. Doug and Billy had been great hosts and cleaned up the kitchen as they went, so she had nothing to complain about, except being late this morning.

Did Henry say what time he was coming over and why was Doug yelling at her?

"Polly! Are you getting up?"

"I'm almost up! What's going on?"

"We're taking you out to breakfast. Now hurry!"

She had to think about it again. What? Why? She ruffled her fingers through her hair and then remembered that she had showered before heading to Boone last night. She'd be fine and at least this meant she didn't have to creep across the upstairs hallway while people were up and running around. Oh, she was going to be glad when she could finally get into her own apartment.

One look around the room, confirmed it was a disaster. Oh well, that could wait until later. She grabbed a pair of jeans and slipped into a flannel shirt. She scuffed her feet into the shoes beside her bed and looked for her phone and her purse. Hmmm, she must have left them in the kitchen. At least she hoped so. She took a quick inventory and decided she was pretty much all together and walked outside her room. There was activity in the apartment across the hall, so she walked that way.

Henry and Ben were inside the door checking things out.

"You're up and moving early today," she said to them.

"Earlier than you are. Sounds like you guys had a heckuva party here last night," Henry commented.

"Really? I didn't notice," she shrugged. "So, how does the floor look to you?"

She could already see that she was going to love it. The wear of the old wood coming through the lacquer was beautiful and she could hardly wait to make this her home.

"It looks really good. I'll be glad to get the next couple of coats on it and then it should be strong enough to take just about anything you've got to give it," he replied. "Ben here is interested in doing some of this on his own, so I've enlisted him to stick close to this project."

"Cool," she said. "It looks wonderful. I'm glad we went with these boards. I can't wait to bring Brad and Lee up to see what you've done with them."

"I think they'll be happy." Henry nodded towards the steps. "Sounds like the boys have some plans for you this morning."

"I know!" she replied. "Where do you go to have breakfast in this town?"

"Probably Joe's Diner uptown. Try the chicken fried steak and eggs, you'll be glad you did. His gravy is terrific."

"Okay! Thanks. See you later!" Polly headed down the steps.

When she got to the bottom, Doug and Billy were there waiting for her.

"Come on! Let's go! We want to take you out to breakfast!" Doug said, filled with enthusiasm.

"Alright, just a minute, though. I need my phone and my purse. I think they're in the kitchen." She walked around behind the stairs and could see no sign of the gaming party from the night before. The trash cans were filled in the kitchen, but everything else had been put away.

"Guys? Did you see my purse and phone?" she called out.

"Oh yeah. We put them in the first cupboard there. On the bottom shelf." Billy called back.

Polly opened the cupboard and sure enough, there were her things. She checked her phone and saw that she had calls from an 857 area code. That had to be Joey. She was going to have to deal with this today. She couldn't take it any longer. But, for now, she was going out to breakfast.

"Are we going to Joe's Diner? Henry said it's pretty good." she said when she walked back out to see the boys.

"Yep and it's on us. We really appreciate you letting us have everyone here last night and we all loved the food and even the cookies you made. So, let's go!"

They were practically dancing to get out the door.

Henry and Ben came down the stairs at that same moment.

"Are we all out of here, then?" she asked.

"I think so." Henry replied.

When everyone was outside, she doublechecked her purse for her keys and pulled both doors shut, tugging on them to make sure they were locked.

Doug turned to Henry, "Are you guys going to breakfast? You know everyone will be there."

Henry looked at Ben, "Breakfast?"

"No, I'd better get home. Amanda told me she'd have something for me when I got there and I'd be dim-witted to not show up when she cooks."

"You're a smart man," Henry said. "Thanks for coming out this morning. We'll see you Monday."

"Thanks, man," Ben said and walked to his car.

"Do you want me to drive?" Polly asked Doug and Billy.

"Nope, we're taking you!" Doug said. She didn't say a word as she waited for him to unlock his beat up red Grand Am. "This is Bellingwood, Polly. We never lock our cars." Billy opened the door and crawled into the back seat and Polly got in the passenger seat. Doug turned the key and said, "You know ... it looks terrible on the outside, but my Dad and me? We've got this thing tuned up on the inside."

He turned the key and then revved the motor to prove to her how nice it sounded. She smiled and nodded.

Doug went on. "We're going to redo the body next summer, but until then, I'm cool with it." He patted the dash of the car and smiled with pride at Polly.

"Very nice," she said.

They only had a few blocks to go. Sure enough the parking spaces in front of and across the street from Joe's Diner were filled. They parked around the corner and walked up to the restaurant. Big glass windows had red-checked curtains drawn back. Polly looked inside and wondered if they would even be able to find a place to sit.

"Oh, don't worry," Doug said. "There's always room. Come on!"

The room seemed alive with chatter. She could smell grease from bacon and sausage, pancakes and whatever else happened back in the kitchen. Three waitresses were bustling back and forth laden with coffee pots and plates of steaming hot food. A few people looked up and nodded, but the conversations must have been important because they never stopped talking or listening to each other.

Doug spied a table right in the middle of the room where an elderly couple were getting up to leave. They walked past them on their way to the door which opened as Henry walked in.

"Henry!" Polly heard from around the room. He shook the hands of everyone at the first table, spoke for a few minutes and then moved on. It seemed like he knew everyone in the place.

Doug steered her to the table and said, "Look, do you mind if Henry eats with us? It's either that or he has to sit at the counter."

She shrugged. "No, that's fine. I don't care."

Polly sat down and Billy sat beside her with Doug taking the seat across from her.

Doug called out, "Henry! Over here!"

Henry waved and nodded, then turned back to the table of folks he was chatting with. Finally he made his way to them and sat down across from Billy, just as the waitress was setting down dripping glasses of water on the chipped, multi-flecked, greenish hued table top. She pulled four napkin wrapped place settings out of the pocket of her apron and set them down in front of each person.

"Do you need menus?" she asked.

"Polly might," Doug said. "She's never been here before."

"No," Polly said. "I think I know what I'm supposed to have."

"Well, the specials are on the board up there," and she pointed behind Polly to a large board over the window to the kitchen. "They're the same every weekend, but they're still the specials. Do you want coffee?"

"Bring us a pot, Lucy," Henry said. "We're all going to need it this morning."

"Alright, I'll be back in just a minute." She came back with a wet dishcloth and wiped the table down as each person picked up their water and silverware. "Sorry about that," and pocketed the change that had been left as a tip. A few moments later, she was back with cups and a thermos pot filled with coffee. "Let me know when you need a refill. Now, what do you want to eat this morning?"

She winked at Henry, "Do you want your regular, Henry?"

"Absolutely. And if Polly has what I told her to have, she'll do the same."

"Polly? From the school, Polly? I've been hearing about you," she scratched some more on the ticket she held in her hand.

"What have you heard? I hope nothing bad." Polly said, then remembered. "If Henry is having the chicken fried steak, I want that and I want my eggs over medium, is that alright?"

"Sure honey, what kind of toast? We have wheat, sourdough, white, or an English muffin, but that's 25 cents extra."

"Oh, wheat is fine."

"Boys? What are you having?" Lucy asked.

Doug said, "I'm having the Sunrise Special, sausage patties, hash browns, over easy and white toast."

Billy looked up and when she nodded at him, he said, "I want the Farmer's Omelet with hash browns and white toast, please."

Lucy said to Polly. "I hear you've had some wild things happening over there at that school. Who would believe you had dead bodies in the bathroom upstairs."

"I know!" Polly replied. "Let's just say it's been a busy week or two. I'll be glad when it all settles down."

"I'll get these orders in," Lucy said and walked to the kitchen.

The man at the table next to theirs who was next to Billy said, "Hey Henry. Is this the Polly you're working for right now?"

"It sure is - and I think you know Doug Randall and Billy Endicott here, don't you, Nate?"

"Sure do," he replied and then said, "So what's up with all the rumors going around about that old school? First you find bones of those poor little Stevens' girls and then you uncover a treasure trove of stolen stuff from before the school got shut up?"

Henry laughed. "Yeah, I think that Polly got more than she bargained for with that purchase." She smiled and let them chatter. Soon a few more chairs had gathered around and then the table on her side was also involved in the conversation. Everyone wanted to know what they were finding in the crates and who they thought was the thief.

Polly stayed pretty quiet. It didn't seem like any of the conversation was directed at her, though it seemed to be about her. Doug and Billy were lapping up the attention, telling about the scratched lock and why they were staying at the school.

There were many observations regarding who the thief might be, but the general consensus was that it had to be old Doug Leon. Everyone agreed he was weird and since his retirement, he had gotten stranger. He walked around town with a beat up old wagon, picking up bottles and cans, turning them in for the five cent bottle refund. Most people admitted that they left bottles out on the street, knowing he'd pick them up. They were just trying to help the old guy out. He wore a big overcoat, except in the heat of summer when he wore his always dirty overalls. He didn't talk to many people and if they tried to engage him in conversation, he would grunt and walk past them.

Lucy came over with their food and announced that the old man came into the diner every Wednesday at ten thirty after the place cleared out from morning coffee time. He always ordered the same thing: two slices of bacon, extra crispy, one egg over hard on a piece of white toast. She said Joe worried he wasn't getting enough food, so he always put something extra on the plate, but Mr. Leon paid with a five dollar bill each week and told her the extra was her tip. He'd done that every week since she could remember.

From there the conversation turned to the deaths of Kellie and Jill Stevens. Polly could tell that many of the people sitting around talking were about the same age and some had gone to school with the girls.

From the booth behind Doug, she heard, "I always thought it was that boyfriend of hers, what was his name, Buddy something."

"Buddy Landers," said someone else.

"But, they didn't have enough to pin anything on him. He stuck around and everyone thought the girls had left town. He looked so sad that his girlfriend had left him. Everyone felt terrible for him."

"What if he killed them, though? He would have looked sad about that, especially if he felt guilty. Why didn't they push him any harder on it?"

"I heard he had a good alibi for the night they went missing."

"Her parents never accused him of doing anything wrong. They always said he was a good boy and had been nice to both of the girls."

"I heard someone say that Jill didn't like him very much," Polly interjected quietly.

"You're right!" said a woman sitting at one of the other tables. "But we never knew whether she was jealous because Kellie was dating someone or if she really didn't like him. And then when they went missing, no one thought about that anymore. The two girls kind of became a single unit."

"Do you remember all the talk about white slavery?" someone asked.

"Yeah, we were all supposed to keep an eye out for the girls in town because if the slavers came in and took Kellie and Jill, they might come back and take anyone. We all knew those girls were probably in some country far away in a harem or something having to put up with unspeakable things. It was hell on their family."

Aaron Merritt entered the diner and everyone turned to look at him.

"Well, Polly," he said. "It looks like you've gathered a conclave!" He laughed and moved through the people to set his hand on her shoulder.

"I didn't do it!" she protested. "It was Henry. He's the one that knows everyone here."

"So, Sheriff," one of the men asked, "Is the thief and the murderer the same person?"

"We don't know anything yet, Jake. We're still working out all the details. You know we'll tell you what we can when we can."

"Lucy?" he called over the sea of people.

She made her way through the cluster of people and handed him a full cup of coffee. "Your regular, Sheriff?"

"Sure," he said, "Why not."

He gestured to one of the men who passed a chair over the heads of a few people to him. Grabbing the chair, he set it down between Doug and Polly. "Do you guys mind if I join you?" He laughed, then looked around the room, "So have you all got it figured out yet?"

"We're pretty sure you need to talk to old Doug Leon about those crates," one of the men said. "He had keys to everything and was always there before anyone else and stayed after everyone left. He was the one who spent most of the time in the basement messing with those boilers."

"You're right," Aaron said, "We are planning to talk to him. We just haven't been able to track him down."

"Lucy?" he called out. "Was Doug Leon in this week for breakfast?"

"He sure was, Sheriff," she said as she brought another pot of coffee to their table. Polly watched her weave through the people like a pro. She seemed to notice how they were moving and slipped in and out of the open spaces until she got to their table. That was impressive.

"Well, he's still in town, then." Aaron said. "I suppose it is probably time to get a little more forceful at his front door. I had kind of hoped he would come out and talk to us. Oh well," he shrugged. "It will all come together when it does."

He turned to Polly. "Is this your first time here?" She nodded, with her mouth full. "How do you like the food?"

Polly smiled at him and swallowed. "It's terrific. Even better than that pork tenderloin I ate last night."

"I've been meaning to talk to you about that, Polly. Can you come over for supper tonight? Lydia asked me to grill steaks."

"Okay." Polly said and glanced up to see that Henry was watching their conversation intently. "Sure, steaks sound great. What time?"

"Why don't you make it around 6:30. Can you get to our house on your own?"

"I think so. If I get lost in this big town, I'll just call."

The conversation had resumed around them and people moved their chairs back a bit to allow them to eat. It didn't take long, though before another question arose.

"What's going to happen to old Mr. Leon if he did steal all that stuff?" someone asked.

"I don't know for sure, Dan. I guess that's for the lawyers to decide. My job is simply to figure who did it and prove it so the suits can deal with it. A lot of it depends on whether he stopped taking things after the school closed down or whether he's still up to his old tricks." Aaron stopped. "We haven't got any idea if he's the one who stole that stuff, so let's not gossip, okay?"

Polly laughed. It seemed like this place was rife with gossip, and while none of it was terribly spiteful, it also seemed like it was a grand place to get in on all of the news from around the community. She remembered her Dad talking about a local coffee shop. He went there every Saturday morning while Mary took her to piano lessons. Huh. She'd forgotten all about that. But now, here she was stuck in the middle of a Saturday morning session at a diner. My goodness she loved being in Iowa.

Lucy brought four checks to their table and passed them out. Just as she handed Polly's to her, Doug snatched it and said "We've got this, remember?"

Aaron looked at him and laughed, "Are you trying to date Polly, Doug? You see her panties once and now you're trying to do something about it?"

Doug's eyes got huge and his entire body seemed to stop in mid-motion. "Absolutely not, sir! I mean, not that you wouldn't be a great girl to date, but, but …" He slumped and looked at Henry. "Help me," he pleaded.

Henry shook his head and said, "I didn't see her panties. You're in this alone!"

Doug turned back to Aaron. "No sir. Billy and I are treating Polly to breakfast. She let our friends come over last night and play video games and she fed everyone. We're only saying thank you."

Aaron patted him on the back. "That's nice, boys."

Polly creased her forehead in thought. "Aaron, tonight's Halloween. I was going to watch for any trick-or-treaters. Darn. I didn't want them to come to the school for the first time in years and not find anyone."

Aaron asked Doug, "Would you guys mind tending the home front tonight or were you planning to go out?"

"Well, we had kind of thought we'd head down to Boone to see a movie, but it's no big deal," Billy interjected.

Polly put her hands on the table, "Guys, I'm sorry to be taking up so much of your lives right now." She glanced at Aaron, "I wish I didn't have to make you guys stay with me."

Aaron stopped her, "As long as you are staying in that building, with all that's going on around you right now, you're keeping them. Got it?"

The boys grinned when Polly said, "Okay. Got it. A girl can't get a break around here.

"Well, guys. You get to choose whatever you want to do tonight. I'll pay for it. If you want to rent movies and order pizza, that's cool. If you want to have Davey's bring you food, I'll pay for it. Whatever you want."

"We'll figure something out, Polly. Don't worry about it," Doug assured her.

She laughed. "I'm not sure what I'd do without you. You're kind of my own Luke and Han."

"Star Wars! That's what we should do tonight. We should do all six of the movies! Billy, you have those at home, don't you?"

"Yes! I do! And remember those robes our moms made us wear for the church pageant? We should totally dress up like Obi-Wan and Luke. We can paint some light sabers this afternoon! So cool!"

"We're on it, Polly."

Aaron sat back and said, "Handled. We'll see you at 6:30."

CHAPTER EIGHTEEN

Henry, Doug, Billy and Polly waited while Aaron finished his breakfast, then when he got up to wander around and chat with other patrons, they left the diner.

Before getting to Doug’s car, Henry took Polly's arm and pulled her aside. "What happened last night, Polly?"

"Henry." her voice took on a warning tone. "I'm fine. Nothing happened. Joey and I had a conversation that didn't go well and Aaron and the Musketeers were there to watch it happen. Now, don't do this again."

He released her and said, "Fine. But, would you tell me if there was something I needed to worry about?"

Polly looked up at him in confusion. "I'm not sure what to say to you. You've gotten protective of me and it doesn't make any sense. I know we work together and I know we're friends, but Henry, this is too much. Just let me work this out, alright?"

He put his hands up in surrender. "I guess I'm a worrier. But, do you not understand there are people here who care about you now?"

"Oh, I understand perfectly. I'm not used to it and I really am trying, but some of these things I have to work out on my own."

"I don't think you're going to be able to do this alone, Polly. As I understand it, this guy is stalking you and he came here even after you made an attempt to hide your location from him."

"Wow. You have all the details, don't you?" she sneered.

"It's a small town, Polly," Henry said patiently. "There are no secrets around here. And if I hear something about someone I like, then I'm going to pay attention. Did he follow you out here after tracking you down?"

"Yes, Henry, he did. There's a stupid little girl back in Boston that is going to get her head taken off her shoulders if I have anything to say about it."

"Well, keep yourself safe. This isn't going to go away easily."

Then, he glanced over at Doug and Billy standing in front of the hardware store, peering in the window trying not to look obvious about waiting. "Your knights await you. Have a good rest of the weekend and I'll see you Monday morning."

"Thanks Henry," Polly said. "You, too."

"Alright boys, are we heading back to the barn?" she asked as she approached them and slipped her hands into their arms. They got in the car and Doug said, "Did you have something else you wanted to do this morning? Because we've got time. Mr. Allen said we didn't have any work this weekend, so we're free as birds!"

"Well," she drew the word out, "What about driving me around town and showing me the sights?"

"Sure!" Doug replied. "Do you mind if we stop by my house to pick up our costumes?"

"That would be wonderful. I'll get a chance to meet your mom again."

Doug's house was a little two story home with an immaculate front lawn. There were flower beds surrounding and a big tree in the front yard. "Mom loves her gardens. Next summer you should come see the back yard. Dad doesn't complain because it cuts down on what we have to mow. I complain because she makes us weed it with her. She plants flowers out here and then the whole back yard is filled with vegetables. Then, she starts canning in late summer and doesn't stop until all the apples have fallen out of the tree and the pumpkins are all gone.

He got out of the car and ran up the front steps, opening the door and yelling, "Mom! Mom! Polly and Billy are here with me. I need those robes. We're going to be Jedi Knights!"

The short, little lady from Lydia's party came up from the basement. "Stop your yelling, Doug. This house isn't big enough for that mouth. I can hear you."

"Hi, Polly!," she said. “So, my boy isn't making you terribly crazy staying all these nights with you?"

"Oh, I love having him there," Polly assured her. “He and Billy clean up after themselves and are great fun to have around."

"It's been awfully quiet with him gone," Helen lamented. “Just me, Frank, Sue and Junior."

Polly looked sideways at Doug. "Junior? You only told me about your sister."

He started laughing. "Oh, Junior is the dog. Mom named him Frank after Frank Sinatra. The dog howls all the time. Dad wasn't too fond of the dog having his name, too, so she started calling him Frank Junior and then it just became Junior."

"I guess that makes perfect sense, then!" Polly smiled at Helen Randall. "Well, I do appreciate him and it seems to keep everyone from worrying too much about me being there by myself."

"I knew someday he'd move all the way out, so maybe this is good training for us." Helen Randall looked up at her son, "So, what was it you were screeching about when you came in the front door?"

"Polly has to go over to the Merritt's tonight and we're going to be Jedi Knights and take care of her trick-or-treaters. Do you have those robes we had to wear for the church pageant?" He turned to Polly. "We were shepherds. We were the best shepherds ever," then rolled his eyes.

"Everything is downstairs in the storage room. You should be able to find the tub marked costumes. There will probably be some ties in there as well."

Doug and Billy took off at a dead run down the steps.

"Someday he'll quit moving so fast, but I have no idea when that will happen," she said and gestured to the sofa. "Come on in and sit down. Can I get you something to drink?"

"No, thank you. We just came from the diner. Doug and Billy took me out to breakfast to say thanks for letting them have game night at the school last night. They're such good kids."

"They are good kids. We worried some when they were in high school, but whatever strange phases they were in always went away," she said. Jerry Allen is good to them and they enjoy working for him. That's really helped."

Doug and Billy came back up the stairs. "We found them. Thanks mom."

"Did you put everything back the way you found it?" she asked.

"Of course I did. You'd have my hide otherwise, wouldn't you?" He laughed and bent over to kiss his mother on the forehead, then said, "Are you ready to go, Polly? We've got things to do!"

Polly smiled at Helen, "I guess we've got things to do! I'll see you later."

They left the house and spent the next half hour driving around Bellingwood, while Billy and Doug pointed out things that had been important to them when they were younger. She saw the ball fields and drove past the cemetery. They drove around the elementary school and past a few homes that had belonged to teachers the boys had enjoyed. They told her stories about climbing the water tower and spray painting it. Then having to climb back up and clean it.

When they got back to the school, Doug asked if it would be alright if they took off for a while.

"Sure," said Polly. "I think I'll be safe in my own place for a little while."

"We're going over to Henry's to see if he'll make us some wooden light sabers. Then we're going to get fluorescent spray paint for the blades and black paint for the handles. These are going to be epic!" he declared.

She unlocked the front door as they roared out of the parking lot. She leaned against it and surveyed her surroundings. Even with everything happening around her, this was a pretty nice little place to live. She shut and locked the door, then went upstairs. All of a sudden weariness took over. The boys would be gone for a while and she had time for a nap. That would be perfect.

Polly walked into her room, kicked off her shoes and plopped down on top of the bedding. She looked at the clock. 1:30. Yep. Perfect. The next time she looked at the clock it was 3:15 and there was laughter and clattering coming from downstairs. She went to the midpoint of the stairs and looked over into the hallway.

Billy and Doug were waving their arms in an apparent fake light saber battle. They were both wearing brown robes with ties pulled around their waists. Two freshly painted light sabers were drying on newsprint off to the side. They actually looked pretty good. The fluorescent paint made them shimmer in the light. She shook her head.

"Nice looking weaponry there, boys."

They stopped dancing around each other and looked up. "I know! Henry did a great job once we told him what we wanted. We had to run to Boone to get the paint, and there might be some sprayed on your grass outside. I hope that's alright," Billy said.

"Sure. That's great. They do look awesome. I'm going to take a shower and then I'll be down. Are you guys hungry yet?"

"We ate at Taco Johns in Boone. We're good," Doug replied.

"Alright. I'll be down in a while."

Polly took a shower and put on some fresh jeans and a nice blouse. She pulled her hair back into a braid, then checked her phone. There were no more calls. Then, she grabbed her laptop and headed down the steps. The guys were back at it, perfecting their moves, she supposed. They followed her into the kitchen.

"Thanks for letting us do this," Billy said. "We'll be the talk of the town once people see our awesome costumes. That was a great idea!"

"Here is all of the candy I've got," and she opened the cupboard. There were several bags of various types of candy. "Use whatever you want and when you run out, then I guess you run out."

"We don't have that many kids in town," Billy said. "I think we'll be fine."

"Then, eat whatever you want to eat." She opened the freezer and pulled a shepherd's pie casserole out, then set it inside the oven to begin defrosting and the boys wandered back out into the hallway.

She walked over to the table and sat down, opening her laptop. There was an email from her friend Drea. It had been sent Thursday night.

"Polly, I just heard Joey is looking for you. Girl, I think he's gone off the deep end. You know that little twit at the library? She found MY number and called me because she knew we were friends. She told me that he had her doing some research and it was all about you. She was checking public records in Boone County, Iowa for the building you bought.

Let me know that you're okay and he hasn't gotten to you. I'll send my brothers out there if I have to! Take care of yourself."

Polly replied:

"Don't worry about your brothers, I've got a lot of people out here who think they are responsible for the care and keeping of my skin. But, thank you.

"I'm going to get hold of my old supervisor and get that little twit fired, though. How dare she use her job at the library to help someone stalk me. It wasn't enough that she broke into the supervisor's office and searched my file to get my old phone number, but now this?

"He is here in Iowa. We kind of had it out last night, but I managed to record some of his rantings and one of my friends here is the Sheriff, so tell your brothers not to worry too much. This time the law is in my pocket.

"Love you! I'll call you next week sometime. Polly."

She checked the rest of her email and there was nothing else needing her attention, so she wandered around the internet for a while. Her stomach rumbled, so she got up to make some toast. She buttered her toast, shook some cinnamon sugar on it, pulled a Diet Dew from the bottom shelf of the cooler and sat back down. One other item in her email was the one she sent to herself last night with the phone numbers from Joey's phone. The first number was his mother's cell phone. Without giving it any extra thought, she dialed the number and was surprised to hear the woman's voice answer the call.

"Hello?"

"Mrs. Delancy? This is Polly Giller."

"Yes, dear. What can I do for you today?"

"Mrs. Delancy, did you know I've moved to Iowa?"

"I heard that, dear. I didn't know why, though. Is everything alright?"

"Mrs. Delancy, one of the reasons I moved to Iowa was to get away from your son. Did you know he was obsessed with me?"

"Oh, Polly dear," Polly could hear the disgust in the woman's voice. "I'm sure that isn't true. I know he went through something with you last spring, but he is certainly over that by now. He has many other things in his life to occupy his time. So many important things."

"Alright, so you didn't know. Well, Mrs. Delancy, your son is in Iowa trying to get me to come back to Boston."

"That's a great idea, Polly. You had a terrific job here in Boston and great friends and you were a good companion to Joseph. His father and I like you very much."

Polly put her head in her hands. This woman was as delusional as her son.

"Mrs. Delancy. Your son is threatening me and I might need your assistance. I do not want to return to Boston. I want to stay here and I want him to go away and leave me alone."

"I'm not sure why you are telling me this. You should be talking to him about it. For goodness' sake, Joseph is an adult now. I don't have any influence over him. If you don't want him around, why don't you say that to him?"

"I said that to him many times last spring and he wouldn't leave me alone. He assaulted a patron of the library and when I broke up with him, he refused to acknowledge that it was real. He asked a girl in my library to find out where I lived so he could come out here and drag me back to Boston. He didn't ask if he could come, he didn't even bother to tell me he was coming. He just showed up and now is telling me that he waited his entire life for me and I'm going to be the mother of his children."

"Polly. You'd make a great mother to our grandchildren. You're a very bright and pretty girl. We enjoy having you at the various functions you have attended with him."

"You're not listening to me. Your son is nuts. He's going to do something bad and get himself into terrible trouble. Are you paying any attention to me at all?"

"Dear, I'm sure you think you know what is going on and I'm also sure you are wrong. Joseph may have some anger issues, but he has assured me those are all behind him. He'd be a great catch for you. You might not want to let him come back here without you. He could change your life."

"Mrs. Delancy, I don't even know what to say to you at this point."

"Well, I'm not certain why you thought this call was necessary if you aren't interested in my son. I don't care to have anything more to do with you. So, thank you for calling. Good-bye."

After Mrs. Delancy abruptly ended the call, Polly sat at the table completely stunned by the conversation. She couldn't imagine anyone being more delusional than Joey, but his mother seemed like she was off the deep end. How was she able to maintain all of the activities she did as a volunteer?

That phone call was useless, to say the least.

She plugged her phone into the computer and dropped the audio file from last night into her cloud drive so it would show up in several places if necessary, then spent some more time wandering aimlessly around the internet. Finally she turned the computer off and flipped the lid closed. She stowed it in the cupboard next to the candy and pulled out a couple of large bowls, filling them with candy and setting them out on the counter. Polly pulled the casserole out of the oven and checked it. Practically defrosted. It would be perfect for the boys' supper tonight.

"Doug? Billy?" she called into the hallway.

The guys came in wielding their light sabers. "Aren't these cool?" Doug asked.

She smiled. "Those are way cool. The force is definitely with you." Then she pointed at the oven and said, "I've got a Shepherd's Pie casserole in here. I’ve set the timer, so take it out and eat the whole thing if you want. Okay?"

"Okay." Doug walked over and watched her set the timer, then pulled his phone out and set his alarm for the same time. "Just to make sure we hear it. Thanks."

With them set for the night, Polly left and went to Lydia and Aaron's house. When she pulled in the driveway, Aaron was outside with a plate of steaks sitting beside the grill.

"How do you like your steak, Polly?" he asked, brandishing a large grill fork.

"I think I've spent way too much time out east, Aaron. Medium-rare to rare is perfect. Not quite bloody in the middle, but close."

He shuddered. "Alright, yours goes on last. Way last. Lydia is upstairs getting things ready for dinner. I'll be up in a bit."

Polly went inside and up the stairs. Funny how this house was beginning to feel so familiar. Lydia met her at the top of the steps; hands filled with vegetables.

"I'd hug you, but I might crush tomatoes down your back and that would look like a bloodbath. Not something we want the neighbors to see," she laughed.

"Can I help?" Polly asked.

"Sure. Here, I was going to chop these up for the salad. It's all ready to go." Polly began chopping things up into bite-sized pieces and tossing them into the salad bowl while Lydia continued putting things out on the table.

"It's a simple meal tonight. Aaron doesn't grill steak that often and when he does, I take the evening off from heavy cooking. I've got baked potatoes and a broccoli dish in the oven. Will that be enough for you?"

"That will be wonderful, Lydia. Thank you," Polly assured her.

They got the table set and when Aaron brought the steaks up, Lydia pulled the dishes out of the oven and placed them on the table.

It didn't take long for conversation to turn to the events of the night before. Lydia took great joy in telling Polly how Joey had sat there in obvious shock for a few minutes after she strode out. Soon he picked up his phone, put it in his pocket and looked around, then left.

"What did you get from his phone, Polly?" Lydia asked.

"Oh, I got his mother's phone number and maybe a counselor's number, too.

She went on, "So, I called his mother today to see if she would be any help. Guys, I think she is as delusional as Joey. She told me I needed to tell him I didn't want to be with him, as if I haven't been doing that over and over. Then, she told me I would be a welcome addition to her family. I don't think she heard a single word I was saying. And if she heard the words, she certainly didn't understand them."

"I'm sorry, Polly," Lydia said. "You're going to figure this out and you know we'll do whatever we can to help you."

"I know. I want to drop him off a bridge somewhere and stop all of this. Last night he sounded insane when he was talking to me. I got some of it recorded on my phone. Before I came over here, I put it on my computer too. Just in case I ever need it. At this point, I don't know how I'm going to get him out of my life." Polly sighed and dropped her hands in her lap.

Then her phone rang. She looked at it and saw that it was Billy. When she answered it, she heard his panicked voice. "Polly, you've got to get over here and bring the Sheriff. Some guy, it was probably your boyfriend, beat the hell out of Doug. He's lying on the gravel and I'm worried about him."

Aaron's phone rang at that moment and he picked it up, listened, then looked at Polly.

"Billy, is he still there?" she asked.

"No, he's gone. I hit him with the light saber and a car drove by and he got in his car and left. I called 9-1-1 and they're sending someone. Get here quick!"

She jumped out of her chair and Aaron was right behind her.

"I think Joey beat Doug up at the school," she said to Lydia. "He's gone now, but I have to go make sure they're okay. Aaron? Are you coming?"

"I'm right behind you," he said. "and if you don't hurry, I'll be right in front of you."

The two of them ran down the stairs and out the back door to their cars.

CHAPTER NINETEEN

Tearing through the streets of Bellingwood seemed overly reckless, so Polly let Aaron lead the way. After throwing the truck into Park, she jumped out and ran to Doug, the siren of the ambulance coming down the highway, its mournful wail echoing her concern.

"Doug!" she cried. "I'm so sorry! Billy, how are you doing?"

Doug looked a little chagrined. Billy had wadded up his brown robe and put it under Doug's head, and thrown the blanket from the back of his car over him. He was wiping blood off Doug's face.

"Billy isn't going to let me get up until the EMTs get here," Doug said. "I told him I would be fine. It's just that my head really hurts."

Aaron knelt down beside him. "They're nearly here. You've been beaten up pretty badly. This wasn't what I meant to have happen, boys."

Polly gave a weak giggle, "Yeah. Way to take one for the team!"

Aaron asked, "Can you tell me what happened?"

Both boys started to talk and Polly put her hand on Doug's shoulder. He stopped talking and waited.

Billy started back up again. "Well, we were in the hallway messing with our light sabers, acting all Jedi and stuff. There were a few trick-or-treaters. They thought we were cool. We handed out a lot of candy.

"Then we heard another knock on the door and when we opened it there was a guy standing there. He took one look at us and started yelling for Polly. He accused us of doing bad things with her. Both Doug and me, we were pretty upset at that and told him there was no way we would ever do anything that nasty with Polly.

He stopped and said, "Not because you aren't pretty or anything, Polly."

"It's okay, Billy. Go on."

"He pushed past us into the school and went upstairs, screaming your name and flinging doors open. We thought he was going to open up the bathroom where the crime scene tape was and we told him he couldn't do that. That made him even madder. He ran into your room and I'm sorry, Polly, he started tossing your stuff around. Doug told him to stop it and get out, that he was going to call the Sheriff.

"Well, that made him even more mad and he rushed Doug and smacked him in the face. Doug fell down and I realized I still had my light saber, so I hit him in the head.

"Dude, that didn't even phase him! He went back downstairs and I helped Doug stand up. We followed him and he was in the kitchen, throwing things and pulling stuff out of the cupboards. Screaming about how you were his and he wasn't going to let you live in some stupid little town and you deserved better than this. On and on.

"Then, he saw us standing there and it was like he took crazy to a new level. He came running at us and before we could get our wits, he pushed Doug to the ground and started beating on him. When I went after him with the light saber, he grabbed Doug and started running and dragging him. He pulled him outside, then down the steps and onto the gravel. Finally I caught up with him and wailed on him with my trusty saber here a couple of times.

"A car pulled out of the entrance down the road and he saw the lights and something must have clicked, because he dropped Doug, ran to his car and drove off."

An ambulance, a fire truck and another sheriff's car pulled into the lot.

Two EMTs got out and rushed over to where Doug was on the ground. They took his vital signs, then began checking him over for breaks. The poor kid moaned a couple of times as one ran her hands over his arms. She looked up, "I don't think anything is broken here, but he's been beaten badly and has some nasty cuts and scrapes from being dragged across the gravel. We're going to take him in, get him cleaned up and x-rayed."

Billy looked down at his friend, "Dude. You're getting to ride in the ambulance. They can go really fast, you know."

"Uh huh. This is so cool," Doug's cynical look dampened Billy's enthusiasm.

"No worries," Billy said. "I'll go tell your parents and see if they want a ride to the hospital. I got this."

Aaron stopped Billy, "Son, you go on home. I'll go talk to the Randalls and we'll make sure they get to Doug tonight."

"But?"

"Dude," Doug said. "I'm fine. You did great. You're my best friend and you had my back. Take my car to your house and come down to Boone tomorrow when I'm all cleaned up and in a pretty hospital gown. You can laugh at me and help me hit on the nurses."

Doug turned his eyes up to the EMT. "My keys are in my pocket. Are you going to let me get them or do you want to go after them."

"Which pocket?" she asked.

"The right front pocket of my jeans."

She reached in, pulled them out and handed them up to Billy.

"See what I mean, Dude? I got girls already checking me out. Tomorrow will be great."

Polly caught the EMT rolling her eyes. She had to be Polly's age and stood up to confer with her partner. They got Doug onto the gurney and into the ambulance. Aaron spoke with the officer who had accompanied the team, then turned to Polly.

"Polly, can you tell me what hotel your friend was staying at in

Boone?" he asked.

"It was the one out on the highway. I don't remember the name."

"That's fine, it's the only one down in that area. You don't know what kind of car he was driving, do you?"

"I'm sorry, Aaron. I don't. I don't think I ever saw it."

Billy piped up. "He was driving a maroon Taurus. Probably this year's model. I didn't see the number, but it was a Polk County plate."

Polly interjected, "He rented it in Des Moines at the airport."

"Alright, thanks guys." Aaron said, "That's helpful."

Billy asked Polly, "You aren't going to stay here alone tonight are you? I could call some of the other guys and I guess we could come hang out."

Aaron Merritt stepped back into the conversation. "No Billy, she's coming home with me. She can stay at our house tonight."

"Oh, whew," he said. "I wasn't going to sleep at all if you were here alone with that psycho on the loose."

"Because I'm only thirty-two years old and have lived on my own for the last fourteen years. Good heavens." Polly sniped.

"Quit muttering and go in and pack a bag." Aaron said to her. "You know you'd never sleep anyway if you were here all by yourself, so you might as well come let Lydia take care of you."

"I'll mutter all I want. You people seem to think I'm incapable of taking care of myself," she huffed.

Billy said, "I'm leaving now. If she gets up another head of steam, I want to be behind my own four walls."

The sheriff laughed at him, "Thanks, Billy. We'll get Doug set for the night. If all he had were some bad scrapes and cuts, he'll be home tomorrow sometime, I'm sure. So, call his parents before you head down to see him, alright?"

"Sure, Sheriff. Goodnight."

Polly waved at Billy as he drove away and went inside and up the stairs. Her room was completely ransacked. Bedding had been stripped off and tossed around, things were pulled out of her bags and the laundry baskets. Her box of books was turned upside down and books were scattered across the floor. She didn't even want to look at the kitchen, so figured she would save all of it until tomorrow and deal with it in the light of day. She scrounged around and came up with some clothes and gathered her travel kit, jammed them in the bag and zipped it shut and then turned all the lights off upstairs and went back down to find the sheriff waiting for her.

"I've turned everything off down here and checked the doors," he said. "You're going to want some help in that kitchen. He might have gone a little crazy."

"That's what I figured. I'll check it out tomorrow and figure out what has to happen." She sighed, "Alright. I guess I'm ready to go back to your place. This is kind of getting to be a habit."

"I've already called Lydia and she knows what's going on. I'll follow you to our house and make sure you get inside safely, then go over to the Randalls and let them know what has happened. I'll be home in a bit."

He watched her get in her truck and followed as she pulled out onto the highway, then followed her to his own house. Once she was safely down the driveway, he headed off to deal with Doug's family.

Lydia was waiting for her at the back door. "Aaron said you were driving in. I'm so sorry, Polly."

"You know, Lydia," Polly said as she walked into their basement, "I'm getting tired of things happening around me. I can't fix anything or make it right. All I can do is stand by while everyone else has to clean up my stuff. I didn't ask for any of this, but the splatter keeps making me hide."

"I know, dear." Lydia put her arm around Polly's shoulder. "Sometimes life stinks. You're in that 'just stinks' phase right now. It will get better one of these days. I promise."

She flipped the locks closed on the door behind her and they walked upstairs and ended up in the kitchen again.

"It seems like I was here only a few minutes ago," Polly said.

"Well, it wasn't that long ago, but I put your plate in the oven. Aaron's is in there as well. Are you hungry or is your stomach too upset to eat?"

"I don't want anything right now. Thanks, Lydia." Polly cursed. "I feel so bad for that kid. And his parents are going to be so upset. This is all my fault. How in the world could I have let this happen? Helen Randall trusted me with her son. All he did was take a job installing electricity."

"Stop it, you silly girl. This isn't your fault. You didn't invite that boy to come to Iowa. You didn't raise him up to be a crazy person. You didn't put those bodies in the ceiling of the bathroom and you didn't collect all that junk into crates. There is no way anyone will believe it's all your fault, so stop with the pity party."

"Wow!" Polly blinked her eyes at Lydia. "You don't let much wallowing happen around here, do you?"

"Not if it's useless," Lydia chuckled. "My kids didn't get to take opportunities for it and I'm not going to let a 32 year old woman do it either. Especially when it's only purpose is to make you feel badly about yourself.

"It occurs to me that if you really don't want any supper, we might need to shock your stomach into realizing things are going to be okay." Lydia pulled the lid off a container filled with pumpkin bars. "Would you like some milk with this?"

It was too much. Polly threw her head back and laughed. "Wow. There will be no wallowing around here, will there."

"Not as long as my oven works and I can get to my recipes. You know, my grandmother always cooked and baked when stress was happening around her." Lydia paused. "Actually, my grandmother cooked and baked when there was happiness and joy around her too. I guess she taught me that families and love and kitchens and good food all kind of blend together. So, milk?"

"Sure. That sounds great."

Aaron walked into the kitchen and saw what was happening at his table. "Oh, you pulled out the big guns, didn't you Lydia?"

"What do you mean? I only baked something with cinnamon in it so the house smelled good."

"Yeah. I recognize this. It's the big guns. Did you save my dinner?"

"Of course I did. I haven't been married to you this long without knowing what to do. Polly, are you sure you don't want dinner?"

"My stomach is fully on board now," Polly said. "Dinner would be awesome."

"I knew it would work. I didn't raise five kids without learning a few tricks." Lydia put their plates in front of them and pulled the salad out of the refrigerator and then took the broccoli and potatoes out of the oven.

They sat down and Aaron looked around the table. "Tonight, I'm grateful that everyone is alright. May the good Lord keep us and save us."

"Amen," Lydia responded.

After eating a few bites, Polly said, "Aaron, I don't know how we're going to stop Joey. His mother isn't willing to deal with him. I haven't called his counselor, but probably couldn't get through until Monday anyway. I can't believe there is no one else in Boston who sees what I see in him."

"I'm sorry to hear that, Polly. I guess I was hoping there might be some help there," Aaron responded.

"Well, if it's help you're wanting," she said. "there is a family of Italian boys who are ready to take care of him. But, maybe that's not what you're talking about."

"No, not yet anyway. We've got people out searching for him for him tonight. It's like he dropped off the face of the earth and that makes me nervous. He checked out of his hotel this afternoon and when we called the rental agency, they said he had rented the car for two weeks. They have no idea where he is. It's not like they ask for an itinerary. We've alerted the surrounding departments to keep an eye out for the vehicle, but who knows which way he might have gone. He had a bit of a head start on us before we got the information.

"I know you don't want to think about this, Polly, but I'd like you to spend nights here with us until we know what he's doing."

"Do I have a choice?" she asked.

"I suppose you do, but I'd like you to make this one." Lydia took his hand at the table in support. Polly recognized it was a losing battle against the two of them.

"Alright," she acquiesced. "Until we know where he is, I'll spend nights here. But, I am going to work there during the day."

"That sounds fair." Aaron replied.

He went on, "Oh, I stopped by Doug Leon's place today. He wasn't answering his door and I don't have a good reason to break in yet. I talked to his landlord and it seems like we might have a hoarder on our hands. Old Doug won't let anyone into his apartment, and neighbors have started complaining about bugs and stuff. I'll wait until Monday to open it up, but I want to try one more time tomorrow to see if I can talk to him."

"Is there anything the law is going to do to him or anything they can do for him?" Lydia asked.

"Well, the thefts of the stuff in the school are long past the statute of limitations unless you five come up with something that got stored there in the last three years. Honestly, though, I suspect he's not so much a thief as he is someone who sees something, picks it up and stows it away. It wasn't so bad when he was busy all the time working at the school, but the older he's gotten, I'm going to bet that wagon he totes around has more in it than pop bottles.

"The landlord says he never misses his rent and pays his bills on time. There's no reason to arrest him or anything, so I have to be careful. But, if he needs our help, I want to make sure he gets it."

Lydia looked sad, "That would be too bad. And I suppose it does make sense when you look at it that way. Even if he was taking things out of kids' lockers, he probably thought he was getting them all together in the right place. He spent a lot of time down there in the basement and maybe having all those things around him made him feel like he was part of the kids' lives.

"He didn't have a family or anything, did he?" Polly asked.

"No. Even when I knew him in the seventies, he was a lonely old man. He'd stand by himself at all of the basketball and football games, leaning on his broom. Other custodians came and went through the years, but he stuck around, doing his job and keeping an eye on the place.

"Andy and Sylvie probably remember better than I do, but when they closed that building, he was pretty upset. He looked like he lost the only family he'd ever had. And the worst thing is, if he lost all the memories he'd collected about that family, it had to even be harder on him.

"He seemed to do alright for a few years. I think he worked at the elementary school for a while, so the school could make sure he had some money coming in.

"You know, Aaron. You might want to talk to the principal over there to make sure they don't have something like the cache found in Polly's school." Lydia had been slowly running her hand up and down her husband's forearm while she talked.

He reached across with his free hand and grasped hers. "That's a good idea, love. You're so smart. I'll call her on Monday." Aaron keyed some strokes into his phone and set it back down on the table.

"They finally had to let him retire," Lydia continued her musing. "You remember that, don't you Aaron? The whole community came out for it. That was in, what, 1995? I think that's about right. We still had three kids in school here in town. But then, when he didn't have anything to do, he cleaned up the streets. He picked pop bottles up and recycled them. You know, he was picking trash up too." Her face became pensive. "We all thought he was throwing it in the trash bins around town. What if he took it all home. Oh, Aaron. We have to help this guy!"

"I love you, dear. We will do what we can for him. But, we can't do anything if he doesn't want our help. There's nothing illegal about picking up trash and keeping it," Aaron explained patiently.

"I know that, but it's just wrong! He can't live that way and be healthy."

Aaron rolled his eyes. "Well, it looks like my wife has a new project."

He continued, "Before you go off your rocker, dear, you have to let me talk to him first and make sure he hasn't done anything wrong with all this stuff he's got laying around. If Sylvie thinks he took the coat out of her locker, he could still be taking things from people."

"Oh, you know better than that," she challenged. "She knew it wasn't lost, but who knows if she didn't leave it on a bleacher or in a chair in one of the classrooms. Maybe she went back to get it and it was gone. That wasn't really stealing, now was it? And it was twenty years ago. It was a non-event in her life and you can't turn it into a big event now."

"Well," said Aaron to Polly, "I guess this is my fault. I asked for it and I got it. I can almost guarantee that by Easter of next year, poor old Doug Leon will be living in an immaculate apartment and will somehow find himself participating in social events all over town. Poor old guy."

Polly laughed with him, "And he'll love it or else, won't he!"

"Well!" Lydia said, scowling at both of them. "We'll see, won't we!"

"I am curious, though, about the coat and t-shirt that don't fit the timeline," Polly said.

"So are we. DCI is doing their job and they'll let us know when and if they have something. I suspect we'll know more midweek and I'll be sure to let you know what I can." Aaron replied.

After dinner, they cleaned up the kitchen and Aaron went downstairs to turn on the television. Polly and Lydia followed him down and before too long, Polly found herself nodding off in the big sofa. She jolted awake when Lydia said, "You know, the bed upstairs is much more comfortable."

"What?" Polly said, looking around, "Oh. Sorry."

She and Lydia were alone. "Aaron has already gone to bed. Let's you and I go upstairs and find pillows for our heads, alright?" Lydia turned off the television and followed Polly up to the second floor. "Goodnight dear. I do enjoy having you here. It's like a party every time you show up."

Polly sighed, "I'm ready to have real parties and not nights out because people might be threatening my life."

"We take what we've been given, dear. And I'm glad I've been given a little time with you. Good night, dear. Sleep well."

Polly opened the door to the room she had used before, saw her bag at the foot of the bed, went into the bathroom to wash her face and teeth, pulled her clothes off and put a nightshirt on. When she crawled under the blankets, she remembered that she had immediately fallen asleep the last time she had been in the bed. That was the last thing that crossed her mind until the next morning.

CHAPTER TWENTY

Polly pulled into the parking lot of the school and sat for a moment in her truck leaning her head back and wondering when it was going to get normal again. When would she be able to go home by herself and soak in a long shower or put her feet up and read a book or stretch out and watch television or sit in front of the computer for a couple of hours doing mindless reading? She felt a little tired of having to rely on other people to take care of her and wanted to let everyone get back to their normal lives so she could get back to hers.

Aaron hadn't heard anything about Joey this morning before she left their house and she assumed he had probably hit the road and run. Now that he had another assault in his back pocket, sticking around would be stupid and she didn't think he was stupid. She sighed, reached over and grabbed her overnight bag and got out. The gravel and grass was still scuffed up from the activity last night as she walked to the front door. Putting her key in the lock, she opened it and went inside being careful to relock the door behind her. A quick shower and maybe another nap would help get her head back together before Lydia picked her up to go down and see Doug in the hospital.

She shook her head. Stupid kids. They should have run away. She wouldn't have cared what Joey did to this place as long as they were alright. She dropped her keys on the newel post and walked upstairs to her room. The mess he'd made of that room was enough to make her want to cry last night, but she had time today to get it all back in order.

Polly opened the door to her room and dropped her bag on the floor in surprise.

"What in the hell are you doing here?" she asked. Joey was sitting at the end of her bed. Everything had been straightened up, the bed was made and her suitcase was packed with her clothes.

"It's time to go, Polly. I'm not going to put up with any more of your protestations." He stood up, took the suitcase in one hand and grabbed her arm with the other.

She wrenched away from him. "I'm not going anywhere with you." She fumbled in her purse for her phone and he knocked it to the floor.

"Polly, I have been more than patient with you. But, finding two young men in your house last night was more than even I could tolerate. You have got to stop having all these relationships with other men. You know how jealous I can be and yet you continue to test me."

"You ass," she said. "Those boys are ten years younger than me and they've been staying downstairs because people have been trying to break in. I would never do anything stupid with them. But, that doesn't make any difference," she went on. "This is absolutely crazy. I'm not going with you."

"I was afraid you were going to be stubborn about this." He pulled a small gun out of his jacket pocket. "You see, I knew that eventually you were going to force me to do something rash. I guess we're at that point now. Pick up your purse and your bag. We're leaving."

Polly didn't know what else to do so she obeyed him, scooping her phone into her purse as she bent over to grab the overnight bag.

"Now, we're going out to your truck. Move it," he demanded.

She walked down the stairs and he snatched her keys off the post.

"You'll drive," he said. "Now get in the truck."

He took her purse and bag from her and tossed them in behind the front seat. They both got in and she said, "Well, where are we going?"

"They might expect us to head east. We're going to Kansas City, instead, by way of Omaha. Now, drive."

He handed her the keys and she turned them in the ignition.

"Don't do anything stupid, Polly," he said. "Head over to Highway 17 and go south. We're not going through Boone. We're not going to go anywhere near your precious little friends. There's no one now who will stop me from making you my wife."

"Bet me," she said under her breath, but decided that it wasn't yet time for her to escalate the situation, so she asked "How did you get in the school?"

"Oh you all are so trusting with your stuff. I don't know how you got so lazy and stupid. It must be from breathing all this pig crap out here. You had extra keys in your purse, so I took one of those yesterday morning.

After all the activity last night, I knew you'd run away from this place, so I came back, unlocked the door and made myself at home. You had a pretty nice thing going there, it's too bad you won't be able to finish it. But, I promise that if what you want is a building to renovate, I'll find one in Boston and we'll work on it together. Just think of all the fun we could have. You could do all of your fun little things and I might open up a learning center. Maybe even a museum. I could bring in some artifacts and hire people to spend time deciphering them. We could do everything together and it would be a wonderful life. We'd even build an apartment so our children would grow up in the middle of all of the excitement. That's what you want, isn't it, baby?"

Polly ignored his comment and asked, "So, what happened after Billy chased you off." She turned and glanced at him, "Do you know you put that poor boy in the hospital? This is another assault charge for you! When Sheriff Merritt gets his hands on you, he's going to make sure you don't come up to breathe for a very long time."

"He's not going to catch me, Polly. We'll be long gone before he knows what has happened. And besides, if they were to find me, I'd claim self-defense. I was protecting the property of my wife. How was I to know those boys weren't there to hurt you and destroy everything. They had weapons and it seems they weren't afraid to use them." He rubbed the side of his head, then curled his upper lip, "In fact, I might even press charges against the one who hit me. That was assault with a deadly weapon, you know."

"That's crap, Joey. You attacked them and you know it."

"I was only protecting what was rightfully mine, Polly. If you would simply stop protesting against our love and agree I am right about us, everything would be okay. I don't want to have to hurt anybody, but if they're trying to take you away from me, I have to stop that. It's not right and I can't allow it."

Polly breathed out. She knew better than to expect lucidity from him at this point.

"Alright then, where did you go last night when you ran away from the school?"

"Oh, Polly, these hicks out here are so easy. I parked my car in an abandoned barn down the road. Doesn't anyone ever lock anything? I drove in and there was no one around. Miles and miles of emptiness. I can't believe there isn't more crime out here," he shook his head in disgust, then continued, "I started walking back into town, and this farmer in an old pickup truck pulled over and asked if I needed a ride. He was going up to Webster City and was more than happy to drop me off at the convenience store on the highway. Stupid man thought he was doing some great favor for a poor boy heading into town to see his mama. I spun quite the yarn for him about how I'd come in to Boone from North Dakota on the bus and that my mama was too sick to come down to get me, so I decided to walk home. He asked me a couple of questions about where she lived and since this town is so ignorant and names its streets after presidents and trees, it was easy to make something up. The old man drove off feeling like he'd been a Good Samaritan. I'll bet he went back to his house and told everybody there about what a wonderful thing he'd done.

"I saw all the flashing lights over here and figured that the sheriff was here. Has he been making passes at you too, Polly? He shouldn't do that. He's supposed to represent safety to his constituents and his wife would be upset if she knew he was messing around with you."

"Joey, that's sick. He and his wife are friends of mine. Both of them. And he would never do anything like that. He has honor that you will never understand." she retorted.

"I don't believe you, but that's alright. We're leaving all of that behind. When I finally get a ring on your finger, the whole world will know that you are taken and that I have the right to ensure your safety. No one will ever lay a hand on you again," his eyes got dark as he looked her up and down, "except me. And then, I am going to enjoy every minute I have with you. I've waited a long time for this. And I agree that it was smart of you to make us wait to get physical. It will be that much better when we're finally married. You will find out how much I can give you pleasure and how much I want to do that for you."

Polly shuddered. She couldn't help it. Something in the deepest part of her heart must have kept her away from Joey physically all those months. He'd never tried anything with her, but she'd never encouraged anything either. There had been plenty of other boys in her life who had received her kisses and a little passion, but not Joey. As she thought about it, it occurred to her that was weird. Wow, her brain was smarter than she gave it credit. Or her heart or something like that.

Joey was still blathering at her about all of the functions they would attend together and how he would dress her in beautiful gowns and then enjoy taking them off of her. He went on and on about the nights he wanted to spend with her until she completely shut him out. She didn't want to hear it, but she wasn't going to argue any longer with him.

Polly drove and kept trying to figure out how she was going to get out of this. It was beyond anything her imagination could come up with. They drove through Des Moines and she turned onto Interstate 80 heading west.

It had been years since she'd been to Omaha and that time her Dad drove. He had taken her and two friends from high school over to the Joslyn Museum for a doll house exhibit. They'd thought they were so uptown. He'd made it a big weekend for them. The Joslyn, the zoo, a big steakhouse with Christmas tree lights all over. They'd walked around downtown and had ridden in a horse drawn carriage. It had been a wonderful weekend. She barely remembered those girls now and wondered what they were doing on this Sunday.

Her truck made a beeping sound and she realized they needed gas.

"What was that?" Joey asked.

"We need gas. Can I pull off at the next exit?"

"Well, of course! You stay in the truck and I'll fill the tank."

"Joey. I'm going to have to go to the bathroom," she said.

"We'll deal with that. Let's get gas first and then pull up to the front and we'll go inside."

She did what he asked. She pulled up and he reached over and took the keys. He ran inside and paid for gas, then came back out and pumped it himself. When he got back in, he told her to pull up to the front of the store. They both walked inside, his hand firmly on her elbow. He walked with her to the bathroom and said, "I'll wait right here for you. Please don't do anything stupid. I won't hurt you, but I don't want to hurt anyone in here, either." Before she could walk away, he nudged her with the gun in his pocket.

Polly went in, sat down and tried to think. How was she going to get out of this? She'd heard of kidnap victims who left messages on bathroom stalls, but realized didn’t have any way to make that happen. She was going to have to think about that at the next stop, so she got up and went back out. Joey hadn't waited. He was checking out at the cash register and when he saw her, he stepped away and took her arm again. Walking back with him, she waited while he paid for the items and they went out to the truck. The clerk never looked at either of them and Polly couldn't signal anyone around her.

"You're still driving. I don't trust you. Now get in. I promise things will get better when we get back to Boston. I really do promise, Polly." He tried to reach across the seat to kiss her on the cheek, but she backed up and pushed him away. He moved to his side of the truck and pulled his seatbelt on.

Polly pulled onto the interstate and Joey took two bottles of water out and opened one, placing it into the well in front of her. "Here. I didn't want to get you any caffeine. We're going to make as few stops as possible."

She didn't say anything. She didn't want to talk to him and while she drove, she tried to come up with any possible remedy to this situation. No one knew she was even gone. The clock on the dash read eleven thirty. Lydia was supposed to pick her up at one o'clock to go to Boone, but until then she was on her own and they'd be in Omaha by then. Joey had thrust her purse with the phone in it behind her seat and set the overnight bag and suitcase on top so it was out of easy reach. There was nothing she could do without provoking him, so she continued to drive.

They drove into Council Bluffs and he directed her to cross the river into Omaha. "We've got a couple of errands before we head south," he said.

He directed her through several streets of the city and then told her to stop the truck in front of a used car lot. Damn it. He'd done some thinking about this.

"Do not leave this truck," he instructed, taking the keys. Then he pulled her purse out and dumped the contents on the seat. He slipped her phone into his back pocket and shoveled everything back in to the purse. "Just in case you decided to try to contact your friends. I will let you call them when we get home, but not until then. They don't need to be involved in this, it's between you and me. I want you to know how much I am willing to sacrifice in order to make you part of my life."

He walked into the dealership and in a few minutes walked back out. The dealer led him over to a green SUV and put the keys into his hand. Joey walked back to the truck and told her to get out. He gathered up the bags from the back seat and nodded at her purse, so she picked it up and followed him to the SUV. Now, she had tears in her eyes. That was the last vestige of her Dad and she couldn't believe it was going to end up in a slimy used car lot in the middle of Omaha, Nebraska.

"Joey, why are you doing this?" she asked. "That was my dad's truck. I can't believe you just did that!"

"Don't worry, Polly. You won't miss anything once you are back in Boston. I'll make sure you have everything you need. Get in. You're driving again."

She drove off the lot and once again, he directed her through the streets of Omaha, looking closely at a laminated map. "Wait," he said. "Pull over here."

There was a food truck serving tacos in a parking lot. She pulled in and he got out, made the transaction and came back. "We're lucky they were open. They usually aren't on Sundays, but there was some big run happening in town today. They were just getting ready to close."

He opened the paper wrap on the taco into a pocket and handed it to her. She pushed it back at him.

He took her hand and wrapped it around the taco, then said, "Honey, I love you so much. You're going to have to eat because you need to keep up your strength. We still have a long day ahead of us. Now, if you don't eat this, I will make you pull over to the side of the road and force you. I don't want you being faint or anything. So, either eat and drink on your own or I will help you, only because I want you to be okay."

She took a bite. It wasn't the worst thing she'd ever tasted, but she was certain it was going to sit in the bottom of her stomach like a rock. He kept watching her until she took another bite. Then, he opened the bottle of water and handed it to her. "This will help wash it down. I wish it were a lobster dinner, but, like everything else, that will have to wait until we get home."

They crossed the river back into Council Bluffs and headed south to Kansas City. Joey tried to engage in conversation with her, but she was having nothing to do with that. She remained silent. Enough time had passed that by now someone knew she wasn't where she was supposed to be. Every once in a while her emotions tumbled up into her throat and a tear squirted out one of her eyes. She reached up to brush them away and once, Joey tried to pat her leg. She pushed him away and said, "Don't you dare touch me."

"I'm sorry you feel badly, Polly. I want to make you happy. One of these days, you'll see. You will have everything you want and I will be the one to give it to you."

Polly ignored him again and kept driving. When they got into the Kansas City area, he directed them to the airport, where she put the car in long-term parking.

Now what! She started to panic. She had no frame of reference for the Kansas City area and couldn't imagine how she was going to get help. Joey couldn't take a gun into the airport, but she didn't know what else he would do. If she tried to flag down a security guard, all hell could break loose and she didn't want to be the cause of that. Polly sighed. Maybe she should just get on the airplane and try to reach out to her friends in Boston. She knew plenty of people there and she knew the city well. So far, Joey hadn't hurt her and that was a good thing.

Joey pulled the gun out of his pocket and pushed it into the glove compartment. "I hope that gun wasn't the only thing that kept you behaving like a normal person today," he said and she rolled her eyes.

"There are only a few hours left before we're home. If you can hold out until then, I promise you will be able to call your friends and tell them where you are. Everything will be alright then. Can I get you to promise me that or do we have to sit here a while longer."

She didn't say anything.

"Polly," he said "I don't want to hurt you, but if you try anything, anything at all, I will make your life a living hell and I promise you I will go after every person you've ever known in your life. Now, do we have a deal?"

Polly set her jaw. Her lips were moving over her teeth as she pursed them together. One more time for the weekend, she breathed deeply and tried to collect her thoughts.

Then she said, "I will go with you today because you seem to be in control. But, I promise you. Your life is over. This is the last day you will ever see freedom. I will do everything I can to see you rot away in some hole. Yes. I will go to Boston with you. Yes, I will stay quiet in the airport. And this is the very last time you will get any acquiescence from me. Do you understand?"

"That's all I needed, sweetie. We have a deal."

She looked at him. Her threats hadn't penetrated his mind at all.

They got on a shuttle to the airport and it seemed Joey had already purchased their tickets and printed them out. The flight was taking off in one hour. He carried her bags onto the plane for her, stowed them in the compartment above their seats, then sat beside her.

"I bought three seats for us so you would have room to stretch out and relax. I didn't think you would want to sit by some huge, ugly person who smelled bad."

"No, because I want to sit by some crazy person who hurts people," she retorted.

"We're going to have the best life," he said and tried to take her hand.

She pulled it back and snarled. "I told you not to touch me."

CHAPTER TWENTY-ONE

Over the loudspeaker, the pilot announced their descent into Logan International Airport. Polly had attempted to sleep, but it quickly became apparent her mind wouldn't allow her to relax, so she kept her eyes closed. Anything to avoid talking with Joey. After the announcement, he tentatively touched her arm. "Polly? Honey? We're almost home. My car is waiting in short-term parking and soon we will be able to have everything I've always wanted. I'm so excited to begin our new life together. Just you and me with no one to interfere."

Polly opened her eyes and glared at him. "I told you not to touch me. Get your hand off my arm or I will make an incredible scene. I don't think you want that to happen while we're still on the plane, now do you?"

He retracted his arm and said, "I love that you have so much spirit. I don't want you to ever lose that, because I believe it will make our children successful, but you are going to have to find it in your heart to forgive me for the things I did last spring. Maybe that will finally allow you to show me how much you truly love me. I've been patient this summer and I can afford to be patient a little longer, because I know in the end we will be together forever."

Polly could barely contain her shudder. His words seemed like some hideous parody of an awful movie, in which the serial killer dressed dead bodies in wedding gowns. She could barely wait to get on the ground, even if it was to get in his car. There would be opportunities to get away from him and now they were on her turf. She had friends in Boston and she knew how to get to them.

The plane landed and taxied to a gate. It was an interminable wait, but Polly did her best to stay calm. From this moment, she would be on high alert, looking for any opportunity to break away. Joey had to be exhausted since he hadn't slept the night before. Soon, he would begin to relax and let his guard down.

They waited while other passengers disembarked, then he stood and pulled their luggage out of the overhead compartment. She took her purse from him as he handed it to her and then accepted the overnight bag as well. Walking in front of him, she exited the plane. As soon as he was able, he once again grabbed her elbow. Polly tried to pull away, but his fingers dug in and held on. "Don't try to get away, Polly. You're the love of my life and we'll soon be home where you can be happy."

She did what she could to maintain her composure and continued walking. Polly glanced around, looking for anything that might allow her to get away. Then, she saw it. Drea Renaldi was there with her brothers standing beside her. Polly nearly collapsed with relief, until she saw Drea's nearly imperceptible shake of the head. She was telling Polly not to do anything.

What in the world did she mean by this? Drea's brothers dropped back and followed them, while Drea turned aside so Joey wouldn't see her. He guided Polly through the crowd and she allowed him to continue, wondering what might be happening.

They exited the terminal and he began to walk toward a shuttle for long-term parking, but as soon as they cleared the doors and were on the street, Polly heard a thump and felt him drop away from her. He was on the ground, out cold, with two smiling Renaldi brothers standing over him. Drea ran up and pulled Polly in close.

"You're here and you're safe," she cried. “Oh, Polly, I've been so worried."

Polly's eyes filled and she began to sob uncontrollably. Then she leaned over into the gutter and retched. She looked at Joey on the ground and retched again. Drea, pulled a bottle of water out of her bag and some wet wipes. She wiped Polly's face and asked, "Did you get it all out? Are you better yet?"

"I think so," Polly said. Her legs were trembling and bile filled her throat.

"Swish some of this around in your mouth and spit."

Polly obeyed, then said. "I'm so sorry" and began sobbing again.

"It's alright, Polly." Ray came up to stand beside her. He reached out and patted her on the shoulder.

She looked at him and said, "Oh, I'm a pretty sight, aren't I?" then giggled.

"You're fine, Polly. You're always fine. Don't you worry about a thing." he replied.

She looked down at the man slumped on the street in front of her and bile rose in her throat again. Without a second thought, Polly pulled her left leg back and kicked him right in the balls, and then she picked up her suitcase and turned back into Drea's arms. A Boston police car drove up, two cops got out and spoke for a few minutes with Drea's brothers, obviously laughing at what had just happened. Then they picked Joey up, pulled his arms behind his back, placed handcuffs on him and put him in the backseat of the car. Joey had come to when he was kicked and he struggled to maintain his posture, but doubled over on himself.

"We'll need you to come in tomorrow morning and file a complaint, Ms. Giller. Jon and Ray here will bring you and I'm sure they'll take care of everything else for you. Don't worry, we've got this. Go get some rest."

Ray, the older brother, whistled for a taxi, and put his sister and Polly in the back seat. "We'll be by first thing in the morning, Polly girl. You're alright now."

"Wait!" she said. "I don't know what just happened. Thank you. Oh, thank you." and she began to cry again.

"Don't worry, Polly," Ray said. "Drea will tell you everything tonight, I'm sure. She's your savior, we're only the muscle." He punched his brother in the chest. "And that was fun!"

Polly watched them through the back window as the taxi pulled away and into traffic.

"Drea," she started, then slumped into the seat.

Drea scooted next to her friend, pulled her close and held on while Polly cried.

"You need to call your friends in Iowa," she said finally, picking Polly's purse up off the floor of the taxi. "They're worried about you."

"How did? How do you? What happened here today?" Polly stammered.

"I tell you what. It's a great story, but first you make a call to your friend, Lydia. She's probably started walking east already. Tell them you're safe. We'll go back to my apartment, pour a few glasses of wine apiece and tell each other what happened today."

Polly opened her purse and dug around for her cell phone. It wasn't there. Then, she remembered. "I don't have it anymore. Joey took it and it's in his back pocket."

"Oh, alright." Drea replied, "Here, use mine. Lydia's number is probably the last call on there anyway." She scrolled through the call list, pressed 'send' and handed the phone to Polly.

"Have you found her yet? Did he take her to Boston?" Lydia's voice came ringing through the phone.

"She found me, Lydia. I'm with her right now. I'm alright." Polly said, her throat choking up at the sound of her friend's voice.

"Oh, Polly. I'm so glad to hear your voice. We've been worried sick today." Lydia pulled away from the phone and said, "She's alright. She's with her friend!" Polly heard shouts and yells in the background.

"I have a houseful of people, Polly. It's not a party without you, though. I'm not going to ask you for all the details tonight, but tomorrow. I want you to call me and tell me everything, then tell me when you're coming back home, alright?"

Lydia took a breath, then continued, "Oh, Polly. I'm thankful you're safe. We're all so thankful you're safe." She paused. "Doug wants to say something to you."

Polly heard her say to Doug, "Here you are, honey. Tell her you're doing fine." Then Doug's voice was in her ear.

"Polly. I wish I would have been stronger. I'm so sorry we didn't take him down last night. I'm so sorry he messed with you."

Polly began to sob. "Doug. Thank you. You did everything right. I'm fine and I'll be home soon and then, I swear to you. I'm taking you out for steak. Are you all right?" She snorted and sobbed through the words and hoped he'd be able to understand.

"I'm okay. The doc says I'll be good as new in a week. Take care of yourself, Polly. Here's Lydia."

Lydia's voice returned, "What did you do to that poor boy. His face is all red ... Oh, there, now he's crying. What a bunch of soggy we've got going on here." She blew her nose loudly on the other end of the phone and said, "Beryl says to tell you that first thing when you get back, she's taking you to Victoria's Secret, because you have to attract some better men than that thing. Everyone wants you to know they're happy you're alright and that you are supposed to come home soon. Got it?"

"Okay, Lydia, got it. I'll call you tomorrow. Thank you, it seems, for everything."

"Good bye dear."

Polly pressed the button to end the call and handed the phone back to Drea, who exchanged it for a wad of tissues. Then, Polly leaned her head back on the seat and shut her eyes. She reached her hand out and Drea gripped it. They sat in silence until the taxi came to a stop in front of Drea's apartment.

The two girls went up the steps and into the building where the night receptionist recognized Polly. "Hi, Polly! Welcome back to Boston! It's been too long."

"Hello, Frances. It's nice to see you."

"I hope you have a good stay with us. Good evening, Miss Renaldi."

"Good evening, Frances." Drea replied.

They took the elevator to the fifth floor and didn't see anyone else. When they reached Drea's apartment door, she unlocked it and motioned Polly inside. Drea flipped the lights on and Polly kicked her shoes off in the foyer. She'd been here often enough to know that Drea didn't appreciate shoes on her carpet.

"Come on in, Polly. Sit down and I'll be right back with some wine."

Polly sat down on the end of the sofa, curling her legs underneath her. In a few moments, Drea returned with two glasses of white wine, knowing Polly's aversion to anything red and a plate with some soft cheese and Italian bread slices.

Drea set everything on the table in front of the sofa, tossed a blanket over Polly's lap and then curled up on the other end, sharing the blanket.

"Are you doing alright, now?" Drea asked.

"I am. It's good to be here with you."

"Do you want to talk about your day yet?"

Polly took a sip of wine. "Really, I think I want to hear about your day. How did you know to come find me?"

"Well, I will be glad to tell you, but first you have to eat something or else that wine is going to seriously mess you up." Drea leaned back in the couch with her glass and began to tell her side of the story after watching her friend take a slice of bread and a piece of cheese.

"My understanding is that Lydia went over to your school to take you to the hospital for that boy Joey beat up. When she couldn't get in, she refused to accept that everything was fine. She called her husband, who still had a key and he came right over and opened up the school. She ran upstairs and saw all of your clothes were gone and made him start calling people. Then, she called everyone in town ... it's not a big town, right?"

Polly laughed. "No, it's not a big town at all."

"She called your friends and they went to the school to create a plan of attack. Her husband wanted to call the FBI because he was sure you'd been kidnapped, but of course there's that whole 48-hour thing and he didn't have enough to prove your life was threatened and you hadn't gone somewhere on your own.

"Then, Lydia remembered you saying something about putting a recording on your laptop and some boy remembered seeing you put the laptop with the candy?

Polly nodded. "Billy. I did that ... wow, was that just last night? I jammed it down in the cupboard to get it out of the way."

"Anyway, another friend opened it up and found the file. Then, Lydia also remembered you said you had emailed yourself numbers from Joey's phone, so this other friend opened your email.

"When they scanned through it, they saw my name and read the email I had sent about Joey. Then, Lydia remembered you mentioned something about some Italian boys and put that together with my last name.

"They found my phone number and called me and told me what they thought had happened, so I called Jon and Ray, who called their chief of police friend. He contacted Aaron and they began setting it up.

"Polly, we've been watching every flight from the Midwest come into Logan today. I was so afraid we had missed you or that he would stay somewhere tonight and not come in until tomorrow or there could have been a million other things he might have done, but I counted on him being dumb and predictable and showing up here as fast as possible.

"When I saw you get off the plane, I didn't want you to react, because I guess that anything that happens inside the terminal would be handled by the FBI, not that they aren't going to be involved anyway. We had to get him out of the terminal and onto the street so that Boston PD could manage him. I'm not sure anyone planned for Jon to drop him right there, but my brothers didn't want you to get hurt, so they took care of it the best way they knew.

"And girlfriend, you had a little anger in you when you kicked in him the balls."

Polly finished her wine and smiled. "Yeah. He had that one coming."

Drea went back out to the kitchen and brought the bottle back with her. She poured some more wine into Polly's glass and got comfortable again.

"They found your truck in Omaha," Drea continued.

"Oh!" Polly said, "I need to call Aaron back. There's a gun in the glove compartment of an SUV in the Kansas City long-term parking. Here, just a second. I've got the ticket. Can I borrow your phone again?" Polly set her glass down and drew the ticket out of her back pocket. "I don't know why I took this with me and didn't give it to Joey, but they need to have that. It will be more evidence against him."

Drea said, "I doubt they can get anything done tonight," but handed her phone to Polly.

Polly dialed Lydia again, "Hi Lydia."

"Polly, is everything alright?" Lydia's voice sounded concerned.

"Oh, I'm sorry. Yes. I'm fine. Is Aaron there?"

"Sure, just a moment, dear."

It took a minute and Polly could still hear noises in the background, then Aaron's voice came through. "Hello Polly," he said.

"Hi Aaron. Say…" she started.

He interrupted. "I'm glad you're safe, Polly. You had us all worried sick."

"I'm sorry, Aaron. I tried to find ways to let you know where I was, but I couldn't."

"Oh, Polly. I didn't mean that. I'm just glad you're alright. What can I do for you?"

"I have a ticket for a green SUV in the Kansas City airport long-term parking. It's the car Joey bought from the lot in Omaha. There's a gun in the glove compartment. That's how he got me out of there."

"You know what? That's terrific. Tomorrow morning, when you go to the police station with the Renaldi boys, give it to the detective in charge and we'll get our hands on it right away. Good thinking, Polly."

"Thank you, Aaron. I'm sorry. I suppose it was silly of me to call you again tonight."

"No way, Polly. Not silly at all. But, you go ahead and trust those friends of yours and their police force. We've got you covered on this. Oh, and Polly?"

"Yes, Aaron?" she responded.

"I have your laptop. We're going to pull that recording off that you made. Is that alright? We're awfully lucky you stowed that away instead of taking it back upstairs to your room. I don't know how else we would have found you today."

Polly gave a weak laugh. "I guess sometimes lazy works out for the best, doesn't it!"

"Now, you relax for the night and tomorrow will be a better day. Come home soon to us, Polly."

It was all she could do not to start sobbing on the phone again, but she sucked back her tears and said, "Alright, Aaron, I will. Thank you."

Polly handed the phone back to Drea. "Well, that was stupid. I didn't need to bother him."

Drea rolled her eyes, "Stop it. It wasn't stupid. He's the person you know and he's in communication with the police out here. It's fine."

Polly shook her head. "Just yesterday, I was whining at all of them about how they couldn't leave me alone and let me be the adult that I was. My 32-year old self was getting a little tired of them being so protective. And now I don't feel like I can make a single decision without consulting someone."

"You'll be fine," Drea said. "You need a couple of days to get over the stress of everything."

"No kidding on the stress. Drea, you can't believe how bat-shit crazy that family is! How did I never see it?"

"None of us can really figure that out, girlfriend." Drea retorted.

"Do you know I called his mother yesterday and she sounded like a total headcase, too?" Polly said. "I was so floored when I got off the phone with her I didn't know what to think. She thought it was completely appropriate for her son to stalk me and she kept talking about what a great wife I'd make for him. Why are these people not locked up somewhere far, far away?"

"You're starting to feel better, aren't you?" Drea laughed.

"It might be the wine," Polly said, taking down the last of her second glass. She wiggled it in front of Drea, who filled it again. "This is probably going to hurt in the morning, isn't it?"

"The boys are coming over about 9:30 to take you down to the police station. I've canceled my class tomorrow, so I will be around all day to help you get things sorted out."

Polly snuggled deeper into the couch.

"I am starting to feel a lot better," she murmured and shut her eyes.

"Polly? Are you about to fall asleep?"

"I don't think so. This has been a wild day and my adrenaline is still running high, isn't it?"

"I don't think so," Drea remarked. "Let's get you into bed."

"Don't make me move," Polly whined. "I don't want to move again. I'm fine right here. That way you won't have to change your sheets when I leave."

"I made the bed up for you, my friend and you are going to sleep in it, not here on this couch. Get up!" Drea took the wine glass away and set it on the table in front of them.

"Polly, you have to help me," Drea said when she tried to pull Polly up out of the couch. "I am not big enough to throw you over my shoulder."

"Ray is," Polly giggled. "He could throw us both over his shoulder and then probably run a marathon."

"Too much wine and not enough food. Let's go, Polly. Stand up straight."

Polly stood straight up and then began to lean. She caught herself by placing her hand on the arm of the sofa. "You're right. Too much wine. Let's take me to bed."

She snickered. "If I said that to Ray, it would mean something different entirely. Why didn't I ever say that to Ray?" she asked.

"Because you're my friend and I would have had to kill him. It's much better this way. Love him from afar, girlfriend." Drea wrapped her right arm around Polly's waist and guided her down the hall toward the bedroom.

"Wait!" Polly exclaimed.

"What now?"

"I need to pee. He didn't let me pee but once today and I think I'd better pee."

Drea giggled, "Of course you do. It's right here. Go on in and I'll be here waiting when you're finished."

"Drea?"

"Yes, Polly."

"I love you, thank you for helping me today."

"I love you too, sweetie. Now, go pee."

Polly went into the bathroom and shut the door. Drea waited a few moments and realized this might be taking too long, so she opened the door and peeked in. Polly was still sitting on the toilet with her pants down around her ankles, and her head resting on the counter, gazing off into space.

"Polly, are you finished?"

"Sure! OH! I was supposed to come back out, wasn't I! But, the seat is so comfortable."

"Let's get you into bed and you can tell me tomorrow morning how comfortable my toilet seat is."

Polly giggled again. "Wow, that wine went to my head, didn't it!"

"Yes it did. I'd forgotten what a nut you were when you've had too much to drink. Let's go."

Polly stood straight up again and reached down to pull up her pants, then decided against it and walked out of them. "I'm just going to have to take them off in the bedroom in a few minutes. I'll save a step." She bent over and held on to the counter. "Oh look," she said, "I had my purple underwear on. Doug would be so proud. Maybe that's what saved me today." She picked up one leg, then the other and slipped those back on and left her jeans on the floor of the bathroom.

Drea helped her get into the bedroom and pulled the covers back, then watched as Polly crawled in between them.

"I'm in someone else's bed again." Polly said, "I can't wait until I can sleep in my own bed every night, but this is nice."

For a moment, lucidity seemed to return to Polly's eyes.

"Drea. I'm sorry I'm such a nut, but thank you for everything. You saved my life today."

"Polly, I love you. You're my best friend, even if you live clear on the other side of the Mississippi River. I'd do anything for you. Now, go to sleep and tomorrow will be a new day."

CHAPTER TWENTY-TWO

One more uncomfortable plane ride and she'd be home. Finally Polly chose to close her eyes, even if she couldn't sleep, and try to ignore the rest of the world. The week had been exhausting and she was glad to be on her way home. That seemed funny, considering that for the last nine years she had considered Boston her home. She'd had lunch with both Sal and Bunny and everyone was able to catch up on their worlds, but she missed her new friends, her own bed and even the craziness of construction.

Yesterday had been fascinating. Polly had gone to the Library to talk to her old boss and deal with a stupid little girl who seemed to have no brains. At the end of the conversation with her boss, Margaret, that stupid little girl no longer had a job. It had been one thing to help Joey stalk Polly through online searches, but breaking into Margaret's office to get a phone number from a personnel file was more than she could justify. Polly knew she was only young and gullible and Joey was smooth and could talk anyone into anything, but that was no excuse and the girl needed to figure out what real life looked like before she damaged someone else's life. Margaret felt awful for all Polly had gone through, but she assured Polly that she finally looked happy and healthy and wished her the best. Polly spent time talking to her friends who worked at the library and left feeling as if she was heading for a new life, not leaving her old life.

Ray and Jon, true to their word, picked her up Monday morning and helped her get through the day at the police station. Aaron had been on the phone with them several times, and sent two of his deputies to Kansas City to pick up the SUV. She gave her statement to different people during a very long day and again on Tuesday, but by the end of Tuesday they assured her there was enough information to keep Joey in prison for a while. His mother hired lawyers for him, while his father stayed completely away from the situation.

Tuesday afternoon, Polly had gotten her cellphone back and the first call was from Joey's mother who begged her to see his side of the story and understand his need for Polly in his life. She couldn't seem to comprehend that Joey had done anything wrong in bringing Polly back to Boston. The detective who had been interviewing her at the time the call came in, listened to the conversation with laughter in his eyes and a smirk on his face.

"She'd be great on the witness stand," he laughed. "Not that Delancy's attorney would be stupid enough to allow that to happen. If someone offers her the opportunity to speak for her son, she'll get him a certain sentence to the crazy house. That boy didn't have a chance, did he!"

When all was said and done, Polly felt like she was truly finished with the city. She scheduled the flight for Thursday when everyone was busy so she could quietly leave town. A quick flight change in Chicago and she would be in Des Moines before five o'clock.

The flights were uneventful. Polly pulled her luggage from the overhead compartment when they landed in Des Moines and entered the terminal. Lydia had begged to be allowed to come get her and when Lydia saw her, she ran to her for a hug.

"I'm sorry no one else came with me. I thought maybe we could go out for dinner and make a big spectacle of having you back, but it seems like everyone had things going on!" Lydia exclaimed.

"Oh, please Lydia," Polly responded. "I'm so glad to be back in the Midwest and on my way home I don't know what to say. I'm glad to see you and know everyone here is alright. I was worried about Doug and his mom being upset at me and what a mess Joey had made of everything. It will be good to get home, see everyone and look in their faces and reassure myself they don't hate me."

"Polly, you have nothing to worry about. Good heavens, nearly everyone has a nut somewhere in their past. Yours just happened to show up and get public with it. No one blames you for his actions. In fact, we all wondered what else we might have done to help you avoid this. But, no worries. It's in the past now and you've got a school to finish!"

"Have they heard anything more about the murder of those two girls, Kellie and Jill?" Polly asked.

"Not yet, but Aaron says he has some thoughts. He's keeping it close to his chest until they get more information back from the DCI. Waiting on them is like waiting for water to boil. It's going to happen when it happens and if you worry too much over it, time seems to slow down.

"Oh!," Lydia went on, "Aaron did finally corner old Doug Leon. He went to Joe's Diner yesterday for breakfast like he always does and my old man was sitting there waiting for him. They went back to his apartment and sure enough, it was a hoarder's paradise. All of the trash and things he'd picked up over the last twenty years were in there. He hadn't heard Aaron knocking on the door, it's so well insulated, and the doorbell had quit working years ago.

"It was a classic story. Piles of newspaper and magazines, stacks of paper and plastic bottles everywhere. There was a small path leading from the door to the living room. Mr. Leon is living in a very tiny amount of space.

"But, they had a long talk. Mr. Leon assured Aaron he never stole anything, but he did pick up everything if it was left around for very long. It seems as if he hadn't been too out of control while working at the school. He picked things up and created a crate for them every year. When they closed the building down in 1992, he was pretty upset about losing his stash, but I guess that before too long, he'd started another one in his apartment and that brings us to today.

"What about the jacket and shirt?" Polly pressed.

"He doesn't know anything about that. He was confident that each crate was specific to one year. He said he was pretty obsessive about that." Lydia responded.

"Did anyone else know about the room?"

"Yes," Lydia replied, "From what Aaron says, there were several high school kids who spent time down there. Mr. Leon doesn't remember them well, but they're planning to meet at the library tomorrow to look through old yearbooks. There's some reason my husband believes that coat is connected to the bodies found in your bathroom, but he hasn't seen fit to tell me what it is."

The two of them talked about Polly's time in Boston and got caught up on news from Bellingwood.

"I can hardly wait to get home," Polly said. They had turned west on to the county road leading to town. “Everything looks familiar to me again. Like it is where I belong. Like the road is taking me home.”

"It won’t be long now,” Lydia said. “I think some of the guys are still working. Henry had last minute things he was trying to finish before you got home and there's plenty of food in the cooler. More than a few people wanted to make sure you knew how glad we were that you had moved into town and how bad we felt we welcomed you to Bellingwood with death."

"Oh, Lydia, I haven't been able to get my head wrapped around how people out here are so friendly. That's so nice!" Polly said.

"And you know Andy. She has everything marked and labeled and organized. She'll take care of returning all the dishes for you, so you have nothing to worry about."

Polly shook her head. "I can't believe how lucky I was to land in Bellingwood. It could have been any other place in Iowa..."

"And you would have gotten the same type of treatment, my dear. You would have gotten the same type of treatment." Lydia responded.

She pulled into the driveway and parked in front of the front steps, letting Polly out.

"Do you want to come in for a minute?" Polly asked. “I'm sure if the guys are still here, there's coffee.”

"Sure!" Lydia said. "I'll be right in. Why don't you go on upstairs, dump your stuff in your room and I'll pour a couple of cups in the kitchen and wait for you."

Polly went in and headed right up the steps. When she got to the first landing she looked around, taking in the familiarity of the place. One of these days she needed to spend some quiet time and come up with a name for the school. She had fallen in love with every square inch of it, even the bathroom with its crumbled ceiling. This was her home now.

She made her way up the second flight of steps and heard noise coming from the apartment. Polly wondered if they had gotten the flooring finished while she was gone. Maybe she'd peek in and see.

She opened the main door to her apartment. The floor in the entryway looked amazing. Then, she heard rustling as Lydia came up and stood beside her. "They did a beautiful job with this didn't they? You can go on in. Henry has been letting people walk on it since last night."

Polly walked through her new entryway into what would be the living room and blinked.

"Welcome home, Polly," Lydia said.

At that, the room exploded with people and noise. Her furniture had been carried up from the basement and arranged in her apartment and it seemed like everyone she had met was coming out of the bedroom, in from the bathroom, up from behind furniture and around corners.

They converged on her, hugging and shaking her hand. All she could do was laugh and before she knew it, tears began to spurt from her eyes. Helen and Frank Randall pulled her into a tight hug. "We're awfully glad you're back and safe, Polly. Doug would have been destroyed if anything had happened to you."

Polly held on for a moment until Helen released her. Doug was standing beside his parents.

"How are you doing, Doug?" Polly asked.

"Oh, I'm fine. Heck, that was clear last Sunday! But, Dad can't make me do anything and I'm getting out of all sorts of work." He laughed and then hugged her.

Polly waded through the morass of people to Aaron, who said. "I'm glad you're alright, Polly girl. You shouldn't work so hard to give an old man a heart attack."

"Thank you for everything, Aaron. For everything."

"Your truck will be back tomorrow. I'm sorry it wasn't here today, but the boys down in Boone told me they needed to check a few more things on it."

"I didn't think I was ever going to see it again. That was one of Dad's favorite purchases. He'd waited for years to buy a brand new truck." Polly's emotions were running so high, she began to cry again. She looked up at Aaron, whose face had turned a little pink. He kept his arm around her and looked over her head for his wife, who smiled and waved at him and continued with her conversation, turning her back so she didn't have to see his pleading eyes.

Polly blubbered a little and Aaron reached in his back pocket for his handkerchief. "Here, keep this. You might not be done blubbering yet this evening." He pressed it into her hand and steered her toward another cluster of people waiting to greet her.

She finally made her way into the kitchen. Several card tables were set out with drinks and cake, appetizers and other goodies. Beryl looked up from the cake she was cutting, dropped the knife on the table and rushed to hug Polly.

"I told Lydia we were coming to get you back if you weren't on that plane today. I have friends in Boston, too, you know and I was ready to call them all to make sure you were alright out there. Then, Lydia told me you mentioned something about hot Italian boys and I figured you had it covered."

Polly blushed. She remembered her comments to Drea in her exhausted, drunken state about her friend's older brother. Drea had only teased her about it a few times, ensuring that Polly would never forget she had exposed her unspoken passion for Ray.

"OH!" Beryl exclaimed, then poked Polly's hot cheek. "I may want to hear more about your hot Italian boys!"

"Stop it," Polly sputtered, "Sheesh."

Andy and Sylvie were in the kitchen, chuckling as they watched the encounter. Both women hugged her and welcomed her home.

Sylvie said, "Lydia wouldn't let anyone but us deal with your bedroom and clothes. Tell us if you want some help rearranging things, would you? We did what we could, but don't know what you want."

"Oh, you guys. This is too much! I can't believe what you've done here," Polly said.

"Henry was all worried about scratching the floor up because we were moving too fast, so the furniture is up on heavy felt pieces and if you look, no one has any shoes on," Andy said.

Polly looked around at the feet of the people in her apartment and laughed. "That's hilarious!" she said. "I spent the last few days with my friend, Drea, who won't let anyone into her apartment with their shoes on. She worries about her white carpet. I will never have white carpet because of that." She glanced around and said, "So, where are all of the shoes?"

"Downstairs in the auditorium, all locked up tight. The Sheriff wouldn't let us in there because of the crates on the stage unless he or Stu was there to make sure no one bothered them," Andy said, "Did you see Stu out there? He brought his cute little wife along. He's the sweetest thing ever."

"Have you guys done any more work on the crates?" Polly asked as she peered around the people looking for Stu. He caught her eye and waved.

"We sure have. I suspect we're about 80% finished. Oh!" she exclaimed. "Aaron says that when we're done and if we haven't found anything else, the crates are probably yours to deal with since they came with the school and there wasn't any theft involved."

"What are you going to do with all of those things?" Sylvie asked.

Polly thought about it a moment and said, "Wow. I hadn't given that any thought at all. I dunno. What should we do with that stuff?"

Beryl stuck her head into the conversation. "I think we should get yearbooks for all these years, maybe the library will let us borrow them. Then, we photocopy the pages, put them in the crates where we think they belong and start advertising around here to let people know we have their stuff. We'll get rid of things we can, then auction off the rest and do something way cool with the funds here in town." She stopped and said, "Oh, I'm sorry, Polly. It's your stuff. You can sell all of it on eBay if you want and take the money."

Polly responded, "That's a great idea, though! I don't want this stuff, it's not mine. Anyone who wants a memory should have it and after that ... do you guys know any good charities here in Bellingwood?"

"Welcome home, Polly. I'm glad you're back and safe." Polly spun around as Henry's voice spoke over her shoulder.

"Henry! Hi! The floor is amazing." Looking around at all of the woodwork that was up, she said. "Actually, everything is amazing. This is so much more than I could have ever expected."

"We do good work around here," he replied. "How are you doing?"

"I'm fine. I'm glad to be home."

"You've got some good friends here, Pol. You can't believe the number of people who showed up today to haul your stuff out of the basement and get this party ready for you."

Polly put her hand on his forearm. "I can't believe this. I've never known anything like it." She paused for a moment. "You know, that's not true. When Dad died, there were a lot of people taking care of a lot of things for us, but I wasn't paying attention. It seemed like it all happened so fast and before I knew it I was back in Boston and the whole world was upside down.

"Dad's brother, Clyde, and his lawyer were the ones who took care of everything and got Dad's house packed up and in storage. I just realized," she said, "I have more furniture over there. I'd completely forgotten about that!"

"I didn't know you had family still around here," Beryl said. "Oops, sorry, was I not supposed to be listening in?" she giggled.

"Clyde's family lives over east of Story City. He bought Dad's part of the farm when Dad wanted out. Their kids were a lot older than me. You know ... Mom and Dad were older when I was born. They didn't think they'd ever have kids, so they didn't plan on it. It was kind of a surprise when I was born. Clyde and Ivy weren't terribly happy with me when I moved to Boston and I guess I didn't figure they'd care whether I was back in Iowa or not. After Dad died, they never called or tried to stay in contact with me. Maybe one of these days I will let them know I'm here. We'll see."

"Polly, oh Polly!" Lydia's voice rang out across the hubbub. "I think you might want to come see this!"

Polly went back into the living room and saw Billy peek out from the bedroom door, then quickly close it. Everyone in the room was whispering.

"What?" she said.

"It's not quite as inappropriate as this is going to sound, but you need to go see Billy in the bedroom."

The entire room giggled as Polly went to the bedroom door and timidly opened it. Billy stood there with a huge bundle of something in his arms. She got closer, trying to figure out what it was.

"I know how much you and Big Jack like each other, Polly, and Doug and I thought maybe you'd like to have someone strong around when we no longer live here, so we went down to Ames to see if we could find another German Shepherd and Labrador mix like him and we did! We got him before you left and have been training him for the last couple of weeks as a surprise. He's getting a lot better about telling us when he needs to go outside. What do you think?"

The words had come spinning out of his mouth and Polly could tell he was terrified she would say no, but when both the dog and the boy looked at her with anticipation in their eyes, she realized she was thrilled with her new best friend. She took him out of Billy's arms, the dog turned to look up at her, and then slurped her right across the face. She grinned and hugged him close and the room erupted in applause.

"Thank you guys," she said, her voice choking up. "This is the best homecoming present. Did you give him a name?"

Billy looked a little sheepish. "Well, we called him Obiwan," then he rushed ahead and said, "But, he's still young and you can call him anything you like. He'll learn it. He's smart." He rubbed the dog's head.

"Obiwan it is. I love it. Those are my favorite movies in the world, anyway."

"Really?" Doug said. "Really? Oh, you're just so cool."

Polly laughed, then turned and looked around the room at the people who were gathered.

"Thank you all for everything," she said, her voice rising to be heard. "I always thought that I had great friends, but nothing compares to this. I'm not very good at speeches, so I'll say thank you and you are welcome here any time."

She blushed and turned back to Billy. "This is the best gift, Billy. I love him!"

"Doug helped me pick him out. The shelter just got a litter and we couldn't believe it! He might shed a little." Billy paused. "He might shed a lot. But, we got you a brush for him and there's a bunch of food here. They said he has his first shots and when it's time, there's a certificate to neuter him." Billy shuddered and said, "I know it's the right thing to do, but man, it seems wrong. Anyway, that's all in a package on your desk over there."

Polly buried her face in Obiwan's neck and smelled the joy of dog in his soft fur. He wiggled and wiggled and she could feel his tail trying to wag.

Doug came over with a purple leash. "We can take him outside and walk him if you'd like, Polly."

"Cool," she said. "If you think he needs it. Oh, nice leash, Doug," and she laughed.

"What?" he asked innocently.

"Purple?" and she pointed at the leash.

"Oh," he said. "Billy, why didn't you stop me?"

"Because, dude," Billy said. "It's funny!"

Billy took the dog out of her arms. "This has been a lot of excitement for the little dude. He'll settle down when the two of you are alone. He and Big Jack already like each other, so it will be cool when we bring him over too."

"You guys are my Jedi Knights," Polly said. "Thank you."

CHAPTER TWENTY-THREE

Rousing early the next morning, Polly was ready to get moving. The party hadn't lasted too late and everyone pitched in and cleaned things up. There were several things she wanted to move around and she discovered the extra boxes containing her decorations were still across the hall, but she was thrilled. The kitchen was still empty of appliances, but Polly didn't think she needed to be in too much of a hurry to finish that since she had that great kitchen downstairs.

She sat up and heard a strange sound coming from the end of her bed, so she pulled on some sweats and a shirt, slipped into her tennies and unlatched the kennel. Obiwan bounced out and she picked him up.

"Good morning, Obiwan! Look at us, living in our own place." Her things were all in one place, her dresser and bedside table, her vanity and chair. "It's our home. You and me, Obiwan. All ours. This adventure is actually going to happen!"

She grabbed the leash and clipped it to his collar, then let him down to the floor. He wiggled his entire body and headed for the door.

"That's right, Obiwan, we're going outside. Are you ready for this?"

The two of them went down the steps and headed out the front door.

The morning was crisp and darkness still held its own against the day, but Polly's front lights came on as she and Obiwan walked to the side of the school. She knelt down and praised him over and over, remembering her Dad's admonition to always talk to animals, using their name often so they could make the connection. After walking around the school, by the time she returned to the front door, she was a little chilly.

"Can we go in now, Obiwan?" He stood at the front door as she unlocked it and headed for the stairs. "You are such a good boy." She sat down on the third step and he came back down to nuzzle her face. "Okay, okay. Let's find us both some breakfast."

Before heading back upstairs, she trotted to the kitchen and flipped the coffee pot on. Then, she ran back up the steps with him, poured food in his dish and went into the bathroom to shower and get ready. She left the door open so she could hear him moving around and when she came out of the shower, he sat in the doorway to the living room as if waiting for her.

"Well, either you're a really good dog, Obiwan, or Billy and Doug are good trainers. We'll see how this goes the rest of the day."

She put Obiwan back on leash and they walked downstairs. The coffee was ready and she opened the cooler to forage for breakfast, not surprised at all to find a container with a label that said, "Eat me for breakfast, Polly." Inside was a sausage biscuit and instructions for microwaving it, as well as a large chunk of breakfast casserole. "Welcome home," she said, "to the town where food shows up in your refrigerator."

Polly looked down at the dog, who was standing patiently, while panting. "It's a good thing you're around, Obiwan. We're going to have to go for a lot of walks to keep up with the food intake." She warmed the sandwich and sat down at the table to eat, looking out of the window. They had started destroying the playground. As soon as everything was hauled away, she would have the ground tilled and seeded. It would be wonderful next spring.

Her front door chimed and Obiwan jumped up and pulled at his leash, barking at the sound. "It's alright. You're going to have to get over that. Let's go see who it is."

Three of Henry's workmen: Ben, Leroy and Marvin were standing at the door, tools in hand.

"Good morning and welcome back, Polly," Leroy said. "Ben and Marv said you had a great party last night. I'm sorry I couldn't be there. Something came up."

"Thanks guys," she replied. "You're a little early this morning." Polly checked her watch, it was only seven fifteen, but she stepped back to let them in.

"I know, but Henry wants to get going on the flooring in the rooms upstairs. We lost all day Monday, what with everyone being worried about you. We're going to spend a long day today and maybe work tomorrow, too. I hope that's alright. Didn't he talk to you?" Ben apologized.

Obiwan sniffed at all three, then sat down. Ben reached over to scratch his ears, Leroy ignored him and started up the steps and poor Marvin looked lost, as if he didn't know which way to go.

"Oh, that's alright, and Henry doesn't need to talk to me about scheduling time here. Go ahead, and thanks!" She watched as they headed up the steps. "Oh," she said, "Coffee is done already, so come down any time."

Polly tripped the locks open on the front doors and went back into the kitchen to finish her breakfast.

"Here's the deal, Obiwan. Today's going to be a busy day and there will be a lot of people in and out of here. I don't want to leave you alone up in the apartment, but you're going to have to be good, got it?" Polly put her hand on his head and rubbed it down his back.

The puppy panted and shivered under her hand. Before she could pull it away, he licked it again.

"So, that's a promise? You'll be good today, Obiwan?" she asked.

He stood up and wagged his entire body.

Polly ruffled the fur on his neck and said, "Alright. Well, then. Let's get going!"

The two of them walked out to the foyer and out the front door. Doug and Billy pulled into the lot and jumped out of Doug's car.

"How was he, Polly? Did he cry all night or anything?" Doug asked.

"No, was he supposed to?"

"Oh, no, I just wanted to make sure you guys were fine."

"We were absolutely great, weren't we, Obiwan," she said to the dog. "We've already walked the perimeter of the building once this morning and were about to head back to the creek before everyone arrives and gets started. What are you two working on today?"

"We're back in the bathrooms first thing this morning," Billy said. "Doug wasn't too sure about it, but," he punched his friend in the arm, "we decided he wasn't going to be a scared wimp, so he got to go in first. We're nearly done up there. After that, we'll be back in the auditorium to finish wiring the place."

"Great. It looks like I'm back on stage today with the girls. See you guys later."

Polly took off at a slow trot around the side of the school with Obiwan following close behind her. They headed for the creek which ran through the edge of Bellingwood behind the school. It was never very full, but big Sycamores lined the banks. There was a beautiful grove of them that she could see from her windows, so today she thought she might go exploring.

Obiwan began sniffing around and marking trees and bushes, rocks and grass as the two enjoyed being out. The sun was coming up and it occurred to Polly that Sunday would mark the end of Daylight Savings time. More sunshine in the morning and less in the evening. Fabulous. The sunrise was spectacular, filled with pinks and oranges and deep reds. "So, you're going to make me be outside in the morning, eh. I might have to start bringing my camera with me."

They continued to walk the outer boundaries of the land on which the school resided, stopping every so often so the dog could again leave his mark. Polly hoped that would help as he began to explore his territory. She watched more and more vehicles arrive and figured they should probably head back in and say hello.

She walked back in the front door to the sounds of people talking and clattering around. Saws were humming, hammers pounding, electric nail guns slamming. Polly leaned on the door sill and smiled. It would be fine with her if these were the sounds she was greeted with every time she opened her front door. Obiwan barked as Leroy came around from where Henry's makeshift shop was and headed up the steps.

"You're going to have to get used to people, Obiwan. There will be plenty of them showing up around here, I hope. Let's go upstairs and see who is here." Keeping him on the leash, she started up the steps. He followed her, then ran ahead of her and attempted to pull her after him. "Oh no you don't, Obiwan. I'm the alpha on this team." He stopped on the step, turned around and looked at her and waited since she'd pulled the leash taut and he could no longer move. As soon as she got closer, he took off again and she stopped him. "Stop, Obiwan," she commanded in her sternest voice. He sat down on the next step and waited for her.

"Yep, we have some training to work out, don't we? But, we'll both get there, I promise." She ruffled his fur again and walked into the first classroom. Obiwan greeted the workers and moved from person to person waiting long enough for a scratch or a rub. They all greeted Polly and then went back to work, so she headed back dowstairs. Stu Decker was walking in the front door. "Right on time," she thought to herself.

"Did you have a nice evening, Polly?" he asked, then knelt down to look at the dog.

"It was a great evening. I'm so glad you were there. Your wife seems very nice." Polly responded.

"Thanks. I love her." He stood up. "Well, I suppose I had better get things opened up. The girls said they were going to be in early today. They want to get this project finished." She followed him as he walked to the stage door, pulling out his keys. "By the way, what do you think you're going to do with all the stuff?" he asked.

"I don't know," she replied. "If we can get it back to anyone who wants it, great. Otherwise, Beryl had a good idea about donating money from an auction to a local charity. Maybe I'll keep a few things to display around here. Who knows?"

He unlocked the door, walked in and flipped on the light. "Would you like some coffee?" he asked.

"Oh! I'll get it," she said and turned around to the counter, pouring out two cups of coffee and carrying them up the steps. Obiwan seemed content to be on the leash with her and until she was more comfortable with him being around, that was right where he was staying. She handed a cup off to the deputy and walked around the room. They were right. Most of the crates were now filled with bags and had been tagged. They might even finish the job today.

Sounds of laughter accompanied footfalls on the floor outside the auditorium and grew louder as Polly's friends approached the stage door. "We're here!" Beryl cried out. Lydia and Andy were with her. "Sylvie will be here after lunch. She's working at the store until then."

It took a few moments for everyone to get their coats off, pat the dog and get their coffee, but before too long they were all working steadily away. The morning passed and after lunch, Sylvie joined them on stage.

"Have you decided what you're going to do with all of this, Polly?" she asked.

"Do any of you have a good idea for a charity? I don't know how much we'd raise, but there are some pretty cool pieces here and if we did an online auction, too, I suspect we could make some decent money." Polly said.

Lydia commented, "You know, Polly. The library is in desperate need of some work. The old building could use help."

Polly perked up, "The library? Of course! Why didn't I think of that! Does anyone else have a better idea?"

Beryl said, "There are always a bunch of things in town that need money. Some of them have better patronage than others. You just need to pick one and do it. Lydia, who is on the library board that we can introduce to Polly?"

"We'll find someone. But, that's a good idea." Lydia said.

All of them worked and chattered about things they found in the crates. Knowing now who had picked the items up made their task more interesting as they attempted to discern why a particular item caught his eye. Today, Polly logged a retainer that seemed to be from some time in the eighties, a couple of cassette tapes that had been recorded. One of them was marked, "For Mindy. I Love You. Ted." She wanted to put that in a cassette player and see what the poor guy had thought would fill his lady love's heart.

Polly was curious about the single saddle shoe. Lydia thought the things in that crate had to be from the mid-seventies, everyone wore saddle shoes for a while. There was a pair of spats tucked inside a band cap, more t-shirts and a well-worn copy of Jonathan Livingston Seagull that Beryl cackled over. There were a number of books that had been bagged up and logged, some had names on the inside and there were even a few with library card envelopes sealed to the inside cover. Polly couldn't believe she was the curator for such an interesting collection of items. Once they got everything dated, this would be a fascinating look at pop culture from the latter part of the twentieth century.

They worked and all of a sudden, Obiwan barked. It made everyone on stage jump. No one had been paying attention to anything other than their task. Aaron was walking up onto the stage with a grim look on his face.

"What's up, Aaron?" Lydia asked.

He shut the door behind him and said, "We're certain the murderer is working here at the school. The only way to know for sure is to fingerprint everyone, but we can't do that, so we need to get a little creative."

"How do you know that?" Polly asked. Her stomach flipped upside down and instinctively she reached down and picked Obiwan up to her lap. There had been a murderer in and out of her school for the last month or so working in her space and seeing how she lived.

"You also need to know that the coat and t-shirt you found was probably his as well. We matched fingerprints from the girls' purses and some that we found on their bones to an old key found in that coat."

"But, you have no idea who it is?" This came from Sylvie. All of the women had stopped working and set their items back down in front of them. They gathered around Aaron and Stu.

"We're becoming more and more certain it was Buddy Landers, but somehow he has become someone else. We don't know when or how that happened. We have no record of him after he left here in the seventies and there are no fingerprints on file anywhere that match to the ones we've got. Since his parents are gone, we've got nothing. But, we have also taken some fingerprints from around here and he's on site.

"Polly, I would guess he's also the one who took your key and tried to get in the front door. His fingerprints are all over that lock.

Polly shuddered. "Alright, I'm not going to complain any more about your insistence that Doug and Billy stay here or that you made me spend some nights at your house. I can't believe he's been so close to all of this. Why would he come back here now? And why would he stick around once the bodies were found?"

"My guess is that he's made his home here and after all these years, he doesn't want to give that up again."

"Oh, the poor boy," said Lydia.

Aaron scowled at her. "Stop it. He killed two girls, two girls that you knew very well. Then, he hid it and got away with it for forty years. Don't you think they should have some justice?"

"But, still. That poor boy. Just think about what he has had to live with. He had to run away and leave his family. When they died, he wasn't around. Then he comes back here with a new name and a new life wanting to be part of a community that he loved all those years and," she sighed, "that poor boy."

This time it was Beryl who scowled at her friend, "Poor boy, my ass. He's my age by now. He's had forty years of living free while those two girls were dead and their family didn't have the opportunity to watch them grow up and have kiddos of their own. Think about Linda and Sandy. They've missed having a great big family because of him and he wasn't man enough to admit what he did.

"Think about all those lies he told and how many people felt sorry for him and pitied him and helped him. He spent an entire year finishing his schooling with everyone thinking he was some poor lost soul whose girlfriend had run away from him. Poor boy? Not in my book."

Andy was quiet, then said, "We can't tell Linda and Sandy until we know for sure."

Aaron interjected, "We can't tell anyone until we know for sure. The only reason I'm here this afternoon telling you is that I need your help."

"How can we help," Polly was puzzled.

"Nearly everyone drinks coffee around here. We need to identify some cups and get them taken away for analysis. I brought a big box of cookies up from the Dutch Bakery in Boone. They're on the counter. Polly, what if you were to invite small groups of the workers to come in and have some coffee and cookies. We'll change out the trash and at least start limiting the possibilities."

"Oh!" she exclaimed. "I can do that! Girls, are you ready to be hostesses?"

"Any way you can separate the cups so I can more closely identify them will be great," he said.

"We're on it big guy," Beryl laughed. "I have an idea." She opened up her bag and pulled out some Sharpie markers. "Let's get busy, girls!"

Polly went upstairs to the bathroom where Doug and Billy were working. She invited the team down for cookies. Jerry Allen looked at her oddly, but it was close enough to a break time, he scooted them out and downstairs, following behind his people. Everyone was interested in the new dog and between the cookies and petting Obiwan, the time went quickly. She moved around from room to room, gathering Henry's group, then the team putting drywall up and finally the group that was tearing up the yard behind the kitchen.

After each group, Lydia, Sylvie and Andy bagged up the empty cups and put a new bag in the container. When they were finished, Beryl handed Aaron a tablet with marks and names on it.

"I marked each cup, then wrote down who took which cup with which mark. Each bag is numbered and I've numbered each piece of paper." She grinned and with a little bit of a cocky attitude said, "I'd make a helluva detective, wouldn't I!"

They all laughed and Aaron put the bags in a larger trash bag. "Thank you so much, ladies. I'll let you know what we find. Since we only have to do comparison, I'm hoping this goes quickly."

"Well!" Beryl said, "I'd call that a good day. I'm done." She looked at Polly. "You have got to be finished with all of this insanity around here soon. It is certainly playing havoc with my creativity. I keep choosing to hang out here and I need to make better choices. One more day. You get one more day and then I have to get to work! Shall we make that day tomorrow and be finished then?"

Polly laughed. "Well, I'm sorry! If I'd known we were cramping your style, I would have," she paused, "done nothing differently." She went on. "I'll be here tomorrow if you guys want to finish up."

Beryl hugged her, "I'd have done nothing differently either. But, one more day. That's all it's going to take and we'll be finished with that stuff."

Andy said, "It's been interesting, but I'm tired of looking at other people's stuff, too. I'm ready to be finished. Tomorrow is a great idea."

"Me too," Sylvie said. She looked at her watch. "Oh! I told the boys we could have tacos tonight. I suppose I'd better get home and start cooking. I don't know what my schedule is, but if I'm free, I might bring the boys over with some video games. It would be good for them to get out of the house."

Lydia said, "Well, sure, then! No one in my life has anything going on. Nine o'clock?" Everyone nodded, then she asked Polly, "Are you doing anything for supper tonight? We'd love to have you over?"

"No," Polly said. "I think Obiwan and I will stay at home. Now that my things are in the apartment, I can turn the television on, sit around and play on the internet, turn on my music or sleep in the living room on the couch!"

"Alright then, I'll see you all in the morning!" Then, they looked at Stu, who stood there shaking his head. "I'll talk to Aaron tonight. I doubt that I need to be here any longer. I will leave a hard drive and SD card with Polly and unless he sends someone up, you guys are on your own. Just keep the door locked until then, okay?"

"Whoops! Sorry about that," Polly said. "Oh, we could have gotten ourselves in trouble!"

Everyone closed down their work and left for the evening. Polly took Obiwan outside again and as they walked around the yard, she watched cars taking off from the lots. Then, she saw Billy and Doug walking toward her.

"So, we were wondering," Doug asked as they got closer, "what would you think if we brought our friends back and hooked up to your internet and played games tonight?"

"Oh!" she replied, "You like my school?"

"Yeah," he said. "It's great. There's all that space and all those plugs we've put in the walls. We'll bring pop and food tonight, you don't have to supply that. But, can we put stuff in the cooler?"

"Absolutely. Obiwan and I will be up and down. Have fun!"

"Thank you! You're the best! And, we're bringing pizza in. You can have pizza with us if you want."

"Cool. I'd love that." she said. "See you later."

The two boys went tripping along back to Doug's car. Obiwan and she walked around the creek for a little while longer as the sun went down and then went inside.

CHAPTER TWENTY-FOUR

Getting up early wasn't quite as easy as she'd hoped, but since most of the workers were planning to be at the school to catch up, she started moving. Marvin had cleaned up the coffee pot and gotten it ready last night before he left, so all she needed to do was turn it on. The kids had played games until after midnight and she wasn't sure what she would find downstairs, so she opened the kennel to a very happy Obiwan and they went for a long morning walk. Polly was glad the weather was still fairly mild. She wasn't afraid of the cold weather, Boston had its share of bitter temperatures, but this was a nice way to spend an early morning. The stars were out and she was still thrilled by the fact that she could see them again. They walked across the highway into the park, greeting one other jogger who was out with his dog. Obiwan got very excited to see someone his own size, but the jogger waved and ran on down the road. After forty-five minutes, she and Obiwan found themselves back at her front door; he was still bouncing with anticipation.

"It's going to take a lot to wear you out isn't it, little guy. Alright, let's get things going. She went back to the kitchen and turned the coffee maker on. The kids had done a great job cleaning up, she saw that the trash can was filled with pizza boxes and empty bags of chips. Other than that, the place was clear. Obiwan was bouncing at her feet.

"Oh, that's right. I should probably feed you first. Alright, let's go, Obiwan," and they went out and up the stairs to her apartment.

Polly put food in his dish and while he was eating, figured that was a great time to take a shower. When she came out, he was sitting in the doorway of the bathroom waiting for her again.

"Really? I can't get over this," she said and reached down to pat his head. He leaned into her hand. "Yes. I know. We're the best friends on earth." She bent over and picked him up, snuggling her face into the nape of his neck. "I'm so glad you're here."

While she dressed for the day, she set him on her bed. The first thing he did was to race back and forth from the base to the headboard, and then he burrowed under her pillows and stuck his head out at her, panting the entire time. "If you get too used to this bed, I'm going to feel guilty every time I put you in the kennel," she said. "Alright, it's time for me to find breakfast. Let's go."

They went downstairs in time to open the door when she heard it chime. Obiwan barked at Leroy, Ben and Marv, who all stopped to say good morning and then went up to begin working. Henry was pulling into the lot out front and Polly waited at the door for him.

"Good morning!" she called.

"Good morning to both of you!" and as he approached them, he knelt down to stroke Obiwan's head.

"That's how it is going to work, isn't it!" declared Polly.

Henry looked up, confused.

"I will stand here and the dog will get all of the attention. It's over for me now, isn't it!"

"Well, I suppose I could pat you on the head when I say hello. It seems a little odd, though." Henry retorted.

"Uh huh. Your guys are already upstairs. They just got here."

"Terrific," he replied, "we're going to finish laying and sanding the wood today in the front apartment and at least get a good start on the back apartment. I might have them haul your boxes to that corner of the hallway by your kitchen, if you don't mind."

"Oh, sure! I hadn't even been over to check things out on that side."

"Don't worry about it. We'll get them out of the way and then you should be able to dig through them whenever you have time. I wanted to get as much wood put down today as possible so we could start finishing it early next week."

"Thank you, Henry. I appreciate all the work. One of these days we'll have to sit down and figure out what you project the end of some of these projects to be. I'm going to have to start thinking about timing on the next steps. There's a lot to process on before I can start advertising an opening date."

"Maybe we should go out for dinner some evening soon. I'd love to take you to a little place I know over in Ames." he said.

"That sounds great."

"Time to get started," Henry said and he bent back down to rub the happy puppy. Then he went upstairs.

Polly and Obiwan wandered out to the kitchen. She thought about baking something for the guys who were working today, it only seemed fair, since they were working on Saturday. Her laptop was upstairs though and most of her recipes were in there. She was going to have to buy some more technology around here soon. The only recipe she could confidently bake from memory was chocolate chip cookies and that didn't feel right this morning. While she thought, she sliced two pieces of bread and dropped them in the toaster, then poured a cup of coffee.

Her toast popped up and she buttered it, thought about it a minute and said, "I've got plenty of time. Let's go back upstairs and enjoy the new apartment. There's no reason to sit down here by myself. She and Obiwan went up the stairs, unlocked her apartment, completely ignoring the sounds coming from across the big hallway, went in and curled up on her sofa together. She watched mindless television while snuggling with the puppy. "This is the life, little guy," she said. "This is the life."

At nine o'clock they went back downstairs. She grabbed a blanket for Obiwan. He had fallen asleep on the stage yesterday and she couldn't bear to see him be uncomfortable, "Good heavens," she thought, "I'm going to be one of those pet owners." Then she giggled and thought, "and I love it."

She unlocked the stage door and turned on the computer when she heard shoes click-clacking across the hall. Soon, Beryl and Andy came in. Sylvie followed close behind them with her two boys, Jason and Andrew. Andrew squealed when he saw the puppy and ran up to him, only to be stopped by his mother's firm voice, "Andrew. Stop."

He stopped, but not before startling Obiwan, but Polly had a close rein on his leash.

"Slow down, Andrew," his mother said. "Go very slowly and ask Miss Polly if you can pet the puppy."

By now, both Andrew and the puppy were wiggling in their attempts to get to each other.

"May I pet the puppy, please?" the little boy asked Polly.

"You sure can," she said, as she knelt down beside the two of them. "Just go slow and let him sniff your hand first, like this." She put her hand out in front of Obiwan's nose and he slobbered all over it. Andrew's hand was right in there beside hers and collected some of the slobbering tongue's action.

He giggled and then began petting the dog. Polly released the leash a little and Obiwan rushed the boy, who opened his arms and took the puppy into them. Soon they were sitting together, Andrew with his legs crossed and Obiwan in the crook of them. Jason sat down beside his brother and asked Polly if it would be okay for him to pet the dog, too.

"Absolutely," she said.

By this point, Lydia had arrived and the girls had all filled their coffee cups.

Beryl asked, "Well, do you suppose Aaron knows yet who done it?"

Lydia said, "He hadn't heard anything when he left this morning. I still feel badly for whoever this is. They obviously haven't gotten into any more trouble since then and it seems a shame."

"Stop it, you old softie. You'd empty out all of the prisons and let those criminals return home to their mommies. I don't know how your husband puts up with you," Beryl scolded.

"I've got a big heart. He says so all the time," Lydia smirked. "So there."

"Told me, didn't you!" Beryl laughed.

"Can we take Obiwan outside?" Andrew asked Polly, holding his hand out for the leash.

She looked at Sylvie, who shrugged.

"Sure, if you'd like to. A couple of things, though. Don't go into the trees by the creek, okay? You have to promise."

"We promise!" Andrew exclaimed.

"And you can't go past the street on either side. Stay near the school and come get me if anything happens."

"Nothing's gonna happen! Come on, Jason, let's go!"

The two boys ran out the door, slamming it behind them. Everyone heard them slam through the front doors.

"I'm sorry about that," Sylvie said.

"Oh nonsense," Lydia replied. "This old school has seen its share of children running through the doors and the halls."

"No kidding," Polly laughed. "And all the energy of Obiwan's they use up will only help him sleep better tonight."

Sylvie chuckled. "It will help them sleep better, too. Sometimes I feel badly that I live in a small apartment. They're boys and should have lots of room like this to run around!"

"Sylvie," Polly said. "Your boys can come over here any time. The dog seems to have fallen in love with them and there's plenty of room for them to run, even in the winter. You and I are going to have to talk! I'll bet I could use some help with snow and the yard and all sorts of things."

"That would be awesome. It's only five or six blocks and they could walk that on their own." Sylvie replied.

"We'll work something out and maybe later, I can ask them to come dog sit once in a while, too."

Sylvie smiled and her eyes filled a little. "Wow. They'd love that. It would be good for them to have some more people in their lives. Thank you, Polly."

The morning was going well and they could see the end of the task approaching. Polly had gone out into the hallway for another cup of coffee when Aaron and Stu came in.

"Good morning!" she said. "Are you here for coffee?"

Stu looked at his boss, who grinned. "Yes, we're obviously here for coffee. How are you girls doing?"

"We're nearly finished in there. We'll be done by the end of the day. Then, everything will be photographed, tagged and logged," she said. That seems kind of incredible, doesn't it?"

"We saw Sylvie's boys out playing with your puppy. They look like they're having fun." Aaron said. "Would you mind keeping them busy for a while? We need to go upstairs and take care of something."

Polly's face fell. "Oh no. Not one of them. Just tell me it isn't Henry."

Aaron looked shocked. "Oh, no, not Henry. We'll be back down in a minute."

The two men headed up the stairs and Polly couldn't help herself. She followed them, paying no attention to anyone else. She couldn't imagine which of Henry's guys it could be. Probably Leroy, he was such a jerk. Ben was a nice guy and Marv was helpful and a hard worker. Damn.

They went upstairs and Aaron walked through the open door to the room where the men were laying floor. Polly watched as each of them glanced up. Henry came over to stand by Aaron and said, "What's up, Sheriff?"

"Just a moment, Henry. I'm sorry to bother you here today." He walked over to Marv and said, "Marvin Davis? Or Buddy Landers? You are under arrest for the murder of Kellie and Jill Stevens."

Polly slumped. It felt like the breath had been kicked out of her. She sat down on the floor and watched as Marv put his face in his hands.

Huge, gulping sobs erupted from his body. "I'm sorry. I'm so sorry. Oh Sheriff, I'm so sorry!" he cried.

Stu went over to help the Sheriff bring the man to his feet. Both Ben and Leroy had stopped working and were shaking their heads. They looked as awful as Polly felt and both sat down on the floor where they were working.

Stu guided Marv out the door and down the steps. When he could, he read the Miranda rights to the man and before they left the building, he placed cuffs on Marv and led him to the car, putting him in the back seat. Henry and Aaron followed them downstairs and out the door.

"I'll take him on down to Boone and get everything started, Sheriff," Stu said. "We'll see you later."

By this point, Lydia, Beryl, Andy and Sylvie had come into the hallway.

Lydia was the first to say anything, "That poor man. That poor man. Aaron, he has no one to help him out. What is he going to do?"

"Lydia. We've got processes in place for this. Stop worrying about it."

"But, Aaron," she started.

"I said, don't worry about it."

"Are you sure it's him?" she asked.

"We're sure," he said. "Now, I'm going to Boone and help get him settled. Lydia, that man has known this day was coming for forty years. You need to be glad that it's me taking care of this and not someone who doesn't have a wife like you. I'll be home tonight."

"I can't work anymore," Beryl said. "That about did me in."

Everyone agreed with her, so they went back onto the stage, their feet dragging. No one said anything more, they closed the work down and turned out the lights. Polly pulled the door shut behind them and locked it, then walked to the front door. Ben and Leroy came down the steps.

"Boss?" Ben said to Henry.

Henry's face was as grim and morose as the rest of the group.

"You guys take the rest of the day. We'll see you on Monday. Thanks for coming in."

"We closed everything up. We didn't figure you'd want to work anymore today." Leroy said. He clapped Henry on the back and then put his other hand on Ben's back as they walked to their trucks in the lot.

"I feel like I need to go down to Boone and make sure Marv has legal counsel or something," Henry said. "I never put this one together. How did none of us see it?"

"There are going to be a lot of questions from everyone," Andy said. "It's best to get the answers we can and move forward, I guess. Do you want someone to go with you?"

"No. I'll be fine," he replied. "I'll wait about an hour and then call Aaron to see what I can do." He walked down the steps and through the lot to his truck. They watched as he drove away.

Jason and Andrew had brought the dog back to the school. Jason asked, "Mom, why did they take that man away?"

Sylvie hugged her sons. "Because they think he might have killed those two girls a long time ago."

"And they found him today? Here at the school? That's pretty cool!" Jason turned to his brother. "We got to see them catch a murderer today! That's not something every kid gets to experience."

Sylvie looked up at her friends, with huge eyes! "No boys, that's not something you see very often and I hope you never have to see it again. Now, give the leash back to Polly and go get in the car. I'll be right there."

Andrew handed the leash to Polly and said, "We walked him good, Miss Polly. He pooped and peed all over the place! He should be good to go for a long time!"

Polly giggled. "Thank you so much boys. I might have to hire you to come over and walk him more often. I'll bet he loves playing with you."

Jason perked up a little, "We'd do it for cheap! You call Mom and set it up. We'll come whenever you need us!"

They ran off to the car. Jason yelled, "Shotgun!" and jumped in the front seat. His brother's shoulders drooped a little and said, "I never remember," but he got in the back seat.

Lydia said, "Can you get a sitter tonight, Sylvie?"

"Why do you ask?" Sylvie said.

"Because I feel the need to sit around with my friends, some wine and a fire. Would you all come over for supper and some friend time?"

Polly nodded. "Me too, but I have a better idea. Just a second."

She pulled her phone out and stepped away while she dialed. "Doug? I have a huge favor. I'll pay you and Billy if you'd come over to the school tonight. Bring Big Jack and some of your video games. Sylvie's boys and my dog need someone to hang out with them while we go to Lydia's house. Would you mind?"

She paused while he asked a question. "I do not know how you heard the news that quickly. But, yes. Sheriff Merritt arrested Marvin Davis this morning for the murder of those two girls. They believe he is Buddy Landers. No, I don't know anything other than that. Yes, they're already gone and headed for Boone." She took a breath. "So, are you free tonight? I'll make something terrific for dinner."

"What time?" She looked over at Lydia, who mouthed 'six thirty?' "How about you guys show up here around six o'clock. Sylvie will bring her boys by and you guys can play games. Thank you so much! See you later."

She turned back, "How's that? Is that alright with you, Sylvie?"

"Well, that was easy! Yes, that's alright. Those are good boys and Jason and Andrew will have a great time with them, games and the dogs. Thank you! And I'll help you pay them."

"Oh, they're cheap. But, sure. You can help. Is there anything your boys love to eat?"

"I'll tell you what. Let me cook and I'll bring it with me."

"Fabulous. Well, Lydia, what shall we bring to your house tonight?"

"Nothing," Lydia said quietly. "I'm so upset that the best thing I could do today is prepare a big meal tonight. Just come over and help me wallow in sorrow."

"Great. We'll see you then."

They split up and Polly walked back inside with her dog. She shut the door, listened to the absolute quiet of the building, locked it behind her and let Obiwan off the leash. He bounded up the steps and she followed him. They went in the front door of her apartment and he jumped up on her couch waiting for her to join him. She turned the television on, pulled a blanket over the two of them, leaned her head back and fell asleep.

CHAPTER TWENTY-FIVE

Until six o'clock, Polly and Obiwan played in her apartment. Then they went downstairs and opened the front door to see Doug drive into the parking lot. Big Jack barreled out and headed for Obiwan, followed closely by Billy. Polly held on to the leash as the two dogs met on her stoop, sniffing and wagging. Sylvie pulled in behind Doug and her two boys leaped out of the car and ran to the dogs. Andrew pulled up short and looked at Billy and Polly.

"May I pet the dogs," he asked the two of them.

Billy looked a little stunned. Polly laughed and remarked, "Kids are easier to train than dogs."

She handed the leash to Jason and took two groceries bags filled with chips and snacks from Sylvie who carried in two casserole dishes in slings.

"I made enchiladas, is that alright?" she asked.

Doug said, "Awesome! That's wonderful!"

"I have everything else you'll need in the bags." She turned to Polly, "Including paper plates and stuff. No one needs to do dishes tonight."

They carried everything back to the kitchen and Polly put the casserole dishes in the oven. "I'm not turning the oven on, guys, but these are already hot and they should stay that way in there for a while."

Billy came into the kitchen, carrying twelve-packs of Pepsi. "Is it all right if they drink soda tonight, or would you rather they have something else?" he asked Sylvie.

She smiled at him, "Thanks, Billy, but soda will be great. It's not a school night and they're here to have fun."

"Polly," she asked, "would you like to ride over with me?"

"Sure!" Polly responded, "I'm ready to go. It feels weird not to take something, though."

"I told you before," Sylvie said, "these ladies don't care whether we bring anything or not, so let's go."

When they arrived at Lydia's house, they discovered they were the last ones there. The fire downstairs was already going and the bar was filling up with platters of food, from snacks with dips to fried chicken. A buffet warmer held mashed potatoes, gravy and beans. Beryl stood up from behind the bar as Polly walked toward it.

"Comfort food anyone?" She asked, holding two bottles of wine in her hands.

"Wow. That's some serious comfort going on here," laughed Sylvie.

Lydia walked down the steps with a basket of sliced bread and Andy followed, carrying two plates of cookies and bars.

"Is all this for us?" Polly asked.

"Aaron will be home in a bit and he knows he doesn't get to go hide until he has told us everything, so I thought it would be nice if I plied him with food. These are his favorites." Lydia put the basket of bread down and waved her hand over the food, "Not that it won't be obvious or anything!

"Thanks so much for coming over," she continued. "I didn't want to be alone in this house with nothing to do tonight."

Beryl scooped a finger full of mashed potatoes from the side of the dish, "This is what happens when she has nothing to do. I vote we strip her of all her…" she paused and leered a little, "ummm, other activities. Yeah. That's what I was going to say. Then she'll have nothing to do but cook good food for us."

"I'm fine with that, too!" Andy said.

"Who wants wine?" Beryl asked.

Affirmatives all around and Beryl opened the bottles and began pouring.

"Shall we wait for Aaron?" Andy asked.

"I'm right here," he responded, coming in the sliding glass door. He glanced at the bar and then at his wife, "Alright. What do you want?"

He looked around the room, "You girls should know I never get this food unless she's about to ask for something I probably don't want to give her."

"Lucky for you, you give me everything I want or you'd never fit in your uniform!" Lydia laughed and hugged her husband.

"I bet you want information. I'm not going to leave this basement alive without telling you what happened today, am I?"

They filled their plates and sat in chairs and on the sofa in front of the crackling fire. No one spoke for a few minutes as they ate chicken and drank wine.

Beryl broke the silence, "Say, did you all hear they arrested some guy for the murder of those girls forty years ago? I wonder how that all worked out."

Polly picked up on the not-so-subtle hint, "Well, after that kid pulled dried up bones down on his head in this poor girl's construction zone of a home, you'd think they might release a few details."

Beryl said, "I heard that the Sheriff who arrested him is stingy with those things and has to be bribed with fried chicken and it can't be anybody's fried chicken …" she looked at Aaron, "or can it? Because I'm willing to go to Hy-Vee and pick up their chicken if that would get your lips a flappin'."

He scowled. "No. Only Lydia's. Her chicken is the only chicken that counts and we don't need to be letting the world in on that secret, either, got it?"

Beryl smirked, "Secret? I have nothing to say, but how long are you going to make us wait for the details?"

Andy got up and walked over to the bar, picked up the platter of chicken and walked back to the group. She waved it a couple of times in front of Aaron's face, fanning the scent toward him, then sat down in her seat. "I'm holding it hostage. Every part of the story you tell me will earn you another piece of chicken. If we aren't satisfied, we're eating it all ourselves." She picked up a wing and ripped it apart, then began tearing the meat off. "Like that," she said.

"Okay, fine," Aaron relented. "I'm not stupid enough to hold out on you girls, but I am enjoying my dinner. Give the poor old guy a break!"

Andy picked up a leg and dangled it in front of Sylvie. "Don't you need another piece, girlfriend?" Sylvie took it from her, grinned at Aaron and began eating.

Beryl walked over to the platter, looked down and took a piece, glanced at Polly, took another and then dropped it on her plate. "We're emptying the platter, big guy. Spill."

Aaron shook his head and looked piteously at his wife. "Don't look at me," she said. "I'm not sure how you thought you could come home this evening and not tell us what happened today."

"But, you made chicken!" he pleaded.

"I certainly did," she said. "And I invited everyone over to watch you fall apart because of my magic. Now talk."

Aaron set his plate down and sipped from his glass. He sat back, closed his eyes, rolled his head, stretched his neck and slung his arm over the back of the couch. He leaned his head back, then stretched his legs out in front of him. Each of the girls watched as he attempted to elongate the time. He opened one eye to peek at them, then chuckled and said, "Fine."

Sitting up straight in the couch, he began telling them the story.

"Forty years ago, Buddy and Kellie snuck out one night after everyone had gone to bed. They were going to Boone to walk the rails. Jill caught them leaving, so decided to go with them. Buddy had rolled his truck away from his house and the girls had walked out to the highway to meet up with him so no one would hear the vehicle. They were walking along the tracks when a train came through. It scared them and they jumped off, but Kellie tripped and began rolling down a hill. She hit her head and had died by the time they got to her.

"Jill started screaming at Buddy, accusing him of doing it on purpose. He says she went nuts. He was in a panic because no one knew where they were, he could see Kellie was beyond help. Jill continued to yell and scream at him, hitting him on his back as he bent over his girlfriend. He says he lost it, picked up a rock and slammed her in the head. She crumpled and before he knew what had happened, he had two dead girls on his hands.

"Being young and stupid, the only thing he could think to do was to try to hide the evidence. He dragged them into the trees, went back to his truck and got an old shovel, then dug a deep hole and buried them and everything they had with them. He drove away, tossed the shovel in the Des Moines River, then came home. All he had to do was roll back into his driveway, sneak back into the house and get up the next morning like nothing had happened.

"For a while he thought he'd pulled something off. He had a secret that no one else had, but you all saw what that did to him. It destroyed him, though he couldn't tell anyone why.

"He left after graduation and headed for Florida. After his parents moved away, then died, he thought about coming home. He had changed his appearance, so was fairly certain no one would recognize him. He moved to Boone, changed his name and started doing odd jobs and household repairs. In the early nineties, he got a job working for a construction company and then one year, probably 1995 or so, they got the contract to clear the land and put up a development right where he had buried the girls. He knew the bodies would be found, so before the process started, he dug them up."

Andy looked at the others in the room, who nodded. She put a piece of chicken on his plate and said, "Would you like something more? You're doing well so far, Aaron."

He picked up the plate, looked over at the bar and said, "Oh, no problem. I can get it." He stood up and walked over, while the rest looked around in confusion.

"How did that happen?" Beryl asked. "He was doing so well and then he left us! Oh, hurry back, Mr. Storyteller. We're not finished with you yet," she sang out.

"Oh, let's all get a quick refill," Polly said, "I could use some more wine. Especially since I'm not driving tonight," and she winked at Sylvie.

"Drink up, Polly. I'll get you home. Tomorrow morning is your own problem." Sylvie chuckled.

Lydia stayed on the couch with her knees tucked up underneath her.

"Are you alright, Lydia?" Sylvie asked.

"I feel like I'm hearing a horrible story about someone else. But, I knew those girls and I knew Buddy. I didn't recognize him as Marvin Davis. How did I miss that?"

"We all missed it," Andy said. "He was in my class. I should have recognized him right away, but I didn't."

"Oh, girls, who knows why we missed it. But, honestly, why would we have ever expected him to come back to town? After he left and everyone lost track of him there's no way we would look for him again. He got so weird his senior year no one wanted to hang out with him anyway. No one missed him when he left." Beryl said.

With their plates and glasses refilled, everyone returned to their seats.

Polly asked Lydia, "Are you sure there isn't anything else you'd like? Some more wine? I'll get it for you." She stood back up and took Lydia's glass from her, walked back to the bar, refilled it and returned it.

"Thank you, Polly." She put her hand over Aaron's, "Alright, dear. Talk and eat. Talk and eat. Just like we taught you when the kids were little."

He laughed and took another bite. Deliberately speaking with a mouth filled with potatoes, he mumbled, "But you told us not to talk with our mouths full!"

Then he winked at his wife, swallowed, and began again.

"Marvin … or Buddy, heard that the school here in Bellingwood was closed and boarded up.

Aaron stopped, "Oh, and this part makes sense after talking with Mr. Leon yesterday. We went through yearbooks together and he pointed out some of the boys who spent time with him, working on small projects around the school. He gave them a little extra spending money if he thought they needed it. He thought Buddy needed it because he seemed to be so far out of his league with Kellie Stevens and then after the twins' disappearance, he felt badly for the kid, so he let him spend time in the boiler room when he couldn't sit through another class."

He nodded, while thinking. "He said he did that with several boys over the years, just to give them a little extra push in their lives so they wouldn't feel quite so alone."

Lydia interjected, "See. I knew that old guy wasn't so bad. Now, we're going to have to find a way to help him out."

"I'm not sure he's going to be very excited about you helping him out, Lydia," Aaron said.

"Like she'll give him a choice," Beryl laughed. "She's already talking about ways we can all get in there and start hauling crap out. I'm going to have to buy a haz-mat suit before she gets me in there."

"We'll get you all haz-mat suits," Aaron said. "It's probably not sanitary. There's at least twenty years of filth and stuff built up." He turned to his wife, "Don't you go in there before talking to me, okay?"

"Alright," she acquiesced. "But we are going in and we're going to get him back into the world. Deal with it."

"Anyway," Aaron continued, "Mr. Leon remembers that Buddy did know about that extra room under the school. He pulled old comic books and other books out of crates and sat down there reading when he couldn't handle being in class."

"I can't believe people let him get away with that!" Andy exclaimed, "If I hadn't been in class, they'd have called my parents."

"Well," Lydia said, "They probably did call his parents, but those two didn't have any idea what to do with their son. They couldn't believe he was such a mess because his girlfriend and her sister were gone. Since everyone assumed they'd been kidnapped for whatever reason, they figured Buddy felt bad because he hadn't been around to protect them."

"Now, back to Buddy's story," Polly said, waving off commentary from her friends.

Aaron continued. "Buddy knew how to get in and out of that school. He'd been over it many times with Mr. Leon and then on his own. No one ever paid any attention to him. They ignored him because they didn't want to deal with his grief, so he went everywhere in the school when he was still there. He pried the door open back by the stage and left it that way, watching it for several weeks to see if anyone noticed. No one did."

"What in the hell had he done with the bodies?" Beryl asked. "That's creepy!"

"They were just bones by the time he pulled them out of the ground," Aaron said. "He bought a couple of big plastic tubs and stowed them in his garage. Who would pay any attention to that?"

"When he realized that absolutely no one investigated the opened door at the school, he took the tubs in and spent the next couple of months sealing the bones into the ceiling of the upstairs bathroom where Doug found them. He said he rinsed out the tubs and still uses them for storage."

"Then why did he put his coat down in the crate? I assume that was his coat and t-shirt?" Polly asked.

"I'm not sure exactly what his reasoning was behind that. I asked him and he stammered around a little bit about it. He'd worn the coat every time he came up here to work on the ceiling and he changed out of the t-shirt the night he finished the project so that he could leave it all behind. He found the crate of stuff from his senior year and stowed it in there, thinking it was safe. Then, he left the school, figuring he'd never see any of this again.

"Five years ago he hoped it had been long enough and moved back into town. He was right. No one recognized him and we accepted him as

Marvin Davis. He made friends, getting to know some of his old classmates and was glad to be back.

"Until this last summer when Polly bought the school. The poor guy said he hoped he'd be dead before anyone got back in that school. When he found out that Henry was going to be doing the wood working and floors, he had enough background to apply for a job. I think at some point he knew it was nearly over and he wanted to be on site when everything fell apart around him.

"He nearly confessed to you, Polly, when he was talking to you about death in the kitchen. But, things happened so fast, that it didn't seem to be the right time. He's also the one who took the key. He told me that he opened the newel post that day they were dropping off the boards for the flooring. I think he was rather startled when the lock was changed so quickly. And then no one suspected him, so he kept working."

Beryl snarled, "I want to know how he lived with himself for the last forty years. I know I couldn't if I had done something like that."

"Let's hope you never have to find out, honey," Lydia said.

"What's going to happen to him now?" Sylvie asked.

"Well, the county is going to press charges for Jill's death, for sure. They'll probably go ahead and press forward on Kellie's death, but he didn't seem to be lying. In fact, I think he was glad to get it all out and be finished. They couldn't have saved Kellie's life, so I didn't recommend negligent homicide or anything there." Aaron responded.

"What about Linda and Sandy? Have you told them yet?" Andy asked. "I should probably go see them."

"We have a counselor meeting with them tomorrow afternoon. They know it was Buddy ... or Marvin, now." Aaron said, "The remains will be released to them in the next couple of weeks."

"They will probably appreciate your help planning the memorial service, honey," Lydia said to Andy.

"Alright," Andy responded. "I'll give Sandy a call tomorrow night after this is all over. Oh, what a mess this turned out to be."

Beryl stood up and went to the bar, returning with wine bottles. She refilled Polly's and Lydia's. Sylvie and Andy both refused any more, then she poured the rest of the open bottle in her glass and set the other on the table.

"Polly, you certainly have stirred this town up in the last few weeks," she said.

"I don't know what to say to that. Sometimes it felt as if I opened a closet door and everything fell out on top of me!"

Beryl lifted her glass, "Well at least you weren't the one under those bones!" She shuddered.

Lydia turned her body so she could snuggle into her husband, "Like it or not, Bellingwood is better for knowing this little mystery is solved. I bet everyone in town had pretty much forgotten about it, except for Linda and Sandy, and now they can have closure and people around here can support them one more time.

"Andy, you'll let us know how we can help, right?" she asked.

Andy was staring off into space, running her index finger around the rim of her practically empty wine glass. "What?" she said. "Oh. Sure. I don't know what they'll want to do, but hopefully they will let us do something nice for them. There are still plenty of folks around who remember those girls."

"Do you have coffee made, Lydia?" Andy asked.

Lydia moved to get off the couch, "No, but I can make some up in a hurry."

"No, you sit. It's all over here at the bar, isn't it?"

"Yep. The coffee is in the refrigerator and you know where the pot is." Lydia tucked herself back in beside Aaron. "How was the chicken, sweet-ums?" she asked.

"You know it was wonderful." He reached over to take another piece from the platter Andy had placed on the table.

"Oh, no you don't!" exclaimed Lydia.

"What? I told you everything!" he whimpered.

"You've eaten three pieces of that stuff and two helpings of everything else. You are going to be miserable when you go to bed and I don't want to listen to your moaning all night."

Aaron put his plate on the table and slumped back in his seat. "Fine," he moped. "Just fine. Will you let me have some dessert?"

"I've got it!" Polly jumped out of her seat and went to the bar. She picked up the two platters of goodies and brought them back to the table, which was filled with the dinner plates. Beryl stood up to clear things off for a space and the two of them carried the dirty plates and the chicken platter upstairs.

"Don't worry, Lydia!" Beryl called back down. "We're not going to do the dishes or anything like that. We'll just get these out of the way."

Upstairs, they scraped the dishes and placed them into the sink. They headed back for the stairway and Beryl caught Polly's arm.

"We're all glad you are here, but you're going to be good for Lydia. She needs some young friends around who don't treat her like a big important town matriarch. She's gotten comfortable with you and I like it. You're not like a daughter to her, even if she says that. It's not true. You're a friend. She needs more of those. Let her take care of you when you need it, but tell her to back off when you're done. Okay?"

"Alright," Polly said, hesitantly. "I think I get it."

"Good," Beryl replied, "I intend to keep you around for a while because I like you too." She suddenly pulled Polly into a hug, then released her and acted as if she were racing her back down the steps.

"I won!" she called out when she hit the last step. "Is that coffee done yet, Andy?"

"What? No more wine for you?" Andy asked.

"If I had any more wine, old fart over there would make me do something I didn't want to do." Beryl grinned.

"Yeah?" Aaron asked. "Like what?"

"Like let you drive me home or make me sleep upstairs or some other horrible thing." she retorted.

Lydia started to speak and Beryl interrupted her. "No, none of us are spending the night here tonight. We'll sit around and eat your goodies and drink coffee and then go home to our nice little houses. You've had your sad day cooking marathon and now your sweet-ums is home for the night, so when we've stuffed sugar in our tummies and cleaned up the mess, we'll leave you two to run around the house nekkid or something."

Aaron dropped his head in his hands, "I didn't marry all of these women, how is it they are in my life?" he mumbled.

"What was that, Aaron?" Polly asked.

"Nothing. It's just that Lydia's friend list keeps growing and NONE of you have burly men around to keep me sane. Will one of you try to find a man in the next few months, please?" he begged.

Beryl's eyes rolled, "Well y'all know it isn't gonna be me. There isn't a man this side of the Atlantic that I'd tolerate in my house."

Andy and Sylvie both giggled into their coffee.

"What are you two giggling about?" she asked.

Andy replied, "Well, I, for one, was thinking about a burly Russian man trying to wrangle you into obedience. It made me laugh. A lot." And the whole room burst out into giggles.

"And you, smart stuff?" Beryl asked Sylvie.

"Honestly, I was thinking that I didn't want a man in my life either. I have two boys and that is plenty of testosterone for me. But, I like the Russian man image better."

The rest of the evening passed as the women laughed at their war stories from old dates. Aaron fell asleep sometime after his third glass of wine.

At ten o'clock, Sylvie said, "I need to get the boys home. Are you about ready to go, Polly?"

"I sure am," Polly said. "Let's get some more of this stuff upstairs."

"No way," Lydia replied. "I've got this. I'll leave the old man here while I clean and then stir him when it's time to head upstairs."

Aaron growled, "The old man is awake. I'll help you take the stuff up."

"Everyone grab a handful," Beryl called out. "It will be done in one trip that way, then we can all go home guilt free."

The lights were all on at the school when they drove up and Sylvie said, "I love seeing it all lit up like this again. Thanks for doing this, Polly."

"Wait until you see all of the plans I have for it. We're going to have a great time!" Polly replied.

They went inside and both dogs rushed to greet them at the front door. Obiwan jumped into Polly's arms and she carried him around the steps. The boys were sprawled out on the floor in front of the kitchen, playing video games on laptops and handhelds. Plates and cups and wrappers were scattered on the counter.

Doug leaped up and said, "Oh! You're back! Did you guys have a good time?"

"Not as good a time as it looks like you had!" Polly said.

Andrew ran up to his mom, who reached out to hug him close. "This was the best mom, can we do it again?"

"I'm sure we'll figure something out. I'm glad you guys had fun. Now, let's get this mess cleaned up and we'll head home. You have to get up and go to church in the morning!"

Jason looked up from the game he was playing, "Aw, mom. I'm not done yet. Can't we stay a little longer?"

"Nope, not tonight, Jason. Save your game and let's get going. Don't argue with me."

He was obviously accustomed to that tone of voice and rapidly did as she asked. The six of them gathered the trash and Sylvie's dishes, making quick work of the kitchen. Doug and Billy gathered up their things.

Billy said to Polly, "I've had a good time hanging out here. I think you've got a good thing going. Thanks for letting us play here with our friends."

She squeezed his shoulder. "Thank you." Polly pulled cash out of her purse and Billy stopped her. "No, me and Doug talked about this. We're not taking your money. We have as much fun as anyone and you let us bring our friends over here, so we still owe you."

"Alright, then. But, I haven't forgotten about dinner!" she said as everyone walked to the front door. Big Jack leaped out of the door as soon as it was open and Obiwan tried to follow. Polly grabbed his collar and held on.

They said their goodnights and drove away. Polly shut the front door and walked around, turning lights off. She and Obiwan walked up the stairs and into her apartment.

"This has been a wild few weeks, little guy. What say we have a nice, calm day tomorrow? Would that be alright?"

He licked her face in affirmation.

CHAPTER TWENTY-SIX

“Yes! Yes! I’m up!” Polly felt a cold tongue on her face and opened her eyes. Obiwan was lying beside her in the bed.

"How did? Oh, I forgot! Oh dear!" She sat straight up and looked around the room. Nothing was out of place and the door was shut. The dog tucked himself in beside her and looked up expectantly. "You slept here all night, didn't you?" He stood up in the bed and she ran her hand down his back several times, then pulled his bottom close to hers so he was sitting beside her. "Well, as long as you can be good, I guess there's no reason for you to sleep in the kennel."

By now both of them were fully awake and she stood up. "It's supposed to be a beautiful day. Let's take a long walk this morning by the creek, okay?"

He wagged his tail and she picked him up and set him on the floor as she pulled on jeans and a t-shirt. She put a flannel shirt on over that and then tugged a sweatshirt over her head. Thick socks and her hiking boots went on and Polly snagged ear muffs and a pair of gloves out of a box on her floor. "I'm ready now and I think you have everything you need. Let's go."

They went downstairs and out the back door of the kitchen and headed for the copse of trees that led to the creek. Polly's eyes were caught by the bark on the trees that was pulling away in the late fall air and showing the mottled wood of the tree itself. "Sycamore," she thought. Then she realized and said, "OH! That's why it's called Sycamore Creek." It was only a trickle, there hadn't been a lot of rain this year, so she and Obiwan crawled down over the bank and walked the creek. She let him off the leash and he ran ahead of her and then back to see if she was going to catch up. The creek ran under the highway, but she crawled back up and walked around, continuing to follow it. The trees had been losing leaves for quite some time and she picked up some of the prettier ones as she walked, looking at their veins and appreciating the peace of early morning in a small town in Iowa.

This was the right decision. Sometimes she felt as if she'd fallen into everything, but it seemed like every step she'd taken had been the right one, even if weird things had happened along the way.

Polly thought about her new friends. They were so different from the girls she knew in Boston. Their careers had been all-encompassing, and while Beryl's art was nearly an obsession for her, she was still pretty laid back. Polly knew she would miss her life in Boston with all of the excitement of the city and the easy access to activities on the East Coast, but this slower life was nice. She would enjoy this.

She picked up a few more leaves and looked at the symmetry. The sycamore trees lining the creek covered everything in falling leaves.

Polly's mind took her back to her elementary Sunday School class. "Zacchaeus was a wee little man, and a wee little man was he. He climbed up in a sycamore tree, for the Lord he wanted to see. And when the Lord came passing by, he looked up in the tree. And he said, 'Zacchaeus! You come down! For I'm going to your house today. I'm going to your house today.'"

A few of the trees were huge and through the fog of her memory she saw an immense tree spread out in a field, with soldiers and horses standing under it for shelter. "Hmmm," she thought.

She turned the sycamore leaf over and over in her hand while she and Obiwan walked home. They'd been out for forty-five minutes and she was getting hungry. She also wanted to spend a few minutes doing research on the internet. It took nearly as long for them to walk back to the school. Obiwan had to cover all of the territory he'd already marked, to ensure nothing had interfered with his efforts, and then explore new territory as well. They walked back in through the kitchen door and she snagged her laptop before heading upstairs. Dropping it on her coffee table, she poured food into Obiwan's bowl, then stripped her sweatshirt and boots off.

"Whaddya think, Obiwan?" she asked. He looked up from his food dish and wagged, "I think it will work quite well."

Flipping her computer's lid up, she sat down, pulled it on to her lap and began to search.

"Exactly!" she shouted. Obiwan stopped eating and turned his head to look at her. "Oh, sorry, little guy. Go ahead. I'll try to be more respectful."

At the Battle of Brandywine in Pennsylvania during the Revolutionary War, both Lafayette's and Washington's armies took shelter under the tree.

Polly did a little more research and choked up when she read that it was a seventy year old sycamore tree which saved St. Paul's Chapel across the street from the Twin Towers after the tree fell and its branches protected the chapel from falling debris.

In America, the sycamore tree stood as a symbol of strength and protection … exactly what Polly hoped for the future of this building.

Her mind began racing as she pictured big sycamore trees lining the driveway and the sidewalk along the highways. More trees would fill the yard and over the years as they grew, would offer incredible shade.

People would stop calling it the old school when she put the sign out front: Sycamore House.

That was perfect.

Obiwan jumped up on the couch beside her and she hugged him close. "Sycamore House," she whispered to him. "Sycamore House."

THANK YOU!

I hope you have had a wonderful time visiting Bellingwood and getting to know some of Polly's new friends.

Check out Polly's Facebook page: https://www.facebook.com/pollygiller for news of upcoming novels. Tell me about your favorite characters and what you remember collecting when you were in high school. Would Doug Leon have found some of your things lying around?

Diane Greenwood Muir's website, http://nammynools.com might be under construction for a while, but will also be home to more news from Bellingwood. Come back often.

The next book featuring Polly and all her friends will be published in April 2013, but never fear, there's more before you go. Turn the page and find a short Christmas story.

POLLYS

FIRST CHRISTMAS

AT SYCAMORE HOUSE

A BELLINGWOOD SHORT STORY

CHAPTER ONE

Standing still was not an option, so Polly paced back and forth across the hallway. This was the first time she had ever done anything like this and she was absolutely terrified. She smoothed her sweater once more, and then checked her hair again in the reflection of the window to the office. Obiwan sat against the wall of the auditorium watching her. She paced around twice more, then stopped beside the dog and bent over to scratch his ears. In the month they'd been together, he'd grown quickly and she didn't have to bend over quite so far.

She walked away, then went back to the office, stepped in and turned the light on. She walked through the other two offices, checking to ensure everything was neat and tidy, turned the light off, thought about it and turned all of them back on. She stopped at the conference room table, straightened a folder at the end, nudged the chair in closer to the table, then nudged it a little to the left.

"Breathe, Giller," she said out loud. "You can do this. You're in charge. This is your place. You'll be fine." After her personal pep talk, she took two deep breaths and walked back out into the hallway. "Benches would be great out here," she thought to herself. "I should talk to Henry about that." Before she could pull out her phone to send herself a note, the front door opened and a young man walked in. He was over six foot tall, with dark, curly hair and was dressed in a well-cut charcoal suit, with a burgundy shirt. His tie was conservative, but Polly caught a glimpse of color in his socks as he walked. She pushed her phone back into the pocket of her jeans and strode over to greet him.

"Welcome to Sycamore House," she said. "I'm Polly Giller."

He met her and they shook hands. "It's nice to meet you, Miss Giller," he paused. "It is Miss Giller, isn't it?"

"Yes, it's Miss. Actually, I prefer Polly." She took her hand back. He had a nice, firm, confident grip. "And you're Jeff Lyndsay?"

"Yes I am!" He glanced at the dog. "Is he yours?"

Polly couldn't help herself and giggled. Why else would there be a dog patiently sitting here watching, but she said. "Yes, that's Obiwan. He's my shadow."

She gestured to the office and said, "Shall we go on in and get started?"

He followed her through the outer office into the conference room and took a seat. She sat down at the end of the table and pushed away the folder she'd left there. Polly hoped this worked out. She'd talked to eight different people and none of them had seemed to have the right mix of personality and creativity, business acumen and excitement about her dream. If she was going to hire a full time coordinator, she wanted someone who would fall in love with Sycamore House as much as she had and after talking on the phone several times to him, she really wanted it to be Jeff. He had flown in this morning from Columbus, Ohio so they could finally meet and do a live interview and seemed like the perfect person to get Sycamore House going.

"You know," she said, "I'm not sure why we're sitting down in here. I want to show you what I've been dreaming about for the last six months. Come on, let's talk a walk around."

Jeff smiled and nodded, then followed her back out into the main hallway.

"I was thinking before you walked in," she said, "that we need some benches or something out here. It's pretty barren." Polly pointed at a painting series on the wall in front of her. "That's by my friend Beryl

Watson. Isn't her stuff great?"

He nodded and didn't say anything, continuing to smile.

Across the hall, they entered a room clearly still under construction. "This is where Henry Sturtz, my contractor and wood guru has been working. When he's finished with everything else, he'll do this space. It will be split into four rooms, so we can have classes and small gatherings, maybe some computer space and a lounge area."

They walked around the corner and she headed for the kitchen. "This was my big dream. I have appliances in here no woman should have unless she is serving hundreds of people every day." Polly giggled, "That might be an exaggeration, but I had a great time putting it all together. The open counter is from the days when school lunches were served. It’s awfully convenient."

She pulled out her key and opened the door to the auditorium. "This will be for large gatherings and events. Nearly anything can happen in here." She pointed to the walls. "Within the next week these will be fully baffled for sound and then we will also bring down the ceiling a bit because of all the ductwork that needs to go in. It will be finished before Christmas.

"Behind the stage are the bathrooms and storage. You can get to it from the far hallway and from the kitchen."

"So, if you are in one of the classrooms, you have to cut through the auditorium to get to the bathroom?" he asked.

"I suppose so," she responded. "There weren't too many options."

"Alright," he said. "What's upstairs?"

"Let's go up! It's one of my favorite places."

They walked up the steps to the landing and looked out over the main floor, then took the left stairway on up to the top level. On their right was Polly's apartment with its extruding entryway. Polly pointed at it and said, "That's my apartment. I'll show you that in a minute, but over on this side are the three rooms I would like to keep filled. I am hoping to make them longer term rentals, say, for an author who needs a month away from their life, or an artist who needs something new to look at. We're still working on the interiors, but they are pretty much finished."

She opened the door to the smallest of the three at the front of the building. It was one immense room. Light streaming in from the tall windows illuminated the patterns in the flooring and the knots and burls of the wood in the bookcases and trim around the room. A small sink was tucked into a corner behind a closet buildout and there was a large king-sized bed in the room, but otherwise it was empty.

"The other two rooms are similar to this one," Polly said as they left and moved to the center room. They glanced inside, and then went to the last room.

"No bathrooms?" he asked.

"Well, there wasn't a good way to incorporate those into the room plans, so we converted the old boys and girls bathrooms up here," and she pointed to the end of the hall, "into two spa bathrooms, figuring we were going to have no more than three guests at a time, so it shouldn't be a problem."

"Alright, last stop on the tour is my private apartment," Polly unlocked the door to her entryway and led him inside. She had just finished outfitting the kitchen and had moved the eight-foot table and chairs up to the dining area. It was still a bit sparse. One day she would move the items in from her father's home which were in a storage unit in Story City, but she had done well with the space and was pleased to finally be settled.

"This is quite nice," Jeff said. "You have a good eye."

"I read a lot," she responded. "Read and look at a lot of pictures. It might take a while, but I finally decide what it is I like and then I figure out how to make it happen."

They walked back to the main hall and she pulled the door shut.

"That's the inside, for the most part. We have a lot of outside work yet to do, but I won't start that until spring."

Polly stopped before they headed back down the steps. "Tell me why you are interested in leaving Columbus, Ohio for a little town in the middle of Iowa?" she asked.

He began walking down, then stopped on a step, "I wanted to do something different with my life. I could get into a hotel chain and make my way up, or manage restaurants or even get into corporate work, but this looked intriguing to me. Your offer is a good one, enough so that it shouldn't be ignored." He started back down again, then, turned around.

"How cosmopolitan is this little town?"

Polly laughed out loud. "Bellingwood? It wants to be bigger than it is, but there are still too many of the older generation who like things the way they are. We're close enough to Ames and Des Moines to have a pastiche of cosmopolitan life, but it doesn't happen ... not really. I suspect if we make a name for ourselves, we'll draw from around Iowa and maybe into the states surrounding us, but as much as I'd like to think we would bring people in from the coasts, I'd be fooling myself.

"The people are ... genuine," she said. They continued down the steps. "Some of them are extraordinary and most have education beyond high school. They are genuinely interested in you and many will accept you as you are. I've been surprised at how easy their acceptance of me has been. Things were a little weird when I moved in, but they've opened up and let me be who I am."

"Here," she said as the hit the main floor, "do you want some coffee?"

"Coffee would be fine," he replied.

"Go on back in and I'll get it." She poured out two cups of coffee and went back to the conference room.

"What would you want me to do, specifically?" he asked.

"Everything and anything." Polly replied. "I'll take care of management and financial decisions and I want to know everything you are doing and planning, and I would want to be notified of any major decisions, but what I'm looking for is someone to handle this entire place, from making sure we have the guest rooms full to keeping guests happy and content; from scheduling and organizing parties in the auditorium, to any classes we have going on, from helping me with decorating, to landscaping. I'd want you to be practically a partner with me in this endeavor."

"What about hiring decisions, cleaning and lawn work and all of the nitty gritty details." he continued.

The two of them continued to discuss the job and what Polly

envisioned for Sycamore House and before he left, she realized he was probably the right person for the job, but knew she needed to be able to think about it a little more.

"When are you planning to head back to Columbus?" she asked and stood up. The two of them walked out into the hallway again.

"I have a flight scheduled for tomorrow afternoon. I thought I'd spend the evening and tomorrow morning looking around the area since I've never been in Iowa."

"Where are you staying?"

"I'm at a hotel in Ames and I haven't checked in yet, so that's my next stop! Thank goodness for GPS in the cars these days, right?" He laughed a little uncertainly. "Oh hell," then he laughed again. "Well, that language was probably inappropriate for the first time I meet you. Anyway, Iowa can't be that big and scary. Can it?"

"That's funny. I returned six months ago from living in Boston for fourteen years. Iowa really isn't that scary. Enjoy your evening and I'll be in touch. Is there anything else you'd like to ask me?"

He looked her in the eyes and said, "Is there any reason you wouldn't offer me the job right now?"

Polly was taken aback. She swallowed, blinked and looked back at him. "Honestly, no. It just scares me to make that kind of decision in a hurry."

"Then, offer me the job. I'll accept it and you can take me out to dinner somewhere in Ames to celebrate. I'll fly back to Columbus, pack a few bags and come back by the end of the week and help you get ready for a terrific Christmas season. We can have a huge party here. I'll do all the work. You can introduce Sycamore House ... and me ... to the area and then I'll find a place and move out here after the first of the year. Tell me why that couldn't work?"

"Wow." Polly said. "Let me do it this way. You go away. I need to think … "

He interrupted and said, "What do you need to think about? I'd love this job and you will love me. I can promise you'll love the way I do the job, at least."

"I need to think. I don't rush into decisions like this."

"If you had found anyone else, this job would already be filled and you wouldn't have paid for me to fly out here. You need me, Miss, I mean, Polly Giller."

Polly looked around, then said the first thing that came into her head. "We need benches in this hallway. I need to sit down and put my head in my hands for a few minutes."

"No you don't. You're fine. And this is going to be great." He threw his arms open wide. "This is already great and I am going to make it grand! Sign me up, Polly. Let me do this job."

Polly laughed a little hysterically. "Alright. You're on. I had plans for tonight, but I can cancel them. I need to do a quick run with Obiwan here, then go upstairs and change. The contract is in that folder on the conference table and we'll sign it over dinner. If you want, you can make the computer in the far office yours. Feel free to wander around and dig into anything you'd like to see." By this point, she was practically hyperventilating, so she slowed down and took a breath.

Jeff smiled at her and nodded again, the turned around and walked into the office while she took the leash hanging on the newel post and attached it to Obiwan's collar and opened the front door, walking outside into the mild December weather. "Alright, bud, mama needs a walk. Let's go."

She hadn't gotten around the side of the building when her phone rang. It was Lydia. "How did the interview go? I figure you wouldn't answer if you were still in the middle of it."

"Oh, Lydia!" Polly laughed. "He hired himself!"

"He what?" Polly heard Lydia laughing on thc othcr cnd.

"Yep. Apparently, I'm taking him to dinner in Ames to celebrate. He's flying home tomorrow, then back by the end of the week to help me get holiday festivities ready." Polly sighed. "Lydia, I didn't even know I was having holiday festivities. I haven't given any thought to Christmas decorations!"

"It sounds like you just hired a character in this one, Polly!" Lydia said.

"Yes I have and I think he's going to be as much of a surprise to Bellingwood as I was, but there's no reason it can't all work out, right?" Polly heard her voice escalate as panic began to set in.

"Right, dear. You're a smart girl and you've probably made a really good decision. Calm down and enjoy it," Lydia said to assure her friend. "I was only checking on you and I knew you wouldn't call me to tell me about it. So, when do we get to meet him?"

"Oh, I can't wait for that. Let's plan something this weekend when he's in town. Wait!" Polly said, "Where is he going to stay?"

"Why don't you ask him that," Lydia responded. "I'll bet he's got some ideas."

"Okay. I'll talk to you later. I'm going to walk this dog and think through my decision before I sign anything!" Polly hung up and picked up the pace. "Come on, dog. I need to put a little distance between me and Sycamore House right now. I need to think. Rushing me into a decision. Bah. This one's going to be trouble, I can tell right now!"

They followed the tree line by the creek while Polly processed on what had happened. He was right. She needed him if she wanted to make Sycamore House bigger than a little mom and pop place on the side of the road. He was coming in pretty inexpensively and if he could pull off what he thought he could, his salary would be well worth it. She needed to man up and make this work. She'd sign the contract, get him in position and let him have at it.

It still freaked her out to have had to make a decision like this so quickly. Polly kicked a small rock in front of her and as it skittered out of the way, Obiwan lurched after it. She followed and thought about her Dad. He'd been fearless when it came to making business decisions. He never seemed to second-guess himself or worry about things, but she wished he were here to encourage her and tell her she was doing the right thing now.

When she'd gotten the scholarship to Boston University, he hadn't hesitated. It was the right thing to do and she was going, even if it meant they'd be far apart from each other. When she was offered the job at Boston Public Library after graduation, he only asked her one question - did she want to work there. When she hesitated, he told her she needed to respond with whatever her gut told her to do.

Then Polly realized that even though for some it might seem like she had run away from Boston because of the terrible situation with her ex-boyfriend, Joey Delancy, in truth, she had been ready to make a change and the best change she could have made was to return to Iowa. When her Realtor offered the opportunity to buy the school in Bellingwood at a ridiculously low price, she grabbed it without hesitation.

That was what she needed to remember and that's what Jeff asked of her this afternoon, to be fearless when making the right decision. He was correct. She needed him and he was the best person for the job. She was lucky to have found him and he would bring a lot of value to this little company she was building. It was time to quit worrying and get started.

She turned Obiwan around and they jogged back to Sycamore House. Jeff was walking around the outside of the building, looking around and taking notes.

"What are you thinking about?" she asked as she walked up to him.

"Just planning the Christmas lights. You know we're going to have to get on that right away. Can you organize ladders and cranes and extra help? I know where I can get the lights. They'll be shipped here by Thursday afternoon. I'll be back in town then and if we can get a crew working on Friday, I'll have this place ready to go by the weekend.

"Umm, okay?" she said. Then with a little more definition, she said, "Alright! Will you let me make a few phone calls right now? I need to find someone who can bring in a cherry picker for us."

"I've signed the contract," he said. “It's on your desk. And thanks for the computer. It's great. But, I'd like to get a tablet, if that's alright."

"Sure. We can do that in the morning, if you don't mind not wandering around the city."

Polly walked into her office and opened her cell phone. She called Henry. He was the only person who could help her pull this off and if he didn't know who to contact, she was going to have to scramble. She wasn't sure what Jeff was used to, but Iowa didn't move that fast. Hmmm, she guessed they would move that fast now!

Henry assured her he would take care of it. While they were talking,

Jeff walked into her office and rubbed his fingers together as if asking for money, she looked at him and he mouthed, "credit card for lights." She stood up, pulled her wallet out and handed him her card, thinking, "This could be a huge mistake." In a few minutes, she heard the printer running and he walked back in with a receipt and her card, leaving them on her desk.

She finished speaking with Henry, who said he would have plenty of people there on Friday to hang lights and then she opened up the folder with Jeff's contract. He'd signed and initialed everything. She signed the rest of it and walked out into the main office. He was already on the phone in his office, so she waited. He waved her in. He said good-bye to whomever he had been speaking with and she laid a copy of the contract on his desk.

"We're ready to go."

He stood up and shook her hand. "Polly Giller. We're going to make a helluva team. You've got something amazing started here and I'm going to rock your socks, girlfriend! Are you ready?"

Polly winked at him. "I'm ready, Jeff. It's time."

She ran Obiwan upstairs to the apartment, changed her clothes and came back down. Jeff was on his phone again, rapidly taking notes. He held his finger up and when he clicked his phone off, said to her, "There isn't much time, but we're going to give this town a great Christmas. They'll be talking about it for at least a month!

"I have a twenty foot tree coming here on Thursday for the main hall, just past the landing. Two more trees will be coming for the front steps, then you and are I going to talk about the party."

"What party? I'm almost afraid to ask!" Polly declared.

"Your all-community Christmas event. We need to set a date and make sure nothing else in town conflicts, then we'll spread the news. Do you know someone who can cater this thing?"

Polly sighed, "Let's go to dinner. I'll lead you down to Ames, take you to dinner and I'll think about it on the way."

She got in her truck, he ran to his rental car and followed her as they made their way out of town and headed for supper.

CHAPTER TWO

Temperatures seemed to be dropping more every night and made it that much more difficult for Polly to crawl out of her bed in the morning. She was eternally grateful for radiant floor heating. At least she could put her feet on the floor without shivers radiating up her spine. She bundled up and snapped the leash on her dog. Obiwan didn't seem to care about the temperature, he was happy to be outside as long as she was with him. They walked out the front door and had it not been for the street lights, it would have been dark. "It's known territory for us this morning, Obiwan. I'm not tripping into the creek so you can have an adventure." She patted her coat pocket to ensure she had her phone and a flashlight.

They turned right and walked beyond the school to the concrete pad where the old gymnasium had once stood. Andy told her it had come down the year after the school closed. It was practically crumbling, so the city razed it due to safety concerns. They walked as far as the trees lining the creek and then followed the treeline back to the school. Obiwan sniffed at every leaf grassy patch. As they passed behind Sycamore House, Polly saw lights from a car, then flashing lights and heard a crunch of tires in her lane as two vehicles pulled in. She and Obiwan continued to walk toward the lane, wondering what might be up. Obiwan took a few sniffs as they got closer and pulled her faster and faster to the vehicles.

When she realized who was getting out of the sheriff's car, it made more sense. Stu Decker had been to Sycamore House several times after her coming home party and Obiwan recognized his familiar scent.

"Good morning, Stu! You pulled a rotten shift!" she said.

"Ah, I took over for a buddy who wanted to go to his girlfriend's Christmas party last night."

"I told them you were a good guy, no matter what anyone says!" she laughed.

"I know that! You keep standing up for me," he replied. "Just a minute, though. I need to deal with this guy."

"Okay. When you're done, if you want to come in for coffee, it's already brewing."

"I might do that. A cup to go would help this night end well."

He bent over to the driver, who had rolled his window down and was handing him paperwork.

"Just a second sir, I'll be right back." Stu said, as he carried it back to his car.

Polly and Obiwan were walking past the car, when the dog pulled away from her and headed for the rear tire.

"What are you doing, Obiwan? Stop that!" she shouted and pulled back on his leash. He continued to drag her toward the car and began digging at something in the wheel well.

"Obiwan! Stop!" The dog pulled something to the ground, then sat in front of it and looked at Polly as if to say, "I found this, is that okay?"

She flicked her flashlight on and saw a package on the ground. Stu left his vehicle and bent down to see what it was. He picked it up, dropped it into a bag he pulled out of his pocket and then went back to the driver.

"Sir, would you get out of the car?" he asked.

The driver's door opened and lights came on in the car. Polly could see a woman in the front seat, rubbing her eyes, as if she were trying to wake up. In the back seat were three small children, all sound asleep. The youngest looked to be around a year old and the other two were several years older than that.

"Sir, I am about to place you under arrest for possession of illegal narcotics, would you please walk around behind the car?"

The man began walking and Polly could see the look of shock on his face. He looked up, peered at her, looked away, then back at her and said, "Polly Giller? Is that you?"

Polly looked more closely and realized she had gone to high school with this man. He dated her best friend, Marsha for two years. "Bruce McKenzie?"

"Polly, I don't know what is going on! I don't know anything about drugs."

Obiwan kept trying to get back to the car, but Polly pulled his leash tight and sternly told him to sit. He sat.

"Please get into the car, sir." Stu walked Bruce around to the back seat and opened the door.

Just then, a third vehicle pulled into the lane in front of the car. Aaron Merritt got out and strode over. Stu took a moment to explain the situation and Aaron walked to the passenger side of the vehicle. "I'm sorry, ma'am, we need you to step out as well."

Fear flitted across her face as she looked into the back of the car. The children were still asleep, as she pulled her sweater tight and stepped out. "What is it? Bruce, what is going on?"

Aaron asked the two of them, "Do you have any family around here who could take your children? This is a serious offense. We need to process this vehicle for further drugs and will be taking you to Boone ."

Bruce said from the back seat, "We were going back to Story City to see if my father would consent to let me work for him. Things have been tough in Denver."

The girl broke in, "He doesn't know we're coming. If Bruce had called to ask, he would have said no, but we were hoping he couldn't say no to our faces. Sheriff, those aren't our drugs!"

"I'm sorry. We have no choice," Aaron replied.

She began to weep as he placed cuffs on her and walked with her back to his own vehicle. At that point, the oldest boy woke up and saw what was happening. He started yelling for his mother, which caused the other two to awaken and begin crying.

"Sheriff, what are you going to do with the children?" Polly asked.

"We'll wait here until Child Protective Services shows up, then we'll let them take care of this." he said.

"Oh, come on!" she protested. "Let me take the kids inside. I'm calling Lydia." She pulled her phone out and dialed, then pressed send. Lydia assured her she would be right there and they would set this straight.

Sheriff Merritt shook his head and sighed. "You aren't helping me do my job, Polly."

"I don't intend to help you do your job," she said. "I intend to take care of some very frightened kids. Let their mom come over here and tell them it's alright to go with me."

He brought the woman back to the car and opened the back door.

"Sammy, this is Polly," and she nodded at Polly. "She is going to take you into this great big old school and you are going to help her with Emma and Tyler, alright?"

"Mom! What's going on?" the boy cried. "Why is Bruce in that car and why is this Sheriff trying to take you away! Mom!"

"I don't know what's going on right, now, Sammy, but we have to go with them and clear things up. It is all going to be alright. And Polly is going to make sure that you three are taken care of while we're dealing with this. Will you be good?"

"Mom!" he began wailing and jumped out of the car, grabbing at her waist. She leaned over and rested her face on his head. The baby and his older sister were now wailing inside the car.

Polly handed the leash to Aaron, then reached in to unsnap the seat strap and pulled the little boy out with his car seat.

"Sammy," his mother said. "I need you to be a big boy. You've done such a good job all the way out here and both Bruce and I would appreciate it if you could continue taking care of them. Can you do that?"

His wailing calmed down to snorting sobs, "Okay. I'm scared, though. Will they let you come back?"

"As soon as we get this figured out, we'll be back. I promise. Would you get your sister out of the car, so she can go with Miss Polly, too?"

She turned to the Sheriff. We have a couple of their bags in the trunk. Tyler's diaper bag and a package of diapers are right there in the back seat. Can Polly take those, so the kids have some of their things?

He looked at the little boy. "Pick out a toy for each of you to play with today, and tonight I will bring the rest of your things." Aaron reached into the back seat and grabbed the diaper bag. He opened it up, rifled through it and thrust it at Polly. "Hug your mom one more time, Sammy, then she needs to get in my car."

Sammy and Emma both hugged their mom and after he handed Obiwan's leash back to Polly, Aaron escorted her to his vehicle. Once she was inside, he walked back over to the car where Polly and the kids were standing. "I don't like this any more than you do, so don't get pissed at me. These two have a lot of explaining to do and I'm guessing that since Obiwan is still trying to dig at the car, there's plenty more where the first package came from. Why they'd carry three kids with drugs in their car, I have no idea. People make me angry some days.

"By the way, how did you train him for that?" he chuckled, nodding at Obiwan.

Polly looked at him and grimaced. "Are you kidding me? I have no idea how he did that. A good nose, I guess."

"We might have to hire him," Aaron replied, "That's a hell of a nose!"

He took Obiwan's leash and the diaper bag back from her and she reached for Emma's hand. The little girl looked up at her tentatively with a tear-streaked face.

"Come on kids," she said. "I have breakfast and a great big room for you to play in today."

She turned back to Aaron, "And I have absolutely no idea what I'm going to do." She reached down, took Emma's hand and began slowly walking across the lawn to the school.

"I'll have CPS call you later this morning and we'll get everything settled. Lydia will be here soon and you know how I love it when she gets involved." He shook his head.

They got to the front steps and he opened the door. Aaron unsnapped Obiwan's leash, who went dashing in and up the steps.

"He thinks it is time for breakfast, everyone. Do you agree?" Polly looked at each of the kids. "Go on upstairs and he'll show you which one is the right door. It's unlocked. Go inside and I'll be right there."

The baby was still crying and the older children were sniffling and sobbing. Somehow, a floppy dog, though, had grabbed their attention and they followed him up the steps.

Polly took the diaper bag back and said, "I've got it now, Sheriff."

"Alright," he said. "We're waiting for a team to come up and take their car to Boone. As soon as they arrive, we'll be cleared out."

He placed his hand on her forearm. "And thank you. This might not be procedure, but there's no reason to upset these kids any more than they already are. We'll get 'em taken care of today."

"No hurries. We'll be fine."

She started up the steps and heard the door shut behind her. Walking in the front door of her apartment, she saw that the two older children had found a place on the floor and were playing with the dog. He ran up to her, wagging and wiggling.

"I know, I know," she said. "It's breakfast." He dashed out to the kitchen and stood in front of his food dish. "Kids, I'm going to put his food in a dish and then get things started for you, would you like to watch some morning cartoons?"

They simply nodded. Polly put the baby down on the floor and walked over to the couch where the remote was sitting. "Do you want to sit on the sofa? It's a lot more comfortable?"

Both children quietly got up and sat on the edge of the sofa. Polly turned the television on and flipped the channel to Nickelodeon. She knew for a fact there were cartoons being played on that channel, she watched them every morning.

"Do you guys like SpongeBob?" she asked, looking at the clock. Yep, almost time. "I watch him every day," she said. The two nodded and watched the television.

"Alright, I'm going to feed Obiwan and then see what we have in here for your brother. His name is Tyler, right?"

Sammy got up off the sofa and walked over to pick up the diaper bag. "I can do it. I help Mom all the time. She has some formula already mixed up in here." He took a bottle out and walked over to the baby whose seat was on the floor.

"Would you like me to carry him over to the table in front of the couch?" Polly asked as she reached for the car seat.

She got the kids set up and watched as Sammy began to feed his brother, stroking his head and talking to him.

"Thank you Sammy," she said. "I appreciate it. I think you're doing a great job and your mom would be proud of you."

Polly then walked out into the kitchen and opened the cupboard, grabbing the container of food to fill Obiwan's dish. His entire body wiggled with glee as food poured out and he was munching kibble before she got the container put away.

There was a knock at her door and she assumed it was Lydia, "Come in!" Polly called.

Lydia walked in, her arms laden with bags and boxes. Polly ran over to help her. They unloaded everything onto the dining table. "What did you bring?" Polly exclaimed.

"Oh, a little bit of everything," Lydia laughed. "I have so many things at the house for my own grandkids, I thought maybe you could use some of them here today. Andy is coming over in a little bit to help us and I talked to Sylvie. She said she'll bring the boys over after school."

Polly peeked inside the two bags she had taken from Lydia and saw games and toys. However, since the kids were completely occupied with their little brother and television, she hoped they might be able to keep some of these things for later. She nodded to the bedroom and Lydia followed her in. Dumping everything on the bed, they shook the bags empty and unflapped one of the smaller boxes. There were cars and dolls, stuffed animals, a small train set and a few board games.

"Wow, did you bring your entire stash?" Polly asked.

"You'd think so, but this doesn't begin to make a dent in the toy closet. My grand babies won't even know these things are missing."

Polly gave Lydia a sideways glance and said a bit sheepishly, "I don't know what I was thinking. I've never spent any time around children. When I was in high school, Dad thought it would be a good idea if I got some experience as a babysitter. He set me up on a job with one of his buddies, who was the doctor in town. That was one of the weirdest evenings I ever spent with anyone."

Lydia giggled, "What happened?"

"Well, their little baby girl had been sick and of course, the doctor had given her some kind of medicine. When it came time to change her diaper, I ran into two issues. One, I had never changed a diaper in my life. Ever!"

That made Lydia snort a little. "You're kidding!"

"When would I have done it?" Polly protested. "I was an only child."

"Anyway, the smell was so bad, I knew I had to do something. I could have called Mary, I suppose, but I found the box of diapers and lo and behold, there were directions on the back. So, I propped it up on the changing table. Then, I pulled the diaper off and holy smokes, but it was runny and I'm not kidding when I tell you it was dark blue. That was some awful stuff. I cleaned her up and all I could think was that I was so glad she was a baby and would never be able to tell anyone that I had used the directions on the box to know what to do. I managed to get a new diaper on her and then I prayed she wouldn't need to be changed again before her parents got home."

"So," Lydia chuckled, "I'm guessing you aren't much better now?"

"Yeah, no," Polly said. "The only other time I had to deal with a diaper, Mary came over to rescue me because it was cloth and the little girl had taken it off herself!"

"We're going to make sure you have help today, Polly, and maybe a few lessons, too!" Lydia walked out of the room laughing.

Polly followed her and said to the two older children, "What would you like for breakfast this morning? I have cereal or I can make oatmeal." When she said the word oatmeal, both kids curled their upper lip. "Alright, oatmeal is unacceptable. I can make pancakes. Would you like that?"

Emma's face lit up. "Can you make Mickey pancakes?" she asked.

Polly thought for a moment, saw it in her mind and replied with, "Yes! I think I can! But, only if you eat the whole thing!"

"Mickey! Mickey!" Emma chanted and jumped off the couch to wrap her arms around Polly's leg.

Polly reached down to pick the little girl up in her arms. "Would you like to keep me company while I cook?" she asked, trying not to let the tears that threatened, drip past her eyelid.

"I help! I help!" Emma curled her fist in Polly's hair as she walked into the kitchen. Polly plopped her little bottom on the counter top and said, "Sit right here while I gather the ingredients, okay?"

"Okay!" Emma replied.

Polly glanced back at Sammy. Lydia looked up at her and smiled as if to say, "I've got this." The two were playing talking quietly while Sammy fed the baby.

"Sammy, would you like some Mickey pancakes as well?" Polly asked.

"Regular pancakes would be fine," he quietly said.

"What do you think, Emma," Polly said to the little girl who was trying hard not to stick her fingers in the batter. "Shall I make them all Mickey pancakes?"

"Sammy's sad." Emma said. "We're both sad. Mommy didn't do anything wrong and that policeman took her away. Will we ever see her again?"

Lydia stood up and walked toward the dining area. "My husband is the sheriff who took your mommy away. I've told him that he has to do everything he can to make sure your mommy comes back as soon as possible. He's a good man and I love him. You don't need to worry."

"Why did he take her away, then?" Sammy asked.

"Because they found something bad in the car, Sammy. Something that shouldn't be there. However, they're going to check everything out and they will do the right thing." Lydia replied.

"I still don't get it," he whimpered.

"I know you don't," Lydia said. "And I'm sorry about that. But, for now, you get to eat pancakes and watch television and play with a big puppy! How's that?"

"I wish my mom were here."

"Yes, you do. You should keep wishing and praying until she gets back, alright? Then you can tell her how much you were thinking about her and you can tell her everything about your day with us."

Polly had been flipping pancakes while they talked and after plating the first two, set them down on the table. She picked Emma up and looked around. There was no way this child was going to be able to sit at the table and Polly didn't have a big Boston telephone book to put under her bottom. Lydia took in the situation and gathered up the pillows from the sofa. Polly moved the two chairs with arms together and draped a dish towel over the pillows and the kids were set. She turned away and went back to the stove to make some more pancakes.

"I can't eat this!" Emma said.

"Why not, honey?" Lydia asked.

"Mommy always cuts up my pancake."

Lydia giggled at Polly who stood poised at the stove with a scoop of batter.

"What do you want to do, girlfriend? Cook or feed?"

"Uh, Uh ..." Polly said, which made Lydia giggle even more. At that moment, there was another knock on the door. Sammy spun around in his chair.

"Do you want to go answer the door, Sammy? It is probably our friend Andy."

He jumped down from the chair and ran to open it. "It's a lady!" he said.

"Hello!" Andy called out. "Hi there," she said to the little boy.

"But, they said it was Andy. You're a lady!" Sammy replied.

She bustled in with a couple of bags and said, "Both of those things are right. Andrea is my name, but everyone calls me Andy."

"Oh," he responded, then announced. "The sheriff took my mommy away."

"I heard," Andy said. "I'm sure they are going to work everything out. You shouldn't worry." She reached down for his hand, which he willingly gave to her and the two walked to the table. Andy placed her bags on the floor, then helped him crawl back up on top of the pillows. She took her coat off, dropped it on top of her bags, put some butter and syrup on Emma's pancake and began cutting it into pieces. Emma's eyes got big as she watched it all happen! Andy sat down beside her and handed Emma the fork. "Do you want help eating this or do you have it?" she asked.

Emma took the fork, her eyes still big and scooped up a piece of pancake.

"Wow," said Lydia. "I didn't see that one coming."

"Bill has kids this size. You don't want to let them get too far out ahead of you!" Andy laughed.

Polly shook her head and continued to flip pancakes. "Emma and I made a big batch of batter. I hope everyone is hungry," she said.

Lydia brought the baby in from the living room and set his seat on the table so she could sit beside Sammy. "I'm ready for pancakes," she said and stood her knife and fork up in her hands. Sammy looked at her and Polly saw a smile try to lift the corners of his little mouth.

"Andy?" she asked.

"Sure, I'll have a couple. It smells great in here."

Polly served up the pancakes and everyone settled into eat.

CHAPTER THREE

After a fun night playing with more kids than she could ever remember having around, Polly woke up the next morning to a bed filled with two of those kids and a dog. She smiled to herself and slid out from under the covers. Walking to the bedroom door, she peeked into the living room where Sylvie's boys were camped out on the couch and a small cot Lydia had brought over. Those boys had been a godsend with Sammy. He thought Jason was pretty wonderful and Andrew quickly became his very best friend. Little Emma hadn't gotten too far from Polly, but that was alright.

Sylvie had brought her boys over after school and they had spent the rest of the day playing, taking the dog out to run and showing Sammy all over the school as if they were part owners. When Sylvie came to pick them up after she was finished working, they begged to spend the night. After a short conversation, she agreed to allow them to stay, as long as they were a help to Miss Polly and not a problem. They promised to be helpful and had ended up being everything Polly needed in order to keep Sammy from spending too much time thinking about his mom. The evening had ended up being a fun party, with everyone in pajamas in front of the television watching Christmas shows.

Andy had borrowed a travel bed from her son for the baby which allowed Polly to keep an eye on him. Sammy was fairly attuned to Tyler's needs and they made it through the night with him only waking up a couple of times, fussing until Polly changed his diaper. She'd made Lydia watch her do it twice and finally felt comfortable enough to manage on her own.

Aaron and a woman from Child Protective Services had stopped by in the afternoon in order to get the children processed. Polly was fairly certain Aaron and Lydia had both been involved in allowing the children to stay at Sycamore House until something settled out with their parents. She discovered that Bruce was not the father of Sammy and Emma; he had married their mom a few years ago, but had been caring for them as if he were. When Marian Tally from CPS asked about their real father, Sammy simply said, "He died," and hung his head. Emma had obviously never known the man because, pointing to Aaron, she told the woman "that man over there took him away last night."

After spending time in the school, asking questions of the kids and of Polly, she seemed satisfied the children were safe.

Polly asked the sheriff, "How long do you think this is going to take? Do you really believe those two were transporting drugs?"

He replied, "I don't know how I could believe anything else, Polly! The back of that vehicle had nearly $80,000 in cocaine packed in there."

"But, that doesn't make sense?" She pressed. "Why would they be coming out here to beg for a job with his dad if he was carrying that?"

Aaron shrugged, "I know. There are some inconsistencies, but for now, we have to keep them until we can uncover the truth."

"Does Bruce's father know they're in Iowa? Do they have a lawyer? Can they get out on bail? Who is helping them through this?" Polly asked.

"Bruce didn't want us to call his father. At least not yet. And yes, they have a court appointed lawyer who is doing everything possible for them." Aaron replied.

"So, Bruce is fine with sitting in jail while I have his children? Is he nuts?" Polly lowered her voice to a whisper and guided Aaron into the kitchen.

"He's upset about the kids, but I assured him you had everything in hand and they would stay with you until things were settled." Aaron shook his head. "Bruce has no money, so he can't pay his own bail. He won't let us call his father for help. I don't want to keep them until this is all over, but right now, I don't have a choice."

Polly thought for a moment, then said, "I'll pay to get them out. They shouldn't have to be away from their kids."

"Polly,no." Aaron said. "It's enough that you're taking care of these little ones. I won't let you become financially responsible for those two. If they are transporting these drugs, you'd lose your money if they bolted."

"Aaron, you know full well they wouldn't put these little ones in danger …" Polly began, but Aaron interrupted her.

"Are you kidding me? They've already put them in danger, just by putting them in the same vehicle! No, I'm not going to let you set yourself up like this. You can't." Aaron said.

"Bet me!" she announced. "Now, are you going to tell me who their lawyer is or do I have to call your wife and get her involved?"

Aaron looked at her, rolled his eyes, then pulled his telephone out and made a call. Within a few moments, her phone beeped and she saw that a man's name and phone number had been texted to her.

"Thank you," she smiled.

"I don't know if I like it when you're not the one in trouble. You used to be much more amenable," Aaron muttered.

Polly laughed. "I always try to play by the rules, but I'm not much of a pushover." She dialed the phone number for the McKenzie's lawyer and after he spoke with the sheriff, he promised her he would do everything possible to get them out on bail the next day. As long as they could get in to see a judge, he thought they would be free to leave and be with their children. She told him to call her and she would arrange for their transportation and a place to stay.

When she got off the phone, she wondered what in the world she had done and those feelings must have shown up on her face. Aaron chuckled and put his hand on her arm, leading her to the table where she sat down.

"It's not so easy taking on the weight of the world, is it Polly girl?" he said.

"Oh shut up, you old grinch," she said. "Now, help me figure out what I'm going to do!"

"First, Polly, you have to get Bruce and his father together. He will need a lot more support through this than you can give him."

"Aaron, I remember them in high school. Bruce was like the prodigal son. His older brother, Kevin, was always the star. He played football, had girls hanging on him, and he played up to all the teachers. Kevin chose to be a farmer. He loved working with his dad and he loved working on that farm. Bruce hated it. He wanted to do so many different things. He loved racing cars and fixing them. When Kevin and his Dad were in the fields, Bruce was at Phil's Shop in town, rebuilding cars. His dad thought both boys would be there to help him out as he got older and Bruce couldn't stand even thinking about it. As soon as he graduated, he took all the money he had saved and left town.

"He was always a good guy. I think he spent too much time in the shop to get into trouble. But, he was so obsessed with all of that, he didn't do well in school. Teachers would find him daydreaming and sketching away. He was drawing engines and cars. None of them cared about it, so they tried to flush him out. He pulled enough grades to graduate, but spent any extra time in school, down in the Industrial Arts room. It was there he got great grades. Oh, and in Art Class too, I guess.

"His dad was furious when he left. They had a big public fight at graduation. It was awful. He was supposed to have a graduation party like the rest of us, but he went home, packed his clothes and left. His mom cried and cried, Kevin tried to find him, but he was gone. My dad was good friends with Lyle McKenzie and he just quit talking about Bruce. If anyone asked, he ignored them. Mary said she saw his mom several times in the grocery store and around town. She asked about him and I guess Bruce called her several times a year, to let her know he was fine, but Lyle never did ask or seem to care. It was like Bruce had disappeared from the face of the earth."

Aaron processed all of that and said, "Well, this little fiasco isn't going to help Bruce's father feel good about letting him come home."

"I know," Polly said. "This breaks my heart."

Aaron had also brought the children's bags to Sycamore House. She was glad they had their pajamas and a change of clothing. The rest of the day had passed in a blur and Polly felt as if no day in her life had been more exhausting. Four kids and a baby were nearly too much for her to manage, but with some help, she finally landed in bed with the two youngest and got a little bit of sleep once everyone else had sacked out.

She took one more look at the children in her big bed, grateful for its size. Emma and Sammy were snuggled together, with Obiwan at their feet and the baby was still asleep in the travel bed. Jason opened one eye and waved at her when she peeked out. She waved him back to bed and as quietly as possible, pulled clothes out and went into the bathroom. After a quick shower, she dressed and tiptoed back to her bedroom. Obiwan raised his head and looked up at her. Then, as if he knew he shouldn't wake the kids, slithered to her side of the bed and off onto the floor.

When they walked into the living room, Jason was up and dressed. "I'll take him for a walk, if you'd like, Miss Polly," he said. That way you don't have to leave the kids alone."

"Jason, wow!" She said. "That would be great. Thank you." He picked up the leash, Obiwan ran to him and the two went out the door. Polly watched them leave the front door from her kitchen window and started her coffee brewing. She had a feeling the day would be long.

Her phone buzzed in her back pocket. It was Jeff Lyndsay. Whoops, she'd forgotten completely about the Christmas party. He was planning to be in today to start decorating the auditorium for the party which was in three days. "Oh no!" her mind screamed. "What in the world was she going to do?" She shook her head to get rid of her fuzziness and answered the phone, "Hello?"

"Hi Polly! Are you ready for today?" Jeff's voice was much too chipper for that hour of the morning.

"Oh, Jeff. I'm not," she sighed. "What was I supposed to be doing?"

"I've got wreaths and trees showing up in two hours. You were going to have people ready to string lights on the trees and then we were going to start popping corn so we could string cranberries and popcorn. Remember? You thought it would be quaint."

"Right. Quaint." she said. "Jeff, why didn't you stop me from saying that?"

"Because you were pretty sure you could pull it off. And I'm only the employee," he chuckled. "So, I take it you aren't ready?"

"No, it's fine. Bring on the trees. I'll get people here to start working on this. Is there anything else I'm supposed to do?"

"I think I've got the rest of it. The string quartet and guitar duo, which will play Christmas carols all evening, are scheduled." he said. "By the way, have you heard anyone in town talking about this? I've got flyers all over town and the newspaper is running a short article tomorrow."

"It seems like everyone is talking about it, so I think the place is going to be packed. The whole town wants to see the school, and I'm afraid it is might be a little crazy."

Andrew stirred on the cot and sat up, rubbing his eyes. Polly walked over and handed him the remote to the television. She assumed this made her a terrible parent, but things were going too quickly for her to manage all the niceties of parenting.

"Just a second, Jeff," she said as she checked on the bedroom once more.

"What's going on there, Polly?"

"Oh, you wouldn't even believe it," she said. "While you were running around Ames and Des Moines yesterday, I became a home for wayward children."

"What exactly does that mean? How many kids do you have there?" he asked.

"Five," she said as she walked back to the kitchen. Polly told him about the events of yesterday and he moaned.

"Well, I guess that will teach me to be out of touch with you for a day," he said. "What are you going to do with all these kids?"

"Hopefully their parents will be back by tonight. But, don't worry, I'll still round up help to decorate the trees." Polly said.

"Alright," he responded. "I'll be there when the deliveries start coming in. You go be a mommy, now, alright?" he teased.

"Thanks for your support," Polly laughed. "I'll see you later."

Jason had come back in with Obiwan, who was jumping up on Polly's legs as she ended the call with Jeff.

"Okay, okay!" she said. "I'll get food for you! Patience, my little Obiwan, patience!"

Jason was standing at the counter. "I think it's totally cool that you named him Obiwan. Do you like Star Wars?"

"Do I like Star Wars?" Polly laughed out loud. "I can't even begin to tell you how many times I've watched the original trilogy. Hey! Do you guys want to watch it this morning? I'm always up for a little Luke Skywalker!"

She walked over to a bookshelf and pulled out her Star Wars videos. "Here," she said to Jason as she handed him a disk. "This is the version originally shown in 1977. There are no strange updates to it. Han shot first."

He looked at her quizzically.

"Oh, never mind. Just put it in the player." Polly peeked in the bedroom again to see Emma looking at her. She whispered to the little girl, "Are you ready to be awake?"

Emma's stage whisper seemed loud enough to wake the dead, "I am, but Sammy said he doesn't want to get up yet."

"Is Sammy awake, too?" Polly asked.

"He's hiding it, but, he's awake."

Polly whispered back, "We're watching Star Wars out here, do you want to come out in your jammies and watch it with us?"

Sammy jumped up, "I love Star Wars! I watch that all the time with

Bruce!"

"Come on out," Polly said. She pulled the blanket off the end of the bed and looked in at the baby. Tyler was still sleeping.

"Be very quiet so you don't wake Tyler up," she whispered. The two children tiptoed out of the room and once they broke the threshold, ran to the sofa. She carried the blanket over to them and tucked it around them, including Andrew in the crowd. Obiwan had seen all of the activity and jumped up on the couch, landing on Emma and Sammy's laps. They laughed as he ran across them to lick Andrew in the face. He finally settled down beside Andrew, and Jason tucked himself in on the other side of the dog. Polly's heart could hardly stand it. She pulled her phone out of her back pocket and clicked a couple of pictures. This was definitely a memory she wanted to keep.

Once breakfast was ready, Polly pried the kids away from the movie so they could eat at the table, then sent them scurrying to get dressed for the day. Tyler finally woke up and she gathered him into her arms as she fed him breakfast. Soon, everyone was dressed and ready to go. There was a knock at the front door and all of the kids looked at her expectantly.

"Go ahead!" she laughed. "One of you get the door!"

Lydia and Andy came in behind Sammy and Emma, who had raced for the entryway. "Good morning, everyone!" Lydia said. "We're going to steal you away for the day so Polly can get some work done."

"Where are we going?" Emma asked.

"How would you like to go see a train?" Lydia said.

"I love trains!" Sammy exclaimed.

"That's great, because we're going to go ride a Christmas train today. Someone told me that Santa might show up, too! What do you think about that?"

Jason and Andrew sat on the couch, not saying a word.

"Oh, boys," Lydia exclaimed. "You're going too. Don't worry. We wouldn't leave you out!" Both of their faces lit up.

Lydia went on. "Your mom will be here in a few minutes and we'll all drive down to see the train. She decided you could take the day off from school. Do you know where your winter coats are? Go get 'em!"

Emma and Sammy dashed into the bedroom as Lydia came over to take the baby from Polly's arms. She said to Polly, "Aaron says you need to get down to the courthouse in Boone this morning, if you're going to bail them out."

"Oh, Lydia, thank you!" Polly said, then remembered something and cried, “Oh no. Jeff has Christmas stuff showing up here in a couple of hours."

"Why in the world did you hire him if you can't trust him to take care of it?" Lydia asked. "Call him and tell him you're busy. He's a smart boy. He'll manage fine without you."

Polly called Jeff and told him what was happening. He assured her that he would take care of everything. As soon as Sylvie showed up, the three women got the children all packed into cars and took off for the train in Boone. Polly changed into something a little more professional, spent a few minutes looking at the map online for the County Courthouse, then took off, not knowing at all what would come next, but hoping someone would steer her the right way.

By one o'clock that afternoon, Polly was on her way home with Bruce and Hannah McKenzie in her truck.

"Polly, I can't thank you enough," Bruce had said over and over.

"Don't worry about it, Bruce. We'll get this figured out." she replied.

"How are my kids?" Hannah had asked the moment they were out of the courtroom.

"They're doing fine. I've probably let them watch way too much television, but otherwise they're fine. A couple of older boys I know came over yesterday and spent the night with us in the apartment and I think Sammy had a great time with them. They love my dog and everyone slept well.

"Lydia, the wife of Sheriff Merritt, took everyone down to the Santa train today. I don't know if they'll be back when we get there, but I texted her to let her know you guys were going to be with me at Sycamore House." Polly had come up with everything she could to assure Hannah McKenzie that her kids were alright.

"They miss you guys, but they're safe and healthy," she said.

"Polly," Bruce said after a lengthy silence. "I need you to believe that neither Hannah nor I know anything about those drugs in the car. I have no idea how they got there. I don't want you to think we'd ever expose those kids to something like that."

"That's fine, Bruce," Polly replied. "It's not up to me."

"No, really, Polly," he said, "You have to believe me. Someone has to believe me!"

"Sheriff Merritt is the most fair, honorable men I've ever met, Bruce. If there is any proof that you didn't do this, he'll find it. So, don't worry about what you can't fix today. Let's figure out what is going to happen next. Are you going to call your Dad?" she asked.

"Gah!" he spat. "I can't imagine what he'll say when he hears this. He's never going to let me work for him. In fact, I wouldn't be surprised if he won't even let me see Mom." His shoulders slumped and Hannah reached over and put her hand on his knee. He covered it with his own hand.

"This has been the worst year," he said. "First Hannah lost her job when Tyler was sick. Then, my hours were cut. We lost everything. The house, the car. Everything. I scraped enough money together to buy an old beater and pay for food and gas to get out here. We packed up the clothes we had left and started driving. And now this."

If his shoulders could have slumped any lower, they did.

Polly started to open her mouth to say something, closed it and thought to herself, "I'm in for the whole thing, I guess."

Then she said out loud, "I have a room at Sycamore House. You and Hannah and the kids can stay until you figure out your next steps. It's Christmastime and you don't need to be homeless when I can put you up. This is all going to work out. It has to!"

CHAPTER FOUR

Rain had begun falling when Polly pulled up to Sycamore House and parked beside Henry's truck. She wished it was snow, but temperatures weren't supposed to fall for another day or so. When she and the McKenzies walked in the front door, the scent of pine filled the room, making it feel more and more like Christmas.

"Welcome to Sycamore House!" Polly said. "You're my first guests! Let's take your stuff upstairs and then I'll show you around the place." They followed her up the steps and she wasn't surprised to see a large tree standing in the hall between the two bathrooms. She was, however, surprised to see Henry walk out of her apartment.

"Hi Henry. Umm, what are you doing?"

"Hi Polly," he snickered. "We had an extra tree, so we found a place for it in your apartment. I think you'll like it."

"Okay," she said. "Henry, these are friends of mine, Bruce and Hannah McKenzie. They're going to be spending a couple of nights in the room across the hall." Henry strode over to them and put his hand out to shake Hannah's hand, then Bruce's.

"Welcome to Bellingwood," he said. "You'll like it here."

"Henry did all of the woodwork in the place," Polly remarked. Hannah and Bruce both looked around in awe.

"Nice work!" Bruce said.

"Oh, I had a lot of help," Henry said. "And Polly lets me get away with doing what I want to do. It's a fun job."

He started to walk away, then turned and said. "We've nearly got all the trees standing up and some of the guys are hanging wreaths on doors. It's getting pretty festive, around here! Nice to meet you guys. Hope to see you at the party Saturday night."

Henry walked down the steps as Polly led the McKenzies to the front room. She opened the door and said, "I'm sorry it isn't finished. There's still a lot to do here. I have a bed in there and that's about it. The two bathrooms at the end of the hallway are both open and ready to go, though. You can have your pick. I don't use either of them. My apartment is on the other side there," and she pointed to the entry way across the hall.

As they went into the room, Hannah sighed, "This is wonderful, Polly. Thank you so much. I can't believe you are doing this for us."

"Well, you've got three adorable children and they should have fun right now rather than worrying about where they're going to sleep. They're scared enough as it is, so it's probably just as well they'll stay somewhere familiar for a couple of nights."

"Polly, I don't know how to thank you," Bruce echoed.

"Bruce, promise me you're sticking around and going to work this out and I'll be fine." she responded. "Why don't you guys take some time to settle in. Unpack your bags, take a nap and I'll be back in a little bit to show you around the rest of the place. Oh, and while you're here, I might put you to work helping me string lights on all of these trees! I guess this party is going to happen whether I'm ready or not!"

She pulled the door shut behind her as she walked back out into the hall. Then, she remembered that Henry had been in her apartment, so she though she ought to check it out. He hadn't rearranged much, but there was a lovely tree in front of one of the living room windows. Obiwan was sitting on the sofa, wiggling with excitement at seeing her.

Polly sat down beside him, stroked his back and looked at the tree.

"What am I going to do with this, Obi?" she asked. He laid his head on her lap and turned over for a belly rub.

She knew her Christmas decorations were in the basement somewhere. Maybe she'd find time to dig them out and decorate the tree before Christmas arrived. Polly continued to stare at the tree and imagine her favorite ornaments filling it. Last year her friends had purchased way too many Star Wars ornaments for her. She chuckled at the memory, then thought about putting a smaller tree in her bedroom, or maybe even her office, for sci-fi ornaments. The Death Star probably shouldn't be the tree topper, though, but maybe crossed light sabers would work. That would be awesome.

A knock at the door broke her out of her reverie, and when she answered, Jeff was standing there.

"You should come downstairs and see what we've done to the auditorium," he said. "Just in case you want to move anything around before the guys leave."

Polly followed him downstairs and when he opened the door, she smiled and nodded. "This is great. This is just perfect!" There were tables scattered around the rooms, intermixed with trees of various sizes. Her first concern was that there be enough space for people to walk, but she saw that it would be fine. Chairs for the musical groups and a podium were arranged on the stage.

"What are you doing about electricity for lights on the trees?" she asked.

"I have battery operated LED lights," he said. "Trust me, I think of everything!"

"Well then, I think this is perfect! It's going to be so festive!" Polly replied.

"Great, I'm going to let everyone go. Are you sure you don't need help with decorating the trees?"

"I'm not sure at all, to be honest with you. But, I'll make it work. We'll be fine," she assured him.

Henry approached the two of them, "Does she like it?" he asked.

"She does." Jeff responded.

"That's good. She's pretty hard to please." Henry laughed.

"Hey!" Polly paused. "Am I really?"

"No," he said, "Not at all. Which makes it all that much more fun to do good work for you. You seem to expect it."

Henry took her arm and turned her away and began walking with her. "So, I was wondering, Polly. Are you busy tonight?"

"Well," she hesitated, "I've got people staying here and there are children and ..."

"Polly," he interrupted. "I got the story from Jeff. I think they can take care of themselves. They'll probably just be glad to be together again. Bring in a pizza or something, the kids will love it."

"I don't know, Henry." Polly continued to protest.

"Come on. Let me take you out to dinner tonight. Christmas is going to be here soon and my family will all be coming home. It's been crazy nuts trying to get this place finished. Let's go somewhere quiet and enjoy a nice dinner."

"Do I have to dress up?" she asked.

Henry thought about it and then said, "Yes. You have to dress up. Put on a dress and look nice. Not black tie fancy, but a nice dress. I'll be in a jacket, but no tie. How's that?" He took a breath, then said, "And I'll pick you up at 6:45."

"Is this a date, Henry?" she smirked.

"Yes. It's a date." He grinned at her. "You're my date for tonight."

"Alright. I'll do it," Polly replied. Her heart seemed to beat a little faster and she felt her face flush, but was saved any further embarrassment at her own behavior with noise from the front door. Everyone had returned.

Lydia brought them all into the auditorium and looked meaningfully at Polly, who nodded in the affirmative, then glanced toward the ceiling. Lydia smiled as Sammy and Emma stood in the doorway with their mouths open.

"It looks like a Christmas forest!" Sammy exclaimed.

"It's so pretty!" said his sister.

"We're going to put lights on these trees and it will be even prettier!" Polly told them. "But, first. Let's go upstairs. I have a surprise for you!"

She turned back to Henry. "I'll see you later."

"I'm looking forward to it, Polly," he said as she walked away.

Lydia whispered at her, "Are you going out on a date with Henry?"

Polly whispered back, "Yes, I am. He's making me dress up."

They walked out into the hallway and Lydia said to Andy, who was holding the baby. "Henry asked Polly out and she's going!"

Andy chuckled. "Well, it's about time. Wait until Beryl hears this. She's been saying all along that the two of you should just do something about it."

"It's only a date," Polly protested.

"Uh huh, that's what I told my friends after my first date with Aaron!" Lydia teased.

"Wow!" Polly said, "I'm nowhere near that. Let's not get us married for a very long time, alright?"

They were laughing as they went up the steps.

"Sammy and Emma, I have something I want to show you in this room over here. Come with me," Polly said.

She knocked on the door. When Hannah opened it and saw the children, she dropped to her knees and hugged them both close to her.

"Mommy, you're here!" Sammy cried.

Emma began to cry, her tears choked out in sobs. "Mommy!"

The three of them held on for a moment. Bruce came over to the doorway and set his hand on Hannah's shoulder, waiting patiently. The kids saw him and Sammy pulled away from his mother, "Bruce, you're here, too! I was so scared!"

"I know, Sammy. I was too. But, Polly here made sure we were able to be with you tonight."

"She's great, Bruce. She likes Star Wars, too."

Bruce looked up and laughed. “I’d forgotten about that. It was you and me and Marsha who watched Star Wars together, wasn't it!"

"It was," Polly laughed. "We rented it at the video store downtown to watch the whole thing before the first Special Edition came out. I'd forgotten about that."

Hannah took Tyler out of Andy's arms and pulled him close to her chest. Bruce swung Emma up into his arms and she laid her head against his shoulder.

"Thank you for everything Polly."

"Look," Polly said. “There's a bunch of stuff over in my apartment for the kids. There are some toys they've been playing with, a travel crib for Tyler to use and all of their clothes. Let's gather up what you want to use and bring it on over here."

In a few minutes, the kids' things had all been moved across the hall and the extra cot was set up for Sammy. Polly let Obiwan out and started the tour with Bruce and Hannah.

After showing them where everything was located in the bathrooms, she took them downstairs to the kitchen. "You can use anything in here you like," Polly said. "I'm going out tonight, but I thought we could bring pizza in."

Hannah was looking at the pantry shelves and wandering around the kitchen. "This is amazing. I've never seen anything like it!" she exclaimed.

"The pantry is full and so is the refrigerator. If you see anything in here you'd rather cook up, I'm fine with that," Polly said.

"Could I? I love to cook and we've been eating nothing but junk for the last couple of days." Hannah replied.

"Sure! Do you think you need anything more?" Polly asked.

Hannah opened the refrigerator and then the freezer. She glanced over at the pantry and said, "Honestly, you have enough here to feed an army.

I'll find something to make for tonight. Thank you!"

"Then make yourselves at home. If you want to take a few of the folding chairs upstairs, that's fine. If you want to eat in the auditorium, that's fine, too. Feel free to do whatever you'd like while you're here." Polly said.

She scratched Obiwan's head and said, "Now, I need to run this dog for a bit, take a shower and get ready!"

Lydia and Andy followed her outside with Obiwan. "You're doing a good thing, Polly," Lydia said as she patted her arm.

"I hope so. I knew Bruce pretty well when we were in high school. And Hannah seems like a nice girl. I hope it all works out." Polly replied.

"You know me," Lydia said, "I see the world through rose-colored glasses. I think we're going to have a wonderful little Christmas miracle."

Andy snickered as the two women walked back to Lydia's Jeep. Polly took off at a slow jog with Obiwan by her side as Lydia and Andy pulled out of the lot.

Later, Polly laughed as she came out of the bathroom. She hadn't taken that long to clean up in months. She'd clipped nails, shaved hairs, fussed over her makeup and had somehow managed to curl her hair into what she considered a relatively attractive coif. Now, she needed to find something to wear. Obiwan was curled up in her pillows and watched as she began pulling clothes out of the closet.

"A dress," she said out loud. Obiwan cocked his head as if listening to her. "Huh. He's not wearing a tie, so nothing terribly fancy." She flipped through the hangers and then flipped through them again. "You wouldn't think it would be this hard. I've been out on dates before."

She finally settled on a belted, forest green dress with velvet cuffs on the sleeves. A pair of black pumps and some black drop earrings and she felt pretty comfortable with her ensemble. Spinning around, she said, "So? What do you think, Obiwan? Too much? Not enough?"

The dog got up, stretched and walked to the end of the bed. He sat back down and put his paw out. She shook it. "I'm going to take that as confirmation that it's alright. Now, because I don't want to deal with your hair all over me, you stay here and I'm going downstairs. Polly bent over and kissed him on the head. He jumped down and followed her out of the bedroom, then sat and watched as she lifted her coat off the coatrack and grabbed her purse. "I'll see you later," and she walked out the front door of her apartment.

When she got downstairs, she was greeted by both Sammy and Emma.

"You're beautiful!" Emma gushed.

"Wow, you look like an angel," Sammy echoed.

"Thanks, you two. What are you doing down here?" she asked.

"Mommy's in the kitchen making dinner. We're supposed to stay down here with her while Bruce and Tyler take a nap upstairs." Sammy told her.

Polly walked back into the kitchen, the kids closely behind her. "Are you finding everything you need?" she asked Hannah.

"Oh, Polly. This kitchen is wonderful! Thank you for letting me use it." Hannah responded.

"I'm glad you are. When they finally got my kitchen installed upstairs, I quit spending so much time in here." Polly looked around. "It is pretty nice."

The front door opened and Polly called out, "I'm back here in the kitchen!" Henry came around the steps and walked up to her.

Emma asked, "Are you taking her out on a date?" then giggled.

"I am," Henry responded. "Since she looks so beautiful, I should probably make this a very nice date, shouldn't I!"

Sammy looked at the two of them, "I'd take her out to a fancy dinner, then for a ride in a boat!"

Hannah laughed, "That was a 'date' we all took this summer."

"Well, it might be a little too cold for a ride in a boat tonight," Henry said, "but I might have some other ideas. We will start with a fancy dinner, though. I promise."

He took Polly's hand and tucked it into his elbow, "Shall we go?"

"Have a good evening, Hannah!" Polly said, then knelt down to get closer to Emma and Sammy, "And you guys be good, okay? I'll see you tomorrow morning."

"You look wonderful, Polly," Henry said as they walked out the front door.

Polly looked him up and down. He looked pretty good in his nice slacks, a black turtleneck and a jacket. "I don't think I've ever seen you in anything but jeans," she said. "You look pretty fabulous yourself!"

"See, this was a great idea," he chuckled. "We get to see that the other person actually owns nice clothing."

Instead of his truck, a beautiful older model teal car sat in front of the school. "What is this?" Polly asked.

"It's my pride and joy. I never bring it out in the winter, except for special occasions." Henry opened the passenger door and held it while Polly entered and waited as she pulled her feet into the car. He shut the door and walked around to the driver's side and got in.

"This car has been in our family since my grandpa bought back in 1955. It's a Ford Thunderbird."

Henry seemed proud of that and Polly smiled. She knew it had to be a pretty great car since he was so happy about it.

"Cool!" she said.

"It is cool," he replied. "I guess you don't like old cars?"

"Well, I've never been around anyone who does," she giggled a little sheepishly.

"I've been taking care of this baby since I was in high school. As soon as Dad would let me, I was under the hood figuring out how it worked. Both he and grandpa took pretty good care of it, so I haven't had to do any restoration. It sits inside the shop unless I'm going out for a drive and I kind of thought that since tonight was special, it would be fun to show off a beautiful girl in a beautiful ride!"

She ran her hand over the dashboard. It was the same color as the outside paint job. "Alright, this is pretty cool," she said.

"It's even more fun in the summer with the no top, but we'll leave it up tonight. It's cold out there." He winked at her.

"Tell me what's special about the car," Polly asked.

She smiled as Henry began describing the engine and telling her about the very first year the Ford Thunderbird had been built. As he talked about the history of the car and the dreams of its creators, she realized how comfortable she was. She hadn't been on a date since the breakup with Joey Delancy last spring and Henry was animated as he compared the Thunderbird to other Ford cars of the time.

As he pulled on to Highway 30 and headed for Ames, he stopped talking. "Did you hear anything I said? You look as if you were a million miles away."

"No, I was listening. I was just thinking about how nice it was to be out with someone I enjoyed. I'm hoping you won't get all psychotic on me tonight, okay?"

"I promise. No psychotic. And if I do, you can kick the wheels of my baby here."

"Thanks," she said. "Where are you taking me?"

"There's a nice little restaurant on Main Street. I've only been there once when Mom and Dad were in town. I think you'll like it."

"So," she said. "A fancy dinner and then a boat ride?"

He chuckled. "No boat rides tonight. Maybe we'll drive around and look at Christmas lights. And I'll be sure to get you home on time, I promise. I know tomorrow is a school day."

"That sounds great." She placed her hand over his which was on the steering wheel. "Thanks for this, if I forget to say so later. This is really nice." She left her hand there for a few moments and when she pulled away, he took it in his. They rode in silence, then he let go to turn on the radio.

"I'm kind of a sucker for Christmas music," he said. "I figure that I only get to listen to it once a year, so it's always on in my truck." He fiddled with the knob until he tuned in "Holly, Jolly Christmas." He glanced back down at the seat to find that Polly had left her hand where he could take it again. He took it in his and before either of them knew it, they were humming along to the music.

Henry took an exit and wove his way through the streets of Ames until he pulled up in front of a small restaurant across from the old train depot. When they went inside, they were greeted by a hostess who seated them after Henry gave her his name. The ambiance was warm and comfortable and their waiter was on hand with a menu and wine list. After they ordered, he disappeared, returning with bread and wine.

They talked all through supper, only stopping to acknowledge the food that arrived and the waiter's short interruptions regarding any needs they might have. Henry told her about his family, growing up with a father who knew how to do nearly everything. At one time or other, it seemed the man had actually done everything, from raising and training horses, to working for the county roads department. When he finally had enough of working for others, he turned his part time job as a fix-it man and cabinet maker, into a full-time business. Henry grew up helping out in the shop, learning his father's craft, went away to college for four years and then decided he was going to be just as happy working with his dad.

Polly told him about growing up on the farm and losing her mother. When he asked how hard that had been, she thought for a moment and said, "You know, I realize that it should have been awful, but Dad, Sylvester and Mary did everything they could to keep life normal for me. Mary was there and she had always loved me, so it wasn't that difficult."

"Did your Dad ever date again?" Henry asked.

"I think he did while I was in college, but I don't think it was ever serious. He never introduced me to anyone as being special in his life." She paused and thought about it. "You know, that's too bad. I never thought about it, but he should have found someone else so he could have been happy. I wasn't around enough to be with him when he was lonely and he was always available when I was home. Wow, I must have seemed very self-centered to him."

"Oh, I can't imagine that's true," Henry replied. "If he had wanted to do something else, he would have. You're his daughter and you know what you want and know how to go get it."

Polly laughed. "I suppose you're right. I never thought about it before."

They talked some more about her friends in Boston and how much she had enjoyed living there. "Have you ever been on the east coast?" she asked Henry.

"No. Not really," Henry said. "Maybe someday I'll be a tourist. It didn't ever seem like something I wanted to do all by myself."

It was Polly's turn to wink. "I'll take you out there someday and show you all up and down the eastern seaboard."

"Now, that's a date!" Henry laughed.

After dinner, they walked back to the car and he opened the door for her again. Polly snickered. "You're going to make me feel all girly."

"You should," he responded. "You look all girly tonight." As she put her left foot into the car, he bent in and kissed her lightly on the lips, then took her hand and helped her into her seat.

Polly went still when the door shut beside her. He'd kissed her! It was nothing like the possessive kisses from Joey. Polly could feel the blood rushing to her face and hoped Henry wouldn't notice when he opened his door and the light came on.

He got back into the car and backed out of the parking space, putting his right arm up over the seat back as he turned to look out the rear window. Polly felt like a kid again, wondering if he would touch her shoulder. The bucket seats kept them separated unless she sat on the little center hump. She decided to stay where she was. Henry left his arm there brushing her shoulder and neck with his fingers as they began to drive around Ames.

They oohed and aahed and talked about Christmas lights until Polly yawned.

Henry laughed, "I've never bored someone to sleep before, so it's probably time to start heading back to Bellingwood." He turned a corner and began heading west.

"No," she said. "It's not that. I had two little kids in my bed last night and a baby in the room. I don't think I got nearly enough sleep."

"Oh, that's right!" Henry exclaimed. "I forgot about that. So, who are these people staying with you?"

Polly told him about her past with Bruce and found herself telling him everything that had happened since Bruce and Hannah drove into town.

"It seems like you're becoming the focal point for crazy stuff in Bellingwood, Polly. We've never seen this much activity!" He laughed.

"That's not funny," she said. "I lived a pretty quiet life in Boston, too, you know. Nothing crazy ever happened to me until I moved back to Iowa."

"It's alright, Polly. I'm kidding you, but, you are certainly upping the level of entertainment for us poor 'ole country folk!" Henry's speech pattern slowed to a drawl.

"There you go," Polly chortled. "Feeding into the Iowa stereotype. A bunch of slow, country hicks who couldn't find their way around a big city, much less be smart enough to deal with high powered business men."

"I'll bet you heard a lot of that while you were in Boston, didn't you!"

"Oh, you have no idea," she said. "I was in Filene's once when I first got to Boston. I was at the checkout counter and because my finances were still in flux, I wanted to write a check from my Iowa account. I asked the clerk if I could write a check from a bank in Iowa and she stuck her nose in the air and said quite primly, "Out here, Miss, we pronounce that O-HI-O!" She took my check, though, and I laughed and laughed on my way home. She had no idea that anything existed west of the Mississippi River. Sometimes it felt as if they still believed we traveled in covered wagons and had to battle wild Indians to get from our home to work every day."

Polly shook her head. "It wasn't always that bad, but I did discover that Iowans ... well, probably people from the Midwest ... had a much better grasp of the entirety of the United States than those in Boston did. All they paid attention to was their little corner of the world. It extended from Maine down to Hilton Head and sometimes out to Pennsylvania and the Great Lakes, but anything beyond that was wilderness in their eyes."

"I made some good friends, though," she giggled. "One of these days, I'll convince them to get on a plane and rather than fly over the Midwest to the other coast, stop and see what's going on out here."

As they drove, he left his arm on the back of the seat. Polly didn't pull away, but the closer they got to Bellingwood, the more awkward she began to feel. She liked Henry, but wasn't ready to start a full-out relationship with him. It had been so long since anyone had paid attention to her like this, she wanted to take her time and not hurry it along.

He finally pulled up in front of the school. All the lights were on and the white twinkling Christmas lights around Sycamore House looked wonderful. Polly thought they would look even better if it snowed.

Henry put the car in park and reached for his door. Polly stopped him. "This was a wonderful evening, Henry. Thank you."

He smiled and his eyes seemed to light up, "I had a great time, too, Polly. I hope you will let me take you out again someday soon."

"That would be nice," she said. "Well," and she turned to look at the front door of Sycamore House, "I probably need to make sure everything is still standing."

Henry opened his car door and got to her side just as she was pushing it open. He took her hand and helped her stand up, then walked her to the front door, which unlocked as she approached it.

"This bluetooth door locking system has been a real lifesaver," she said. "I couldn't take any more key stress after the fiasco this fall. This is better. I love that I can just send a key to your smartphones. I'd hate to have to come downstairs every time somebody wanted to get in the place."

"You're quite the tech geek, Polly," Henry laughed. He opened the door and waited as she stepped inside.

"Well, good night, Henry. Thank you again ... so much." she said.

He stepped in and kissed her again, another light kiss on her lips. Before she could do anything more, he stepped back and let go of her hand.

"I'll see you tomorrow, Polly."

"Good night, Henry. Thank you."

She watched as he walked back to his car, then waved as he drove away. She shut the door to Sycamore house and heard it lock behind her, then walked back to the kitchen and saw that it was clean and the lights were off. Heading back for the stairs, she flipped the main level lights off and walked upstairs, her mind chasing itself around and around about Henry. She turned off the lights in the hall as she opened the door to her apartment. Glancing back at the first bedroom, she saw light coming out from under the door and smiled. She hoped they were happy to be together again.

As soon as she walked into her apartment, she was greeted by a bouncing Obiwan.

"Well, darn it!" she exclaimed. "I forgot all about you! Alright. Let me get some real clothes on and we'll go outside."

Polly quickly changed into her sweats, snapped a leash on Obiwan, grabbed a flashlight and ran downstairs to give him a quick run around the school. She was going to be glad to drop into her own bed, all by herself tonight.

CHAPTER FIVE

When Polly and Obiwan got to the front door of her apartment the next morning to go outside, she noticed a piece of paper had been slipped under the door. She opened it and read, "I'm making breakfast downstairs in the morning and I'd love to cook for you. We'll be ready for you about 7. Thank you, Hannah."

"Well, Obiwan, it looks like I'm being pampered for another meal. Come on, let's get the morning going." She snapped the leash on him and went out the door, down the steps and out the front door of Sycamore House. Obiwan walked patiently beside her as she headed for the south side of the building. As soon as he saw the open field, he pulled on the leash. Polly said, "Alright, let's go," and took off at a jog. They ran to the end of the lot where Sycamore Creek crossed under the road and then wandered the creek back toward home. They walked to the other end of the lot, where the creek passed under that county highway and by then Obiwan was looking to make the morning a little longer.

"No, I don't think so," Polly said to him. "Let's go back in. I tell you what. After school today, I'll see if Jason and Andrew can come over and play with you. I'm sure they'll be ready to do some running around after sitting all day."

She pointed him back to the house and he picked up the pace again. They jogged to the front door, went in and up the steps. By the time she was at her front door, he began to wiggle with joy.

"Oh, the life of a dog," she said. "You have it pretty rough, don't you!" They went inside, and after unsnapping his leash and releasing him, he jumped on the couch to wait. Polly poured food in his bowl and he dashed across the room to enjoy breakfast while she took a shower and got dressed for the day.

"Good morning!" Hannah called out as she saw Polly come across the foyer. "I hope you like french toast. It's the kids' favorite and it's so easy, I don't mind making it. I found some bacon in the freezer and it's in the oven."

Polly smiled and walked into the kitchen. "That sounds great! I'm glad you've found your way around in here! Do you guys like coffee?"

"Oh, I do and Bruce drinks more of it than one man should."

Polly laughed. "Oh my goodness that’s right, we learned to drink the stuff together when we were in high school! Mary was forever trying to get me to stop drinking it; she always told me it would stunt my growth."

"You two spent a lot of time together, didn't you?" Hannah said.

"Well, he was dating my best friend, Marsha, during our sophomore and junior year and part of our senior year. They broke up after Christmas because she wanted to go out with some college guy her sister set her up with. Poor Bruce was so upset. I thought she was rotten, but I guess life goes on."

"He never talks about those years," Hannah remarked. "I don't know what he was like back then before everything got ugly with his father."

"Well, he was always a good guy," Polly said quietly. "Just a really good guy. He didn't deserve all the crap that happened to him that last year he was in Story City. It wasn't right. And when I left for Boston I totally lost track of him. It's good to see him again and it's good to see him with you and the kids."

She filled the large coffee maker with water and coffee, then flipped it on. "So, if I'm not being too nosy, where is Sammy and Emma's dad? I guess I figure Tyler is Bruce's boy. He got his lips."

"It's alright," Hannah sighed. "Yeah, Tyler is mine and Bruce's. We met in a bar in Boulder. I was a waitress there. Bruce started to come in regularly and he was such a nice guy and loved talking about cars. My old beater had some trouble and before I knew it, he was fixing it up. I made dinner for him to say thank you and Sammy and Emma fell in love with him. Pretty soon, I did too."

Hannah pulled the bacon out of the oven, flipped it over, and then put it back in. She looked up at the clock and went on, "Their daddy drove a truck. He was never home, which was alright, I guess. He wasn't much for kids. He never hurt them or anything, just didn't pay any attention to them. Finally, he told me that he hadn't intended to be a dad, and since I was going to be a mom, he wanted out. We got a divorce and have both moved on. I'm just glad the kids were little enough to not know who he was. Bruce is pretty much their daddy now.

"He says he wants to adopt them, but we don't have the money to pay a lawyer to do the work. One of these days, we'll get all that figured out and then we'll all have the same name." She paused, then sighed again. "As long as this mess gets cleared up. I swear to you, Polly. We have no idea what is going on. Bruce may be unemployed and be looking to beg his father for work, but he isn't a drug user or a dealer or a criminal at all."

Tears began streaming down Hannah's face. She looked so strained and beaten.

"And I don't know how we're going to have Christmas for the kids. Oh, and I don't know why I'm even telling you this. You have done so much for us. I can't believe we have a warm place to stay until we can get to Bruce's family's house and I can't believe you've taken such good care of us. I'll quit crying and whining now." She let loose a small, pathetic chuckle. "It doesn't do me any good, anyway. I'm sorry."

Polly put her arm around Hannah's shoulders. "It's alright. Lydia says she believes everything is going to turn out fine and I trust her instincts, so I'll tell you that everything is going to turn out just fine."

Hannah brushed tears away and they heard the clatter of feet tripping down the stairway. Sammy and Emma raced into the kitchen. "Mommy, guess what we did!" Sammy said. "We took a bath in a great big tub. It had water spouts and everything!"

Emma tugged her mother's apron. "I didn't want to get out, but Daddy said I'd turn into a prune. What's a prune?"

Before anyone could respond, she ran back to the stairway and said, "Hurry up! We're hungry!"

She waited a few moments, then Polly heard her run up a few steps. "Hurry up!" she yelled again.

Polly laughed as she saw Bruce, carrying the baby, round the corner and walk to the kitchen. "It looks like you are late," she said.

"I guess so!" He took his hand out of Emma's little hand and ruffled the hair on her head. "Is there anything I can do?" he asked his wife.

"Nope. You've got the baby. I need to get out the juice and milk, then set the table and we'll be ready."

"I'm on it," Polly said.

Before she knew it, breakfast had happened, was finished and cleaned up. Bruce had run back upstairs to get the baby's car seat and propped it up on the counter while they cleaned up.

"So, guys," Polly said, "We're going to be decorating Christmas trees for a big party tomorrow night and I was wondering if you wouldn't mind helping. At this point, I'm begging everyone I see."

"Absolutely!" Bruce replied. "We're glad to do whatever we can to help you out. Are you really decorating all of those trees in the auditorium?"

"Well, we're going to put lights on them. Jeff got a great deal on some battery powered LED lights and we'll put those up today. Then, during the party, we're going to string cranberries and popcorn and decorate all of the trees, and then we'll draw names for people to take home a decorated tree at the end of the evening."

"There have to be twenty trees in there!" Jeff said.

"Yep. There are a bunch. Hopefully we'll have a great turnout and everyone will have fun." Then she had a thought. "Oh, Hannah! My friend Sylvie is going to be here all day today and tomorrow working in the kitchen to bake cookies and hors d'oeuvres for the party. Would you mind spending time in the kitchen with her? Her sons, Jason and Andrew, were the boys who helped me out with your kids the other night. She's terrific and I think you guys would get along."

"Thank you, Polly! I'd love to!" Hannah said. "This is such a great kitchen to mess around in, I'll have a blast."

“Thank you. I know she wasn't worried about it, but I think it's an awful lot of work for one person." Polly replied. "Everyone should be here around eight thirty, and I can promise you there will be plenty of people who want to hold Tyler and make sure he is entertained. You might have to tuck him away in a corner if you don't want him passed around from person to person."

Bruce said, "I'll bring down the portable crib and put it in the back of the kitchen. That way Hannah can keep an eye on him and I'll check on him whenever I can. Will it be alright if Sammy and Emma help me out with lights?"

"They'll be fine," Polly said. "They're good kids."

Bruce went upstairs to bring things down for the baby, then made another trip for toys for Sammy and Emma.

Promptly at eight o’clock, Jeff walked in the front door and smiled at Polly. "Are you ready for the next couple of days?" he asked.

"I don't know!" she exclaimed. "I'm a little afraid of what you have planned."

"Let's go on into the office and I'll show you what I'm thinking." She followed him into his office and waited as he woke his computer up. A few keystrokes later and he had a 3D representation of the auditorium on the screen.

"Alright, that's cool," she said.

"Oh, it was nothing. Just call me a geek and be done with it."

"You're a geek! And that's pretty amazing."

"Okay. What I'm thinking is we've got the trees set up here." A flick of a key and the trees were in place. "And we've filled these spaces with tables and chairs," another flick and round tables with chairs around them showed up on the screen. "Since the kitchen is so close, we don't have to waste any space in the auditorium for food tables. That makes it better for traffic. I have coat racks showing up this afternoon and we'll put them in the hallway. We're going to stack those crates on the stage and drape them with some dark material. There will still be plenty of room for the musicians and the podium. So, now are you ready?"

"I'm ready, Jeff. This is a great job you've done. Next thing we need to have you do is start making me money instead of spending it, but it's the Christmas season, so let's spend away!"

He laughed and said, "I'm all ready to start doing that too, but I kind of thought we might wait until next week to discuss those plans."

"Okay!" she said, then looked up and listened, "I hear Sylvie out there. I want to introduce her to Hannah. Do you need me in here any longer?"

"No, I'm good. I'll see you in the auditorium later on."

She trotted out to the hallway and stopped Sylvie as she was walking around the steps, "Can I talk to you for a minute, Sylvie?"

"Sure! Good morning!" Sylvie responded.

"Oh, sorry ... Good morning to you! I wanted to talk to you about Hannah McKenzie."

"The gal who is, ummm, married to your old friend?"

"Yep, that's the one." Polly chuckled. "Nice save, there. Anyway, she's a great cook and loves being in the kitchen. Could you put her to work today?"

"Sure," Sylvie shrugged. "That sounds fine. It's a great big kitchen and there shouldn't be any reason the two of us can't work in that space. I'll find plenty for her to do and it will probably be a big help to me in the end." She looked sideways at Polly. "You were worried about me, weren't you?"

"Nah," Polly said. "Why would I worry? You only have hundreds of cookies to bake and whatever else you're going to put out tomorrow evening for everyone to eat. Of course you should be able to do it all by yourself." Then she laughed, "Okay, I was a little worried. But, I think Hannah needs to help you more than you need her help. So, is it alright?"

"Of course it is. Heck, I know what it's like to be all alone out there wondering what you're going to do next. I still can't believe you hired me to do this job."

"And now I've given you an assistant. See how wonderful I am!" Polly shook her head and chuckled. "Let's go on in so I can introduce the two of you."

Sylvie followed her into the kitchen. Hannah was pouring a cup of coffee and looked up.

"Hannah McKenzie, this is Sylvie Donovan. She's going to be the head chef this weekend and is ready to put you to work!" Polly said.

Hannah set the coffee cup down and put her hand out to shake Sylvie's. "Thanks for letting me help you. I can't wait to see what you're going to do today!"

Sylvie shook her jacket off and pulled an apron out of her bag. "I can't either." She turned back to look at Polly, "Oops! Maybe I shouldn't let her think I don't know what I'm doing."

"Can I leave you two alone and trust that nothing will explode in here?" Polly asked as she moved to step out of the kitchen.

"You can leave us alone," Sylvie responded, "but if there's an explosion, it's her fault."

Hannah giggled and said, "I'm already in trouble, I guess an explosion can get added to the list!"

Polly left them to their work and went into the auditorium where Jeff was placing packages of lights underneath the trees.

"Can I help?" she asked.

"Sure. I think three strings of lights per tree should do it. They're over there," and he pointed at some brown cartons. She pulled a carton out and drug it across the room to the furthest tree, setting three strings on the table beside the tree. Bruce came in and saw what they were doing and helped finish the task, then began breaking open boxes and wrapping lights around a tree. When he was finished, Jeff turned the lights on. "What do you think," he asked. "Too thin or just right?"

Polly looked at the tree. "That looks great," she shrugged. "What do you think?"

"It'll do." he said. "These look great. Thanks, Bruce."

Bruce nodded and walked to the next tree. Henry came in followed by his four assistants, all carrying ladders.

"Good morning, Polly! Hi Jeff," he said. "We'll start back here and move to the front of the room," he told his guys as he walked over to where Polly and Jeff were standing.

He winked at Polly, "Did you sleep well last night?" he asked.

"I did," she said. "Thank you for a wonderful evening. Oh, you know what! I should get you and Bruce together. He's been a car nut as long as I can remember!" She glanced over at Bruce who was wrapping lights around a third tree. "Yeah. I'll do that later. Or ... you can, whenever you get a moment."

"Where are all of the lights you want hung from the rafters, Jeff?" he asked.

"Let me show you," Jeff said and walked over to the cartons of lights.

Henry started to follow him, then turned back to Polly. "I had a great evening too and slept like a baby. Thank you."

Jeff started to speak, then realized no one was near him. He looked up, as if confused, then shrugged while he waited for Henry to join him. The two men opened cartons and began pulling packages of white lights out. The ladders were up and Jimmy and Sam were elected to run up and down. While that project was going, Polly heard more activity in the hallway and walked out to see all her friends laughing and giggling as they came around the staircase.

Beryl was the first to say something, "So, I heard you had a hot date last night, girlie. Are you going to finally be the one who gets Henry Sturtz to settle down?"

"Oh, gah!" Polly cried out. "No, we're not settling down. Whatever gave you that idea?"

"Maybe the way you've been mooning over each other every time you're in the same room."

"We do not, nor have we ever mooned over each other," Polly said disgustedly. "Ewww. That's for girls with no brains."

"Wow," Beryl laughed. "I thought that's what falling in love did to a girl. Well, at least some girls. Like Lydia. She loses her brains when her boy is around."

Lydia rolled her eyes.

"I'm not in love with Henry. For heaven's sake, Beryl. Don't turn this into the romance of the century. It was one date, it was nice." She winked at the three of them, "In fact, it was very nice. But, I'm not falling in love with him and he isn't falling in love with me. Now, grow up." Polly stomped her right foot when she said it and all three of them laughed.

"So, what are you guys doing here today?" Polly asked.

"We're going to make the table decorations." Andy responded. "Jeff got these adorable wooden candlesticks and some Christmas plates, so we're going to make dessert trays and all sorts of things. Bring on the glitter and spray paint!" she laughed.

"I'm a celebrated artist all over the country," Beryl announced, "and I'm not too good to play in glue, glitter and glam for you, Polly, my friend. So, you be nice to me."

"I love you guys," Polly laughed and snorted. "Oh, what would my life have been without knowing you?"

"Let's get busy, then! Onward, my artistic troops!" Beryl pulled her right knee up and stuck her right arm out, pointing toward the auditorium. "Come on!" she commanded. "Onward."

Laughing, they all entered the auditorium.

Jeff showed them where the items were they would use to create the decorations and Lydia pulled Polly aside.

"You and I are going to take a quick trip this morning," she said under her breath.

"What? Where are we going?"

"We're going over to see old Mr. McKenzie and his wife and we're going to talk to them about their boy and those little kids. That old man is going to come off his high horse today or I'm going to kick it out from under him and he'll find out how black the dirt in this state is, face first."

Polly's eyes grew wide in shock. "I've never heard you talk like that. Are you sure you want to get in the middle of this?"

"I'm already in the middle of this. You can't spend a few hours around those kiddos without falling in love with them and that stupid old man doesn't know what he's missing. I'm going to take a few moments of his day to remind him and you're going to help me."

"I don't want to," Polly said, drawing space out between each word. "He scared the crap out of me in high school and I'm pretty sure I'm not over it yet."

"Then you will talk to Bruce's mother while I talk to old man McKenzie. I know his type and he doesn't scare me."

"I'm betting there aren't too many people who scare you, Lydia." Polly remarked.

"Well, there's that," she said. "So, are you driving or am I?"

"Okay!" Polly said. "I guess we're going now?"

"Yep, might as well get it over with early in the day so we can think about something else later on." Lydia said.

Polly spoke up, "Jeff, Lydia and I need to run an errand. We'll be back in a bit. Call me if you need anything."

Before he could say anything, Lydia took Polly's arm and propelled her out of the auditorium and into the foyer. "Don't give them a chance to protest, it messes with their mind," she said.

"Mine too, just in case you were wondering," Polly laughed. "Alright, let's get this over with. I'll drive. I know the way to their house."

CHAPTER SIX

As they drove down the road, Lydia lamented, "I wish we had some snow. A white Christmas is so much more festive."

"Snowstorms in the northeast can get pretty wild," Polly remarked. "But, if we get crazy snow in Boston, at least I don't have to drive. It's been so long since I've driven on county roads in the winter, I'll probably turn into a wimp."

"I know, I know," Lydia said. "I do hate having Aaron out in the stuff and he's always the first one to go. But, when he's home and the fire is roaring and I know where all my friends and family are, I love it."

She looked sideways at Polly, "That means you have to stay put, you know. I don't want to be worried about you this year. Got it?"

"Got it," Polly giggled. "I promise to stay put." She pointed at a cornfield to the south where cattle were grazing on the leftover stalks. "I'd forgotten how beautiful the fields in Iowa are. Whether I'm looking at little green seedlings in the spring, or row after row of corn waving in a summer breeze or fields recently harvested, it's amazing. I can't wait to start experiencing the farm cycle from beginning to end again. I had no idea I would miss it and honestly, I didn't know I was missing it until I got back and started seeing again." Polly lifted her left palm off the steering wheel and waved at an oncoming pickup truck.

"I can see you didn't forget how to be neighborly," Lydia remarked.

"I know, right!" Polly laughed. "The one thing I noticed first off out east was that people walked around with their heads down, barely acknowledging anyone else on earth. Out here, you are expected to pay attention, and to say hello. I don't know any of these people and it's like they simply want to tell me it's good I'm alive. Pretty wonderful, eh?"

Lydia smiled, then reached over and patted her arm. "It is good you are alive. And yes, it's pretty wonderful." They rode in silence, then she asked, "So, how long would it have taken you to come back to Iowa if things hadn't fallen apart with Joey last spring?"

"I don't know. For a while after Dad died, it seemed like there was no reason for me to ever come back. I was building a life. I guess I figured I would finally meet someone and end up in Massachusetts for the rest of my life. The family I have back here doesn't care if I'm around, so there was no reason to visit for holidays or vacations.

"But, then all of a sudden, I felt claustrophobic in the city. There were people everywhere. Not just in my space, but everywhere. The only place I ever found real solitude was in my apartment and even then, I had to listen to stomping upstairs and music from downstairs and I could hear people walking in the halls and fighting and screaming next door. Sirens wailed down the street and cars crashed outside my windows. It was noise all the time.

"The day I got out of the truck in front of the old school, I breathed in fresh air and heard birds and insects and nothing else. It actually took a few moments for me to hear a car drive by. I felt every muscle in my shoulders relax and I didn't have any more questions. I was going to live here forever.

"We don't know what we've got, do we?" Lydia commented.

"When I was in high school," Polly said, "I told Dad I would never marry a farmer. I didn't want all of the hassle involved in running a farm. The early hours; worrying about corn prices and fretting over the weather. It seemed like the worst life in the world. Dad made it easy on me, but I saw what he did and I didn't want to live like that. I wanted something exciting! I didn't want to stay in my little town and see the same people day after day. I wanted to experience what I thought would be a great big life, meeting new people all the time, going to museums and galleries. I wanted the hustle and bustle of a big city. Well, I got it and for a lot of years, I loved it.

"But, I don't want that any more. I've had my fill," she finished.

"You know we have museums and galleries around here." Lydia smirked.

"Yes, and an amazingly talented artist right there in town!" Polly exclaimed. "It's such snobbery to think that Iowa doesn't have everything necessary to make a great big life. I'm glad I'm home."

"I'm glad you are, too." Lydia said. "So, do you know where we're going?"

"Well, it is weird, coming back here without planning to stay with Dad. I feel like a tourist driving into what used to be my home town." Polly stopped talking, then said. "And in answer to your question, I know where we're going. I'm taking the direct route and staying on good roads, rather than driving around the back way. It's been long enough that I'm sure I would make a wrong turn and we'd end up driving in circles."

"You know, you could get GPS." Lydia said.

"Uh huh. I don't think so. If I can't figure my way around Iowa roads, I will give up my navigator's badge." Polly retorted.

"Really? You're that stubborn about it?" Lydia asked.

"I'm really that stubborn. Give me a map and some time. I hate GPS systems. That woman is always yelling at me and she gets so mean when I make a wrong turn. 'Recalculating, recalculating' sounds more like. 'Stupid girl, you should have listened to me.' I gave my last GPS to Drea because I nearly tossed it out the window on the interstate one day."

"You could have turned it off."

"Right. Well, it found a new home and I'm perfectly happy without it," Polly laughed. "Alright, their home is that big white house over there on the hill. Are you ready for this?"

"Not really," Lydia breathed, "but let's get it over with. Then I vote we go get ice cream."

"It's a deal!" Polly said. She took a deep breath and pulled into the lane.

"Damn it," she said.

"What?" Lydia asked.

"I'm worrying about it again. Do I go to the front door or the back door?" Polly turned to Lydia with a pout.

"Figure out where the cars are. Go to that door." Lydia said and pointed to the back door.

"You're knocking first, then," Polly said and parked the truck.

They got out of the truck and Lydia walked up to the door. As she raised her hand to knock, Polly recognized Mrs. McKenzie already walking toward them. Lydia stayed her hand and waited until the door was opened.

"Mrs. McKenzie?" Polly said, "I don't know if you remember me, but I'm ..."

"Polly Giller!" she said. "What are you doing here today? I heard you were back in Iowa and bought the old school over in Bellingwood."

"I am back," Polly said. "And yes, I did buy the old school. I've been having a lot of fun renovating it."

"What can I do for you today?" she asked Polly and Lydia.

"May we come in? We'd like to talk to you about a few things. Oh, and this is Lydia Merritt, a friend of mine from Bellingwood."

"Sure! Where are my manners? Come on in." They followed her in through the mud porch, up three steps and into the kitchen.

"Oh, this is lovely!" exclaimed Lydia. "What a beautiful view you have!"

"Thank you," beamed Shirley McKenzie. "We renovated the kitchen three years ago and I like to spend mornings in here." She pointed at the table. "Go ahead and have a seat. Can I pour some coffee for you?"

Lydia nodded at Polly, "I'd love some," Polly said.

Then Lydia asked, "Mrs. McKenzie, I'd like to speak with your husband. Is he here this morning?"

Shirley McKenzie's face took on a look of concern. "Is there something wrong? I guess I don't understand why you're here?"

Lydia assured her, "There's nothing wrong. I'd like to speak with your husband and Polly here wants to tell you a story."

"Well, alright. He's out in the shed working on the old mower." She poured coffee into two cups, setting one down in front of Polly and holding on to the other. "That's what he likes to do when harvest is finished. I keep trying to talk him into taking a vacation, but he won't hear of it. Tells me there will be plenty of time for that in the future."

She set her coffee cup down on the table, pulled her cellphone out of her pants pocket and said, "Here, let me call him. He'll be on the lookout for you."

"No that's alright," Lydia stopped her with a hand upraised. "I can find him." Polly knew that she didn't want the man to know what freight train might be coming at him."

Shirley McKenzie looked a little dazed and slipped the phone back into her pocket. Lydia walked back outside and headed for the shed.

"What's going on, Polly? Tell me why you are here today?" the woman asked.

"Sit down, Mrs. McKenzie. I feel a little silly sitting here all by myself."

After they were both seated, Polly asked, "When was the last time Bruce called you?"

"Is he alright? Has something happened? What about Hannah and the children? Are they okay?" Worry filled the woman's voice.

"He's fine. Hannah and the children are fine. So, you know about them?" Polly asked.

Mrs. McKenzie nodded. "I do. He called me when they got married and then when they had that adorable little baby. We exchange emails, so I've seen pictures of them. Lyle doesn't know that I talk to him. It just breaks my heart, but that husband of mine has a stubborn streak a mile long and when Bruce walked away from him, he hurt his dad pretty badly. It was one of those things I could never fix."

"Bruce needs you right now, Mrs. McKenzie …" Polly started.

"Oh, please call me Shirley. We're way past the Mrs. McKenzie age, I think," Shirley McKenzie interrupted.

"Alright ... Shirley. What I was trying to say was that Bruce and his family need you. He has nowhere else to go and nobody else he can turn to. He's been trying to make it alone and I think they are finally at the end of their rope." Polly said.

"What do you mean? I thought he had a good job out in Colorado!"

"Well, he did and Hannah had a job too, but the economy finally got to them and they've sold everything and packed their entire lives into a car and were on their way back to ask your husband for a job on the farm."

"Oh." Shirley's shoulders drooped and she let out a sigh. "I don't know what my husband will do. This wasn't a great year on the farm either."

"Mrs. Mck ... Shirley. They are at my place right now." Polly said.

"What? They're in Iowa and they didn't come here?"

"Well, there was some trouble and they ended up at my school. Neither of us knew the other was there until we recognized each other."

"What kind of trouble? You said the children were alright?"

"Everyone is fine. They are all staying together in an extra room I have there. Hannah is a wonderful person and Bruce seems to love all of those children a lot."

"Oh, I know he does. He talks about Sammy and Emma like they were his own." Shirley said. "But, you said there was trouble. What kind of trouble?"

"I should probably let Bruce tell you himself, but while he was stopped for speeding through Bellingwood, a dog found drugs hidden in his car." Polly stopped as the poor woman gasped. "He says they aren't his drugs and Hannah assures me he would never do anything like that. I tend to believe her, but right now, the sheriff is investigating. They arrested both him and Hannah and both are out on bail right now and staying with me until the sheriff can figure out what is going on."

"Arrested? Bail?" Shirley McKenzie put her elbows on the table and dropped her head into her hands. "What is happening?"

"What is happening is that your son needs help from his parents and you are going to have to figure out how to get your husband to come down off his self-centered high horse and think about someone else." Polly took a breath and realized she might have pushed too far.

"I'm sorry," she said. "That was a little extreme. I shouldn't have said that."

"No, that's alright. You didn't say anything I haven't said to him over and over again throughout the years. He let my boy go and wouldn't budge because of his pride. I hoped one day he would finally mellow out about all of this, but obviously, I can't wait any longer. I don't know what I'm going to do, though."

She thought for a moment. "I need to talk to Kevin, I suppose. He's never said much about Bruce leaving, but I know it's been hard on him having to be the only one responsible for everything around here."

"Is there anything they need right now?" she asked Polly.

"Nothing other than a place to live, a job and a family to help them get through this. I think that's enough," Polly said. It occurred to her to wonder when she had gotten that snippy with people. Lydia must be rubbing off on her.

"Is this what your friend is talking to Lyle about?" Shirley asked.

"Yes it is. Her husband is Aaron Merritt, the Sheriff. He's gone out of his way to keep the family together while all of this is going on and she has fallen in love with those little kids." Polly responded.

"I hope she has more luck than I do with him. He usually just walks away and keeps walking until I can't follow him any longer. By the time he gets home in the evening, we're both too tired to talk about it and neither one of us wants to fight at that point, so it's been easier to let it slip aside."

Polly opened up her mouth to speak again, but stopped when she heard the back door slam open and Lydia stomp her feet up the steps. "Come on, Polly, we're not welcome here any longer. I think we need to go."

"But, wait!" Shirley McKenzie said. "What happened?"

"Your husband," Lydia spat, "is a rude, rude man who doesn't deserve to have small children around to tell him that he is a good grandpa." She took Polly's arm and pulled her up out of the chair. "I'm sorry for being rude right now, but foul words are going to come out of my mouth and it's not fair for me to do that to you."

She propelled Polly down the steps and out the door with Shirley following close behind, who said, "I'm so sorry he was rude to you. I'll try to talk to him and get him to see reason. I think it's about time I exercised a few rude behaviors of my own."

"I do apologize for my behavior," Lydia said. "I'm generally not like this, but that man is one angry old cuss and when he treats a woman like he treated me, my mouth comes unglued and gets me in trouble. I hope to meet you under better circumstances another time, so you can find out that I'm not quite such a bitch."

She got in the passenger side of Polly's truck and slammed the door. Polly looked at Mrs. McKenzie and raised her eyes, "I've never seen her like this and I'm sorry that we've upset your family here. We're having a big Christmas party at the school tomorrow night for the whole town if you'd like to come over and see Bruce and Hannah and the children. You're more than welcome and we'll keep trying to figure something out, alright?"

"Alright, dear. Thank you for stopping by to tell me what's going on." Shirley McKenzie pulled Polly into a hug. "I'm so sorry this has happened. Tell your friend she doesn't have to apologize to me. I know Lyle can be an insensitive jerk."

Polly got in the truck and backed out of the lane. When they got on the road, Lydia threw her hands up in the air. "Polly I'm so angry right now, the only words I can think to say are mean and ugly and well ... filled with curses. That man has his ass so tightly bound up, he can't see for all the shit filling his body. I want to curse everything about him. And then I want to do it some more."

Polly tried not to giggle. Listening to prim and proper Lydia curse was more than she could handle with a straight face, so she kept quiet.

"Well, aren't you going to ask me what happened?" Lydia demanded.

"Would you like me to go to Dairy Queen for some ice cream?" Polly asked.

"Hell no. I'm too angry to eat ice cream." Lydia responded. "But, go there anyway. I might change my mind."

Polly chuckled and turned east and drove into Story City. "Okay, what happened out there? I was having a perfectly pleasant and, shall we say, polite conversation with his wife."

"That jackass told me I had no business bothering him about a son he had written off years ago. If said son couldn't be bothered to let him know that he was even still alive, there was no way he was going to offer any assistance or help. He didn't care if Bruce had a family. He was so wrapped up in starting his own life without his parents, he could damned well live out there on his own and make it with or without them. He, the old man, had made it on his own, there wasn't any way he was going to take that from a self-centered son who thought he could do it without him.

"I might have reminded him that he was farming a family farm and hadn't ever done it on his own, he'd had a good solid start, when that set him off on another tear about how he'd been responsible to his family and had stayed here to work when everyone else took off and then he decided to tell me about his wonderful son, Kevin, who chose to stay and help with the farm.

"That is one bitter old man and all I wanted to do was kick him in the balls just to watch him groan on the floor while I stood over him and spat. However, I restrained myself and asked about grandchildren. He told me that his perfect son, Kevin, had three children and those were enough in his life and he didn't need any more draws on his finances. If Bruce had gone out and gotten a woman pregnant and couldn't support her, that was his problem, not his father's problem.

"Oh Polly, it was awful. It was like he couldn't see any reason at all. All he could see was that he had been betrayed by his son. It was almost as if he had wanted to leave when he was Bruce's age and because the kid actually did it, the dad can't forgive him.

Lydia took a breath. "Wow, I never get that angry. I'm usually the mediator in these situations. That man worked me up. I couldn't find anything in him anywhere that would give his son a break. I kept trying and trying to find a soft place and it just wasn't there." Lydia rolled her shoulders and neck, and then slumped back in the seat. "I have probably made it worse and that wasn't my intention. And then, I was mean to his poor wife. How does she live with a jackass like that?

"And you know what he said before I walked away from him? He told me I was a nosy old woman who probably had better things to do than try to fix his life. Old? I am NOT old. I might be nosy, but he was rude!"

Polly glanced at her friend, "Are you done?"

Lydia shook her head. "Oh, I'm done, alright. I should never have started this morning."

"Well, Mrs. McKenzie knows about Hannah and the kids. She talks to Bruce and emails back and forth with him. She knows her husband can be a jerk and it seems like she loves him anyway. Crazy, I know." Polly laughed.

"I told her everything. She's going to talk to their other son, Kevin, today. I think. Don't give up on this yet. I vote we wait and see and pray for one of your Christmas miracles."

"Yeah, throw my words back at me," Lydia snapped. "I'm not feeling much like a Christmas miracle today. I feel more like Scrooge and the Grinch all wrapped up in one shiny package. Now, where's my ice cream."

Polly laughed. "I love you, Lydia Merritt. You're the most normal person I've met in my life."

They pulled into the drive-thru at Dairy Queen and discovered that both of them loved nothing more than a simple twist cone. Chocolate and vanilla ice cream could work wonders when savage beasts needed soothing.

CHAPTER SEVEN

Ready or not, the time was finally here. All the insanity of the last few days and it was time for Polly to begin welcoming people from Bellingwood to Sycamore House for the first time. She and Obiwan had taken one final walk before the evening began and now she was standing in front of him in her bra and slip attempting to pull her hair back into yet another artful arrangement that would hold throughout the evening.

"I need more bobby pins," she said and pulled drawers open to find where she had stowed her stash. "There are no more bobby pins. Where are they, Obiwan?"

He laid his head on his paws and reached out to lick her toes. "Oh, alright. I'll calm down." She opened another drawer. "See? There they are. Right where I put them." He thumped his tail on the floor.

Polly walked back into the bedroom and picked up her new dress. Now, this was a beautiful dress. She'd found the dress in Des Moines several weeks ago and knew she couldn't leave the store without it. It was midnight blue and floor length with a sheer, floral patterned lace covering the solid skirt and bodice. Tiny, little sequins sparkled throughout the lace, flickering in the light. Though it was strapless, she had a short matching velvet jacket with pearl buttons. Floral lace also covered the collar of the jacket. She felt elegant when she had purchased it, and knew it was a must have for her first Christmas at Sycamore House. Slipping it on, Polly stepped into her pumps and said, "What do you think, Obiwan?"

He thumped his tail again. "Thank you. It means a lot to me," Polly said. "I will be back later. If it gets too late, I'll see if one of the boys will come up and take you outside again, alright?" His happy tail seemed to signify his approval of the plan and Polly headed out her front door.

She knew she was downstairs early, but wanted one last look at the auditorium before it filled with people. Jeff and Lydia, even Henry and Aaron had all assured her the town was buzzing about the party and they would have a full house. Polly opened the main doors to the auditorium and took a breath. The scent of pine was redolent throughout the entire building, but it was beautiful among the cinnamon and vanilla scented candles which had been lit in the room. It looked like a winter wonderland with the trees lit up. Now, if only there was a bit of snow falling outside the windows, it would be perfect.

Smells from the kitchen filled the foyer and the auditorium and she smiled at Hannah and Sylvie, who were setting food out on the long counter. Tables along the walls of the foyer were filled with cups and plates, and different types of drinks. Several high school girls were bustling about, making sure everything was perfect.

Jeff came out of the office, looking resplendent in his tuxedo. He had found a cummerbund to match the blue in her dress and was grinning.

"What do you think, boss?" he asked.

"Oh Jeff. This is amazing. I know what you showed me, but every step has brought it that much closer to perfection. It's like a dream in here.

"Well," and he let out a breath. "We're ready for action any time. As soon as I give the nod, the music will start and we're off. Are you ready?"

"I am," she said "It feels like I've been ready for this for a long time. It's just the first in a long line of great things to happen here. Thank you for making this real for me."

He smiled. "My pleasure." Then, he looked at his watch. "Okay, 7:20. Shall we begin?"

Polly nodded at him and made her way to the front door. She saw car lights pull in the driveway and waited while they parked. Opening the front door, she wasn't surprised to see Aaron opening the door behind behind the driver's seat for Andy, then come around and open the other side up for Beryl and Lydia.

"How did I know you would be the first ones here tonight?" Polly called out across the parking lot.

"We wanted to make sure you had everything you needed!" Lydia said. "And besides, Aaron has some news."

"Good news?" Polly asked.

"Why don't we wait and see," Lydia said. "Just wait and see, right, Polly?"

They came in the door and there were quick hugs all around. Four young people stood ready to take coats and exchange them for tags that Aaron stuffed down in his suit coat pocket.

"Where are Bruce and Hannah?" Aaron asked.

"Hannah's in the kitchen and I think Bruce is upstairs with the kiddos. He was going to stay with them until they fell asleep, then Sylvie's boys would head up and keep an eye on them." Polly responded.

"Lydia?" he said.

"Yes, I know. I'll make my way to the kitchen and work my fingers to the bone while you talk to Hannah," she sighed. "I tell you, a girl can't even go out for a party with her husband anymore."

Lydia and Andy went back to the kitchen and Beryl took Polly aside. "Could I borrow two of your young people for a minute? I have something out in Aaron's truck I want to bring in for you."

Jeff stepped up, "Sure, is it heavy?"

"Not heavy, just awkward, I suppose." Beryl replied.

"Dave? Joe? Could you give Ms. Watson a hand?" he called across the foyer. Two of the boys came over and went outside with her.

Hannah walked up to Aaron and said, "Is something wrong? Lydia told me you needed to talk to me."

"Let's go upstairs, so I can talk to both you and your husband at the same time."

Her face fell and she looked at Polly, pleading for help.

"Can I come with you, Aaron?" Polly asked.

"No, it's alright. Come on up with me, Hannah. Polly should stay here and greet her guests."

Polly watched helplessly as the two of them mounted the steps. Hannah was dragging her feet, and kept turning around to look at Polly. But, as they hit the landing, more people arrived and Polly put her happy Christmas face back on to greet her guests. Lydia joined her at the door and made a few introductions for her, then guided people into the auditorium. She came back and put her arm around Polly's waist, "It is good news, Polly. Don't worry."

Polly let out a sigh of relief. "Oh, he scared me so badly. Alright. I can wait to hear it from them, then."

Beryl came up the steps followed by the two young men who were carrying a six foot by ten foot wrapped gift.

"Oh, Beryl! What is this?" Polly asked.

"It's my gift to you," Beryl said.

"But, but. You shouldn't have gotten me anything."

"I didn't GET you anything. I painted you something. Here boys, set it down over against this wall. Now, Polly rip the paper away and you'll see what I'm talking about."

Polly began pulling paper away and she must have been going too slowly, because Beryl started ripping from the other end. When she uncovered the painting, Polly's eyes filled with tears. "Oh Beryl," was all she could say and she crossed over to hug the woman.

Beryl had painted a beautiful sycamore tree, spreading its branches across the canvas. The branches changed color across the piece, from the new green of spring, to the full growth of summer, the leaves of fall to the empty branches of winter. In the background of the painting, behind the tree was a very light image of Sycamore House.

"No matter the season, Polly, Sycamore House represents more than an old school building. It is filled with life, now. Life that you brought to it, life that you bring to Bellingwood.

"Thank you, Beryl. This fills my heart. I have no words." Polly turned to Jeff, "Can you get this onto the stage, maybe prop it up on some of those crates under the draping?"

"I'm on it," he said and beckoned to the two boys to help him carry it in.

"Thank you, Beryl. I can't believe I own one of your originals. It means the world to me."

"Good. Now I am going to find some food and drink and start this party." She looked sideways at Polly. "I bet there's no alcohol tonight, is there."

"Well, I didn't want Sycamore House's first event to be a drunken brawl."

Beryl laughed. "I'm only messing with you." and she took off.

Polly continued to greet people at the door until eight o'clock, when Jeff came to get her. Many of the people she had worked with were there and she recognized friends from the party at Lydia's house. Lydia's daughter and family came in from Dayton and Andy rushed over to introduce Polly to her sons. The hall was filling up and Polly was having a great time. Henry had snuck in past a group she was speaking with and winked as he went into the auditorium.

Jeff said, "We'll leave the kids out here to greet and take coats, but you need to get the evening started."

"Alright," she said. "Let's do this."

He escorted her to the podium. The music stopped and within a few moments everyone ceased talking.

"Welcome to Sycamore House," Polly said into the microphone. "We're glad you could join us to celebrate Christmas and the beginning of new life for this building. My name is Polly Giller and I hope that over the next year, we will find a lot of time to have fun together, both here at Sycamore House and in town. I'm glad to be back in Iowa and can't wait to get to know all of you better."

As she took a breath, scattered applause began around the room until everyone was clapping. Jeff held his hand up and Polly went on.

"This evening, we're going to decorate these trees around the room. Find a table, get comfortable and you will see that there are cranberries and popcorn to be strung, paper to make snowflakes or other decorations ... anything you'd like to do. But, each tree is a team effort. We will give the trees away before the end of the evening. There are signup cards on your tables if you'd like to enter your name to win a tree. It will then be delivered to your house and set up by some of your very best workers. They've promised to get them to you over the next couple of days.

"Now, if you know someone who needs a tree and can't afford one, do me a favor. Write their name on a card and hand it to me or Jeff here. We want everyone to have a little bit of Christmas this year.

"Enjoy your evening and let's decorate!"

More applause followed her as she walked down the steps, music began again and Lydia caught her. "Come with me, alright?" she said quietly.

Polly followed Lydia out to the foyer and then into her office. Bruce and Hannah were standing there, smiling.

Bruce said, "Polly, thank you for believing in me. Everything is going to be alright now."

"What do you mean?" she asked. "What happened?"

Aaron said, "Well, Bruce told us who he'd bought the car from and we started investigating backwards. It seems that an old buddy of his set him up as a transport. Denver police caught him and he admitted to everything. When Bruce started talking about driving out here to Iowa to beg his dad for work, this guy figured it would be a great way to move things across a few states. Once, Bruce got to Story City, another guy was planning to steal the car and move it on to Minneapolis. We're working on that one. A young family would never be suspected of moving drugs or so he thought. So, everything is good. We've got all of the McKenzie's stuff in storage until they find a place to live. They're free to go."

Polly hugged Hannah. "I'm so glad it has worked out. Oh, your kids are going to be happy that everything is alright."

"Sheriff Merritt has already taken care of that, Hannah said. “He spent some time with Sammy and Emma and told them there was a misunderstanding and they shouldn't worry anymore. Neither of the kids was sure what to do with him, but since he didn't have his uniform on tonight, he wasn't quite so scary," she laughed, a little uncomfortably.

Lydia poked Polly, "See, I told you. A Christmas miracle."

Polly smiled and said, "You guys can stay here until you figure out where you're going to live. I haven't been able to finish those rooms yet to rent them out, so there's no reason you shouldn't have the room. And it's Christmas time, for heaven's sake. There's room in this inn."

Lydia squeezed her and said, "You're a good girl, Polly."

"Now that this is over, I'll start looking for a job on Monday," Bruce said. "Maybe I can find something to do around here." His lips turned down. "I just wish ... " then he stopped. "Nope. I'm going to be happy this is behind me and my family has a warm place to sleep. Everything else will come in time. Thank you Polly. I can't believe that of all places for me to be pulled over, it was in your lane."

"I know. It’s kind of unbelievable. But, like Lydia keeps reminding me. Christmas miracles happen!"

Hannah looked up, "I need to get in the kitchen. Sylvie has to be going crazy," and she took off. Then, she turned around, hugged Polly tightly, then hugged Aaron, then Lydia. "Thank you all for everything! This is a Christmas miracle!" With that, she bolted out the door of the office and headed for the kitchen.

"Are you all coming in now?" Polly asked. "We can't hide out in here all evening." She strode out of the office and went back into the auditorium, where people were chattering and working away to decorate the trees in the room.

As she walked around the room, commenting on the trees and the strings of decorations that were filling them, she was stopped several times as cards were pressed into her hands. Many people complimented her on the renovation of the old school. She stopped to talk to some of the women she had met at Lydia's slumber party a couple of months ago, when she heard her name being spoken behind her. She nearly turned around, but stopped as she realized they weren't necessarily being complimentary.

"I heard she got involved with the mob in Boston and is hiding here in Iowa. Can you believe she's going to bring that type of trouble out here?

"Well, I can't believe anyone would spend all of that money to fix this old place up. I thought her daddy was a farmer and would have given her more sense than that.

"What does she think she's doing giving away these trees? People can buy their own trees; they don't need to get free trees that we decorate. That's just stupid.

"Have you even seen her downtown very much? I'll bet she does all her shopping online or in the big cities. Did you see that dress she's wearing? She probably spent more on it than I did on groceries for the last two years. Imagine.

"I think that Jeff Lyndsay is homosexual. Did you see how flashy he is? Can you believe she brought one of those to town?

Polly's ire began to rise and then she felt a cool hand on her forearm. She looked up and it was Henry.

"Ignore them or confront them, but don't let them get to you." he said quietly.

"Are you kidding me? They come here and eat my food and listen to my music and think they can say those terrible things? And so what if Jeff is gay, does that mean he's poison? I'm getting angry, Henry. I want to kick them out."

"Breathe, just breathe. Then think about how you want to handle them. You are always going to find these people around you. This probably isn't the only table of people here who are saying bad things."

Polly took a couple of deep breaths, then said, "Okay. You're right. I know this type of person. I went to school with these people. I worked with these people. I even went to church with these people. It still doesn't make me like them, but you're right."

She took another deep breath, then stood up a little taller and walked over to a table filled with several couples. Both men and women had been spewing ugly gossip and she had finally figured out how she would handle it. "Good evening! I'm so glad you're here. I don't think I caught your names earlier."

Henry was standing beside her as she walked around the table and greeted each person as they introduced themselves to her. "Are you enjoying yourselves?" she asked.

"Oh yes," said one woman, "You've done a beautiful job with the old place. We were talking about how much you've invested in it."

"Were you!" Polly said. "Well, I hope the investment pays off soon. My father would have been so happy to see the money he left me used to make this dream come true."

Polly zeroed in on one of the more snide looking women. "What a lovely dress you're wearing this evening! That shade of green looks wonderful on you!" she gushed.

"Do you think so?" the woman responded. "My husband here never tells me what he thinks about my clothes. You have a very nice dress, too."

"Did any of you come up with someone you thought should get a Christmas tree? Surely you know people in town who aren't going to be able to have a tree this year? Wouldn’t it be just awful for there to be kids with no Christmas tree when we could help them out?" Polly went on.

"Well, if you think of someone, please write it down and hand the card either to myself or to Jeff over there. Isn't he gorgeous?"

She spun away and walked off and heard Henry giggling in her ear.

"Now, that's the way to handle a group, Polly. You're good at that." Henry said.

"It was either that or kick their chairs out from under them, but I wasn't ready to pay for eight new hips and at their age, I'm guessing every one of them would have broken when they hit the floor."

"Well, they aren't sure what just hit them, and they're going to be very confused for a while." He turned around and glanced back at the table. "Look, they're working on the popcorn string now. I wouldn't be at all surprised if you get a card with a name on it before the end of the evening."

"Oh, that reminds me," Polly said. "I have a few here. Tell me if these names are all good ideas." She pulled the cards up and handed them to Henry.

He glanced over them and said, "Yeah, these are all good."

"Let's see what Jeff has," she said and walked over to her associate.

"Have you gotten any names of people to receive trees?" she asked.

"I have. I don't know if we're going to have any extra trees to give away," he said.

"That's fine. I'd rather they all went to someone who could use a tree." she responded.

He slipped the cards into her hand and passed them on to Henry, who glanced at them and nodding, handed them back.

"How are you doing, Jeff?" Henry asked.

"I think we're doing well. There was a stack of brochures about hosting events here at Sycamore House out by the front door and those are nearly gone. The business cards I left on the counter are also gone, so maybe we'll start getting some calls. And Polly, the food is great. Your friends have done a fabulous job."

"I'm going to talk to Sylvie. She needs to think bigger about her life. Working in a grocery store doesn't nearly begin to tap into her talent." Polly remarked.

They chatted for a few more minutes until Lydia walked up to Polly and said, "You aren't going to believe it, but I need you again."

Polly turned to Henry and Jeff, "I'm sorry. I'll be back in a bit. Hold down the fort, okay?"

CHAPTER EIGHT

Stepping out into the foyer, Polly asked, "What's going on? Is something wrong?"

"No, just someone who wants to see you and I figured it was easier for you to come out rather than bring them in." Lydia giggled a little. "You aren't going to believe this. I'm beginning to think you might have a new career ahead of you!"

"What!" Polly exclaimed. As they entered the hall, she recognized two people she hadn't seen for a while.

"Brad! Lee! I'm so glad you were able to make it up this evening!" she said.

"We would have been here earlier, but Brad decided at the last minute he needed to transfer some hay around and then he lost all sense of time. He drives me nuts sometimes," Lee said, while shaking her head. Brad just smiled.

"You don't say much, do you Brad?" Polly laughed.

"Maybe not," he replied. "But we brought you a gift!"

He held out a large covered basket. The blanket moved around a little and Lydia stood beside Polly snickering.

"What did you do?" Polly asked, then made a sound in the back of her throat as she pulled back the blanket. Two kittens were wrestling with each other in the warmth of the covered basket. One was black and white and the other predominantly white with a little color on her ears and as Polly saw when she lifted her out of the basket, her tail.

Lee said, "The boy is already been neutered and they have their first year shots. We didn't want to take them away from their mama right away, but I know that little boys need to be neutered early so they don't turn into tom cats."

"They're adorable! Have you named them?"

Lydia snickered again.

"What? What do you know?" Polly demanded.

"I might have been talking to them for a while about this little gift," she responded. "They named them Luke and Leia."

Polly snorted as she laughed out loud. "Oh, I'm already getting a reputation, aren't I? That's perfect. I wonder what Obiwan's going to do with these little guys!"

She put her foot on the first step, "I've got a few minutes. Let's go upstairs and find them a home and you can see the wood floors. They are beautiful, but thank you so much! This is a wonderful gift!"

As they walked up the steps, Lee laughingly said, "We weren't sure if you would be happy getting two kittens after you already had a dog, but Lydia told us it would be alright. Brad had called Henry to make sure and he hooked us up with her and well, it's been a plan in the works, I guess. I hope you have fun with them."

"I'm going to have a blast with them. The more furry little things in my life, the better, I guess," Polly said as they stopped in front of the door to her apartment. "I think Jason is in here with Obiwan, so, he should be in good shape."

She opened the door and stepped in, then started laughing even more. Henry was standing there beside an immense cat tree with a big red bow on top. Aaron, Beryl and Andy were on the couch with wrapped gifts in front of them.

"We've all been in on this," Lydia said. "I think you'll find everything you need to incorporate these two little kittens into your life."

Polly's eyes filled with tears as she hugged her friend. "I can't believe how fortunate I am. Eight months ago I was trying to figure out what next to do with my life and now here I am with all of you as friends, animals filling up my house and a home that is more than I ever could have dreamed of. Thank you all."

She turned to Brad and Lee, "Have you met everyone?" They nodded and she continued, "Thank you for bringing me these little guys." Brad held the basket out to her and she put it on the floor. The kittens looked around and scrambled out of their basket, making their way onto her floor. Beryl tossed her a lightweight package which, when she opened it, was found to be a soft, bright purple mat. She put it in front of the kitten, who made his way to it, flopped down and promptly went to sleep.

"Well, I guess he has been working hard making his way up here," she remarked. His sister followed him, curled up in front of him and went to sleep as well.

"Now what do I do with them?" Polly asked. "I don't want to move them and disturb 'em!"

She stood back up and laughed. "Where's Obiwan?"

"Oh!" Henry said, "Just a second. This will disturb them for sure!" He opened up the bedroom door and Obiwan bounded across the room toward Polly, coming to an abrupt stop in front of the two kittens. Polly knelt down and reached her hand out for him to sniff. He sniffed her hand, then began sniffing at the kittens. He nosed them once or twice and they didn't respond to his attention. Finding that they were uninterested in him, he began trotting around the room, looking for attention from anyone who would give it to him.

Jason had followed him out of the bedroom. "Oh, you've got kittens, too! This is the best place, ever!" he said.

"It sure is," Polly responded. "Now, would you mind babysitting all of them while we go back downstairs and finish up the evening? Maybe your Mom would even let you and Andrew spend the night in my apartment with all of the animals."

"Really? Would you ask her? That would be awesome! Andrew is over watching the McKenzie kids sleep, but he will love these kittens!" Jason said.

"I'll ask. I'm sure it will be alright." Polly said. "Thanks for taking care of them. Oh, did you get some food from downstairs?"

"Bruce brought us food and cookies. He's a nice guy," he replied.

"Thank you and I'll see you later," Polly said as she placed her hand on his back. "Check in on your brother, will you?"

"I will!"

Everyone went back downstairs. Brad and Lee made their way in and found some people they knew, so they sat down and helped finish decorating a tree.

Jeff found Polly and said, "I think it's time to wrap up the evening and get everyone headed home. Have you looked outside lately?"

She looked out the window and smiled. Great big snowflakes were glinting in the lights lining the driveway as they fell from the sky. "It's beautiful!" she said. "But, you're right. Let's do this. Do you have any more cards with names on them?"

"Just two more." he replied.

"Alright, I'll head for the stage." Polly made her way onto the stage and the musicians wound down as she approached the podium. She turned and smiled at them. Such beautiful music for a beautiful evening. "Thank you," she mouthed, then stepped forward.

"Excuse me!" she said into the din filling the room, then waited. It took a few moments, but soon the room had quieted enough for her to speak.

"I hope you've all had a wonderful evening. If you'll look outside, we're having our first snowfall of the winter. I think it's a perfect way to end this evening. Before I say goodnight, though, I want to talk about the Christmas trees you've been decorating. This evening, we've had thirteen recommendations for people who should get a decorated tree. Some of these people have received more than one recommendation and I think that's wonderful. We will begin delivering them tomorrow. As for the rest of the trees, we're going to draw names from those of you who signed up at your table. We'll deliver them to you as well and hope you have a very merry Christmas!

"Jeff Lyndsay, who has introduced himself to many of you, has been hired to act as my manager and associate here at Sycamore House. All of this is his work and I look forward to working with him as he creates extraordinary experiences for anyone who chooses to use Sycamore House for events in the future. He'll come up in a moment to announce the winners of the Christmas trees.

"I'd also like to thank Sylvie Donovan and Hannah McKenzie who put together all of the food for tonight. Do you think I should hire them as caterers?" At the room's applause, Polly smiled and winked at Sylvie. "Done. Now, you need to find reasons for me to have them in to cook, alright?"

"There are many more people I know I should thank tonight and my heart is filled with gratitude. I can't tell you how thankful I am to be back in Iowa and find myself surrounded by such wonderful people. If there was ever a question as to where my favorite place on earth to live was, you've all answered it."

Polly looked out over the room and her eye was caught by movement in the light from one of the doors. She looked a little more closely and realized she knew who had just walked in. She beckoned to Jeff, who came up to stand beside her at the podium.

"And now, we'll finish up by announcing the winners of the Christmas trees. I hope you all have a safe trip home, a very Merry Christmas and a Happy New Year!"

Applause followed her off the stage as she looked around for Lydia. She was nowhere to be found, so Polly walked out into the foyer and over to the kitchen. Hannah and Sylvie were standing beside the coffee maker, both with steaming mugs in their hands.

"Hannah," Polly said, "Where's Bruce?"

"Oh, I think he ran upstairs again to check on the kids. This has been a terrific evening. It never occurred to me that I would be so relaxed, but Aaron's news for us this evening drained all the stress out of my body.

Even if we don't have a place to live or jobs to go to, I feel like we'll be fine," Hannah replied.

"Hannah, Bruce's parents and brother just walked in." Polly said.

"What? What? How do they even know we're here?" Hannah cried out.

"Well, I might have told them," Polly said.

"I was part of that telling, too," Lydia said as she came up behind Polly. "So you saw them walk in?"

"I did. Bruce is upstairs with the kids. What should we do?" Polly asked, then said, "Look at me. I'm shaking. That old man still scares the crap out of me."

"Well, if you're shaking, then I'm going to fall apart," Hannah said. "But what did you guys do?"

"We might have driven over to Story City yesterday to see if we could talk him into being a decent human being," Polly responded.

"But, I might have sent him over the edge." Lydia chimed in.

"The old man was a jerk to you and just because he's mean and bitter doesn't mean you sent him over the edge. He was already there before we arrived on the scene," Polly declared.

She shrugged her shoulders and looked at Hannah, "Alright, we might have exacerbated the situation with him, but Bruce's mother, Shirley, was the one we told about the party. She knows everything. Well, except that the Sheriff has cleared you guys. But, she was willing to listen and seemed to want to help."

Lydia said, “I suppose we may as well confront the dragon. We certainly don't want to make Bruce do it by himself. So, upstairs or down here?"

"Don't you think it would be better upstairs? We can ask Jason to go over and stay with the kids and do it in my apartment, where there are plenty of places to sit and no one will have to witness this happening."

"Hannah, why don't you run upstairs and give Bruce a heads up so he isn't sideswiped by this."

"I don't know what you're talking about. I'm totally sideswiped."

Lydia patted her on the shoulder, "We're looking for another Christmas miracle here, Hannah. I think it's going to be alright."

Hannah left the kitchen. Sylvie stood there with her mouth open.

Lydia laughed. "Whoops, sorry, Sylvie. Didn't know you were getting caught up in all of the insanity, did you?"

"Umm, no? I guess I'll stay here and keep the ruffians at bay downstairs. But, you have to tell me everything later, alright?" Sylvie said.

"It's a deal." Lydia said, "Ready to beard the lion in your own den, Polly?"

"No, but I suppose I don't have a choice. I walked into this and this is the only way out of it." Polly threw her shoulders back, rolled her neck and walked out into the foyer. Shirley McKenzie saw her coming and rushed up to greet her.

"I don't know how things are going to go, but I talked Lyle into coming over tonight to meet Hannah and see his son," she said as she approached.

"Then, let's go upstairs to my apartment," Polly said. "That way they can see each other without a room filled with people looking on."

Shirley McKenzie said something to her son, Kevin, who looked up and smiled tentatively at Polly. He was several years older and they had only seen each other a few times when she was at their house with Bruce and Marsha. He nodded as if to assure her that things would be alright, then spoke with his father. All Polly heard from him was a grunt. There was no sign on his face that he was going to be pleasant about things, but at least he was here. She figured that was a start.

The family followed her upstairs and she showed them into her apartment. The kittens and Obiwan were nowhere to be seen, so she peeked in her bedroom. Jason had gotten them all up on the bed and wonder of wonders, they were snuggled together sound asleep. The evening was filled with little miracles! She hoped they would stay that way for just a while longer. Quietly pulling the door shut, she turned around as people began entering her home.

"Please, find a seat," she said and gestured to the living room. "I'll go across the hall and get Bruce and Hannah. Lydia?"

Lydia picked right up and said, "Can I get anything for anyone to drink?" They all shook their heads no. As Polly left the apartment, she saw Lyle sit down in a chair he had pulled away from the dining room table, essentially separating himself from the rest of his family. This wasn't going to be an easy evening.

She knocked on the door and Bruce answered it, holding Hannah's hand. Jason and Andrew were sitting on the floor quietly playing with some video games they'd brought.

"Well?" she asked, "Are you ready for this?"

"Not really," Bruce said. "This was NOT the way I'd planned to see him again."

"Well, he's here. I think that says something, don't you?" Polly asked.

"I suppose so," he moaned. "Ugh. I'm sick to my stomach,"

"I know. Just don't think about it and once this starts it will all be over soon enough. The worst part is getting it started." Polly said.

"Okay. Hannah? Are you going to be alright?" Polly could see that he was squeezing her hand pretty tightly, her knuckles were white.

"I'm fine. We'll be fine. If he doesn't want anything to do with you, we'll figure it out," she said.

"Alright then, let's go."

The three of them walked back across the hallway and into Polly's apartment. Shirley jumped up off the sofa and ran to hug her son. Hannah hung back until Shirley pulled away and said, "Hi, I'm Bruce's mother. I'm glad to finally meet you." When Hannah put her right hand out, Shirley didn't wait, but hugged her as well. She took Bruce's hand and pulled him with her to the sofa.

Kevin McKenzie stood up and stopped him on the way, "Bruce, it's good to see you man," he said.

Bruce's eyes were wary, but he said, "Good to see you too."

Lydia and Polly made their way back into Polly's kitchen, trying to stay out of the way of the family reunion. Bruce sat beside his mother on the couch and Hannah sat on his other side, holding his hand. This time it was her grip that threatened to cut off his circulation. His mother had a firm grip on the hand closest to her and all of a sudden, she began to weep. It wasn't a quiet, pretty weeping and soon grew into loud, choking sobs. She turned into her son and as he took his hand out of hers and wrapped it around her shoulders, she threw her arms around him and held on. Hannah released his other hand as he wrapped his arms around his mother.

Polly glanced at Lydia, who picked up a box of tissues from the counter and handed it to her. Polly mouthed the word, "chicken" at her friend and walked out to the living area. Placing the box on the table in front of them, she glanced at Lyle McKenzie, sitting stiffly in his chair, looking at nothing in particular. Kevin had moved forward in his seat as if to care for his mother, but instead, looked stricken and unsure as to what to do next.

Finally, Shirley McKenzie took a deep breath, pulled a few tissues from the box and patted her eyes. "Excuse me," she said to Polly, "Do you … ?"

"It's right over here," Polly interrupted and led her to the door into the bathroom. The room remained uncomfortably silent while she was gone. When she returned, it seemed as if she had regained her composure and she walked over to stand beside her husband.

Placing her hand on his shoulder, she said, "Bruce, we'd like you to come home. Your father and I will help you get back on your feet. We want to get to know your new family and meet those little children of yours.

"We've discussed it and if you want to work on the farm, there is plenty of work there. Kevin and Lyle were going to hire a new farmhand this spring anyway. If you don't want to work on the farm, you're welcome to stay with us until you find a job somewhere else. Isn't that right, Lyle?"

Lyle McKenzie stood up and walked over to the couch. Bruce shrank back toward Hannah, as if he were unsure as to what might happen next, but then stood up to face his father.

"Son, you hurt your mother when you left town, but she forgave you a long time ago. I'm a stubborn man with a lot of pride, but you're family and no matter how old you are, I guess I'm still responsible for you. If you want to come back, you're welcome to return."

Kevin McKenzie stood up as well and walked over to stand beside his brother. "You know, there is an awful lot of machinery on the farm that could use your touch. Dad's fighting with some lawn mowers right now. We want you to come home."

Polly looked at Lydia, whose eyes were filling with tears. She grabbed a few tissues and scurried to the kitchen, shoving two of them into Lydia's waiting fingers.

"Thank you, Dad," Bruce said. "I would like to come home. That's where we were headed when we got sidetracked. I wanted to do this on my own with you, but it looks like we managed to get everyone else involved."

His father took a deep breath, then said, "I know you have some legal trouble, son. Your mother says we're going to help you out with that, too."

"No, you don't have to. It's all settled. There's no more legal trouble. They have the guy who set us up. We're free and clear to go." Bruce replied.

"You know I'm not an easy man to get along with, but your mother, well, she makes me remember that I'm not the only person on the earth who has pride." He turned around and looked at Lydia. "I'm also supposed to apologize for being rude to you. I suppose I was and if I don't tell you I'm sorry for it, she told me I'm sleeping in the barn for the rest of the winter." He glanced at his wife, who smiled at him. "And that's cold and lonely. I'm not so stubborn that I want to do that and I'm not so difficult that I don't know when I've been rude to a woman. So, I apologize."

Lydia nodded at him in acceptance.

Shirley McKenzie spoke up, "We don't have anything ready for you, though, Hannah." She turned to Polly, "Would it be alright if they spent another night or two here. We'd be glad to pay you. That way we can get the basement ready for them."

"You can stay here as long as you need to," Polly said to Bruce and Hannah.

Shirley took Hannah's hand, drawing her up off the sofa. "Will you introduce me to your little ones tonight before we leave?"

"Sure," Hannah said. "Let's go over to our room."

"Bruce," Polly said, "Go ahead and send Andrew and Jason back over here. I think they're spending the night." She turned to Lydia. "Whoops, I forgot to ask their mom if that was alright. I'd better go do that."

The two went downstairs and discovered that much of the crowd had thinned out. Aaron was waiting at the bottom of the steps for them.

"Is everything alright?" he asked.

"Oh, Polly and I got to witness one more Christmas miracle," Lydia said as she sidled up to her husband and slipped her arm around his waist. "Sycamore House keeps handing them out, doesn't it!"

Polly walked over to stand by the front door which had been opened as people were leaving. Henry came up behind her.

"The snow is beautiful, isn't it?" he asked.

"It is," she responded. "It kind of makes the entire evening perfect."

"You know, I didn't get a chance to tell you before, but you are beautiful tonight, too." He reached down and took her hand in his very warm hand and squeezed it lightly. "I'm glad you're here, Polly Giller. Very glad you're here." Then, he lightly touched her lips with his and they stood together looking at the snow come down.

"I'm glad too," Polly whispered, more to herself than anyone else. "Merry Christmas."

THANK YOU FOR READING

Made in the USA
Charleston, SC
05 April 2013